About the Authors

Nikki Logan lives next to a string of protected wetlands in Western Australia, with her long-suffering partner and a menagerie of furred, feathered and scaly mates. She studied film and theatre at university, and worked for years in advertising and film distribution before finally settling down in the wildlife industry. Nikki believes that the passion and risk of falling in love are perfectly mirrored in the danger and beauty of wild places. Every romance she writes contains an element of nature, and if readers catch a waft of rich earth or the spray of wild ocean between the pages she knows her job is done.

Annie West has devoted her life to an intensive study of tall, dark, charismatic heroes who cause the best kind of trouble in the lives of their heroines. As a sideline she's also researched dream-worthy locations for romance, from bustling, vibrant cities to desert encampments and fairytale castles. It's hard work but she loves a challenge. Annie lives with her family at beautiful Lake Macquarie, on Australia's east coast. She loves to hear from readers and you can contact her at www.annie-west.com or at PO Box 1041, Warners Bay, NSW 2282, Australia.

Michelle Douglas has been writing for Mills & Boon since 2007 and believes she has the best job in the world. She lives in a leafy suburb of Newcastle on Australia's east coast with her own romantic hero, a house full of dust and books, and an eclectic collection of 60s and 70s vinyl. She loves to hear from readers and can be con...

Dreaming of...
COLLECTION

April 2018

May 2018

June 2018

July 2018

August 2018

September 2018

Dreaming of...
Australia

NIKKI LOGAN

ANNIE WEST

MICHELLE DOUGLAS

MILLS & BOON

Published in Great Britain 2018
by Mills & Boon, an imprint of HarperCollins*Publishers*
1 London Bridge Street, London, SE1 9GF

Dreaming of… Australia © 2018 Harlequin Books S.A.

Mr Right at the Wrong Time © 2012 Nikki Logan
Imprisoned by a Vow © 2013 Annie West
The Millionaire and the Maid © 2015 Michelle Douglas

ISBN: 978-0-263-26667-2

09-0918

MIX
Paper from
responsible sources
FSC™ C007454

This book is produced from independently certified FSC™ paper to ensure responsible forest management.

For more information visit: www.harpercollins.co.uk/green

Printed and bound in Spain
by CPI, Barcelona

MR RIGHT AT THE WRONG TIME

NIKKI LOGAN

PROLOGUE

THE droning whine might have been coming from the tyres spinning in defiance of the absence of a solid surface beneath their tread, or from the still cooling engine, or from the air hissing from the deflating airbags.

Or quite possibly from deep inside Aimee Leigh's tight throat.

The brace of the steering wheel against her chest really didn't allow for much more than a whimper, followed rapidly by a shallow, painful breath, but making noise seemed like a priority because somewhere down deep Aimee knew that if she was making noise then she was still breathing. And if she was still breathing then she had something to save.

A life.

No matter how pathetic.

Adrenaline surged through her body as she flicked her eyes desperately left and right. It was pitch-black outside, except for a lone shaft of moonlight which fractured into a hundred different facets in the shattered windscreen of her little Honda. Long lengths of her hair brushed forward across her cheeks, defying gravity. She shook them just slightly, they swung in the open air, and the press of the steering wheel into her chest finally made some sense.

It wasn't pressing into her. She was pressing into it.

Down onto it.

Her world righted itself as she re-orientated and spidered her free hand along her middle to the pain in her abdomen—and discovered the seatbelt carving into her belly, straining against her weight, holding her in her seat.

Saving her life.

The moment she acknowledged it, its ruthless grip became unbearable. Her trembling fingers found the long cross length that was supposed to brace her from hip to shoulder—that had been until the force of the accident had pulled her free of it—and, forcing panic back, she squeezed her free arm up behind her and found the place where the seatbelt locked against its hidden reel. She curled her sticky fingers around it, got a good purchase, took as deep a breath as she could manage...

...and then she pulled.

Her whole body screamed as she forced her torso behind the fabric restraint and pressed herself back into the driver's seat. The release of pressure on her abdomen allowed a rush of blood into the lower half of her body, and it was only then that she realised she'd not been able to feel anything down there before. At all.

The painful burn of sensation returning kept her focused, and as she hung suspended at the waist and chest by her strong seatbelt she audited her extremities, made sure everything responded. But when she tried to flex her right foot an excruciating pain ripped up her leg and burst out into the night.

A bird exploded from its treetop roost just outside her shattered window, and as she slipped back into unconsciousness the urgent flap of its wings morphed in Aimee's addled mind into the hover of an angel.

A heavenly soul that had come to earth to act as midwife between her life...and her death.

CHAPTER ONE

'HELLO?'

The darkness was the same whether her eyes were open or closed so she didn't bother trying.

The disembodied voice that floated down to her made Aimee wonder if maybe she *was* dead, and she and her car and the tree she'd hit when she flew off the A10 had all been transported together in a tangled, inseparable mess into a void.

Some kind of spiritual waiting room.

Her heart battered against the seatbelt that still pinned her to the seat like an astronaut strapped into a shuttle.

Starved of light, her imagination lurched into overdrive. She replayed the slide and crash in her mind, each time making it worse and more violent. One minute she'd been travelling happily along through the towering eucalypts that defied gravity, growing forty-five degrees up out of the Tasmanian mountain all the way to the horizon…

…the next she'd been sliding and briefly airborne, before slamming into the trunk of this tree.

'Hello?'

Her head twitched slightly. Maybe her heavenly number was being called? She prised open her crusted, swollen lids and stared into the darkness that still reigned.

It didn't seem necessary to reply. Surely in the spirit world it would be enough just to think your response?

Yes. I'm here...

She reluctantly released her death-grip on her seatbelt and risked extending trembling fingers out into the dense nothing around her. They grazed against something solid almost immediately, and she traced them across the crusty, papery surface of bark, rolling tiny unbreakable cubes beneath her fingertips like reading Braille.

A tree branch. Riddled with pieces of her shattered windscreen.

She fumbled her touch to the roof of the car, found the interior light and—with only a momentary thought for what might be revealed—depressed the plastic panel and squinted at the sudden dim light.

Her dash had slipped forward about a foot, and buckled where parts of the engine had pushed into it. The roof above her had crushed downwards. But, most terrifying of all, an enormous tree limb had pierced the armour of her little car, through the windscreen and the passenger seat beyond it, and was taking much of the vehicle's weight. Aimee stared at the carnage and tasted the slide of salt down the back of her throat.

If that branch had come through just two feet closer...

The panic she'd been holding at bay so well these past hours surged forth. She plunged the car back into darkness, thicker and more cloying than before, and let the tears come. Crying felt good—it helped—and she let herself indulge because no one was around to see it. She'd never in her life cried in front of someone else, no matter the incentive, but what she did in the privacy of her own car wreck was her business.

'Can you hear me?'

The words just wouldn't quite soak into her overwhelmed, muddled mind, but the voice sounded angelic enough—deep and rich and... concerned. Shouldn't it be serene? Wasn't its job to reassure her? To set her mind and fears at rest and guide her to...wherever she was going? Glowing and transcendent and full of love.

'Make any kind of noise if you can hear me.'

A solitary beam of light criss-crossed back and forth from high above her, mother-ship-style, across the places her vehicle wasn't. It moved too fast for her fractured mind to make sense of what it revealed around her.

'Search and Rescue,' the voice said, sounding strained and uncomfortable and somehow closer. 'If you can hear me, make *any* kind of noise.'

For an angel, he was awfully demanding.

Aimee tried to speak, but her words came out as a creepy kind of gurgle. He didn't respond to her partial frog croak. She fumbled the hand that wasn't pinned behind her and found her car's horn, hoping to heaven she'd preserved enough battery.

She pressed.

And held.

The noise exploding through what had been so many hours of silence made her jump even though she knew it was coming, and her leg responded with sharp blades of protest. The long peal echoed through the darkness, sounding high and empty.

'I hear you,' the voice called back, sounding relieved and professional. 'I'll be with you soon. I'm just securing your car.'

A small lurch and a large clang were separated only by the barest of heartbeats, but then she felt and heard some of the weight of the car shift as whatever he'd used to secure it tightened into position. The move changed the dynamic of all the twisted fixtures in her front seat, and shifted some of the pressure of whatever had been pressing against her injured leg. It protested with violent sensation and she slammed her hand down on the horn again. Hard.

'Ho!' The voice yelled, then again urgently. Somewhere high above she thought she heard the word echo, but not in the same voice.

The tensioning stopped and the vehicle creaked and settled, more glass splintering from her windscreen and tinkling away into the night.

'Are you okay?' the voice yelled.

She swallowed back the pain and also wet her

throat. 'Yes,' she cried feebly, and then stronger, 'Yes. But my leg is trapped under the dash.' She hoped he'd do the maths and make the connection that their securing of the car was making her pain worse. She didn't have the energy or breath to explain.

'Got it.' She heard a thud on her roof but then nothing, no movement. Then some rustling outside the rear passenger side window. 'Any other injuries?' he called, closer. She heard the sounds of a mallet knocking something into place.

'Uh…I can't tell,' she whimpered.

'What's your name?' This time from somewhere over the top of her windscreen.

So they could advise her next of kin? Give her parents one more thing to fight over? she thought dismally. God, wouldn't they both make a meal of this? 'Aimee Leigh.'

He repeated that detail in short, efficient radio-speak to whoever he'd just called up to moments before. 'Are you allergic to morphine, Aimee?' he asked, definitely sounding close this time.

'I don't know.' And she didn't much care. The screaming of her leg had started to make every other part of her ache in sympathy.

'Okay…'

She heard more rustling from beyond the tree limb her Honda was skewered on and she craned her head towards the empty front passenger seat. Suddenly the darkness glowed into an ethereal white-blue light and a glow-stick seemed to levitate through the window, around the enormous branch, and then come to rest on the crippled dash of her car. She blinked her eyes in protest at the assault of blazing light. But as they adjusted the full horror of her situation came back to her. She looked at where her leg disappeared into the crumpled mess that had been her steering console, down at her right arm, which was wedged behind her between the seat and her driver-side door, then back again at the half-a-tree which stretched its grabbing fist past her into the back of her little hatchback.

But just as she tasted the rising tang of panic the man spoke again, from beyond the tree. 'How are you doing, Aimee? Talk to me.'

'I'm—' *A mess. Terrified. Not ready to die.* '—Okay. Where are you?'

'Right here.'

And suddenly a gloved hand reached through the leaves of the tree branch that had made a kebab out of her car and stretched towards her. It was heavy-duty, fluoro-orange, caked in old dirt and had seen some serious action. But it was beautiful and welcome, and as the fingers stretched towards her from the darkness Aimee reached out and wrapped all of hers around two of his. He curled them back into his palm and held on.

'Hi, Aimee,' the disembodied voice puffed lightly. 'I'm Sam, and I'll be your rescuer today.'

Right then—for the first time in hours—Aimee believed that she was actually going to make it.

Search-and-Rescue-Sam couldn't get close enough to do a visual inspection from outside the car, so he had her run through a verbal description of all her major body parts so he could try and assess her condition remotely. He seemed less concerned with her agonising leg than with the tightness in her chest, where her seatbelt bit, and with her forgotten arm—completely numb, immobile, and impossible for her to twist around to see.

'I don't like unknowns, Aimee Leigh,' he murmured as he ducked away to check the tension on the ropes holding the car in place. He kept up with the assessing questions and she kept her answers short and sharp—pretty much all her straining lungs would allow. The whole time he circled the vehicle, equipment clanking, and bit by bit she felt the car firming up in its position.

'I want to get a look at that arm if I can,' he said when he reappeared at the window beyond the tree limb.

'If I can't see it from here how are you going to see it from there?' she gasped.

'I'm not. I'm going to try and get in there with you.'

How? The two of them were separated by three feet of solid tree. And her door wasn't budging.

'Can you pop the hatch?'

She knew what he was asking—could she reach the door release?—but the request struck her as ludicrous, as if he wanted to load some groceries into the back of her brutalised car. She started to laugh, but it degenerated into a pained wheeze.

'Aimee? Hanging in there?'

Focus. He was working so hard to help her. 'I'm just…' She stretched her left arm across her body, to see if she could reach the release handle below her seat. She couldn't and, worse, she puffed like a ninety-year-old woman just from that. 'I'll have to take my seatbelt off…'

'No!'

The sudden urgency in his otherwise moderated voice shocked her into stillness, and she realised for the first time how hard he was working to keep her calm. He might be faking it one hundred percent, but it was working. Why the sudden urgency over her seatbelt? It had already done its job. It wasn't as if she could crash twice.

'I'll come through the back window. Shield yourself from the falling glass if you can.'

It took him a moment to work his way around to the back of the car. She followed his progress with her senses and pressed her good foot to the brake pedal until she could see his legs in her rearview mirror, splayed wide and braced on the failing tail-lights of her hatch, as though gravity meant nothing to him.

Somewhere at the back of her muddled mind she knew there was something significant about the fact that he'd abseiled down to her. But then she was thoroughly distracted by the realisation that he was going to come in there with her—put himself at risk—to help her. Anxiety burbled up in her constricted chest.

'Ready, Aimee? Cover your head.'

She curled her lone arm around her head and twisted towards the door. Behind her she heard a sharp crack, and then the high-pitched shattering of the back window. Tiny squares of safety glass showered down on her and pooled in the wrecked dash. She straightened and watched in the rear-view mirror as Sam folded down her back seats and lowered himself to where she was trapped.

A moment later he appeared between the two front seats of the car, bending uncomfortably around the sub-branches of the tree limb.

'Hey,' he said, warm and rich near her ear.

An insane and embarrassing sob bubbled up inside her at having rescue so close at hand—at having *him* so close at hand—and she struggled to swallow it back. 'I'm sorry…' she choked.

'Don't be. You're in an extraordinary situation. You wouldn't be human if you weren't scared.'

He didn't get it. How could he? She didn't feel scared. She felt stupidly safe. Just because he was here. And that undid her more than all the fear of the hours before he'd come. How long had it been since she felt so instantly *safe* with a man?

'Do you understand what's happened to you, Aimee?'

'I had an accident,' she squeezed out. 'I ran off the road.'

'Yeah, you did. Your car's gone down an embankment. The back is pressed into the hillside and the front has come to rest against a tree.'

'You make that sound so peaceful,' she whispered. The complete opposite of the violence that had befallen her and her car. She twisted around to see his face, but the angle was too tricky and it hurt too much to twist any further.

'Try not to move until I've stabilised your neck,' he murmured gently. He reached past her and adjusted the rearview mirror so that he could see her in it. And vice-versa. 'I want you to look at my eyes, Aimee. Focus.'

She lifted hers to the mirror and met his concerned, compassionate gaze, eyes crinkled at the edges from working outdoors, and the bluest blue she'd ever seen. At least she thought they were blue. They could have been any colour, given the emergency lighting was casting a sickly pallor over everything. He slid his finger up between them.

'Now, focus on my finger.' He moved it left and right, forward and back. She tracked the gloved finger actively in the mirror, but slipped once and went back to his eyes—just for a moment, for a better look. The most amazing eyes. Just staring at them made her calmer. And more drowsy.

'Okay.' He seemed satisfied.

'Did I pass?'

She lifted her head just slightly, so that the mirror caught the twist of his lips as he smiled.

'Flying colours. You're in pretty good shape for a girl wedged in a tree.'

She felt him brace his knees on the back of the front seats and heard him rifling through the kit he'd hauled in with him. 'I need to check you out physically, Aimee. Is that going to be okay?'

The man who'd climbed in here to rescue her? 'You can do…whatever you want.'

In her peripheral vision, in the dim glow of the cabin, she watched him strip off his gloves and twist a foam neck brace out of his bag.

'Just a precaution,' he said, before she could start worrying.

She let her head sag into the brace as he fitted it. Quite a comfortable precaution—if anything in this agonising situation could be called comfortable.

Next, he wedged a slimline torch between his teeth, and then he twisted through the gap between the driver and passenger seats, reaching for her legs. He held himself in place with one hand and dragged her torn skirt high up her thighs with the other. He pointed his torch down into the darkness at her feet, studying closely.

'I felt it break,' she said matter-of-factly—and softly, given how close his face was to hers— amazed that she could be calm at all. Still, what else could she do? Freaking out hadn't helped her earlier.

'It hasn't broken the skin, though,' he mumbled around the torch, sliding her dress modestly back into position. 'That's a good thing.'

He wasn't going to lie, or play down what was happening to her. She appreciated that.

'At least I can manage to break my leg the right way.' She winced. 'Wayne would be pleased.' One of very few things her dominating ex would have appreciated—or possibly noticed—about her.

Sam was eight-tenths silhouette, since the glow-stick was behind him on the dash but suddenly the front of the car was full of the smell of oil and leather, rescue gear and sweat, and good, honest man.

'Are you going to give me painkillers?' she said, to dislodge the inappropriate thought, and because everything was really starting to hurt now that the car was more stable and the pressure points had shifted.

'Not without knowing for sure you're not allergic. And not with the pain in your chest; you have enough respiratory issues without me compounding it with medication.'

'I hate pain,' she said.

His chuckle was totally out of place in this situation, but it warmed her and gave her strength. 'With the endorphins you'll have racing through your system you'll barely feel it,' he said, before twisting away to rifle in his bag again. When he returned he had a small bottle with him. 'But this will help take the edge off.'

She glanced sideways at the bottle. It didn't look very medical. She lifted her curious eyes to him in mute question rather than waste more breath on a pointless question.

'Green Ant Juice,' he said. 'It's a natural pain-killer. Aboriginal communities have used it for centuries.'

'What makes it juicy?'

His pause was telling. 'Better not to ask.'

Oh. 'Will it taste like ants?'

The rummaging continued. He resurfaced with an empty syringe. 'Have you tasted them?'

'I've smelled them.' The nasty, acrid scent of squashed ants.

Again the flash of white teeth in the mirror. 'Your choice. You prefer the pain?'

For answer, she opened her mouth like a young bird, and he syringed a shot of the sticky syrup into it. 'Good girl.'

His warm thumb gently wiped away a dribble of the not-quite-lemony juice that had caught on the corner of her lips. Her pulse picked up in response. Or it could have been the analgesic surging into her system.

Either way, it felt good.

The gentle touch was so caring and sweet, while being businesslike, that it brought tears back to her eyes. When was the last time someone had taken genuine care of her? Had just been there for her when it all went wrong? Her parents believed that prevention was infinitely better than the cure, and Wayne would have just rolled his eyes and scolded her for over-reacting.

As Sam withdrew his ungloved left hand her

eyes were tear-free enough to notice that his ring finger was bare and uniformly tanned. *Yeah, because that's always important to know in life or death situations.* She shook her head at her own subconscious. Her shoulder bit and she winced visibly.

'I'm going to have a look at your arm, Aimee. Just keep very still.'

She did—not that she could feel a thing; her arm had been wedged back there for so long it wasn't even bothering her, although obviously it was really bothering Sam. She heard and felt him changing positions, getting closer to her driver's door.

'Do you remember how the accident happened?' he asked, making conversation while he fiddled around behind her.

She shook her head. 'I was driving the A10. One minute everything was fine.' She filled her strained lungs again. 'The next I was sliding and then…' She shuddered. 'I remember the impact.' *Breath.* 'Then I passed out for a bit.' *Breath.* 'Then I woke up here in this tree. Stuck.'

Her strained respiration seemed unnaturally loud in the silence that followed. When he finally did speak he said, 'Looks like an oil patch on the asphalt. A local passing through slid on it, too, but managed to stop before the edge. He saw your tail-lights down here and called it in.'

Thank goodness he did. I might have been out here for days. Aimee lifted her chin to see better in the mirror what he was doing behind her. 'Sam, don't worry about whether it's going to hurt. Just do whatever you have to do. I'm a rip-the-Bandaid-off kind of girl, despite what I said earlier about pain.'

She felt his pause more than heard it. 'You can't feel this?'

The worry in his voice spiked her heart into a rapid flutter. 'I can't feel anything.'

When he spoke again, his voice was more carefully moderated. 'Your arm is wedged back here. I think it's dislocated. I've freed it up a little bit, and I'm going to try to push it forward, but this will go one of two ways. Either you won't feel a thing even once it's free—'

Meaning she might have damaged something permanently.

'—or the sensation is going to come back as soon as it's free. And if that happens it's going to hurt like hell.'

She felt a tug, but no pain. It was like having a numb tooth yanked. So far so good. 'Won't the ant juice help?'

'It won't have taken full effect—'

That was as far as he got. With a nasty crack her arm came free, and he pushed it forward back into the front seat where it belonged. The pain burst like white light behind her eyes, and came from her throat in an agonised retch as full sensation returned—arm burning, shoulder screaming.

His hands were at her hair instantly, stroking it back, soothing. 'That's the worst of it, Aimee.

It's all done now,' he murmured, over and over. 'All done…'

She rocked where she sat, holding her breath, damming back the tears, sucking the pain in, wanting so badly to be as brave as Sam was in coming down here for her. Then, as the ant juice and her own adrenaline kicked in, the rocking slowed and her body eased back in the seat, not fighting the restraint of the seatbelt as much.

'Better?' That voice again, warm and low just behind her. She lifted her eyes to the crooked rearview mirror, reached for it slowly with her good arm, missed and tried again through a slight fogginess. She adjusted it and found his eyes.

'Thank you,' she whispered, knowing it would never be enough, but just so grateful that she was no longer alone with her thoughts and fears of death.

He knew what she was saying. 'You're welcome. I'm sorry that hurt so much.'

'Not your fault. And it's easing off now.' If *easing off* could describe the deep, dull, throb coming from her right arm and leg. 'And it's made it easier to breathe. Talk.'

Though not perfectly.

'Don't get comfortable. We have a long way to go.'

'Is it time to get out?' God, she hoped so. Every time the car creaked and settled the breath was sucked out of her lungs.

The compassion turned to caution. 'Not just

yet. We have to wait for it to get a little bit lighter. It's not safe to try and haul you out in the dark.'

Given how unsafe she felt staying in, that was saying something. Although that wasn't strictly true; everything had got a whole heap less scary the moment Sam had first called out to her. But every minute she was here *he* was here, risking his life, too. 'You should go, then. Come back when it's morning.'

His eyes narrowed in the mirror. 'But you'd be alone.'

As uncomfortable as that thought made her, it was a heck of a lot more comfortable than something happening to him because of her. 'I've been alone most of the night. A few more hours won't kill me.' Except that it very well might, if things went wrong, her lurching stomach reminded her. But at least it would only be her. 'I don't want you to get hurt because of me.'

The crinkles at the corners of his eyes multiplied. 'I appreciate the thought, but I know what I'm doing.'

'But the hatch isn't open.' So if the car slipped further it wouldn't just slide away from around him, and the harness she guessed tethered him to something above them. It would take him, too. And who knew how steep this embankment was.

'We're secure enough.'

'Do you do this for a living?' Suddenly she wanted to know. What kind of person risked his life for total strangers? Plus talking took her mind off…everything else.

'Amongst other things, yes.'

She tipped her head and spoke more freely than she might have without fifty mils of squished ants zooming through her blood. 'Are you an adrenaline junkie?'

He laughed and checked her pulse, his fingers warm and sure at the base of her jaw under the foam neck brace. Her heart kicked up its pace.

'A little fast…' he murmured to himself, then turned his focus back to her. 'No, I'm not interested in risk-taking for the sake of it. But to save someone's life…'

'I don't want you risking your life for mine.'

Blue eyes held hers in the mirror. 'Why not?'

'Because…' *it wasn't worth it* '…this was my mistake. You shouldn't have to pay for it.'

He looked like he wanted to argue. 'Well, if I do my job right then neither of us will be paying. Excuse me a sec.'

He reached to his collar and pressed a button she'd only just noticed. He had a speedy conversation with whoever was on the other end of the radio at his hip. It was mostly coded medical talk, but she read his thin lips and his deep frown well enough.

'Assess this as Code Three. Will offer hourly sit-reps.' More distant crackles, then his eyes lifted to hers in the mirror and held them as he spoke, a fatal resignation written clearly in them. 'Negative, Topside. Requiring static again. We've just gone Code Two.'

After not much more communication he

signed off, and the silence that followed was the longest that had fallen since he'd scrambled into her beleaguered Honda. When he finally did speak, it was hushed.

He cleared his throat. 'If anyone asks, you passed out just then.'

Her eyebrows shot up. 'Did you just lie?'

'Would you feel better if I said I save them up for very important moments?'

I'd feel better if you didn't do it at all. Her father was a liar, and she didn't like even the slightest connection between the two men in her mind.

She raised both brows for answer. Wow, when had she got so confident? One month ago she never would have challenged someone like this. Driving off a mountain really brought out the best in a girl.

Plus, with Sam, she felt safe expressing herself. On five minutes' acquaintance.

He sighed and relented at her pointed look. 'It seems I'm the only one who thinks I'm better off down here with you,' he said.

'Were you ordered to go back up? Why?'

He considered her in the mirror. Now that her arm was free she could twist her body further around. She did it now, turning to face him for the first time, though it hurt to do it. Her already tight breath caught further.

She hadn't imagined it… Piece by piece in the mirror she'd thought he was intriguing. Fully assembled he was gorgeous. There was something almost…leonine…about the way his features all came together. Dark, high eyebrows over blue almond-shaped eyes. Defined cheekbones, trigger jaw. All with a coat of rugged splashed over the top. As if she wasn't breathy enough…

'Why, Sam?'

His mind worked furiously and visibly. 'Okay…' He resettled himself into the gap between the seats and lowered his voice. As if he was about to share a great secret. As if there was anyone but them here to hear it.

'We're not just resting against a tree, Aimee. Or on a hillside.'

She appreciated his use of the collective. 'We' sounded so much better than 'you' when someone was breaking bad news. And he was. His whole body confessed it.

'Where are we?' she whispered, glancing out at the inky blackness around them and remembering how she'd imagined earlier that it was death's waiting room. But as she said the words she realised… He'd abseiled down to her. And when she'd first tried to move her leg and screamed a bird had exploded from its roost *right next to her window,* not high above it. And she'd heard her wheels spinning freely in space when she'd first slammed to a stop.

Her heart lurched.

'Or should I be asking *how high* are we?'

CHAPTER TWO

SHE saw the truth in the flinch of his dark brows. A tight pain stabbed high in her chest. She was so, *so* bad with heights. 'Oh, my God…'

'Aimee, stay calm. We're secure. But we don't know what damage the impact has done to the tree—if any. That's the unknown.'

She stared at him. 'You hate unknowns?'

His eyes grew serious. 'Yeah. I do.'

'But you're in here.'

'I've made it safe.'

But still he was refusing to leave her. 'You have to go.'

'No.'

'Sam—'

'It's going to get light in a couple of hours,' he pushed on, serious. 'I want to be here when that happens.'

For the rescue? Or for when she could see what was below them—or wasn't—and went completely to pieces? She shifted her focus again and stared out through her shattered, flimsy windscreen, partially held together only by struggling tint film. The only thing stopping her from falling into—and through—that windscreen was her seatbelt.

She turned back to stare at him again. In truth she really, horribly, desperately didn't want to be alone. But she didn't want him hurt, either. Not the man who'd taken such gentle care of her.

'Don't even worry about it, Aimee,' he said, before she'd even finished thinking it through. 'It's not your choice to make. It's mine.'

'I don't get a say?'

'None. I'm in charge in this vehicle. It's my call.'

I'm in charge. How many years had she secretly rebelled against 'in charge' men. Men who thought they knew what was best for her and insisted on spelling it out. Her father. Wayne. Men who liked her better passive, like her mother. Yet here she was crumbling the moment an honest-to-goodness *'take charge'* man told her what to do.

But, truthfully, she didn't want to be alone. Not for one more moment of this ordeal.

'So, what do we do until it gets light?' she asked.

'I'll keep monitoring your condition, make sure the car's still sound. I can radio up for anything you need.'

Silence fell. 'So we just…talk?'

'Talking is good. I don't want you dropping off to sleep.'

But making small talk seemed wrong under

the circumstances. And it was just too much of a reminder that she didn't know him at all, despite the strange kind of intimacy that was forming between them. A bubble she didn't particularly want to burst.

'What do we talk about?'

'Anything you want. I'm told I'm good company.'

She glanced up into the mirror in time to see him flick his eyes quickly away. Maybe this was awkward for him, too.

She scratched around for something to say that wasn't about the weather. Something a bit more meaningful. Something that would normalise this crazy situation. 'You said Search and Rescue is only part of your job. What's the other part?' With every minute that passed, her breath was coming more easily.

He seemed unused to making conversation with his rescuees, but he answered after just a moment. 'I'm a ranger for Tasmania's Parks and Wildlife Service.'

The man who abseiled down rockfaces to save damsels in distress also looked after forests and the creatures in them. *Of course he did.* 'So this is just moonlighting for you?'

He chuckled, and shone the small torch on the fixings of her seatbelt. 'Don't worry. They sent me because I'm the best vertical rescue guy in the district. We don't get enough demand for a full time Search and Rescue team up here.'

'Small mercies.'

He sat back. 'True.'

'Which do you enjoy more?'

His eyes lifted back to hers in the mirror, held them in his surprise. Had no one ever asked him that? 'Hard to say. Search and Rescue is more… tangible. Immediate. But the forests need a champion, too.'

'This part has got to be more exciting, though?' Her dry tongue had made a mess of that sentence.

Sam rummaged in his equipment for a moment, before reappearing between the seats with a sponge soaked in bottled water. He pressed it to her lips and Aimee sucked at it gratefully.

'It's not the excitement I'm conscious of.' He frowned as she sucked. 'Though that's how it is for some of my colleagues. For me it's the importance.' He withdrew the sucked-dry sponge and resaturated it. 'I think I'd feel the same way if it was national secrets I was protecting. Or a vial of some rare cells instead of a person.'

The ants' innards were making her feel very rubbery and relaxed, and the water had buoyed her spirits. She chuckled, low and mellow. 'Just in case I was beginning to feel special.'

He smiled at her. 'Right now you're very special. There's sixteen trained professionals up there—all here for you.'

The scale of the rescue operation came crashing into focus for her. That was sixteen people who should be home in bed, wrapped around their loved ones. 'I'm so sorry—'

'Aimee, don't be. It's what we do.'

Did Sam have someone like that at home? Someone worrying about him when he was out? She could hardly ask that question, so she asked instead, 'How many lives have you saved?'

He didn't even need to count. 'Twenty-seven. Twenty-eight after today.'

Aimee's eyebrows shot up, and she turned in her seat as best she could. Her shoulder bit cruelly. His hand pressed her back into stillness gently.

'*Twenty-seven!* That's amazing.' Then she looked more closely at him. At the shadows in his gaze. 'How many have you lost?'

'I don't count the losses.'

Rubbish. Everyone counted the losses. It was human nature. 'Meaning, *"I'm not about to tell a woman trapped in her car whether or not I saved the last woman trapped in her car"*?'

His smile was gentle. 'Meaning I don't like to think about it.'

No. She could understand that. Given how much of a partnership this rescue was, she could only imagine how he'd feel when he couldn't save someone. Maybe someone he'd bonded with. Like they were bonding now. She smiled tightly. 'Well, on behalf of all women everywhere trapped in their cars I'd like to say thank you for trying. We can't ask for more.'

Ridiculously, just acknowledging that she wasn't the first person who'd been in a life-or-death situation made her feel just a little bit more in control of this one. Other people had survived to tell their tales.

In control. A further novelty. She frowned. *How bad had she let things get?*

'Sure you can. You can ask me for whatever you need right up until they're loading you into the back of the ambulance. Then I know I've done everything I can.'

'Putting yourself at so much risk. It must be hard on…' *Your family. Your girlfriend.* Was she seriously going to start obsessing on his availability? It seemed so transparent. Not to mention hideously inappropriate. In that moment she determined not to even hint for more information about his personal life. 'Hard on you…emotionally.'

He thought about that. 'The benefits outweigh the negatives or I wouldn't do it.'

He reached forward to check her pulse again and she studied the line of his face. There was more to it than that, she was sure. But it would be rude to dig. His fingers brushed under her jaw for the third time and her already tight breath caught further.

'Would my wrist be easier?' she asked, lifting her good arm because it felt like the appropriate thing to do.

He shook his head and pressed tantalisingly into the skin just down from her ear, monitoring his watch. 'You have a nice strong pulse there.'

And it gets stronger every time you brush those fingers along my throat.

'Aimee…?' She looked at him sideways, her lashes as low as his voice. His smile was half twist, half chuckle. 'Don't hold your breath—it affects your pulse.'

Heat surged up her throat around his fingers. Wow. Did ant juice turn everyone into a hormone harlot?

Fortunately he misread her flush. 'Don't feel awkward. I'm trained for this, but I'm guessing this is your first major incident.'

She nodded. 'I've never even been to hospital.'

'Never?'

She grasped at the normal topic of conversation. 'Not counting my birth.'

'Are you super-healthy or just super lucky?'

'A little of both. And it helps when your parents won't let you lift so much as a box without assistance.' The same as every man she'd dated. 'It's hard to hurt yourself falling out of a tree when they are all off-limits. And streams. And streets.'

'Protective, huh?'

'You could say that.' Or you could say her parents were competitive and bitter after their divorce and neither of them wanted to give the other the slightest ammunition. 'They both went a bit overboard in protecting me.' She'd grown up thinking that was normal. 'It wasn't until I left home that I realised other kids were allowed to make mistakes.'

'How old were you when you left home?'

'Twenty-two.'

'So you get points for taking the initiative and getting out of there?'

It hadn't been easy to break away from both of them so, *yeah,* she did get points.

But then she lost them again for leaping out of the frypan into the fire with a nightmare like Wayne.

'Anyway, it's just as well my parents aren't here to see this,' she joked. 'They'd have me locked up for ever and never let me leave the house.' *Or they'd have each other in court trying to score points off me.*

'Give them credit for getting you this far in one piece,' he murmured.

She laughed, and then winced at the pain. 'If you don't count the broken leg and dislocated shoulder. And the bruised sternum.'

'Don't forget the gash on your forehead.'

Really? Her hand slid up and followed the trail of stickiness down to her lashes. That explained the stinging in her eyes earlier. Lord, what must she look like? Black and blue and with the fine white powder from three airbags all over her? She wanted to check in the mirror, but that just smacked of way too much vanity. And it was too close to publicly declaring her interest in whether or not Sam was looking at her as *her*…or just as a person to be rescued.

'Here…' he said, curling between the seats again and bringing his face closer to hers. He efficiently swabbed at the superficial cut with a damp medicated wipe, and then fixed the two sides of the wound together with butterfly tape. Then he gently swabbed up some of the dried blood that ran down over her brow. Aimee stole a chance to breathe in some of his air.

'You'll be back to beautiful in no time,' he said.

The temptation to stare at his eyes close-up was overwhelming, but it seemed too intimate suddenly so she shifted her focus lower, to his lips, before forcing them away for something less gratuitous. Which was how she ended up staring at a freckle just left of his nose while he ministered to her wound.

Freckle-staring seemed suitably modest.

Awkwardness tangled in amongst the awareness suddenly zinging between them, and she struggled for something harmless to say. 'I can honestly say that's the first time anyone has ever said that to me. Especially by the dying light of a glow stick.'

A deep frown cut his handsome face immediately as he seemed to realise that the iridescent emergency light had dimmed to something closer to a sickly, flickering candlelight. He stared at it as though he couldn't quite believe he'd failed to notice, then disappeared into the back to rummage in his bottomless kit.

'It's got nothing to do with the colour in your cheeks,' he said, snapping a second glow-stick to activate the chemicals inside, and reaching forward to place it next to the first. Las Vegas light filled the car, and for a heartbeat the tree outside the windscreen, but the graduated darkness beyond it that didn't show a hint of ground.

Aimee swallowed hard.

'Look at how you're handling yourself,' he said. 'You're very calm, under the circumstances.'

She captured his eyes in the mirror. 'It just means I'm good at denial. It doesn't mean I'm not afraid.'

He stilled, and the intensity in his gaze reached right through the glass of the mirror and twisted around her lungs, preventing them from expanding. 'I'm not leaving you, Aimee.'

'I know,' she squeezed out.

'We'll be out in a couple of hours.'

'Uh-huh.' But it sounded false even to her own ears.

'You don't believe me?'

'I want to. I really do.'

'Do you trust me?'

Did she? She'd believed every single thing he'd said. She'd done every single thing he'd asked, without question, and not just because he'd pulled rank on her. Sam was trained, capable and compassionate, and he'd not done anything to earn her distrust. Even though she'd known him less than an hour she felt a more natural connection with him than some of the people she'd known her whole life.

Wow. That was a bit sad.

'I do trust you,' she whispered. But he'd have no way of knowing how rare that was.

'Then trust I'll get you out of here.'

She looked at him long and hard. 'I know you want to.'

'And I always get what I want.'

As a kid, she'd practised for weeks to teach herself the one-eyebrow lift and she did it now, desperate to retreat from the chemistry swirling smoke-like around them. The butterfly tape over her left brow tugged slightly. 'Such confidence.'

'I don't start something without finishing it. It's a point of principle.'

So how had he coped with those people he'd not been able to save? Maybe sitting in vehicles like this one with them, knowing he'd failed? Her heart ached for the memories he must have. But she wasn't about to ask. For his sake…and hers.

She shivered convulsively. 'Did the temperature just drop?'

'Hang on…' He disappeared for a moment and then squeezed back through the gap with a tightly rolled silver tube. It unfolded into an Aimee-sized foil blanket. Together they tucked it around her as best they could. Down over her good leg. Carefully around her injured arm.

Sam stroked back her hair from the neck brace with two fingers and tucked a corner of the blanket in behind her shoulder. Heat surged where he touched and became trapped beneath the insulation. A perverse little voice wondered if it would be inappropriate to ask him to touch her every ten minutes, to keep the heat levels optimum. She might as well get some use out of the unexpected chemistry between her and her knight-in-shining-fluoro. His heat soaked into her chilled skin.

'God, that's good…' Her good hand was outside the blanket, and she used it to tuck the foil tightly under her thighs to seal more warmth in.

'Don't cover your injured leg,' he said, withdrawing back between the seats. 'The cold is actually good for it.' Then, without asking, he reached forward and took her exposed hand between his and started to rub it. Vigorously. Impersonally. Creating a friction heat that soaked into her icy fingers and wrist. He did the same up and down her bare arm.

'How's that?' he murmured.

Heavenly. And it had nothing to do with the blanket. 'Better.'

He rubbed in silence as the insulation from the foil sheet did its job. But as the minutes went by his businesslike rubbing slowed and turned into a hybrid of a massage and a hold. Just cupping her smaller hand between his own like a heated human glove.

'So…' The unease with which he paused made her wonder whether there was still more bad news to come. 'Is there…anyone you'd like us to call for you? Your parents?' He glanced down at the fingers he held within his own. 'A partner?'

She frowned. Absolutely not Wayne. They were well and truly over. And she'd prefer to call her parents from the safety of terra-firma, when they wouldn't have to see the immediate evidence of what heading off alone into the wilds had done to her and when they'd have less reason to tear each other to pieces. Work wouldn't miss her for days yet—they knew how she got when she got to the transcribing stage of a project. 'No. Not if you truly believe we'll make it.'

'We'll make it.' His certainty soaked through her just like his body heat. 'But is there someone you'd call if you thought you *weren't* going to make it?'

'Hedging your bets, Sam?' Maybe that was wise. She still had to get hauled out of here successfully.

His lips twisted. 'It would be wrong of me not to ask.'

Danielle? That would get a tick in the friend box and the work box at the same time. She folded her brows and tried to make her foggy brain focus…

'It's not like prison, Aimee. You can have more than one phone call.' Then he looked closer. 'Or none at all. It's not compulsory.'

How pathetic if she couldn't even identify one *'in case of emergency'* person. And how ridiculous. She sighed. 'My parents, probably.'

He pulled a small notepad from his top pocket. 'Want to give me a number?'

She stared at him, and then to the floor of the passenger seat. 'Their numbers are in my phone.'

He blinked at that. 'You don't know your parents' phone numbers?'

'I have them on speed dial.' There was no way

that didn't sound defensive. Not when she knew how little wear those two buttons actually got.

'How about a name and address, then?'

There was no judgement there, yet his words somehow reeked of it. She glared and provided the information; he jotted it down, then called it up to all those people waiting up top. Waiting for sunrise. They confirmed, and promised to make contact with her parents. She wanted to shout out so they'd hear her: *Wait until seven. Dad hates being woken.* Sam held the earpiece out so she could hear their acknowledgement.

Then they both fell into uncomfortable silence. It stretched out endlessly and echoed with what he wasn't saying.

She pressed back against her seat. 'Go ahead, Sam. Just say it. We can't sit here in silence.'

'Say what?'

'Whatever's making you twitch.'

Even with full permission, and all the time in the world to tell her what he thought, Sam refrained. It was sad how surprised she was about that. Men in her life didn't usually withhold their opinions. Or their judgement. Not even for a moment.

'I watched my parents raise my brothers and sisters. Eighty percent of it was guesswork, I reckon. Parents don't get a manual.'

She shook her head. 'You're from a big family?'

He nodded. 'And my folks got a whole lot

more right with my younger brothers than with me, so maybe practice makes perfect?'

'What did they get wrong with you, Search-and-Rescue-Sam?' He seemed pretty perfect to her. Heroic, a good listener, smart, gentle fingers, and live electricity zinging through his bloodstream…

'Oh-ho… Plenty. I made their lives hell once I hit puberty.'

She studied him. 'I can see you as a heartbreaker with the girls.'

He smiled. 'No more than your average teen. But I was a handful, and I ran with some wild mates.'

'Another thing I don't have trouble seeing.' Maybe it was the uniform. Maybe it was the torn-out-of-bed-at-midnight stubble. Maybe it was the glint in those blue eyes. He had the bad-boy gene for sure. Just a small one. Not big enough to be the slightest bit off-putting but just big enough to be appealing. Dangerously appealing.

'Fortunately my older brother intervened, and turned me into the fine, upstanding citizen you see before you.'

She laughed, and her spirits lifted a hint more. Insane and impossible, but true enough. She shifted in her seat to remind herself of where they were and how much danger they were still in. 'Tell me about him. I'm sick of talking about me.'

And of thinking about the wrong turns she'd made in her life.

'Tony's two years older than me. The first. The best.'

'Is that your parents' estimation or yours?'

He looked at her. 'Definitely mine. He was everything I wanted to be growing up. The full hero-worship catastrophe.'

She smiled. 'I can't imagine having siblings.'

'I can't imagine not.'

'You want kids? In the future?' she added, in case her breathless question sounded too much like an offer.

He shrugged. 'Isn't that why we're here? As a species, I mean? I like my genes, I'd like to see what else could be done with them.'

She was starting to like his genes, too. Very much. He had a whole swag of good-guy genes to go with the bad-boy one. And the dreamy eyes. Silence fell, and she realised into what personal territory they'd strayed. She was practically interviewing him for the job of future husband. 'Sorry. Occupational hazard. I get way too interested in people's lives.'

'Why? What do you do?'

'I'm a historian. Oral History. For the Department of Heritage.'

'You talk to people for a living?'

'I swing between talking endlessly to people and then spending weeks alone pulling their stories into shape.'

'What for?'

'So they're not lost.'

'I mean what happens with them?'

She shrugged. 'They get archived. Locked away somewhere safe.'

'No one ever hears them?'

'Sure they do. Every story is catalogued by topic and theme and subject, so they can be accessed by researchers into just about anything anywhere in the world.'

'Do you get to see the end results?' he asked.

'Not usually. Just my own research.'

'So your work just goes on file somewhere? To gather dust, potentially, if no one ever looks for it?' he mused.

'Potentially.' She shrugged. 'You think something's missing from that equation?'

'Isn't it a bit…thankless?'

She stared at him, wondering if he realised what he'd just revealed. Search-and-Rescue-Sam liked to be appreciated. This was exactly why she loved to do what she did. For the moments a person let a bit of his true self slip.

She smiled. 'Not at all. Our jobs aren't too dissimilar.'

He frowned at her.

'We both save lives. You preserve their flesh for another few decades,' she said. 'I preserve their stories for ever. For their family. For perpetuity. There's more to people's time on earth than genetics.'

Which was why it was such a crime that her life was only just beginning at the ripe old age of twenty-five. She'd wasted so much time.

He considered her. 'So what's your story,

Aimee Leigh? What are you doing up here in the highlands?'

'Working. I've just finished a history, and the next few weeks I'll be pulling it all together.' She glanced around. 'Or I would have been.'

'You always do that in remote parts of the state?'

'I wanted some time alone. I rented a house at Brady's Lake.'

His eyebrows lifted. 'How's that time alone working out for you?'

Laughing felt too good. She went on longer than was probably necessary, and ended in a hacking cough. Sam reached out and slid his warm fingers to her pulse again, counting, then saying, 'Nothing makes you reassess your life quite like nearly losing it.'

True enough. She'd planned on doing some serious soul-searching while up in the highlands and really getting to grips with how she'd let others run her life for so long. She refused to think it was because she wasn't capable.

Well, she'd wanted space to think and she'd got it. Above, below and on both sides.

The pause fell again. But then she had a thought. 'Can you see my handbag, Sam?'

He looked around. 'Where is it?'

'It was on the passenger seat.' Not any more.

'What do you need? Your wallet?'

'That's all replaceable. But I have someone's life in there.'

'The person whose history you were about to start working on?'

She nodded. 'All my notes on a thumb drive.'

'I'll have a look,' he said. 'Not like I have somewhere else to be.'

He wedged himself between the seats again, but twisted away from her this time, bracing his spread knees on the seat backs and reaching out for the glow-stick. The yellow light moved with him as he stretched down towards the floor of the passenger seat.

But as he did so the car lurched.

'Sam!' Aimee screamed, just as his two-way radio burst into a flurry of activity. But the sudden splintering pain from her chest crippled her voice.

He froze in position and then slowly retreated, his strong muscles pulling him back up, bringing the light with him. He spoke confidently into the transmitter at his collar, but his words were three-parts buzz to Aimee. Her heart hammered so hard against her chest wall she was sure it might just split open.

She might have caused them to go crashing to the ground—who knew how far below? For a handbag! For a story! Tears filled her eyes.

'Sorry, Aimee,' he said, breathing heavily and righting himself more fully. 'I'll get it when the car's hauled up.'

She shook her head, unable to speak, unable to forgive herself for putting them both at such risk.

He looked more closely at her. 'Aimee? Were you hurt? Is the pain back?'

She shook her head—too frightened to speak—though her burst of activity had definitely got her pain receptors shrieking.

'I wouldn't have tried that if I'd thought it would actually dislodge us. That was just a settle. It will probably happen again whether we move or not. It doesn't mean we're going to fall.'

Tell her clenched bladder that. She nodded quickly. Still too scared to move more than a centimetre.

He found her eyes in the mirror. 'Aimee, look at me.'

She avoided his eyes, knowing what she'd just done. *Get my handbag, Sam...* As though they were just sitting here waiting for a bus. Maybe her parents were right not to trust her with important decisions.

'At *me,* Aimee.'

Finally she forced her focus to the mirror, to the blue, blue eyes waiting for her there. They were steady and serious, and just so reliable it was hard not to believe him when he spoke. 'We're thoroughly wedged between the tree and the rockface, and tethered to a three-tonne truck up top. We won't be square-dancing any time soon, but you don't need to fear moving. *We are not going to fall.'*

She looked at the rugged cut of his jaw and followed it down to the full slash of his lips, then up to his strong, straight nose and back to his eyes. Every part of him said *reliable*. Capable. Experienced. And a big part of her responded to the innate certainty in his manner. But an even bigger part of her was responding to something else. Something more fundamental. The something that would never have let him get this close, this quickly under her skin, if not for the fact that the fates had thrown them together like this. She would have followed him out onto the bonnet of her car with no safety harness if he'd asked her to with the kind of sincerity and promise that he was throwing at her right now in the mirror.

And extraordinary as it was, given how slow she was to trust strangers, she realised why.

She believed in him.

'We are not going to fall,' he'd said. She nodded, letting her breath out on a long, controlled hiss.

But deep down she feared that while that might be true literally, she could see herself falling very easily for a man like Sam. And just as hard.

Under these circumstances, that was a very, very bad idea.

CHAPTER THREE

'So who's Wayne?'

Aimee's head came up with a snap as Sam shifted again behind her. He was a big guy, and he had squeezed himself into the small space left vacant by the tree branches in the back of her little car and been settled there for over an hour.

'Wayne?'

'You mentioned his name earlier. Boyfriend? Brother?'

Was this conversation or curiosity? 'Ex.'

'Recent ex?'

'Recent enough. Why?'

'There was a…certain tone in your voice when you mentioned him.'

'A certain sarcastic tone?'

She heard the smile in his voice. 'Possibly.'

Aimee shifted back in her seat. Wayne was not someone she usually liked to talk about, liked even to *think* about, but all bets were off in this surreal setting. Their physical proximity demanded it. 'Wayne and I turned out not to be a good fit.'

'I'm sorry.'

'Don't be. I'm not. I'd rather have found out now than later.' And it was true—no matter how challenging she'd found it to walk away. Even though he'd been giving her clear signals that she was somehow deficient in his eyes. Even though she knew he wasn't good for her. She'd wriggled out from under the controlling thumbs of her parents only to fall prey to a man just like them at a time when she was most susceptible to him. 'If I'd put any longer into the relationship I might have been more reluctant to end it.'

Another long pause. Funny how she'd only known Sam a handful of minutes but she already knew how to tell a thinking pause from an awkward one. This was thinking.

'Not everyone finds that strength,' he finally said.

'You learn a thing or two recording life histories for a living. About achievements. About regrets. I don't want any regrets in my life.'

She'd lost him again. His eyes stared out into the darkness.

What was *his* story?

'Sam,' she risked, after a comfortable silence had stretched out, 'any chance you can lower the back of my seat a bit? Safely?' She didn't want a repeat of what happened before.

He studied the angle of the car and her position in it. His answer was reluctant. 'The seatbelt is working well right now specifically because it's nearly at ninety degrees.'

'Even just a little bit? It's doing my head in, looking straight down, wondering what's down there, knowing that I'd crash straight through if the seatbelt gave.'

His hand slipped onto her shoulder through the gap between the seats. 'The seatbelt is what's keeping your body from putting too much weight on your bad leg.'

Oh.

Her disappointment must have reached him, though, because he said a moment later, 'Let me just try something.' He rummaged in his kit again, and then emerged with a set of flex-straps.

Aimee chuckled tightly. 'You got a decaf latte in that Tardis, Doctor?'

He smiled as he wrapped one strap carefully around her waist and fixed it behind the seat, then the other under her good shoulder and hooked it on the headrest. 'These aren't generally for people, but I'll be gentle with them.'

He pulled the two together and clipped one end of a climbing tether onto it, then fixed the other end to his own harness. If she fell she'd snag on his safety rope. Or pull him down with her.

That was a cheery thought!

'Ready?'

So ready. So *very* ready not to be facing death literally head-on for every minute of this ordeal. She felt him fumbling along the edge of her seat for the recline lever and then suddenly the back of the seat gave slightly—just slightly—and he lowered it halfway to a fully reclined position.

She hung on to her seatbelt lifeline and prepared for the pain of more of her body weight hitting her leg, but the flexi-straps did their job and held her fast to the seat-back. It really wasn't too bad.

'Oh, thank you.' Her view was now the buckled roof of the car. A thousand times better than hanging out over who knew what. 'Thank you, Sam.'

With her seat now reclined into the limited free space in the back of the car, there was nowhere for him to go but into the expanded gap between the front seats. He wedged himself there, with his spine to the passenger seat back, his shoulder pressing against the branch, facing her across the tiny gulf he'd opened up.

Unexpected bonus. She could talk to him front on.

'You look funny,' she said softly. *Though still gorgeous.* 'Your face is back to front without the mirror.'

'You look good.' He smiled, then flushed as she dropped her eyes briefly. 'I just meant that pretty much everything on you is intact. I can't tell you what a relief it was to find that. Just to hear you honk that damned horn.'

Aimee sobered. He must hold some truly terrible images in his head.

'It's always the calmest most compliant people that have the worst injuries. They're the ones I dream about later.' He tucked her foil covering back in, keeping up his part of the conversation. She let his deep, rich voice wash over her. 'It's the guy with a twisted ankle and a golf tournament to get to that makes life hell. We've had hikers activate their EPIRB halfway up a mountain because they're tired and want a lift back down.' He shook his head.

'Where do I fall on that scale?' Was she being too high maintenance? *Get my handbag, Sam. Lower my seat, Sam...*

'You have a scale all your own. All the reason in the world to be losing it, but holding up pretty well all things considered.'

She was—and that was really saying something, given her upbringing. Where the heck would she have learned resilience from in her bubblewrap childhood? But honour made her confess. 'I was sobbing my heart out before I heard you calling.'

That seemed to genuinely pain him. 'I'm sorry I didn't get to you quicker. We had to assess the safety.'

She pinned him with her gaze. 'I'm so glad you found me at all. Imagine if you hadn't.' It hit her then, for the first time, how long, slow and awful her death would have been. She swallowed back a gnarled lump and just stared, watching the play of emotion running over his features. Sadness. Regret. Confusion. But then his eyes lifted and it was just...light. And it changed him.

'How old are you, Sam?'

'Thirty-one.'

'How is it that a man like you who wants children doesn't yet have any?' That was the closest she'd come to asking him outright: *Why are you still single?*

His eyes grew wary, but he finally answered. 'It takes one to want it but two to make it a reality.'

'You don't have women knocking down your door to help you along with that reality? You're gorgeous.'

His eyes grew cautious. But they didn't dull. On the contrary, they filled with a rich sparkle. 'Are you offering?'

She held her breath. Tilted her head. 'Are you flirting?'

The bright sparkle in his eyes immediately dimmed. The smile straightened out into a half-frown.

Her breath caught. 'You are.'

'Sorry. Really inappropriate. Just playing to my strengths.'

His confusion touched her. 'Don't apologise. I'm battered and broken and feeling pretty average. It made me smile.'

'I'm glad I could make you smile, then.'

'Do they train you for that?' she asked pertly.

'For what?'

'Keeping up people's spirits with a sexy smile.'

The hint of colour high in his jaw brought her back to her senses. The man was just trying to keep her alive. He would say just about anything. Flirting included. It probably *was* in his training manual. Which meant it had to end. One of them had to put things back on a more real footing.

She took a deep breath. 'Sorry, Sam. I think that was the ant juice talking. I apologise.'

He brushed it off with a shake of his head. 'It's not generally known for its truth serum properties.'

A blush stole up her cheeks, but this time he was staring straight at her. There was no hiding it. 'A crazy side-effect?'

'It's probably written on the bottle somewhere. *"May cause outbursts of inappropriate confession."'*

A gentleman, too. Handing her as dignified an exit as she was going to get. 'Thank you. For keeping me sane.' *For keeping things light.*

'That's how this works. You're the victim. Whatever you need…'

Victim. The word put an early end to the golden glow of promise that had filled her from the inside out at his gentle teasing. Wasn't that exactly what Danielle had accused her of being? By letting her father and Wayne run her life and others control her career? That hadn't been a fun conversation. But it had been necessary. It had triggered the rapid departure of Wayne from her life and this journey of self-discovery. 'Is that what I am?'

He stared at her—hard. 'No. You're brave and open and the least victim-like victim I've ever met.'

'It's because you're with me. I'd be a basket case without you here.'

Two tiny lines appeared between his brows.

'Sometimes we only find out what we're capable of when we're tested.'

'Well, I think I've failed this test. Maybe I'll do better next time.'

'No.' Immediate and fervent. 'No next times. You don't get this kind of luck twice.'

'Luck?' Was he crazy?

His face grew serious. He glanced at his watch. 'You'll see in a couple of hours. But I'll be right here with you.'

A couple of hours felt like for ever. 'Will the… what do you call it…getting me out…?'

'Extraction.'

'Will the extraction start as soon as the sun comes up?'

'As soon as the sun crests the mountaintops, and assuming there's no fog, yes.'

'How long will it take?'

'Hard to know. We have to stabilise your leg properly and make sure your shoulder is back in its socket before we shift you.'

She swallowed. Both those things sounded very unpleasant.

'And then we'll be pulling you out the back of the car.'

Her face must have paled, because he leaned forward and took her hand. 'I'll be with you every step of the way, Aimee. We'll be tethered to each other at all times.'

'The whole way?'

'Until the top. Until the ambulance.'

She frowned at the finality of that statement. 'Then what?'

He frowned. 'Then that's it. You go to hospital, then home where you belong.'

What if she didn't belong anywhere? And why did she suddenly have the urge never to leave this shattered vehicle and the foil blanket and Sam's gentle touch. 'That's it? I won't see you again?'

He stared at her long and hard. 'I'll see how I go. Maybe I'll drop your luggage back to you when the car's towed up. You'll have plenty to keep you busy before then.'

It was utterly insane how anxious she felt at the thought of that. A man she'd known less than a day. 'I'd like to speak to you again. Under less extraordinary circumstances.' *When I'm showered and groomed and looking pretty*. 'To thank you.'

He nodded even more cautiously. 'I'll see how we go.'

That sounded very much like Wayne's kind of *I'll see*. Her father's kind.

Translation: *no*.

CHAPTER FOUR

'How many siblings do you have in total?' Aimee asked after a while, when her inexplicable and irrational umbrage at his apparent brush off had subsided sufficiently. It wouldn't hurt her to remember that this was business to Sam, no matter how chatty they got waiting for the sun to rise. Maybe rapport development was a whole semester unit over at Search and Rescue School. And maybe the two of them just had more rapport than most.

But it didn't mean he'd want to take his work home with him—even metaphorically.

It just meant he was good at his job.

'Seven,' he murmured, leaning forward and blowing hot air into the cupped circle of her hand, still inside his. He pressed his lips against her fingertips for a tantalising, accidental moment. They were as soft and full as they looked. But warmer. And the sensation branded itself inside her sad, deluded mind.

Wayne had kissed her fingers many a time—and lots of other places besides—but while his lips had felt pleasant, even lovely at the beginning, they'd never snared her focus and dragged it by the throat the way the slightest touch from Sam did. She'd even started to wonder whether she was physically capable of a teeth-gnashing level of arousal, or whether 'lovely' was going to be her life-long personal best.

Please don't let this be the drugs talking. Please. She wanted to think she was capable of a gut-curling attraction at least once in her life.

'I'd definitely want more than one child,' she said, then snapped herself to more attention when she heard her own dreamy tone. 'Speaking as an only child, I mean. I'd want more.'

'Your parents never did?'

'Mum did, I think.' But Lisbet Leigh hadn't been the pants-wearer in their family. 'Dad was content with just me.'

'Why *"just"* you? I'm sure they are very proud of their only daughter.'

She let her head loll sideways on its neck brace. His way. 'You really are an idealist, aren't you?'

Was his total lack of offence at her ant-induced candour symbolic of his easygoing nature or of something more? Was Sam as engaged in her company as she was in his? Or was she just chasing rainbows? Maybe even painting them?

'I'm sure my father will be eternally disappointed that his one-and-only progeny wasn't really up to par,' she continued.

'Define par.'

She shrugged, and snuggled in tighter into her foil blanket. 'You know... Grades. Sports. Achievements.'

'You work for the country's leading science and culture body. That's quite an achievement.'

'Right. And I had good grades. Not record-breaking, but steady.'

'I can imagine.' He smiled, and it reminded her a little bit of the way people smiled at precocious children. Or drunks. She didn't like it.

'You're humouring me.'

'I'm—'

Choosing your words very carefully...?

'—just enjoying you.' He almost fell over himself to correct himself. 'Your company. Talking.'

Well... *Awkward, much?* 'Anyway, nothing short of medicine or law was ever going to satisfy my father. He's had high expectations of me my whole life.' And was constantly disappointed. Ironic, really, when she considered how his marriage had ended. Imploded. And how little he'd done to save it.

'Do you like what you do?'

'I *love* what I do.'

'Then that's what you're meant to be doing. Don't doubt yourself.'

His absolute certainty struck her. 'What if I might love being a doctor, too?'

He shrugged. 'Then that was where you'd have found yourself. Life has a way of working out.'

His assured belief was as foreign to her as it was exhausting. How would it feel to be that sure—about everything? She settled back against the seat and let her eyes flutter closed for a moment, just to take the sting of dryness out of them.

'Aimee—'

Sam was right there, gently rousing her with a feather touch to her cheek.

'I can't even rest my eyes?'

'You went to sleep.'

Oh. 'I can't sleep?'

He stroked her hair again. Almost like an apology. 'When you get to the hospital you can sleep all you want. But I need you to stay awake now. With me. Can you do that?'

Stay with me. Her sigh was more of a flutter deep in her chest. 'I can do that.' But it was going to be a challenge. It had to be four a.m. and she'd left at six yesterday morning. Twenty-four hours was a long haul, even if she *had* had some unconscious moments before he'd found her. And apparently another just now.

'Tell me about your research,' he said, clearly determined to keep her awake. 'What's your favourite story?'

She told him. All about wrinkled, weathered, ninety-five-year-old Dorothy Kenworthy, who'd come to Australia to marry a man she barely knew eight decades before. To start a life in a town she'd never heard of. A town full of prospects and gold and potential. About how poor they'd been, and how Dorothy's husband had pulled a small cart with his culture-shocked bride and her belongings the six-hundred kilometres inland from the coast to the mining town he'd called home. How long love had been in coming for them; about the day that it finally had. And about how severely Dorothy's heart had fractured the day, seventy years later, she'd lost him.

Stories of that kind of hardship were almost impossible to imagine now—how people had endured them—overcome them—and were always her favourites.

'Dorothy reminds me that there is always hope. No matter how dire things get.'

Sam's brow folded and he drifted away from her again. Not because he was bored—his intense focus while she'd been telling the start of the story told her that—but because he'd taken her words deep inside himself and was processing them.

'Why didn't she give up?' he eventually asked. 'When she was frightened and heatstroked and feeling so…alien.'

'Because she'd come so far. Literally and figuratively. And she knew how important she was to her husband. She didn't want to let him down.' His frown trebled as she watched. 'Plus she'd made a commitment. And she was a woman of great personal honour.'

'Is that something you believe in? Honouring commitments?'

'What do we have if not our honour?'

Finally his eyes came back to her. 'Is it her story on your thumb drive?'

'No. It's another one…'

She told him that one too. Then another, and another, sipping occasionally at the water he meted out sparingly and not minding when he shared from the same bottle. She didn't care if Search and Rescue Sam gave her a few boy germs while he was giving her the greatest gift any man in her life had ever given her.

He listened.

He showed interest. He asked questions. He didn't just listen waiting for an opportunity to talk about himself, or slowly veer the subject around to something of more interest to him. He *heard* her. He didn't interrupt. And he wasn't the slightest bit bored.

Just like that a light came on, bright and blazing and impossible to ignore, right at the back of Aimee's mind.

That was the kind of man she wanted for herself. That was the kind of man she'd never really believed existed. Yet here one sat: living, breathing evidence—her already compromised chest tightened—and the universe had handed him to *her*.

How had she ever thought a man like Wayne was even close to worthy? Maybe if she'd been allowed out more as a young girl, had got to meet more people, sample more personalities…Maybe then she never would have accepted Wayne's domination of her. Maybe if she hadn't grown up watching it, until her father had finally forced her mother's hand…

'I can see you love these stories.' His blue eyes were locked on her so firmly, but were conflicted, yet immobile. 'You're…glowing.'

Unaccustomed to the intensity he was beaming at her, and still unsettled by her thoughts of just a moment before, Aimee took shelter in flippancy. 'Maybe it's the glow-sticks.' She smiled and settled against the seat-back, her body begging her to let it drift into exhausted slumber. 'Or the sunrise.'

That seemed to snap him out of his blue-eyed trance. Around them the light had changed from the total absence of any light at all during the night to a deep, dark purple, then a navy. And the navy was lightening up in patches by the moment.

Sam glanced at his watch. A dozen worry lines formed on his face. 'Okay Aimee, the darkness is lifting. We made it.' He found her hand and held it. 'I'm going to need you to be very brave now, and to trust me more than ever.'

We will not fall. She heard the words though she knew he didn't say them.

It only took another few minutes before she realised why a new kind of tension radiated from his big body and from the hand he'd wrapped so securely around hers. The deep blue outside seemed to dilute as she watched it, and darkness began to take on the indistinct blurs of shape. Then they firmed up into more defined forms— the tree branch outside the window, the hint of a

hill on the horizon—as the first touch of lightness streaked high across the sky.

Her heart-rate accelerated as it struggled to
pump blood that seemed to thicken and grow
sluggish.

Around them she saw nothing but emerging
treetops—some higher than her poor battered
Honda, some lower. The front of the car was in
darkness longer than the areas around it because
the nose was buried in a treetop. Literally balancing in the crown of a big eucalypt, which threw
off its distinctive scent as the overnight frost
evaporated. In her shattered side mirror she could
see the angle of the hillside—steep and severe—
that the back of her little hatchback had wedged
against.

And they perched perilously between the two,
staring down into the abyss.

A black dread surged from deep inside
Aimee's terrified body. She sucked in a breath
to cry out but it froze, tortured, in her lungs and
only a pained squeak issued, as high as the elated
morning chorus of the birds around them but infinitely more horrified.

'Hold on to me, Aimee….'

Sam's voice was as much a tether as any of the
cables strapping her into her car, and she clung
to it emotionally even though she couldn't rip her
eyes from the scene she hung suspended over,
emerging through the shattered windscreen, as
the sun threw clarity across the morning and finally lifted the veil of darkness.

Her squeak evolved into a primitive whine and her entire body hardened into terrified rigour. The shadowy blur of Australian bush below them resolved itself into layer upon layer of towering treetops, falling away for hundreds of meters and narrowing to a sliver of water at the bottom of the massive gully she'd flown over the edge of.

Half a kilometre of deathly fall below the tenuous roost of her car, wedged between the treetop and the mountain.

Sam! Sam!

She couldn't even make vowels, let alone call to him. The only movement her body would allow was the microscopic muscular changes that pushed air out of her body in a string of agonised whimpers. Like a dog with a mortal injury.

'Look at me, Aimee...'

Impossible... It was so, *so* much worse than she'd feared even in her darkest moments. *Luck,* he'd called it, but it was more of a miracle that her car had hit the crown of this tree rather than plummeting straight past it and down to the tumbling rapids at the bottom of the gully. She'd have been dead before even getting down there, ricocheting off ancient trees like a pinball. Every single base instinct kept her eyes locked on the source of the sudden danger. The threat of the drop. Horrible, yet she couldn't look away.

Her heart slammed so hard against her ribs she thought they might crack further.

Sam forced himself into her line of vision, stretching across her to break the traction of her gaze on the certain death below. The shaft of pain from the extra pressure on her leg was more effective than anything in impacting on her crippled senses.

'Aimee…!'

Her eyes tried to drift past him, her face turning slightly, but he forced her focus back to him with insistent fingers on her chin.

'At me, Aimee… Look only at me.'

Only at me. She heard the words but couldn't process them. This was like last night all over again. *It's the shock,* something deep down inside her tossed up. It was the shock preventing her from looking at him. Understanding him.

The whining went on, completely independent of her will.

Sam slid both warm hands up on either side of her face and forced it to him. This close, he all but obliterated the dreadful view down to the forest floor. In that moment her whole world became the blue of his eyes, the golden tan of his skin and the blush of his lips.

'Aimee…' Sam's voice buzzed at her. 'Think about Dorothy. Think how frightened and alone she felt out there in the desert—fifteen years old, with a man she'd only just met. Think about the courage she would have had to have to go with him. To get onto that boat in Liverpool and leave her entire family for a hot, hostile country. Think about how hard she would have fought against the fear.'

The most genteel, gentle woman she'd ever

interviewed. And the toughest. Words finally scraped past her restricted larynx. 'She had her husband...'

'You have me.' He ducked his head to recapture her eyes. 'Aimee, you have me, and I'm going to get you out of here.'

This time her eyes didn't slide away, back to the void below them. They gripped onto Sam's.

He sighed his relief. 'There you are. Good girl.' He leaned in and pressed his hot lips to her clammy forehead.

The reassuring intimacy just about broke her again. 'Sam...'

'I know.' He dropped back into his position, lying across her, between her and the awful view. 'But you're okay. Nothing's going to happen to you. Not while I'm around.'

She blew three short puffs through frigid lips. 'Okay.'

Sudden noises outside drew his focus briefly away, and when it returned it was intent. 'Aimee... The extraction team are getting into position. Someone else is going to be taking over, but I'm not going to leave you, okay? I want you to remember that. We're going to get buffeted and separated for moments, but I'll always be there. I'm still tethered to you. Okay?'

She nodded, jerky and fast, curling her hand hard around his, not wanting to let go. Ever.

He stroked her hair back. 'It's about to get really, really busy, and no one's going to ask your permission for anything. They'll just take over.

You're going to hate that, but be patient. You'll be up top in no time and then you're back in charge.'

Her laugh was brittle and weak at the same time. 'I thought *you* were in charge.'

His smile eclipsed the sunrise. 'Nah. You just let me think that.'

She sobbed then, and pulled his hand to her lips and pressed them there. He rested his forehead on hers for a moment as the clanking outside drew closer.

'I wet myself,' she whispered, tiny and ashamed.

He wiped a tear away with his thumb. 'It doesn't matter.'

'I don't think I can do this.'

'You can do anything in this world that you set your mind to, Aimee Leigh.'

His confidence was so genuine, and so awfully misplaced, but it filled her with a blazing sort of optimism. Just enough to get her through this.

Just enough to do something really, really stupid.

She stretched as far forward as the flexi-straps would allow, pulled him by his rescue jacket towards her, and mashed her lips into his. Heat burst through her sensory system. His mouth was just as warm and soft as it had felt on her fingers, but sweet and strong and surprised at the same time, and salty from her own tears. She moved her lips against his, firming up the kiss, making it count, ignoring the fact that he wasn't reciprocating. Just insanely grateful for the fact that he hadn't pulled back.

Her heart beat out its triumph.

An unfamiliar face dropped in spider-like at their side window just as Sam tore his mouth away from hers. A dozen different expressions chased across his rugged features in a heartbeat: pity, embarrassment, confusion, and—*there!*—the tiny golden glow of reciprocal desire.

The man suspended in space outside the car did as good a job of schooling his surprise as Sam did—maybe they were all trained to mask their feelings—and immediately cracked the glass of her driver's side window. One part of her screamed at the intrusion of sudden noise and calamity, but it was just as well.

What would she have said otherwise?

Sam gathered himself together faster. He looked out at the crew now swarming over the Honda and then back at her. And then he smiled. In that smile was understanding, forgiveness, and just a trace of regret.

He brushed her hair back from her face again, and Aimee thought she'd never be able to brush her own hair without imagining his callused fingers doing it for her.

'Okay, Aimee,' he said. 'Here we go.'

And as a second man scrabbled into the back of the hatch and squeezed himself around the tree limb still buried there Sam smiled and winked at her.

'Race you to the top.'

It took nearly three hours for the emergency crew to cut Aimee free, get her safely fixed onto a spine board, and carefully slide her backwards out of her car and up the gully-face to the waiting ambulance.

Sam hadn't been kidding about his crew taking over. She was pushed, pulled, yanked and poked every which way, and only Sam was there to dose her up with ant juice and look out for her dignity, tied to her the whole time by his industrial umbilical cord. But she stayed silent and let them do what they had to do, and closed her eyes for the entire last third of it, because watching her own ascent up the hillside required more strength than she thought she had. She tuned her mind in to the sound of Sam's voice—capable and professional as he gave instructions and followed others.

'Last bit, Aimee,' he said, close and private, as they finally pulled her up onto the road she'd gone flying off. 'It's going to get even more crazy now.'

She turned her head towards him as best she could in her moulded spinal brace and opened her mouth to thank him, but as she did so someone stuck a thermometer into it and she found herself suddenly cranked up onto wheels and rushing towards a waiting ambulance. He jogged alongside like her personal bodyguard, and in the split second before she was surrounded by paramedics she thought how little she would mind being protected by a man if it was a man like Sam doing the protecting.

Yet how ironic that she'd practically run away

from the first two phases of her life because she'd been smothered.

She lifted the pained fingers of her dislocated arm in a limp kind of thank-you, but he saw it, jogging to a halt as they reached the ambulance. He unclipped his tether.

'Goodbye. Good luck with your recovery.' He was one hundred percent professional in the company of his peers, and her stomach dropped. Had she truly imagined the closeness between them?

But then she caught the expression in his eyes—wistful, pained—and he lifted a damp strand of hair from her face, those lips she'd pressed her own against whispering silently, 'Live your life, Aimee.'

And then he was gone, and she was strapped unceremoniously into the back of a clean, safe ambulance, mercifully sitting on four wheels up on terra firma. She craned her neck as much as her tight restraints would allow and tried to track Sam in the suddenly chaotic crowd.

Emergency crew. Farmers with heavy loaders. Onlookers milling around. Presumably all the people who couldn't get along the A10 because her rescue was in the way.

But then there he was—straightening out his kinked back and reaching for the sky with the fingers that had first stretched out to her in the darkness. Even with his heavy rescue gear on she knew that his body would be hard and fit and healthy below it.

An irritating orange blur blocked her view,

and she tried to look around the emergency crew member who had climbed into the ambulance after her.

'Sam said you needed this,' the stranger said, placing her handbag on the gurney next to her.

Aimee's eyes fell on it as though it was a foreign object.

'It is yours?' the man asked, suddenly uncertain.

Aimee made herself remember that this man had spent a freezing night on a mountain to save her life, and that it wasn't his fault Sam had reneged on his promise to bring it to her in the hospital.

'Y-yes. Thank you.'

Sam knew how much she was worried about the oral history on the thumb drive inside. He didn't want her separated from it for longer than necessary. Her eyes drifted back to him again as the stranger shifted slightly in the ambulance and her heart swelled.

Such a good man.

But, as she watched, a fragile, porcelain-featured woman hurried through the throng of onlookers and hurled herself at Sam—*her* Search-and-Rescue-Sam—and threw slim arms around his neck. Those masculine arms that had kept her so safe on the hillside slid automatically around the woman's waist and he picked her up, swinging her gently around as she buried her face into his neck.

The orange blur blocked her view again as the stranger turned to climb out of the ambulance.

'Wait! Please!' Aimee called out to him, and he turned back. 'That woman…with Sam. Who is she?'

It never occurred to her not to ask, and it clearly never occurred to him not to answer, because he turned around, located them in the crowd, and then brought his gaze back to Aimee.

'Oh, that's Melissa,' he said, as if that explained it all. 'Sam's wife.'

CHAPTER FIVE

Eleven months later

Wow. Where had the year gone?

Sam caught the sideways glance of the woman next to him and pressed a damp palm onto his right thigh to still its irritating bounce. He straightened, then shifted, then loosened and re-fixed his tie one more time. What he wouldn't give to be hanging off the side of a mountain somewhere, rather than sitting here today...waiting. To either side of him was a mix of old and young, male and female, trained professionals and passers-by. All nervous—like him. All lined up—like him—to get their handshake from the Governor General and a commendation for bravery.

A commendation for doing what he was paid to do.

He shook his head.

He'd participated in six other rescues in the eleven months since he'd hauled Aimee Leigh's battered car up that cliff-face. Since the ambulance doors had slammed shut on that rescue and raced off down the winding A10. No sirens. The best news in an otherwise crappy day. No sirens meant no critical emergency. No sirens meant his assessment of her injuries and his handling of them as they'd carefully winched Aimee up the rock-face had been correct. Busted leg, dislocated shoulder, chest bruising.

No sirens meant the tree had come off worse than she did.

Thank God.

Her little car had been a write-off. She'd been fond of it, judging by the gloss in its paint work and the careful condition of its interior before nature tore it to pieces, and he'd become pretty fond of it, too, by the time they'd finished examining the towed up wreck. How something that small had managed to preserve the precious life in it against an impact like that...

Pretty miraculous.

'Gregory?' a voice called down from the top of a small set of temporary steps. 'Sam Gregory?'

Damn. His turn.

For lack of any other kind of moral support here today he turned to the stranger next to him and lifted his eyebrows in question. The older woman gave him a quick visual once over and a reassuring nod, then wished him luck as he pushed to his feet, tugging at the suit that felt so foreign on him.

But Mel had nagged him into wearing it.

Not that she'd know if he'd switched out of it

halfway to the ceremony today, as he'd used to when he ditched school. Maybe he could have skipped the whole thing—gone sightseeing in Canberra instead. She'd have no idea.

She wasn't here.

She'd said she would come, but she'd been gnawing her lip at the time, and he knew she had a lot going on at work. Knew she'd be here under sufferance. And that was worse than having no one here.

Or so he'd thought at the time.

'This way Mr Gregory,' the assistant stage manager murmured, walking with him to the edge of the enormous drapes which framed the simple setting on stage. The recipient before him was standing awkwardly in the centre of the stage as the master of ceremonies segued into amateur mobile phone video of a man—the awkward man—dangling by braced legs off the edge of a bridge in the north of their country, snatching survivors from torrential flood waters as they tumbled under it. He'd caught and saved three people that day. No one was talking about those that his numb fingers hadn't been able to hold on to.

That's heroic. A man who'd been servicing a farm truck one minute and was risking his life for strangers the next. No training. No equipment. No crew backing him up. No time to change his mind. The only man left standing as an inland tsunami careened through his town.

Sam flexed his shoulders. Why anyone

thought *he* was worthy of even standing on the same stage as a guy like that…

He'd wanted to knock it back when his supervisor had first told him of the nomination. But his boss had guilted him into coming, warning him that not accepting it with grace was an insult to the men and women he worked with who'd missed out on being nominated.

'Do it for the Unit,' Brian had urged.

So here he was, dressed up in a monkey suit, taking one—quite literally—for the team, walking onstage right after a bona-fide hero to accept an award for just doing his job.

The man by his side signalled to his equivalent on the opposite corner of the stage as the video finished and the lights rose, and Sam's eyes followed across the open space. There were two people over there, the second one mostly in shadow because of the bright stage lights between them, but Sam knew instantly who it would be. His chest tightened.

Aimee.

The other reason he'd come. She was here to hand him his award. He needed to look at Aimee Leigh and know that she'd made it—know his efforts had not been in vain and that she'd gone back to a normal, healthy, *long* life.

He needed closure.

Maybe then she'd quit stalking his dreams.

'Stand by, Mr Gregory…'

A low murmur next to him. The live point in his throat pulsed hard enough to feel.

The MC finished his speech and the farmer on stage stepped forward—every bit as awkward and uncomfortable in *his* brand-new suit as Sam was—and accepted the glinting medal offered to him by the immaculately dressed Governor General.

It hit Sam then what a big deal this was, and how right his boss had been. This gong was for every single one of his colleagues who put their life on the line for others. It really wasn't about him.

Applause—thundering applause—as the Queenslander left the stage, and then the MC glanced their way to make sure they were ready. Then he spoke in dramatic, hushed tones into the microphone. Sam took a deep breath and expelled it in a long, slow, controlled stream.

'Our next recipient spent a long, dangerous night on a cliff-face squeezed into a teetering, crushed hatchback to make sure its driver was lifted to safety...'

Jeez. Did they have to over-sell it quite that much? There had been no teetering, and only partial crushing... Sam used the same techniques he used on rock-faces to control his breathing. *In two, out two...* And then suddenly the venue was echoing with more applause and he was being nudged onto the stage.

Nerves stampeded past his eardrums, merging with the drone of the audience. Hundreds of faces beamed back at him from the stalls, all of them there for someone else's award but perfectly willing to celebrate anyone receiving a commendation that day. The MC was still speaking—going through Sam's service record—but he wasn't really listening. His eyes briefly lifted as the dignitary stepped forward to shake his hand, and he did his best to look sincere through his nerves.

'Thank you, Governor General,' he murmured.

But then his eyes slid of their own accord to the curtain on the far side of stage. The shadow had stepped out into the half-light beyond the spotlight and stood quietly waiting. Perfectly upright. All limbs accounted for.

He sucked in a deep breath. *Here we go...*

'And here today, to present Sam Gregory with his Commendation for Bravery is the woman whose life he saved on that Tasmanian mountainside—Miss Aimee Leigh.'

A spotlight swung round to where Aimee hovered in the wings, and she stepped forward nervously but with determination. Sam concentrated on breathing through his nose. She wore a long lemon skirt and a feminine white blouse, and a killer pair of strap on heels that gave her a few unnecessary inches. He realised then that he'd never seen her standing up. He'd imagined her smaller, somehow, although her height was completely perfect for the strong, brave woman he'd spent the best part of a night with.

In the worst imaginable way...

Her long hair was gone—cut short. One of the things he remembered so clearly about that night was having to slide his hand under her thick crop of sweat-damp blonde hair to check her pulse, but seeing it now, trimmed back to a chaos of wisps around a naturally made up face… It was perfect. Kind of Tinker Bell.

Very Aimee.

For no good reason he suddenly craved a shot of O_2—maybe it would steady him as he stood there under such intense scrutiny from the crowd in the eternity it seemed to take for Aimee to walk across the stage towards him. She'd been dressed down for her drive into the highlands a year ago, and the only thing on her skin back then had been blood and air-bag dust, so he hadn't expected this…*vision*. Perfectly groomed, carefully made-up.

Beautiful.

And, best of all, one hundred percent alive.

But those glistening rose lips weren't smiling as she stepped closer, and she was working hard to keep her lashes down, avoiding eye-contact with him or anyone. Sam's focus flew to the two tiny fists clenched at either side of her. Something about the defensive body-language made his own muscles bunch up. Was she here under sufferance? Or did she hate public displays as much as he did?

'Aimee has asked to be excused from making a speech,' the MC boomed into the mic, 'but we're thrilled she's here to give this commendation to the man who saved her life last year.'

Her high heels drew to a halt in front of the lectern and her green eyes lifted to the Governor

General, who handed her a medal on an embroidered ribbon. Her smile as she took it from him was weak, but it dissolved completely to nothing as she steeled herself to face him. As if she was facing a firing squad.

His gut clenched. He hadn't expected a brass band, but he'd definitely expected a smile. Or something.

'Aimee...?'

She lifted her eyes and they were wide with caution but otherwise carefully blank. Her tightly pressed lips split into a pained smile for the crowd's benefit and she held trembling fingers forward to present him with the medal. Sam took it from her with his left hand and slid his right into the one she offered him—perfunctorily, as if she could almost not bear to touch his hand, let alone shake it.

What the hell...?

This was a woman whose life he'd saved. A woman he'd spent hours talking with, sharing with. Whose pain he'd stroked away. Who'd kissed him in her gratitude. And she couldn't even bring herself to smile at him now. He frowned.

Screw that.

When she went to pull her hand away he held it longer than was necessary, drawing shocked lagoon-coloured eyes back up to his. He locked onto them, and her lips fell slightly apart at his intensity.

'You cut your hair,' he whispered, for her

benefit only. And for something to say. Then he made himself smile through the gravity of this moment.

As if his banal observation was some kind of ice-pick in the glacier of her resistance the blank *nothing* leached from her eyes, and they flashed briefly with confusion before filling with a bright, glinting relief he virtually basked in. Her tense façade cracked and fell away, leaving only the Aimee he remembered from the A10, and before he knew it she was stretched to her toe-tips and throwing her arms around his already tight shirt collar. Completely on instinct his hands slid around her waist and he held her close, returning her embrace.

The crowd leapt to his feet to cheer.

'I missed you,' she whispered into his ear, as though she'd been waiting a year to tell him that. The warmth of her breath against his skin made it pucker. 'It's so good to see you.'

As he held onto a woman who wasn't his wife in front of two hundred people who weren't his friends, Sam realised what those dreams and memories he'd been suppressing had tried to tell him.

He'd missed her, too.

Even though he'd only known her a few hours he'd missed Aimee for *a year,* and kept her close in his sub-conscious. Never quite on the surface—just out of it. As she'd stood in the shadows of the spotlight just now.

Waiting.

His arms tightened further, swinging her just slightly off her feet and forcing her curves more firmly up against him. His commendation dangled forgotten from his fingers.

After all, *this* was all the reward he needed.

Aimee's heart had still not settled twenty minutes later as the two of them stood talking in a quiet corner backstage. She'd dreaded this for so long—but one look from those baffled, wounded blue eyes had totally washed away her resolve, rewound the past eleven-months-nine-days-and-sixteen-hours and thrown them straight back into the place where two complete strangers could feel so instantly connected.

So... It hadn't gone away.

Had she really believed it would?

'You must have people waiting for you?' Aimee hinted at last, giving him a graceful exit point if he wanted one. Just in case she was wrong about the connection.

He shook his head and let the exit slide. 'Nope. I came up to Canberra alone.'

She only noticed she'd suspended her breath when her chest forced her to exhale. 'Your... family didn't come with you?' God, she was such a coward. But she didn't want to ask. She wanted him to volunteer it openly. Honestly.

To prove he wasn't like her father.

'They're all at home. They wanted to fly up but I refused. Too expensive for all of them. I'll go see them before I head back to Tassie. Take the medal.'

'Oh.' What else could she say? There was only one thing she wanted to know, and she couldn't ask it.

Why wasn't *she* here?

He filled the silence where she should have spoken. 'And the Parks Service couldn't spare anyone because they're covering for me being here.' His eyes shadowed briefly. 'And Mel couldn't get away from work.'

Her heart thumped at both the hollow tone in his voice and the unexpected opening. 'Mel?' she asked, all innocence.

'Melissa. My wife.'

It was barely a pause, but it was there. Aimee glanced down at his left hand. Still bare.

He read her expression and his fingers slid in between the buttons of his dress shirt, fished out a gold wedding band on a chain. 'I wear it around my neck. It's too exposed at work.'

Another one of a dozen deluded scenarios crumbled to dust. Like the one in which Sam and his wife were actually divorced but still good friends. Or the one where the orange-clad volunteer had simply made a mistake all those months ago, confused Sam with someone else. Or the one in which they all changed religion and Sam found himself in need of an additional wife.

Anything that meant he wasn't some kind of sleazoid, disguising his married status.

Aimee sighed. The truth was Sam wasn't

hiding his wedding ring, he was *protecting* it. That good-guy gene at work again. 'I'm sure she was really disappointed not to be able to get here today.'

His eyes shadowed. 'Yes.'

The audience burst into applause for the ninth and final recipient on stage and Aimee felt her opportunity slipping away. The ceremony would be over in minutes and he'd go back to his life. Where she wasn't invited.

'Why didn't you mention you were married?' she blurted, and then winced at her own lack of art.

His leonine brow folded. 'Rescue is a—'

Someone rushed past, calling all the recipients together for a newspaper photograph. Sam's lips pressed together to contain his irritation. Then he flicked his eyes back to hers. They glittered with intensity even in the shadows. 'Aimee, are you in Canberra for the day? Would you like to grab a coffee?'

That couldn't be a good idea. Could it? She glanced at her watch and pretended to consider it.

'I'd just like to talk. To find out how everything went after the rescue.'

The rescue. The reason she was here. Surely it wouldn't be civil to throw his medal at him and then run. The man who'd saved her life. She nodded. 'Sure. I have time.'

His broad smile was ridiculously rewarding.

Those white, even teeth. That hint of a dimple on the right. And it was all too easy to imagine that it was relief lingering at its corners.

'Ten minutes!' he said, and then dashed off for his media call.

He's married, a stern voice whispered.

'It's only coffee,' she muttered under the thrum of the ceremony's closing music out front.

But he's married.

Aimee took a deep, mournful breath. She'd been kidding herself if she'd thought she'd put Sam out of her heart as well as her mind. He was always there somewhere, lingering. Popping up at the most inconvenient times. Just waiting to claw his way back into prominence at the first available opportunity.

Reminding her of the kind of man she still hadn't found.

But *married* was more than a deal-breaker for her. Her family had been torn apart when she was a child, thanks to her father applying a rather too flexible interpretation to his vows. She was not about to start messing with someone else's marriage.

No matter how tempting.

Just coffee, though. To say thank you properly, to apologise for the embarrassing kiss, and to wish Sam well with his life… Coffee was public and harmless and agenda-free. Coffee wasn't like a drink at a bar. Or in a hotel room. Or over breakfast. Coffee was just coffee and a little bit of conversation. And then that would be that.

They could part as friends, instead of strangers.

Life would go back to normal.

CHAPTER SIX

'So you were only in for a few days? Amazing.'

Aimee lowered her skirt down her leg, back over the pin-scars high on her calf that she'd just been showing Sam. The only physical reminder she had of her night on the side of a mountain.

'It's good to be able to talk to you about this,' she said, sipping her latte. 'No one else gets it. They look at my little scars and think that somehow reflects the scale of the accident.'

'You haven't talked about it to anyone?'

'The counsellor at the hospital.' *Though mostly about growing up as a human tug-of-war, as it turned out.* 'My friend Danielle.' *Mostly about you.* 'But I only gave my parents the basics…'

'You mean you played it down.' He smiled.

She thought about hedging, but then laughed. 'Only because they were already so freaked out by a two a.m. phone call from your crew.'

'Have you dealt with it at all?'

'Yes. I've gone over it a hundred different ways. Things I might have done differently, *should* have done differently…' She dropped her eyes away. 'I'm pretty reconciled to having handled it as best I could.'

'You were brilliant. You made it so easy for me to help you.'

She lifted her eyes. 'I wanted to thank you. Right after…But you were—' *kissing your wife* '—busy.' She sighed. 'The nomination was the closest I could get.'

'*You* made the nomination?'

She nodded. 'I felt like an idiot. All I knew was the date and location of the accident and your first name. But they did the rest.'

'That changes everything.'

'What everything?'

'I didn't want the award. I thought it was crazy that the state would nominate me for just doing my job. But you…' His eyes warmed the whole front corner of the café and his smile soaked into her. 'You I'll accept it from.'

'Good. You'll never know the difference that day made for me.'

'Tell me now.'

Her eyes flew wide as she lifted them. 'Now?'

'You didn't make a speech at the awards. Make one now. Tell me what it meant to you.'

Words wouldn't come. She opened her mouth to say something pithy, but that wouldn't come either. She shuddered in a deep breath and began at the one place she knew she'd already taken him.

'That night changed me, Sam. You showed me that there was a difference between taking *charge* and taking *over*. I hadn't ever seen that before.'

Three little creases appeared between his brows.

Okay. She wasn't explaining this at all well. She leaned forward. 'It took me a long time to realise that the crash mats my parents surrounded me with as I was growing up was more about them than me. But by then I'd bought into all that care and concern and I'd forgotten how to be independent. Maybe I never even learned.'

Sam frowned at her and waited silently for her to continue.

'Then I met Wayne, and I let him drive our relationship because I'd become so accustomed to other people doing my thinking for me. Taking over. Giving me instructions.'

Sam frowned. 'Like I did.'

She shook her head. 'You showed me that the best kind of capability doesn't come from bossing. It comes from influencing.'

Sam frowned at her again.

'You did it the entire time we were in the car. You wanted me to do things but you didn't order me to. You simply gave me the facts and the reason for your request and your preference and you let me decide. Or you asked. And if I said no you respected that—even when it was the wrong decision. Then you just compensated for my glaring bad calls.'

He looked supremely uncomfortable with the

praise. 'Aimee, I just treated you the way I'd want to be treated in the same situation.'

'Which is how?'

He thought about that. 'Like an adult. With all the facts.' Then his expression cleared. 'Like a team.'

'Yes! I have never in my life felt like I belonged to a team, where we worked together for a solution. It was always about compliance or conflict.' She held up her two hands as though they were scales, with one or other of those words weighing heavily in them.

'Well, I'm glad. We were a team that night. We had equal stakes the moment I climbed into that car, so we deserved equal say on what went down.'

She leaned forward earnestly. 'See—that's a novelty to me. The whole idea of equity. I love it.'

He seemed enchanted by her excitement. But a little bemused. 'I'm glad.'

His gentle teasing warmed her every bit now as it had back in the car. 'Don't laugh at me. This is revolutionary. I don't ever want to go back to being that person who needed permission to get through the day. I still shake my head that I let it happen at all. You saved so much more than my physical self on the mountain.'

'Don't go canonising me just yet. I'm sure you were already halfway to this realisation yourself.'

'What do you mean?'

'You were heading up to the highlands to reassess your life. You'd broken off your dud relationship. You were managing your parents.'

If by 'managing' he meant avoiding… 'Okay, so I wasn't starting from zero, but it took that accident to really spotlight what was wrong with my life. And you were wielding that spotlight.'

He grinned. 'Nice analogy.'

'Thank you. It's the storyteller in me.' She finished her coffee and signalled for another before turning back to Sam, her biggest and most exciting secret teetering on her tongue. 'Anyway, that's why I'm so grateful. It's changed the way I do my work, too.'

He cocked his head.

'I got to thinking about what you said—about how my oral histories collect dust once I'm finished with them.'

Sam winced. 'Aimee, I'm sorry. I probably said a lot of careless stuff that night. I was just trying to keep you awake.'

'You were absolutely right. But I'd been too uncertain of myself before to do anything to change that.'

'Before?'

'That's how I've come to think of things. Before the accident and after the accident.' Actually it was before-Sam and after-Sam, but she wasn't about to tell him that. He'd bolt from the café before his spoon even hit the floor. She pressed her hands to the table, leaned forward, lowered her voice. 'I'm going to write a book.'

His eyebrows shot up. 'Really?'

'Really. I'm going to pull together all the stories I've collected about people who grabbed their futures by the throat and took a crazy chance. People like Dorothy. And how that paid off…or didn't. But the important thing is that they were the navigators of their own destiny one way or another. Oh! That could be the title… *Navigators!*'

He stared at her, bright interest in his eyes as her brain galloped ahead. 'Good for you, Aimee.'

Her lungs struggled to reinflate as the full impact of all that focus hit her. She pushed them to co-operate, and it was almost harder speaking now than back in her squished Honda. 'And it's not because you made me feel like what I do isn't complete… It's because it's *not* complete. These particular stories always resonated for me. I just never recognised it.'

Sam smiled. 'I love the idea, Aimee. Let me know if there's anything I can do to help.'

She straightened, took a deep breath and held his eyes. 'Let me do *you*.'

His whole body jerked back.

'Your story!' she rushed on. 'Oh, my God… Let me interview you for your story.' Heat surged up her throat and she knew there was nothing she could do to change that. Intense Sam was only half as gorgeous as Sam in a full belly-laugh, but he treated her to one now, as she stumbled out of the awkward moment. 'I want to include some more contemporary stories as well, and you're about the most proficient navigator I've ever met. I'd love to include you.'

'My story's not really all that interesting, Aimee.'

'Everyone's story is interesting, Sam. Just not to them.'

He stared at her. 'You're serious? You want to put me into your book?'

'I want to thank you—' She held up her hand as he went to interrupt. 'In a way more meaningful than just an award nomination or a couple of cups of coffee. You were present at the moment that redefined my life and I want to reflect that importance.' She sat up straighter. 'So, yes, I want the man that saved my life in my book.' Such naked insistence still didn't come naturally to her, but she squashed down her instinctual discomfort.

'Can I think about it?'

She took a fast breath. 'No. You'll refuse if you think about it.'

His smile then warmed her heart. 'Look at you, getting all take-charge.'

Her laugh burbled up into an excited squeak. 'I know!'

'Maybe you know my story already.'

'You're a modest man, Sam. It's part of your charm. I understand that you won't want this story to be some kind of reflection of how important *you* think the work you do is, but I really want it to reflect how important that work is— *was*—to me.' She forced herself to keep her stare locked on him, even while every cell of Old Aimee demurred, whispered that her insistence was ungracious. Not feminine. *Scandalous.* 'Please say yes.'

His eyes narrowed. 'What's involved?'

'You'll hate it,' she said without the tiniest pause. 'It involves more coffee.'

A hint of a twitch in his left eye was the only clue that he was smiling on the inside. But it was enough. 'If we're going to have more coffee I need some food to soak it up,' he said. 'Are you hungry?'

'Ravenous.'

Suddenly she was. After months of barely picking at even the most delectable meals. Sam was going to be in her book. Sam was going to share a little bit of himself with her.

And an entire afternoon.

All of a sudden her chest didn't feel large enough for the organs in it as she squeezed out speech. 'What time's your flight?'

He stared at her, his eyes carefully neutral. 'Late enough.'

It was beyond refreshing to see a woman inhale her lunch the way Aimee did, despite their plates being piled high with home-cooked Italian food and herbed bread. He was so used to Melissa and her friends either fussing about the dressing on the tiny salad they were expecting their bodies to function on, or getting stuck into something more substantial and then punishing themselves endlessly for enjoying it.

The kind of unabashed feeding frenzy he was witness to now reminded him of home. Of his family.

They'd taken their meals to a more comfortable booth, and chatted about other rescues he'd worked on in the past year, and about her heritage work, and whether either of them had been in Canberra before, and then, before he'd even looked away from her, a waitress had materialised from nowhere and was clearing their empty plates and bringing more coffee.

'I may never sleep again,' Aimee joked as she blew the steam off her fourth latte.

But there was something about this afternoon: something blindly indulgent that made a bottomless cup of coffee and pasta carb-loading seem as reasonable as his almost gluttonous need for conversation.

Aimee's conversation.

He knew she was intelligent from their hours in the car, but back then she'd been suppressed by pain and medication and—if her epiphany was to be believed—by her own personal demons. But this Aimee had a lightness and an optimism so untrained and raw it was almost captivating. Like a newly emerged butterfly testing out its wings. Definitely engaging. And thoroughly contagious. So much so that by the time she slid a little digital recorder from her handbag into the centre of the cleared table and set it to record he was no longer dreading his decision to help her out.

'You carry that with you everywhere?'

'Yup.'

Her eagerness touched him almost as much as her innocence prickled at his senses. Taunted him. Drew him. 'You really are excited by this book, aren't you?' he said.

Her green eyes sparkled. 'Beyond words. This idea is one hundred percent mine—sink or swim, for better or worse.'

He twitched, but only slightly. Was the mention of marriage vows intentional? A reminder to both of them to keep things professional? If so, it was it was well timed.

'So…' She adjusted the recorder and pointed one end towards him. 'Tell me about your family. You're the oldest of…what was it?…seven?'

'Eight. Second oldest.'

'Big family.'

'Lots of love to go around.'

'That's nice. So no one went wanting?'

He reeled a little. 'Uh…?'

She smiled so serenely it took the edge off his anxiety about where this was going. 'Don't worry—this isn't some kind of exposé. I just want to get to the heart of your background. I like to leap right in. It saves lots of preliminary warm-up.'

Plus, they'd been warming up all afternoon,

technically speaking. 'Okay, uh…no… No one went wanting.'

'How much of that was thanks to big brother Sam?'

He thought about that. 'We all pitched in and looked after each other. Dad worked pretty long hours so Mum needed support.'

'Were you her favourite?'

'There's a loaded question.' He laughed. 'I felt like her favourite, but I'm sure every one of my siblings would say the same. Mum was good like that.'

'Tell me about your parents. How did they meet?'

Sam took her through what he knew of the romance that was his parents' marriage. Some of the challenges, the wins, the losses, their decision to come to Australia and start a new life.

'Sounds almost idyllic.'

'It wasn't without its challenges, but my folks have worked their way through every major bump in their road to happiness. They're great role models.'

'How many of you are married?' she asked.

He blinked. 'Just me and one sister.'

'Too hard to live up to for everyone else?'

His stomach tightened. 'What do you mean?'

'I mean your parents' example. Pretty tough act to follow?'

He struggled against the automatic bristling that came when anyone criticised his family. She was just curious. And she wasn't all that far off the mark, in truth. 'I think we'd all consider it inspirational. Not demoralising.'

She watched him steadily. 'That's nice, then.'

'Yeah, it is.'

'Is that how it is for you?'

His chest matched the tightness in his gut. *Here it comes.* The subject neither of them was mentioning. 'What?'

'Your marriage. Do you aspire to a relationship as strong as your parents'?'

'You're assuming it's not already like that?' And that was a big call on just a few hours' collective acquaintance in which the topic had almost never been raised. He couldn't stop his arms folding across his front.

A hint of colour pinked her cheeks and highlighted the deep green of her eyes. It galled him that his body noticed that even when he was annoyed. He forced his hormones to heel.

'You're right. I am. Sorry. I just…'

But she swallowed back whatever she'd been about to say. So he called her on it: partly to see just how strong her reinforced spinal column really was, and partly because he wanted to see what had made her assume as she had. If he was giving off clues to strangers that his marriage wasn't rock-solid, did that mean Mel might pick up on them, too?

'Just what?'

A dozen expressions chased across her expressive eyes and finally resolved into caution. 'She didn't come. Today,' she added when he just stared at her. 'Today was a really big deal and she didn't come. And I know that the complimentary air tickets were for two because I didn't use my plus-one either.'

She had no one to bring. His antenna started vibrating with a bit too much interest at that piece of information and so he buried it under a land-slide of hastily whipped up umbrage and forced his focus where it belonged. Defending Melissa was second nature.

'She works. Hard.'

'I know. You said.' Then Aimee leaned forward and he got a flash of cream curve as her breasts rose and fell. 'But so does your father, and I'm guessing he would have moved the earth to be there if it was your mother shaking the Governor General's hand and being recognised by his country.'

A cold, twisted kind of ugly settled in his belly. It was sixty percent righteousness, forty percent guilt, and one hundred percent reflex. He'd had *exactly* those thoughts himself. 'Are *you* offering me relationship advice? Seriously?'

His subtle emphasis on *you* didn't escape her, and the hurt and disappointment in her expression were immediate. As if she'd been suspending breath, waiting for something to happen.

And he'd just been that something.

Shame bit—down low.

'No.' She smiled, but it was half-hearted and without the luminosity of before. 'That would be like asking me to get *you* out of a stricken vehicle on a mountain. It's just not in my skill set.'

He hated his own overreaction almost as much

as how fast she was to put herself down when challenged. Both smacked of long-standing defensive tools. So her healing was still a work in progress, then.

She went on before he could. 'But I do know something about people. And subtext. I'm trained to read between the lines.'

'My relationship with Melissa is *not* fodder for your book,' he stated flatly.

'You think your wife is not material to your life story?'

He wiped his hands purely for the satisfaction of throwing his serviette down onto the table. The international symbol for *this discussion is over*. 'I think if you want to include her then we should get her agreement.'

This was where a polite person would step back, oil the waters. Aimee just leaned forward. 'You're protective of her.'

'Of course I am. She's my wife.'

'You love her.'

'She's my wife,' he reiterated.

Her perfect face tipped. 'Why are you so defensive?'

'Why are you so pushy? Are you upset I didn't tell you I was married? I met Melissa through one of my brothers, we were together two years and then we got married. End of story.'

Except that was complete bull. There was so much more to their story.

A hint more pink crept into her cheeks. Or was it just that the colour around it had faded? She leaned forward again, lowered her voice. 'Why didn't you mention her to me before? There were so many opportunities.'

A dangerously good question. Was it because he'd felt the simmering *something* between them in their perilous little nest on the mountainside and hadn't wanted it to evaporate? Was he that desperate for a hint of attraction, even back then?

Uncertainty clenched, tight and unfamiliar, in his chest.

'It was none of your business.' Present tense included. *How do you like that subtext?*

Her face froze and her fists curled into nuggets on the table. She took a moment collecting herself. It reminded him of something…

'I…' She pressed her lips together, sat back.

It hit him then—what he was being reminded of. Aimee looked right now as she'd looked back on that mountainside. Pale…stiff. When she'd been in shock, but trying not to let on. It was such a direct echo of how she'd looked all those months ago, hanging off the side of the A10, that he couldn't help the memories surging in. How close he'd felt to her when she was toughing it out in the darkness. How impressed he'd been at her calmness under pressure. How open she'd been with him about her fears and vulnerabilities. How hard he'd worked to keep her safe.

How connected he'd felt to her.

Apparently mutual.

Even now, after he'd just been a bastard and hurt one of the most open and innocent people

he knew rather than manning up to his own inad-
equacies.

It was palpable.

He shifted to dislodge his body's intense focus.

'You know…' Her face twisted in concentration. 'I owe you an apology, Sam. I've spent so
much time dwelling on those hours up in the
highlands I think I've…' she physically grappled
for the right word '…infused them with too much
meaning. That day was life-changing for me, but
it really was just business as usual for you. No
wonder you're uncomfortable with the nomination. With my obsession on having you in my
book.' She reached forward and turned off the
recorder, her eyes averted. 'I'm so sorry.'

Shame gnawed at his intestines. He was being
an ass. 'Aimee…'

She forced her earnest gaze back to his. 'I
wanted to do something as meaningful for you
as you did for me that day. And I don't have anything to give you other than my interest and the
way I see your story fitting into my book. I can't
offer you anything else to express how much you
did for me.'

'You don't need to.'

'I do need to. For me. I need to…balance the
scales.' She reached for her handbag. 'But I've
forced a connection that isn't there for you, and
I'm sorry.'

Everything inside him twisted. 'Don't leave…'

Her laugh was brittle and her hurried words
were for herself. 'I've already made a fool of

myself with you once. I really should learn from my mistakes.'

That kiss. So she did remember it. 'Aimee—sit…'

A tiny frown braved the storm of recrimination blustering around it. 'I wish you all the best for the future, Sam.' She was on her feet and swinging her bag onto her shoulder, and then a heartbeat later she was stepping away. Walking away. Doing what he should do. What was best all round.

But he knew he wouldn't. He stood.

'So that's it?' The corner of his lip practically curled. *'Thanks for saving my life, Sam. Have a nice life.'* Two people at nearby tables tried very hard to pretend they hadn't heard that.

Aimee slowly turned back to him, her face guarded. 'You want my firstborn in return?'

Frustration ripped at him. He was screwing this up. Royally. 'Don't leave, Aimee.'

She stood like the proverbial salt pillar, indecision etched into her expression. So he battled on. Risked exposing his true self. 'Your rescue was not business as usual—though it should have been. I don't know what that means, and I don't want to read into it, and I absolutely don't want to *do* anything about it.' He sucked in a breath, and the people at the next table abandoned their efforts to not listen in. 'But you of all people asking me about my marriage was just too…'

He ran out of courage. And words. And air.

Her handbag slipped off her shoulder and she

twisted the strap in her hands. 'Do you want to talk about it?'

'No. Not at all.' But, yes, he really did. Aimee Leigh was the last person he should want to talk about his marriage with, but just then she was also the *only* person he could imagine talking about it with.

'All right.' She collected the handbag in front of her. Its next stop was surely back on her shoulder and swinging out through the door.

Suddenly all his priorities shrank down to just one simple one: keeping Aimee in this café. 'But I don't want us to part like this, either. I'm sorry for snapping. I'm…not used to talking about my personal life.'

She smiled, and it was so full of sorrow she might not have bothered. 'No. I think we should quit while we're ahead. I'll pretend you never answered as you did if you'll pretend I never asked what I did.'

'Make-believe works for you?' He hoped so, if it meant her last memory of him wasn't his being an ass.

The handbag was up and on her shoulder now. 'Let's both agree to try.'

She was turning, and he missed her already. 'What about your book?' It was desperate, but if it kept her here…

She paused, but didn't turn back. She looked at him over her shoulder. 'Maybe another time. Bye, Sam.'

'I'll hold you to that!' he called as she moved decisively through the door.

And then she was gone.

Again.

This time it was his fault.

CHAPTER SEVEN

THE universe wanted her to resolve this, clearly.

If it didn't, it would have left well enough alone and allowed her to just walk out of that café and never see Sam Gregory again outside of her dreams. Now here he was, in the rock-hard flesh, leaning casually on the counter of the airport coffee lounge with his back to her, wearing a light, earthy sweater and sinfully snug jeans.

Her throat tightened just slightly. It had to be a bad thing that she knew him so instantly from behind.

The weeks of separation hadn't done a thing to scrub him from her mind. If anything the passage of time had only exaggerated him in her subconscious. And six days of anticipation since she'd agreed to the State Government's request hadn't helped her to be ready for this moment.

If anything they'd made it worse.

She stopped just a few safe feet from him, suppressed her natural urge to get closer, and took a deep, confident breath. 'Sam.'

Nothing.

She stared at his oblivious back. His broad shoulders shifted just slightly and his right foot tapped on the edge of the counter's kick-bar. She caught a flash of a white wire poking from his ear.

Was he…dancing?

While her stomach ate itself from the inside? Clearly this wasn't as big a deal for him.

She cleared her throat and laid her fingers on his warm bicep to get his attention.

He jerked with surprise, then turned and smiled at her, yanking earphones from his ears. He quieted the tinny *tsss-tsss* with the press of a button in his pocket.

Warm eyes rained down on her and her stomach tumbled in on itself. 'You came. I wasn't convinced you'd actually show up.'

She almost hadn't. Should she be trusted with Sam on an interstate flight? Spending her days in close confines with him? Staying in the same hotel? He hadn't got any worse smelling since she'd last seen him, and the texture of his sweater screamed *touch me*.

She tucked her hands behind her back before she experimented to see if the front of it was as soft as the back. 'Your department was responsible for saving my life and it cost them a lot in equipment and manpower. Coming along on this promotional tour is the least I can do to repay them.'

Even if it put her heart at significant risk.

He took her carry-on bag from her and turned

for the check-in area. 'Apparently we made quite a splash with the public that day in Canberra. My boss's boss wanted this.'

'You didn't?'

He chuckled. 'More time in the spotlight? No, thanks.' Then his eyes found hers. 'But I'm not sorry I get to see you again. I hope to handle myself a bit better this time around.'

Aimee frowned. Straight back into awkward territory. Oh, well, since they were already here... She took a quiet breath and asked as casually as she could, 'Melissa not with you?'

Was it wrong that she wanted him to say yes almost as much as she hoped he'd say no? Having his wife along would solve an awful lot of problems.

'Ah... Three days away from work is more than she could swing. Some imminent breakthrough on an ice shelf project.'

'A what?'

'She works for the Australian Antarctic Division. She's been studying fracture patterns in ice shelves.'

He'd said Melissa was smart. Foolishly, she hadn't believed him. She'd thought it was just what people said about their spouses. 'At least I can bring my work with me. Transcription goes wherever I do.' She looked around anxiously for inspiration. 'So... We'll be talking to schools?'

Talking to schoolkids was another tick in the pro column for coming along: the opportunity to share what she'd discovered about herself during that twenty-four hours on the mountain-side. She'd needed quite a few 'pros' to outweigh the big three-lettered 'con' scrawled in the other column.

S.A.M.

'I think so. And some Victorian volunteer groups. Their Parks and Search and Rescue services are separate up there.'

'So this is about more than just publicity?'

'Not for the department, but for me I look forward to the chance to talk to others in the field. Share expertise. Bring something new back to my team.'

'Sounds like we'll be busy.' If there was a God.

'I think there'll be some down time.' His blue eyes seemed to turn luminous.

Oh. *Great.*

Aimee struggled to generate small talk until their flight was ready for boarding. Then getting on the plane and seated and into the air knocked off a good thirty minutes. She busied herself with the in-flight magazine, flicking pages she wasn't reading. It helped keep her from thinking about the way Sam's thigh pressed into hers in the tight seating. And how she was going to survive three days up close with him.

He leaned over the armrest. 'You know, we could probably use this time to get to know each other better.'

If eyes could get whiplash hers would have needed that neck brace he'd once given her.

'What?' she choked, half afraid of the answer. But only half.

'For your book. We never did finish that interview.'

Oh. 'No. I kind of blew that on my last question.'

His lips twisted. 'What question? I thought we were forgetting that. Do you have your recorder?'

She slipped it out of her handbag a little too keenly. When had she started so thoroughly hiding behind her job? She wanted Sam in her book, no question, but she could do it without his wife being in it. Leaping in on his marriage hadn't been premeditated, but her subconscious had definitely acted with intent.

Now Sam was buying into her folly. But, as gift horses went, he was a pretty good-looking one.

'You're sure about this? I'll need to ask you about Melissa.'

He took a breath. 'Why don't we start there? Get it out of the way? I promise not to be reactive.'

A non-reactive man? Another novelty. Assuming he could pull it off. She lowered her food tray, sat the recorder on it gently and pressed the red button.

'How old were you when you married?' she asked over the hum of the jet engines.

'Twenty-one.'

Wow. That made her feel like an old spinster at twenty-five. 'Young. Is that a Catholic thing?'

'It's a Gregory thing. We don't believe in wasting time.'

His smile was gentle, and she grew aware of how big he was in the cramped seat next to her. Her heart kicked up She shook her head to stay focussed. 'How did you even know who *you* were at twenty-one, let alone each other?'

'I knew. Plus Mel had been a fixture in my family for a long time because of her friendship with my brother.' He studied the digital recorder and didn't quite meet her eyes, making her wonder if there was more to that story.

'How does she feel about the work you do?'

Pained creases appeared above his brow. 'It bothers her. The hours. The disruption to our routine. She's a creature of habit.'

'You being at such risk?'

She'd never seen eyelashes flinch, but Sam's did. 'She doesn't like thinking she could be widowed. The financial uncertainty. I get that.'

The warm glow inside her responded to the misery in his voice. Defending his wife was automatic. Could he hear what he was admitting? Melissa wasn't worried about losing *him,* only her husband, and apparently a large chunk of the household income. 'You never considered giving up the Search and Rescue stuff?'

He lifted his eyes. 'When we have kids. Yes.'

'Which haven't come?'

She knew it was a mistake before the words even left her mouth, but he didn't react. Not the way he had to her suggestion his marriage wasn't solid. This time it was totally unconscious—a deep pain in his eyes. It hurt her to see it. She shifted tangent smoothly.

'You live in Hobart?'

He picked up the new direction gratefully. 'Mel's work has its head office there, so it was a necessary move for her research.'

Necessary. Word choices like that often led her to the true grit in someone's story. If only she had the courage to pursue it. On anyone else she wouldn't have hesitated…But every urge she had to dig into Sam's life suddenly felt loaded and a bit wrong. She hedged instead. 'Quite an achievement, given her young age.'

'She was so excited the day she told me she'd been successfully promoted. It had been a long time since I'd seen her so animated.'

'You were happy to move? Away from your family?'

The look he gave her was pointed. And conflicted. 'We both thought it would be a good idea for us to…start our own lives. Somewhere different.'

'Must have been tough.' And there must have been another reason.

The plane engines were too loud to waste effort with empty words. He just nodded.

'But you had each other. That's something.'

His nod continued, shadows lingering around his gaze. But then they cleared as if by conscious effort. He came fully back to the present. She grew almost uncomfortable under his steady regard as his eyes lifted.

'You're very easy to talk to, Aimee.'

The compliment warmed her and filled her body with helium. But she wasn't about to take it to heart. She couldn't afford to. 'People say that. I guess it's because you have no emotional stake in me. Like talking to a bartender.'

He snorted. 'You don't go to many bars, obviously.'

She wrinkled her nose. 'No, not many. Does that not happen?'

'Not outside of the movies.'

'Oh.'

'Besides, it's not exactly true, Aimee.' Blue heat simmered.

'What's not?'

'We're hardly strangers,' he said. 'We've been through a lot. I…we're friends. Aren't we? No matter how unconventional our meeting was.'

She hesitated to speak, fearing that if she opened her mouth the echo of her hard-hammering heart would come out instead of words. She nodded.

'So it's not true that I have no emotional stake in you at all.'

Her breath caught around the thumping in her chest. What in the world was she supposed to say to that?

'Plus there's…' His hooded gaze was crowded with every thought running through his mind as he deliberated. He reached out and turned off the mini recorder. 'The Kiss.'

Mortified warmth flared through her whole body. Had she really expected the topic to never to come up? She'd spent a lot of time analysing that kiss these past months, reliving it. And though she'd had a hard time regretting giving in to the impulse—even once she knew about the existence of *Mrs* Gregory—she was sorry for the way she'd forced it on him.

But she'd never expected it to earn uppercase status in his mind. *The Kiss.* And she'd really never expected him to raise it so openly.

She struggled for the right words. 'That was my fault, Sam.'

'I wasn't chasing an apology. But I think we need to talk about it. Get it out of the way.'

Really? She just wanted to pretend it had never happened. 'I'm not sure examining it is going to explain it. I was overwhelmed with fear and you were the one keeping me sane. I just needed the...human contact.'

Did she get any points for half-truths? Or did she lose one for the half she was hiding?

'Aimee, you don't need to justify why you did it.'

She frowned. 'Then why raise it?'

He glanced around them at the half-empty plane and then leaned in. 'Because it's stayed with me.'

She stared at him, her breath thinning. Her mental oxygen mask dropped down. 'Stayed?'

'I was on the job. You were hurting. I totally understand why you did it. But what I don't understand…' his blue eyes pierced hers '…is why I let you.'

Her tongue threatened to stick so firmly to her palate that it would be impossible to speak. She was sitting on a plane, heading for a hotel in a different city with a married man she'd non-consensually kissed, taking about said kiss….

She squirmed. 'I didn't really give you much option—'

'You were tied to your seat. I could have moved out of your reach easily. Why didn't I?' His stare burned into her. 'And why haven't I forgotten it?'

It was hardly going to be uncontrollable lust—for a woman covered in blood and dirt and soaked in her own urine. She stared at him and shook her head: silent, lost.

The chief steward's even tones streamed out of the overhead speakers, advising passengers that they were commencing their descent into Melbourne. She had no idea what he expected. So she did the only appropriate thing.

She brushed it off with a hollow laugh.

'A mystery for the ages!'

His eyes narrowed. 'It doesn't bother you?'

Time to lie! 'It bothers me that I did it. I'm embarrassed, of course.'

'But that's all?'

Time to run! She unclasped her seatbelt. 'I'm just going to…Before we land. I'll be right back.'

But before she'd made it to the next row she heard him behind her. 'We're going to have to talk about it at some point, Aimee.'

She fled. Down the aisle and into the toilet before the seatbelt light came on. She made the most undignified exit of her life from the most excruciating conversation of her life about the most unforgettable kiss of her life.

She slid the 'engaged' knob into place as if it would save her life.

Sam watched the little unisex toilet symbol flick from green to red and he sighed. Pretty appropriate, really. The little man represented him and the little woman represented Aimee. It only took one conversation to push the two of them from an amiable green to a cautionary red.

Red for embarrassment. Red for anger. Red for incendiary.

Take your pick.

The two of them existed perpetually on the edge of an inflammatory zone. His pulse was still pounding. The chemistry between them hadn't eased off since that day at the awards ceremony. He rubbed his thigh where it tingled from pressing against hers. All that unspent tension had to go somewhere.

Even after weeks apart it was still live.

Simmering. Just waiting for an excuse to flare up.

Enough to rattle both of them. Enough that he'd forgotten himself and started a conversation that he'd have been better off not having. So why had he started it? Was he so desperate to forge a connection between them? Or was it because it was the only legitimate way he could relive that moment? The moment on the rock-face when Aimee went from being his patient to something more meaningful.

Something she wasn't asking to be.

Something he couldn't let her be.

But he did enjoy riling her. The colour that flared in her cheeks... The glitter of her eyes... The defiant toss of her hair...

He adjusted his position in the cramped economy seat as his body celebrated the image.

Or maybe he just regressed to being nine years old in her presence and stirring her up was the equivalent of pulling her plaits to get noticed.

Maybe he really was that lame.

Either way, he needed to get a handle on it. They had three intensive days of promotion to get through, and they weren't going to be any easier if he kept teasing her into hiding. They were both adults, and now colleagues. This was officially a work trip. Attraction or not, if he couldn't count on his own best judgement then he'd have to count on his professionalism to get him through.

He glanced at the little red symbol above the bathroom again.

Assuming she ever came out.

CHAPTER EIGHT

AIMEE curled up in the comfy corner of the L-shaped sofa in her hotel suite at the end of their first long day in Melbourne and let her head fall back on a laugh. 'Are you serious?'

'Right in the solar plexus.'

'And she was how old?'

'Eighty-two. She had the bone density of someone two generations younger.'

'Sam Gregory taken out by a great-grand-mother.' A frightened, bewildered great-grand-mother, who'd had to wrestle with a young bag thief until Sam intervened. 'Can't you go anywhere without rescuing someone?'

'She was doing a great job of holding onto her bag against a pretty big kid. I just evened up the odds for her.'

'And got punched for your trouble.' She laughed again. 'You were supposed to be walking off the craziness of the day. Not hanging out in a police station making a report.'

They'd both run from point to point like mad things since the moment they'd set foot in Tullamarine Airport that morning. Two school appearances, then out to a rescue centre at the foothills to have the same conversations, answer the same questions. To go over and over the events of that night on the A10 in excruciating detail.

'Were you scared?' one kid had asked.

'Did it hurt?' This from a young girl.

'Was your car smashed to pieces?' Always a boy asking that one.

She was so grateful to have him by her side, but every time Sam told the story he used words like 'standard operating procedure' and 'protocol' and 'training'. Depersonalising the entire incident. By contrast, her contribution was all about her feelings, her fears, how much difference Sam's presence and support had made to her.

Not unlike the whole day, really. And the two yet to come.

As an exercise in public relations it was textbook. As a tool to remind her how everyday her situation had been for Sam—how *not* special—it was acute.

'I just wanted to explain why I wasn't at dinner,' he went on.

Reality still haunted her. 'I don't expect you to babysit me every minute.'

'I know, but this is my city. My turf. I feel bad that I left you here alone on our first evening.'

Our. As if they were a couple.

'Don't feel bad. I had Room Service soup and then a long, hot bath. It was blissful.' It had soaked away some of her exhaustion, but not all. She squirrelled deeper into the sofa and got comfortable on a soft sigh. 'Is that why you called? To apologise?'

There was the slightest of pauses before he cleared his throat and continued. 'Getting fresh air was only part of the reason I went out. Mel turns thirty next weekend and I wanted to pick her up something.'

Aimee smiled past the little twang at the mention of his wife's name. She was going to have to get used to those twangs. 'I'm guessing the inner-city constabulary don't offer a lot in the way of fine giftware?'

Her eyes flew to the adjoining wall as she imagined she heard his rich laugh clean through it. Until that moment Sam being next door to her in the hotel had hovered around her consciousness in a kind of abstract way. Talking by phone, he might as well have been across the country.

But that laugh brought him into pulse-racing context.

Right. Next. Door. Her heart kicked up a beat.

'I have no idea what to get her,' he said.

Really? His own wife? 'None at all?'

'Flowers? Chocolates? Something expensive?'

'Lord, don't use price as your primary parameter…'

'Don't *all* women like expensive gifts?'

Aimee smiled at the genuine bemusement in his voice. 'Not if they're in lieu of intimacy, no. We see right through those.'

'My sister says lingerie, but—'

Her stomach curled. *Oh, God, don't ask me about lingerie for your wife.*

'—won't she think I have an expectation of seeing it on her?'

Despite not wanting to have this conversation, Aimee frowned. 'She's your wife, Sam.'

'Right, but...lingerie's a statement. You know?'

She blinked. What kind of marriage did they have?

Before she could worry that particular bone further he went on. 'In the same way that a toaster is a statement. Or slippers.'

'Do *not* buy her slippers.'

His low, rich chuckle down the line had its usual effect on her. Every hair on her body quivered. 'I won't. Even I know that much.'

She blew out a breath. She owed Sam: bigtime. If gift advice for the wife she wished didn't exist was what he needed, then so be it. She wouldn't fail him. 'Okay, so you want intimate, but not *intimate.*'

'Right. Thank God we have this shorthand, Aimee.'

That made her frown. She stretched on her sofa. 'And you have no thoughts whatsoever?'

'I have heaps of thoughts, but I have no idea which is the best one.'

'Want to throw some at me?'

Pause. Long pause. 'Actually, I was hoping

you might help me out…in person. We have a couple of hours' down-time tomorrow.'

Her spine stiffened again, just as it had started to relax. Being together racing around the suburbs of Melbourne on business she could handle. Being on the other side of a thick hotel wall was doable. Shopping together for a gift for his beautiful, talented wife…?

She got to her feet—all the better to roam around the room.

'Together?'

He laughed again. 'That's the idea. Unless you want to phone in your advice like tech-support?'

Restricting themselves to phone conversations might be the best thing all round. Though she doubted that those few degrees of separation would do much to diminish the way he invaded her thoughts—awake or dreaming—it would at least spare her the confusion and frustration and risk of sitting across a table from a man she couldn't in good conscience touch.

Not in the way her body wanted to.

She stalled him as her mind raced for a way out of this. 'What did you have in mind?'

'The markets?'

Say you're busy. Say you have to work on a transcription. Say you're feeling fluey.

A deep shudder left her in a rush of air. 'Okay.'

She did a shabby kind of rain-dance across the carpeted floor of her suite. *Honestly!* She had the self-determination of a lemming.

When it came to Sam she had absolutely none.

'Fantastic. Thank you, Aimee. I appreciate it.'

Sure he did. Why wouldn't he? She was at his beck and call. And that was a dangerously familiar dynamic. But she pressed her fingers to her temple and took a deep breath. It wasn't Sam's fault she'd reverted to the bad old days. It wasn't his fault the gravel of his voice turned her spine to jelly and her mind to hot, long, imaginary nights.

Not seeing him in person these past weeks hadn't done anything to reduce the *thing* between them. Or the fact that indulging the *thing* wasn't acceptable because of his wife. Because of Aimee's own values.

But she'd committed to helping him—she *wanted* to help him. To do something to even the slate. Though this really wouldn't have been her first choice.

As had become her norm, she took shelter behind her book. 'My price for assistance will be knocking off some more of my interview.'

'The pleasure of my company is not reward enough?'

It couldn't be. She couldn't let it be. She shielded those raw, strained thoughts behind her old friend flippancy. 'You have an unattractively high opinion of yourself, Sam Gregory.'

His smile warmed the earpiece of her phone. 'Looks like my days of trading on your hero-worship are well and truly over.'

Aimee frowned. A lesser man might, in fact, have acted on her sycophantic adoration—wife or no wife. A lesser woman might have let him. But for all he'd tried on the plane to get her to talk about *The Kiss,* Sam hadn't once exploited the complicated emotions she had about the man who'd rescued her. He just wanted to clear the air.

'You'll always be my hero.' That much, at least, she could say. Hand on heart.

'And statements like *that*—' he laughed '—are why I have an unattractively high opinion of myself.'

She grasped the humour he threw out and used it to climb out of the dangerous place they'd just found themselves in. It was safer all round if she didn't go back to those days. Those feelings. 'Just a pity all that talent doesn't stretch to gift selection.'

He groaned. 'Thanks for pointing that out.'

'Well, you know you can always count on me for a healthy reality check.'

'Something to look forward to tomorrow. I'll meet you in the lobby at nine?' he said.

'Make it eight. Something tells me we're going to need all the scouting time we can get.' A loud noise from Sam's end of the phone made her jump. There'd been a lot of rustling, too, as they spoke. 'What are you doing, anyway?'

'Shaving. I'm just out of the shower. That was the bathroom cabinet closing a bit too quickly.'

Her whole body flinched. 'Oh… Okay.'

What exactly was she supposed to say to that?

Her ears grew acutely sensitive to every little sound in the next moments. The way the acoustics changed as he left the bathroom. The pad of his feet on the carpet. The flip of the lid of his suitcase and the rustle of him pulling out some clothes. Pyjamas, presumably.

Heat suffused her.

She turned to the big blank wall that stood as all that separated them. It formed the perfect canvas for her vivid imagination to paint him sauntering barefoot and damp across a suite the mirror image of hers, a fluffy white towel slung low on lean hips, the mobile phone at his ear the only other thing adorning him.

Every bit of saliva in her mouth decamped.

'Well,' she croaked, 'I'll let you go. I have some work to do tonight. See you tomorrow.'

He sighed. 'Yeah, I still need to call Mel. Don't want her to worry.' His voice dropped in timbre. 'See you in the morning, Aimee.'

She practically tripped over her tongue in her haste to end the call, then sat with the phone pressed numbly to her head long after Sam had rung off, her ears tuned, desperately, for any further audio hints from beyond the wall.

Just out of the shower.

While on the phone to her.

She wrestled free of the heated visuals that rushed at her like a line of football players and chewed her lip at a niggling afterthought. Having a conversation with someone while you were naked hinted at a certain kind of intimacy. Husband-wife kind of intimacy. Or oldest mate from childhood.

The latter suggested she'd assumed a genderless kind of role in Sam's mind: totally nonsexual, like a sister or an old friend. The sort of non-wife woman you wouldn't hesitate to have a phone conversation with while wandering around a hotel room in the buff.

Aimee frowned. She didn't want to be genderless with Sam. She didn't want to be his sister. Just because she wasn't actively exercising her femininity on him it didn't mean she wasn't keen to remain feminine in his mind. She liked how sexy she felt when Sam was around. She'd had a lifetime of feeling otherwise. A child…and then a chattel.

But the other possibilities bothered her even more—on a much deeper level. There should only be three women that Sam felt comfortable getting naked with—even telephonically. His mother, his doctor and his wife.

And she was none of those.

Her mind whirled. Did it say something that *she* was the first person he'd called on stepping out of the shower? Or was he just getting her call out of the way before stretching out on that king-sized bed for a longer late-night call with his wife?

That set a whole extra set of visuals flickering past her consciousness, and she shut them down hard.

One way or another Sam's unconscious behaviour was telling her something important about the nature of their relationship. Something that had alarm bells clanging deep in her psyche. Unless she was misreading this through inexperience? Maybe it was a Mars-Venus thing? Maybe guys truly thought nothing of getting naked while they had a woman on the phone, and Sam was just keen to relax after a long and chaotic day?

She let the phone slowly slip down from her ear to rest on her straining breast.

Maybe.

Sam flopped down on the sofa in the corner of his room, folded his arms behind his head and stared at the ceiling.

It couldn't be a good thing that he was still struggling to clear his head of an image of Aimee, all pink and soft from a hot bath, curled up in her complimentary bathrobe with papers spread all around her, working diligently on her transcription. Lifting her head as he walked into her room. Smiling and stretching up for the kiss he would place on her hairline before going back to her work and losing focus on everything but her stories. Leaving him to just…watch her.

Okay, now he was just plain fantasising.

It had been bad enough spending all day together—listening to her soft voice talking to the school kids, vicariously experiencing her fear and anxiety about the accident through the memories she recounted for them, sitting with his body pressed against hers in the compact car that his department had sent to move them around Melbourne. Working so well together as a team.

He really didn't need to add inappropriate fantasies to the many different ways he was *not* helping the situation. Yeah—fantasies in the plural. This wasn't the first that had broken through since she'd walked so cautiously back into his life across that stage all those weeks ago. Since she'd exited the café with such dignity after he'd been a jerk. Since her cheeks had flushed so hot this morning when he'd mentioned the kiss.

The harder he tried to keep Aimee out of his mind, the more often he caught her in there. It was never lewd, never disrespectful. Just flashes of her smile, the smell of her hair, the memory of a touch…

But she wasn't here for his amusement. She was here to help out his department. It wasn't her fault she was also the sweetest, freshest, most distracting person he'd met in…

He sighed.

…a really long time.

His mind made the immediate shift to Melissa. The only other woman that he'd ever obsessed about in quite this way. All the more because he couldn't have her at the time. Four long years of teenage angst and hormone-driven focus until his planets had aligned and he'd had a chance with the girl he'd been secretly admiring for what felt like for ever.

By then he'd built her up to goddess status. The sun had risen and set with her. She was perfection.

How could she ever have lived up to that?

The contrast between the intense attraction he'd felt then, for the girl he couldn't have and the beige, comfortable *nothing* he felt now, just a few years later for the girl he'd eventually married… Had he learned nothing since he was nineteen?

He should know all about heady infatuations.

Was that what he was doing with Aimee? Turning her into some kind of new ideal of the perfect woman for him? Since Melissa had failed to achieve it? Since they'd so miserably failed to achieve perfect couple status together?

Back then, his list of non-negotiables had been a heck of a lot shorter. These days it had become more sophisticated: intelligence, compassion, warmth, someone looking to be stronger in a pair than they were on their own.

His needs had grown beyond the shallow.

They'd certainly outgrown his marriage.

Sam's eyes drifted shut. He should call Mel. Not that she'd asked him to, or would even expect it; she wasn't exactly what you'd call needy. She'd probably be at the lab, working on her ice, not even conscious of the time, enjoying a concentrated opportunity to work without having to worry about getting home to him. She wouldn't appreciate the interruption.

He'd gone to do it earlier—picked up the phone and dialled. But Aimee had answered instead, like some kind of cosmic mistake. He glanced at the last call on the phone still in his hand. Yep. He'd dialled her number without realising.

He'd had to come up with something fast to justify his stuff-up. Mel's birthday was the perfect excuse. Totally real—he'd failed abysmally in getting something for her—but he hadn't started the day planning on asking Aimee for her help finding a gift.

He wasn't that much of a masochist.

He let his head roll to one side on the sofa-back and stared at the wall dividing Aimee's room and his. He pictured her sitting there, all languid and relaxed and sleepy, and his body responded immediately with a torturous tingle. It would take just moments to throw on some clothes, heartbeats to be out in the hall knocking on her door, and fantasy seconds more to get those clothes off again.

As if that was ever going to happen.

He was married.

She was Aimee.

Ne'er the twain shall meet.

He pushed to his feet and dialled Mel's number. It started to ring immediately. Aimee reminded him of the best part of his relationship with his wife. The early golden years when the two of them had still been caught up in a spiral of mutual appreciation and new romance. Back before life had got busy, before they'd both found their feet as adults. Did that place even exist any more? And if it did could he possibly find his way back there? Could *they?*

He shuddered in a sigh.

He'd made Mel some promises that day they'd

stood before a priest and committed to each other for ever, and she'd taken him in good faith.

He owed her as much, too.

The call went to voicemail. His wife's impatient, confident tone suggested even a voice message was an interruption.

His eyes dropped shut and he concentrated on the woman he'd pledged his life and allegiance to, pushing out the one who flirted enticingly at the edges of his mind even when she didn't mean to.

The phone beeped.

'Hey, Mel…' he started.

Hey, Mel…what? Hey Mel, I'm miserable and so are you. Hey, Mel, is it possible we got married for the wrong reasons? Hey, Mel, I'm sorry that I'm not better at loving you.

'I…uh…just wanted to let you know we arrived okay—' *your husband and the woman he can't stop thinking about* '—and that…'

He opened his eyes and stared at the blank wall again. Imagined Aimee there. Wanted to be with her so badly he burned with it. But his loyalty—his life—belonged to someone else.

He had to try harder.

'…just that I'm thinking about you.'

He rang off and dropped the phone onto his bed, then followed it in a defeated kind of body-flop.

He was honouring his wife.

Why did that feel like such a betrayal of himself?

CHAPTER NINE

'No! Definitely no.'

Aimee stood with Sam, deep at the heart of the beachside markets, the historic architecture in pronounced contrast to the modern, brightly coloured pop-up canopies littering the busy square.

Around them, buried beneath a surging crowd of tourists and locals, rows of stalls sold fine oils, organic produce, delicately hewn crafts, original artworks, timber knick-knacks and bright handwoven beanies. They offered just about every gift imaginable.

But still Sam had found *this*.

He held up a twisted oddity made from forlorn-looking recycled cutlery. 'It's a spoondelabra. You put candles in it.' He blinked at her lack of enthusiasm. 'It's clever.'

Aimeee smiled at the tragedy of his expression and prised it carefully from his fingers. 'No, Sam.'

He frowned and picked it up again as soon as she'd placed it back on the display table. 'I like it.'

Her laugh graduated to a full chuckle. 'Then

buy it for yourself, by all means. You are not buying your wife a *spoondelabra* for her thirtieth birthday.'

She'd taken to calling Melissa *your wife* as a defence mechanism. Not only did it serve as a healthy reminder to her not to get too entangled with Sam, but it helped to depersonalise Melissa, too. As long as she didn't have a name, Aimee felt slightly less guilty about tiptoeing around with someone else's husband on secret business.

Slightly.

A purple-haired woman dressed almost completely in hemp squeezed past them with a small goat trotting happily behind her on a leash. Sam's free hand slipped protectively around behind Aimee as she pressed in closer to him to let the goat pass. She felt his heat and got a whiff of something divine under the wool of his jacket. Definitely not goat. Her eyes drifted shut.

Focus...

'Fine.' He handed the artwork back to its creator with a reluctant smile. The man shrugged and gave it a quick polish before replacing it on the table.

They moved off again through the thick crowds. 'Seriously, Sam. We're not going to get very far today if you buy every little thing that takes your fancy.'

Sam stayed close to her as they walked, shielding her with his body from the worst of the crowd and lowering his head to be heard. 'Who says?

Could work well... If she doesn't like one gift I can whip out another.'

She laughed. 'Right. She'll never notice that.'

'Well, what do *you* like, then? Since *my* ideas apparently suck the big bazoo.'

'It's her thirtieth, Sam. She's not going to want a novelty anything. She'll want something lovely. Something unique. Something that says you know her.'

His lips thinned. 'I *do* know her and I'm still at a loss.'

Yeah? Why was that? She slid her hand around his forearm and squeezed. 'Don't worry, we have a couple of hours yet. We'll find something this morning.'

But his eyes didn't lighten. 'Pretty sure I'm not supposed to need this kind of support team just to buy my wife a gift,' he muttered.

Aimee was feeling sorry enough for herself without him adding his self-pity to the mix. She braced her fists on her hips. 'Well, you can pout about it or you can get on with it. And you've dragged me out of a warm bed on our morning off, so if you're going to pout I might just wander off and do my own thing.'

He stopped and stared as she was towed ahead of him by the crowd. She turned back against the tide and tipped her head in enquiry.

'You reminded me of my mother just then,' he said as he caught up with her.

'Flattering.'

'In a good way. She's very no-nonsense like

that. She wouldn't tolerate self-pity either. I'm not used to that outside of my family.'

Aimee smiled as they set off again, feeling unaccountably light. 'She and I would probably get on well, then.'

'I know you would.'

She detoured physically—and conversationally—stopping in front of a stall with handcrafted silk scarves blowing like medieval banners in the breeze. 'What about one of these? They're beautiful.' The soft fabric blazed rich colour in the mid-morning light.

Sam frowned. 'What will she do with a scarf?'

Aimee blinked. 'Wear it?'

'On her head? Isn't that a bit...nanna-ish?'

She dismissed the concern with a wave. 'Think less *nanna* and more *catwalk*.' She loosened one carefully from its tie point and caressed the cool, soft silk as it slipped through her fingers. 'She can wear it like this...' She looped it quickly around her throat in a fifties kind of knot. 'Or like this...'

She twisted it into different styles to show Sam the many ways Melissa—*his wife,* she corrected herself—could enjoy a beautiful scarf without it being old-fashioned.

'Or if she's really keen she can wear it like this.' She tipped her head forward and twisted the scarf into a hippy headband, pushing it up the line of her shaggy hair. Then she struck an exaggerated catwalk pose and threw Sam a two-fingered peace sign, smiling wide and free.

Blue eyes locked onto hers, entertained and glittering, and Aimee's breath caught at the fire kindling deep in them. The fire she hadn't seen since the careless, unmasked moment after she'd kissed him on the mountainside. Time froze as they looked at each other. But as she watched his smile dissolved, the flames flickered and extinguished, and two tiny lines appeared between his brows.

Her confidence faltered and she let her peace sign drop limply to her side.

'Very Woodstock,' Sam finally said, carefully neutral, but stopped her as she went to slide the scarf off, curling his warm fingers around hers. 'Leave it. Freedom suits you.'

They stood like that—silently, breathless, his fingers coiled around hers—for dangerous moments.

Freedom did suit her. The year since taking charge of her own life had been the best of her whole life. And the hours she spent with Sam the best of those.

'I'll have to buy it,' she murmured.

'Let me.' His wallet was open and the stall holder's hand was outstretched before she could do more than squeak in protest. He finished the transaction: efficient, no-nonsense. Very Sam.

'Thank you,' she said, too unsettled by the gesture to protest. 'Now we *really* need to get Melissa something.' He slid a curious glance her way. She couldn't help her fingers touching the scarf where it curled under her hair. 'It's going to be really dodgy if the only person you buy a gift for today is another woman.' She laughed weakly.

He took his receipt and turned to face her, eyes serious. 'You're not another woman, Aimee. You're you. This is to show my appreciation. For your help today.'

You're you. What did that mean? Not worthy of 'other woman' status, or somehow outside of the definition? Genderless again. 'We already had a deal. I help you with your gift and you help me with the interview. Quid pro quo.'

'Today deserves extra credit.'

A rare, uncomfortable silence fell between them as they stared at each other but then Sam's eyes drifted over her shoulder, flared, and his face filled with animation.

'What about a kite?' he exclaimed, and was off.

'Men really are just little boys in big bodies, aren't they?'

They sat at a weathered timber table beneath a canopy of fragrant flowering jasmine which defied gravity on the pergola over their heads, tucking into an early lunch of cheese, bread, pâté and something peculiar made of eggplant. Aimee dragged her eyes back off the two enormous kites sticking out of a recycled plastic bag and met the mock offence in Sam's with a grin.

'Kites are timeless,' he pointed out. 'Airborne works of art. And good for obesity.'

'I know. I heard the sales pitch too.' Though

she'd never met a man less likely to have issues with obesity now or in the future than Sam. Or more comfortable with his inner nine-year-old. In truth, his passion for life and his willingness to let himself be open in front of her was dangerously appealing. He wasn't endlessly talking himself up, like Wayne, or angling to get anything from her, or making himself look good. He was just being Sam.

And she liked Sam. She really, really did. Just exactly as he was.

More fool her.

She forced a smile to her lips. 'Given you came up trumps for Melissa, I can hardly begrudge you a kite.' He'd bought his wife the most heartbreakingly beautiful mirror, its artisan-made frame inlaid with luminous crystals and with intricately wrought iron vinework twisting through and around the whole piece. *'Symbolic of both of us,'* he'd said when he chose it. *'Melissa's brilliance and my love of nature.'*

Her heart had swollen with pain then—for the poetry in his words, for the sweet uncertain fear he felt about choosing the wrong gift for the woman he was sharing his life with, and for the truth his words revealed about their relationship. Now and again he'd say something that made her think that maybe things weren't all roses at home, but those simple words spoke volumes about his real feelings for his wife. Her heart weighed heavy in her chest.

'Sam, can I—?' Her own judgement stilled her tongue.

'What? Go ahead.'

She frowned at him and thought hard for the moments that ticked by, wondering if she should back out. 'I want to ask you something, but I don't want to offend.'

'I'm having too good a day to take offence.' He slid one big hand on his heart. 'Ask away.'

'It's about Melissa.'

The hand faltered as he lowered it.

'Is everything okay with you two?'

His whole body stiffened up. 'Why do you ask?'

'You're so passionate in your defence of her, so considerate in meeting her needs, so proud and loyal when you speak about her…'

'But?'

She took a deep breath. 'But…your body language and what you're not saying tells a different story.'

His nostrils flared. 'What I'm *not* saying about her tells you more than what I *am* saying?'

'This is what I do for a living, Sam.'

'Are we in the interview now?'

She sucked back her instinctive reaction to the harshness of his voice. 'See—that's very telling to me. That you get so worked up on this particular subject.'

His cheek pulsed high in his jaw. 'Mel and I are fine.'

'Just *fine*? Not great? Not wildly, crazy in

love?' Although she knew the answer to that. If he were he wouldn't have had such a hard time buying her a gift. And he sure as heck wouldn't be sitting here with *her*.

His simmering eyes told her he was trying very hard not to be rude. 'All marriages go through their rough patches.'

She took a breath, trusted her instinct. 'How long has this patch been?'

He dropped his eyes to the table, and when he lifted them they were predatory. 'I think we should talk about that kiss now.'

It was her turn to stiffen. 'Don't change the subject.'

'Don't avoid the subject. Why won't you talk about the kiss?'

She leaned forward. 'Why is it so hard for you to talk about your wife?'

He met her in the middle of the table. 'Same reason it's so hard for you to acknowledge kissing me. It's personal.' He blinked and his voice softened. 'And terrifying.'

She sat back.

Terrifying. Sam Gregory—the man who seemed to be afraid of nothing—was frightened for his marriage. Everything he'd not *quite* said these past days, every 'fine' instead of 'great' came into crashing focus.

This changed everything.

And nothing.

The tightly reined emotion in his eyes said that he was raw and hurting and vulnerable to suggestion; this was not the time to be careless with the knowledge she'd unexpectedly found herself holding. But she could lead by example and have some courage.

'I kissed you before I knew you were married,' she said.

His eyes flared, as if he hadn't truly expected her ever to return to the taboo subject. Maybe he'd thrown it out there as a distraction, but she grabbed it with both hands.

Fair's fair.

'I'm not someone who would ever knowingly…' Her father's wandering eye had wrecked her family. But she couldn't tell Sam that. That wasn't the sort of thing you revealed over a casual lunch. Even her friend Danielle didn't know the full story about her past. 'I wouldn't have done it if I'd realised.'

Talking about the kiss was somehow self-fulfilling, drawing her eyes to his lips unconsciously and reminding her of how they'd felt so warm and surprised against hers. Her mouth watered with the memory.

She forced her eyes upward only to collide with ones so intense and earnest they stole her breath.

'You remember it. I was beginning to wonder.'

'Of course I remember it. How many men in vehicle wrecks do you imagine I've kissed?'

'Not as many as me.'

'Wh—?'

'Mouth-to-mouth,' he said with a straight face,

but couldn't hold it. His smile undid all the tension of the past five minutes.

Her relief bubbled over. He was making this easier for her. How was it possible she was laughing again so soon after the awkwardness of just a moment ago?

Because this was Sam. 'That's it,' she said. 'That's what I was doing that night.'

He laughed. 'Yeah, let's go with that. Really good mouth-to-mouth.'

And just like that the awkwardness was back. At least for her. Sam didn't seem the slightest bit affected. His eyes strayed to the large parcel that contained the mirror, and he took shelter in a new subject. 'I just hope Mel likes it as much as you and I did,' he said.

Wow—how much had changed that talking about his wife was safer territory between them? 'She will. She'd have to be blind not to see how hard you've worked to get the perfect gift.' No man had ever made an effort to please her as Sam was making an effort to please his wife. 'She's very lucky.'

Her breath sucked in on a tiny gasp at her accidentally spoken words.

Sam lifted his eyes. 'Lucky?'

'That you're going to so much effort,' she stumbled. 'That you care enough to do…all of this…for her. You could have just gone with flowers.'

His lips twisted. 'She has no idea.'

'Then tell her,' Aimee said, locking her eyes

on his. 'Every woman deserves to know she's cherished.'

Sam frowned. 'I can't even *imagine* a conversation between us that would lead to that.'

Her eyebrows lifted. 'You don't talk?'

'Not like that.' He shook his head and his gaze flickered away. 'Not like this.'

Again her breath tightened. So it wasn't only she who found their time together easy and natural. 'That surprises me.'

His eyes lifted. 'Why?'

She shrugged. 'The Sam I met dangling off that highway…That's not a man I can imagine having difficulty communicating.'

'Mel's not really a talker.'

'Have you tried?'

His eyes shaded over. 'Repeatedly.'

She knew firsthand how frustrating it was to try and talk to someone who didn't reciprocate. Except in her case it had been more a case of Wayne not being a listener. He just hadn't stopped talking long enough for her to get a word in, and if she had, his reflex had been to disregard it.

Sam's gentle voice drew her eyes back to his. 'Has someone made you feel like that? Cherished?' The blue of his irises seemed to have grown richer.

Her mouth opened and then closed again without answer. That wasn't a question she could answer without embarrassing both of them.

Silent moments ticked by.

'Is our friendship one-way, Aimee?' he asked out of nowhere, shifting in his seat, not letting up with the eye-contact. Not angry, but rough enough that she winced—just slightly. 'You can ask me personal things but I can't ask you?'

'I…' That was actual hurt in his eyes. Or was she imagining it? Her pulse quickened. 'I've…I must have…'

He leaned forward. 'Everything I know about you I know from that one night on the mountain. Since then you haven't…invited personal conversation.'

Her heart beat in her throat. 'We just had one. About…' *The Kiss.*

'That wasn't personal. We were both involved. I'd like to know more about Aimee Leigh, about what makes her tick. You told those kids yesterday more about yourself in one hour than you've told me since we met.'

Old scars pinched tightly. In her household personal discussions had been discouraged lest they led to…you know…actual caring. She didn't *do* emotional risk. And opening up to this particular man would definitely be risky.

'Why?'

The question seemed to anger him. 'Because we're friends, Aimee. Or at least I think we are. I don't know.' He threw his hands into the air. 'Maybe we're not?'

Her chest tightened. *Friends.* 'We are. Of course we are.' *It's all we ever can be.*

'Then open up. Let me in.'

She matched the lift in his voice, though hers was tighter. 'I can't.'

He pressed his palms onto the table. 'Why not?'

'Because you're not mine to let in,' she half-shouted, her chest fixed with the pain of where they were about to go, of what she'd just admitted.

Neither of them moved.

For entire moments.

Even the birds around them held their breath. 'Opening up means something to me, Sam. I'm programmed to...' She shook her head. 'It means something.'

Her parents had cloistered her so tightly she didn't even know how to take a risk. How to dare to.

He leaned in. 'Aimee, I'm sorry. I'm not trying to be obtuse. I truly do not understand what you're saying.'

Her face pinched, and she recognised somewhere far away, deep inside, that this was not one of her finest moments. Her breath fluttered. 'I don't...open up...easily. But if I did it would be because we meant something to each other. And we don't have that kind of relationship.'

He squinted his confusion. 'You do mean something to me, Aimee.'

She groaned her frustration. 'I'm not talking about friendship, Sam.' Lord, could he not hear her?

He shook his head, as though it might rattle all

the pieces together into an understandable shape. 'Are you saying that you only open up with some-one if you're in a relationship?'

She just stared at him.

'What? So I'm either in or I'm out?' he grated. 'There's nothing in between?'

'You're not someone I could let in just a little bit, Sam.' *Please understand what I'm saying. Please.*

He blinked at her. 'I don't want to be out.'

So innocent in its utterance, so painful in its intent. 'But you *can't* be in.'

And finally it dawned in his eyes. What she was trying so hard not to say. He sat back and took a deep, slow breath. 'This is about Melissa.'

She flung her hands in the air. 'Of course it is.'

'You're keeping a distance because of her?'

'I'm keeping the distance you should be keep-ing, Sam.'

That hit him hard. The colour fled from his face. But he didn't make excuses. He didn't defend himself. And his next words surprised her. 'What have they done to you?'

Two seconds ago he had been under exami-nation. Now he was turning the spotlight on her again. 'Who?'

'Your family. The men in your past. They've made you this all-or-nothing woman. A person who can't even have friendships without rules. Is that truly the world you come from?'

'They've done nothing.' Though that wasn't strictly true. Wayne had run off most of her male friends and dressed it up as his great devotion and focus on just being with her. And her father had been the same with her mother up until the day Lisbet Leigh threw his belongings out in the street. Both of those men and the lessons they'd taught her had had an impact on her. 'I still have values, Sam. They haven't changed just because I've struck out on my own.' If anything they'd crystallised.

'You pursued this friendship, Aimee.'

She sighed, because it was true. She had opened the door for all of this that day at the awards ceremony. It had seemed so doable at the time.

'But you're saying it can only be one-way?' he went on. 'Or superficial?'

God, how could such an intelligent man be so blind? Damn him for making her explain. 'You have a *wife*, Sam.'

He threw his palms up again. 'I'm not suggesting anything illicit, Aimee. There are degrees. Friends have a different level of intimacy. A different role.'

Aimee surged to her feet and slapped her fists on the table, leaning across it. 'Not for me. If I let you in then you will be *in*. Do you understand me? Is that a complication you want?'

Sam stared at the dignity and passion in her eyes. He almost chased the conversation to its natural conclusion, followed the white rabbit deep down into the hole, because for one blazing second—*yes*—he did want that complication.

Very much. But Aimee was right: getting closer to her emotionally wasn't going to do either of them any favours. He should be admiring the strength of her character, or cursing the lack of his own, but all he could think about was that this amazing human being was apparently off-limits to him.

And, God help him, he wanted to be *in*.

'So that's how this has to be? A careful distance between us?' he said.

'Don't you think that's wise?' Aimee slumped back onto her side of the bench and into the shaft of dappled light streaming down through the tangle of flowers overhead. It made her mop of blonde hair shimmer like a halo, like some angelic being. But all that did was make him feel more like playing the devil.

'No. Not if it means I can't get to know you.' She flinched, and he regretted causing it, but Aimee was fast becoming one of the important people in his life and her opting out was not on the cards. 'I like you, Aimee. I like how you think so differently to me in many ways but on the essential things we're in tune. I don't like being told that I can't be friends with you just because of Melissa.'

But he didn't like that he'd referred to the woman he'd married as 'just', either. And he *really* didn't like the resentment that had started oozing through the moment Melissa had become an obstacle between him and getting to know Aimee better. He frowned internally. He'd been working so hard on managing that ugly, unreasonable side of himself, but apparently it was alive and well.

Aimee lifted one prosaic brow and the corners of her mouth tightened. 'It's not actually your call, Sam, whether I'm friends with you or not, or what kind of a friend I am. If that's what you're expecting, then...'

She leaned down for her own shopping bags and her reach had a tremor in it. *Ugh, idiot!* She was breaking away from under the controlling thumb of her family and here he was going all caveman on her. He rushed in to undo his damage.

'I respect you, Aimee.' That stilled her fingers just as they started to pull on the handles of her bags. 'And that goes for whatever decision you choose to make about this. About us.'

She straightened up and brought her green eyes back to his, and he hated the caution he saw there. Partly because he'd caused it, and partly because he knew she was never going to tell him who'd put it there in the first place. One of a thousand things he'd never get to know about Aimee Leigh if she got her way.

He folded his arms in front of him on the table and leaned towards her. 'Keeping our friendship shallow feels like a crime against nature. But I'm not about to force the issue. I know you well enough to know that you'll walk if I do. Like it or not, you're a part of my life now, Aimee, so I don't want you to do that.' He wasn't about to look too closely at why. Not today at least. He smiled and hoped it seemed genuine. 'So, even though I don't agree with you, I'll take whatever you'll give me.'

Her eyes darkened and dropped briefly, but when they rose they were flat. 'I like and respect you, too, Sam. But you have a wife. She's where your emotional investment should be.'

She was right. Of course she was. And Lord knew if ever a marriage needed emotional investment it was his and Mel's.

But he still hated it.

He shook off the growling doubts in his stomach, stood when he should have been reassuring her, and waved a hand towards the bright fabric sticking out of his bag. 'Come on. How long has it been since you flew a kite?'

Kites were superficial. Harmless and pretty. She couldn't be suspicious of a bit of recreational fun, right?

But her eyes could.

'I've never flown one. I think my mother was afraid of friction burns on my hands.'

A long-dormant part of him deep inside roused, lifted its slumberous head. Aimee had been so protected from life…The things she must not know… The things that he could teach her…

If she was his to teach.

But all he said was, 'Come on. Time to add a new life-skill to your repertoire.'

Sam's heart was simultaneously warmed and saddened by the enjoyment Aimee got from her lesson. His urge to protect her clashed headlong with his anger at the selfishness of her parents—raising her in an over-cautious bubble and robbing her of simple childhood joys.

Like flying a kite.

She set off again, in a long-limbed gallop across the open parkland, with the fuchsia fabric eel trailing behind her, lifting higher, flirting with the current. This time it caught and held, and she jogged to a halt and looked back at him across the foreshore, with triumph in her whole body as it climbed.

'It's up!' she cried in astonishment, bouncing on the spot, returning her eyes to the feminine kite wavering and folding in the air high above her.

'She's like an alien,' Sam muttered as he jogged across to her, his own yellow and black kite in his hands. A big-brained alien who existed on learning new things.

'If she starts to drop,' he called out, 'pull on the line. If she veers left, you pull right…'

In under a minute Sam was by her side, staring up into the electric blue above the park, his hawk kite dominating the sky, expertly keeping his strings from tangling in Aimee's.

'You're good!' She laughed as her eel tumbled momentarily.

Sam reached one hand over on top of hers and showed her how to moderate its altitude. Her hands were warm and soft and fitted perfectly in his. He had to force himself to let go. 'I flew kites as a kid. It's like riding a bike. You never really forget.'

'I never learned that, either.' She squealed as the eel cut to the left sharply, but she'd already started correcting it.

'You have good instincts.' He smiled.

'I'm not exactly tearing up the sky.' She laughed. 'I'm too scared to move out of my safe little orbit.'

'You just need the right motivation. Watch out.' A flick of his wrist turned the sharp-winged hawk back towards the eel and he cut it back and forth on her tail like a predator toying with its prey. Its two long ribbons streamed like twin vapour-trails behind.

'Quit it!' Aimee grumbled, laughing.

'Make me.'

She kicked into top gear then, weaving her kite ahead of his, trying to anticipate whatever stunt he'd pull next, her frown pronounced as she concentrated on besting him. She wasn't bad, but half an hour's experience was never going to beat a lifetime love of the skies, and he had plenty of easy time to glance back at what the eel's pilot was doing.

A light sheen of sweat glistened on Aimee's golden forehead and determination blazed in her heaven-lifted gaze. His eyes dropped to her full mouth. Lingered.

'Does biting your lip help?' he teased.

The guilty lip sprang free and she smiled,

broad and brilliant, but didn't take her eyes off his hawk. 'Yes. It improves my aerodynamics.'

Immediately his mind was filled with thoughts and images that she'd have been horrified to know he harboured. He shook them loose and disguised them with a laugh. 'Interesting technique.'

Above, Sam wound his hawk in tight circles around the eel, trapping it in the spiral of the twin-tails, but she broke free and let herself soar high above him, before circling back around and down to meet him from the side. He dodged away and twisted back, to race the eel through the sky.

The two of them moved in parallel, tightly synchronised, and Sam's glance ping-ponged down to see what Aimee's hands were going to do next before shooting back up to watch his hawk respond.

Where she ducked, he dived. When she turned he was right there with her, mirroring her every move.

Her radiant gaze grew large as the beauty and sensuality of the airshow overtook her. Her lips fell open and she sighed. He felt it in his gut more than heard it. Sam took his chance, tightening his strings and bringing the headstrong hawk back under tight control, curling close around the eel but never quite tangling with it. The two kites danced in dreamy synchronicity across the blue canvas sky.

Wild, open, limitless. A place where anything, any future, was possible. His breath grew short.

For one brief moment he raced the hawk ahead of her, hovered in space as her eel caught up, and then twisted in freefall to touch it in a slow-motion aerial kiss before falling away in a showy controlled dive.

Beside him, Aimee gasped.

He steered the hawk back into an ascent and his focus flicked to her, met her gaze head-on. Wide-eyed. Flushed.

Utterly dismayed.

He fumbled his climb, and the strings were yanked meanly from Aimee's hands as the two kites tangled, tipped, and plummeted in a twisted mess to the hard ground in the distance, their sensual skirmish terminally interrupted.

I'll take whatever you'll give me.

That was what he'd said back at the little cafeteria, and he'd meant it to be kind. Some sort of compromise between what he wanted—to really get to know her—and what she needed—to keep a safe emotional gulf between them. But all it did was hurt and mirror her own *patheticism* back to her. Not even a real word—but it summed her situation up perfectly so she was going with it. She was taking whatever *he* would give *her.*

How had she found herself in this situation—again? She marched resolutely back towards the car, her chest balled tight around her anger and pain.

Anger at herself.

Pain because he'd never be able to touch her for real.

What was she prepared to give him? *Everything.* But she wanted everything in return. Not a friend. Not a shopping buddy. She wanted someone she could curl up with at night, see the wonders of the world with, and whose brain she could mine for useless information. She wanted someone to admire and appreciate and get jealous over. She wanted someone to wander the markets with or sail a boat or fly a kite. Or cheer for at an awards ceremony. All perfectly legitimately.

She wanted someone like Sam. She *deserved* someone like Sam. And it was a bit of a first in her life to be thinking that way. But all those things were way, way more than he was free to give.

And so Sam playing kissing-kites had done nothing but mess with her head and cut her deep down inside where she never let anyone go.

'Aimee… Stop.'

'Someone will steal your kites,' she threw back over her stiff shoulder, picking up pace as the park got smaller behind them.

'They'll have to untangle them first.'

Her smile stretched her skin tight. Even his sharp wit got up her nose. Why couldn't he be an egotist? Or as thick as two planks? Was he not even the slightest bit muddled by what had just happened back in the skies? By that little aerial seduction?

Did he not even have the decency to be vaguely rattled?

'Aimee. Please.'

Her feet slowed. Shuffled. Stopped. But she didn't turn around. Either he'd see how mad she was or he'd see the confusion in her eyes, and she didn't want either. She clenched her fists. 'I've got somewhere to be, Sam. I'm not at your disposal all day.'

'You're angry with me.'

Her eyes drifted shut and she turned slowly, marshalling her expression. 'I'm not angry with you. I'm just angry at...' *The universe. The timing.* '...this whole situation.'

'It was nothing. It wasn't supposed to be anything.'

That meant he knew it was something. Her mouth dried up.

He lifted his hands either side of him. 'I just wanted you to have the chance to fly a kite.'

'Why?'

'Because you never have. That seems wrong.'

'Why is it your job to fix the ills of my past?'

He frowned. 'Because...' But his words evaporated and his shoulders sagged. 'I don't know, Aimee. I just wanted to see your face the first time you got the kite up. I wanted to give you that.'

She stared at him. It was a nice thing to do, and it *was* just kites. But then it wasn't. 'So what was with the kite foreplay?'

It was a risk. She watched his face closely for

signs of total bemusement, for a hint that this was all in her head and totally one-sided and she'd just made a complete fool of herself. Or for the defensiveness of a man caught out.

She got neither.

'I don't know,' he murmured, frowning and stepping closer. 'It just happened. And it was kind of...' She tipped her head as he grasped for the right words. 'Beautiful. Organic. It didn't feel wrong.'

It *had* been beautiful and it had started so naturally, but it was wrong. It had felt too good so it had to be wrong. She shoved her hands deep into the pockets of her sweatshirt and took a deep, slow breath. 'This is how we're always going to go, Sam. Even something ordinary like flying a kite becomes—' *loaded* '—unordinary.'

He ruffled long fingers through his hair and stared at her. 'So maybe that's just us? Why don't we just...allow for it?'

Allow for it? 'How?'

He stopped in front of her, looking down with deep, calm eyes. 'It is what it is, Aimee. Neither one of us is going to act on it, so do we really need to stress about it? We could just accept that there's an...attraction...between us, and then just move past it.'

Her lips twisted along with the torsion in her gut. 'You make it sound so simple.'

'I'm sure we're not the first two people who have accidental chemistry.'

Except it wasn't just chemistry for her. Her

mind was involved. Her heart. And that made it very complicated.

'What just happened with the kites...' he started. 'I feel comfortable around you, Aimee. Relaxed. It just happened. I'll be on my guard from now on so that it doesn't happen again.'

Her chest hurt. 'What kind of friendship is that going to make? If we're both constantly guarding our words and actions?' *Our hearts.*

His broad shoulders lifted and fell, but she couldn't tell if it was a shrug or a sigh. 'Our kind.'

Sam's defeat was contagious. Her eyes dropped to the ground.

'Come on. We have an hour before we're due back. Let's go rescue the kites and then go back to the café for that interview.'

The interview. Did either of them believe that excuse any more? But the pages of her book were already established neutral territory between them, so it was good to have it to retreat to.

Just accept the attraction...

Aimee shook her head. He was so easy to believe. He was so certain that this was a good idea. Sam had no doubt that he could put aside whatever this was simmering away between them, and maybe he could.

But could she?

CHAPTER TEN

AIMEE re-read the opening to the oral history spread out on the hotel table before her and stared at the words as though they were prophecy.

She'd first met Coraline McMahon as an elderly woman from the suburbs of Melbourne, but the Cora she was meeting now was fifteen, beautiful, running barefoot and wild in her home on the Isle of Man. Cora had set her cap at tearaway Danny McMahon from a very early age—a young man idolised by the boys, dreamed of by the girls, and *tsked* about by their parents alike, which had only made him all the more desirable. Dark and bold and charismatic. She'd fallen hard and irrevocably for Danny, but he'd left her behind when he'd enlisted in the Second World War.

Broken-hearted. Fifteen.

Pregnant.

Within weeks a shamed Cora had been married off to Danny's younger brother Charley: the responsible one, the tolerant one, the one willing to raise his brother's child to avoid a family scandal. They'd had a sound sort of marriage, living in the McMahon household while the war raged on, until the day Danny got a foot blown off and limped home to a hero's welcome.

'Ugh.' Aimee dropped the sheets of her transcribed story onto the tabletop and slid down further on her chair to study the ceiling.

Every day.

Every day Cora had struggled with wanting a man she couldn't have. Living under the same roof. Watching him making a slow life for himself. It had broken Charley's heart, watching her try to hide it. She'd never so much as touched Danny again, but breathing the same air as him had tarnished her soul and her husband's—even after he'd packed them all up and shipped them to Australia to escape his older brother's influence.

Aimee's subconscious shrieked at her to pay attention. To what, though? What was the right message to take from Cora's cautionary tale?

Was it counsel against the pain of spending time with someone she wanted but could never have? Or a reminder of how damaging it could be to any future relationship she might form? Or was it a living warning about not seizing the moment, of settling for someone less than you wanted? Cora had lived seventy years with second-best, faithful, loyal, accepting Charley McMahon. Yet he'd married her because she was pregnant with his brother's child. Pressured by his parents. And he'd lived his life knowing her heart truly belonged to his brother.

No matter the great affection that had eventually grown between them, each of them lived had long lives knowing that neither was the other's first choice.

That was just…awful.

And yet their story was going in her book. Coraline McMahon had willingly given her life to the brother she didn't love. She'd done the right thing by her family, her son, on her own merit. She hadn't been swayed by the fact that it was the wrong thing for her. Outwardly it smacked of passivity, but there was great strength in the way she'd taken her unplanned future by the scruff and fashioned a reasonable life for herself, and that made her story perfect for *Navigators*.

She'd owned her choices and she lived with the consequences. For ever.

But…oh…how it had hurt her.

Aimee remembered the cloudy agony in Cora's eyes as she'd relived the day they'd trundled away from the McMahon home with their meagre belongings stacked around them. Told her about the momentary eye-contact she'd shared with a broken and war-shocked Danny, standing respectfully to the rear of the group farewelling his brother's family.

Bare seconds locked together. Her first and only glimpse of the saturated sorrow in his eyes. Realising he'd loved her after all.

How had she managed, never seeing him again, never speaking to him…? Aimee studied the yellowed photograph of Cora and her son aboard the ship they'd boarded for Australia. Seeing Danny every single day in the dark eyes of their son?

Was that a comfort or a kind of torture?

She squared up the bundled pages that captured Cora's story and refastened the elastic band around them tight, sealing in all the heartbreak. The cover title was the widow's final words to her on the last day of their interviews: *This Too Shall Pass*.

Except Aimee felt certain it had never passed for Coraline McMahon. She was strong and honourable, and hadn't been afraid to reinvent herself for her son's sake, but she'd carry the secret pain of Danny's loss to her grave.

Aimee slid the documents back into their file and swallowed back tears. Would she have the same strength of character? Endurance? Would she grow to accept Sam's unavailability or, like Cora, would her heart form a callus around the wound so that she could survive?

'Phone, Aimee...'

She jumped at Sam's voice, so close behind her, and reached for her mobile as the special ring-tone he'd recorded on her phone the day before repeated itself.

'Phone, Aimee...'

But just as she went to accept his call she paused, glanced at Cora's notes, and then at the hotel wall between their suites. She tuned in to the heart that hammered in Pavlovian response just to the sound of Sam's voice. The cell-deep anticipation that excited her blood.

'Phone, Aimee...'

And she let it go to voicemail.

She opened the door, expecting hotel staff to collect her bags, and found Sam there, instead, a deep scowl marring his handsome face and fire sparking in his eyes. Her stomach clenched.

'Why are you leaving?' he said.

Because it's not healthy for me to be around you, like this. Because I need to remove myself from the temptation of touching you.

'You don't need me for this afternoon's meetings so I might as well fly out today.' *Without you.*

'But what difference does one more night make?'

Her whole body stiffened up. That was not an easy question to answer. If he knew what she'd be wanting to do right through that night... What she'd wanted to do that first night, with a head full of images of him in his towel... Or last night, fuelled by sensual dream images of his strong, lithe fabric hawk kite twisting around her... How long she'd lain awake taking herself through the mental pros and cons of rolling out of bed and tiptoeing next door... How hard it had been to finally settle on not doing it...

Her arms crept around her front. 'None, to you. But I'd like to get home now that I'm not needed. I've done my part for your department.'

It was more defensive than she'd meant it, but that couldn't be helped. Being strong had to start somewhere.

He frowned. 'You have. You've been amazing. I just…'

'What, Sam?'

'Are you leaving because of yesterday? Because of what I said on your recorder?'

There was nothing too controversial about what they'd recorded at the café. But 'yesterday' could only mean the kites. She tossed her hair back. 'I'm leaving because I'm done.' *Totally.* 'And because staying has absolutely no purpose.'

His eyes smouldered the way they had at the end of their kite-flying. He was busting to say more, but even he had to see the sense in not hurting each other any further.

Aimee's skin stretched to snapping point as they stood there, silently.

'So…good luck this afternoon.' She stood back to close her door.

'I'll call you. When I get back to Hobart.'

Her heart squeezed. 'Why?'

His scowl bisected his handsome face. 'Your book. Don't we need to finish the interview?'

The book. The last remaining thread between them. A totally fake thread.

She pressed her fingernails into her palms. 'I think I got everything I needed yesterday.'

'I'll call you. To be sure.'

She'd seen him angry, amused, confused, delighted. But she'd never seen Sam so…adrift.

Cutting him completely free just wasn't something she could do at this very second. She needed more strength for that.

She sighed. 'Okay.'

No one said she had to answer his call.

The banks of the Derwent were busy as always—even for a week day. Small watercraft under billowing sails glided along its gleaming surface, and presumptuous ducks busied themselves nearby, waiting for any scraps that might tumble from Aimee's lunch. Parallel pairs of prams pushed by athletic mums dominated the shared pathway and cyclists had to rumble onto the grass to go around them.

Aimee sat on her comfortable bench, tucked back into a recess in the thick foliage edging the pathway, munching absently on her chicken sandwich, her eyes very much lost amongst the boats out on the channel. Glorious golden rays of sun sprinkled down, warming all they touched.

Was there anything more restorative? A productive morning in Hobart's research library, a simple lunch by the Derwent and a silent mind. A rare treat after the emotion of the past few days.

Aimee sighed and sipped her apple juice.

A clutch of power-walking nannas passed her, chatting across each other like the ducks grumbling around her feet, and she followed them with her eyes as she ate. She missed Danielle. Not that they'd ever been power-walking-type friends, but she missed having someone to chat to, to share work with, since her friend had gone on a month's leave back to New Zealand.

Maybe that was what she needed? Some more friends. Broader horizons. New people. Non-Sam people.

As if just thinking his name had made him manifest, the gaggle of fast-moving nannas split like a cell, dividing around two people strolling towards her secluded corner of riverbank in the distance, then reformed behind them.

Her tasty chicken turned to ash in her mouth.

Sam.

With his wife.

They stopped in the distance and watched the boats go by, the downward tilt of Sam's head indicating he was listening intently. Eager to see her after his three days away.

Aimee's body reacted as immediately and inappropriately as it always did to the sight of Sam: tightening, anticipating. Going all gooey. But for the first time it wasn't him that dominated her focus.

Melissa was as small and slim as she remembered from the confused chaos of the A10. But she was better lit in the golden noon light than she had been in the dimness of early morning on the mountain, and infinitely better dressed in businesswear rather than the running pants and sweater she'd had on that cold morning. Dark hair tumbled around her shoulders and seemed to blaze red in the sunlight.

She was…radiant.

Aimee's heart pattered harder, and she dropped her eyes rather than be caught staring. Not that Melissa would have a clue who she was. But Sam would, if he turned around and saw her. Her mouth dried.

She hadn't expected Melissa to be so lovely. She'd built an image of a fusty scientist gadding around in a lab coat stained by God knew what in a poor attempt to diminish her. What kind of cosmic injustice was this, that she should get Sam's heart *and* be beautiful, too?

But of course he would pick someone beautiful. Ethereal.

She risked a glance up again. Sam's back was still to her. But she recognised that posture, the slope of his shoulders.

They stood barely separated, barely touching, and watched the boats. Then Melissa turned and peered up at her husband with such unmasked adoration it stole Aimee's breath. Even from a distance she knew that this was not the face of a woman who was unhappy in her marriage. And right then another convenient myth crumbled. She'd built an image of two mutually unhappy people trying to make a doomed marriage work. It had suited her to think that Sam's dissatisfaction wasn't one-sided.

Because that made him a better man.

As she watched he lifted a hand to stroke an errant lock of hair from Melissa's face, but Aimee was too far away to see the details of her expression. Did his wife's eyes drift shut in bliss at that tiny contact? Did her lips fall open on a tiny breath the way hers would have? Certainly her body seemed to sway towards his. Would Sam have *that* smile on his face—the gentle half-twist that matched the warm glow in his gaze? Would he still be smiling as he leaned in to kiss her?

Melissa stretched up onto her toes and Aimee dropped her head, forcing her voyeuristic gaze to the pathway, her stomach churning, her lips tight, her heart screaming.

Damn him.

And damn herself.

She'd fooled herself into believing—stupidly—that they were staying together out of some kind of obligation, that they were physically together but emotionally apart. Where was the obligation in Melissa's devoted gaze just then? Where was the emotional separation in the way Sam gently brushed her cheek with his knuckle? Even faking it wouldn't be that convincing.

She forced her rampant heart back into some kind of regular metre, her breathing easing. But her chest was still tight.

It was not fake. There was love there. Lots and lots of it.

Did it make her a bad person that she really couldn't find it in herself to be happy for Sam? She wanted that love for herself.

When she dared to glance up they were gone, back the way they'd come.

She sagged back into her bench, spared the hideousness of having them bump into her, fresh out of that touchy-feely display. She wasn't sure she could look Sam in the eye and not cry.

She wasn't sure she could look Melissa in the eye at all.

Thinking of her as 'the wife', or imagining her in shabby jogging pants with a severe ponytail, or in that stained lab coat, or as a faceless, nameless person, had all been futile attempts to depersonalise the woman behind the wedding ring. To somehow make it okay that she was coveting someone else's husband.

She didn't need a commandment to tell her it was wrong. She knew it was wrong. For so many reasons.

But try telling her straining pulse that.

She tossed what was left of her sandwich down to the ducks and ignored the fat little birds that raced in to demolish it, staring off in the direction Sam and Melissa had gone.

Delusion, thy name is Aimee.

Somewhere deep down she'd seriously convinced herself that Sam was miserable, holding onto his marriage out of some misguided honour. Because that had made her feel less *dis*honourable about the feelings for him that she was harbouring.

But he was doing just fine in the job of getting past whatever speed bump his marriage had hit, judging by what she'd just seen. If he'd rushed back from Melbourne to stroll the riverbank with his wife on a work day then they weren't exactly at loggerheads.

Which meant Aimee was distracting Sam from a perfectly *healthy* relationship—not a fatally flawed one.

And she knew exactly what else that meant.

Bundling up her rubbish and her empty juice container, and tucking her research under her arm, she hurried down the cycle path in the opposite direction from Melissa and Sam.

There were some fates you just didn't tempt.

CHAPTER ELEVEN

'WHAT do you mean, we're done?'

Aimee stared at him, wringing her fingers under the café table. 'I've got what I need for the book.'

Sam's beautiful face folded. 'So that's it?'

She took a careful breath. 'Your history is nearly complete. Today should be our last interview. It's a good time to wind things up.'

'Including our friendship?'

Yes. 'No. We'll still see each other.' She frowned at the lie. 'From time to time.'

His lips thinned. 'Christmas and birthdays?'

She reinforced her back against the hurt in his eyes. 'Sam…'

'Aimee, we already had this conversation.'

Every part of her wanted to cave, but she forced a resolute expression to her face.

He frowned. 'I thought your book was…'

Just an excuse?

It had been since the beginning, if she was honest with herself.

But he changed tack. 'I thought our friendship was about more than just your book.'

God, why was it so hard to keep things professional when he was sitting there looking so wounded. She forced herself to remember the blazing adoration in Melissa's upturned face. 'Sure it is.'

'Why don't I believe you?'

She took a breath, as though it would help her lie better. 'Our friendship was forged under extraordinary circumstances. Maybe it wasn't meant to outlive that night on the A10.'

'You can't seriously believe that?'

She met his accusation with blank eyes. Not defending or reacting. 'You said you respected me.'

Three little lines appeared at the bridge of his nose. He looked as if he wanted to disagree. But he didn't. How could he, in good faith? 'I do. Of course I do.'

'Then respect my decision. I think we're done…' She squeezed her fists. 'On all fronts.'

He leaned in closer. 'Aimee, why?'

But just then a shadow loomed over their table. They both looked up into a startlingly familiar face. Sam leaped to his feet, his expression annoyed and grateful at the same time. Maybe he needed a moment to regroup. She'd really thrown him, if the paleness of his face was any indication.

'Aimee, this is my big brother Anthony. Tony, this is Aimee Leigh.'

Aimee smiled past her surprise, slid her hand into Anthony's, and lifted her eyes to his. So this was Sam's infamous big brother. He was very definitely family.

'Your expression tells me I wasn't expected,' he said to her, and glared at Sam.

Sam shrugged it off, turned to Aimee. 'I figured it could be useful getting a family member's perspective on me. For your oral history.'

Oh, the timing. She'd just told him the history was finished. But Anthony didn't deserve to get dragged into their sorry mess. *The sins of the brother...*

'Ah...very useful,' she agreed. And she wasn't entirely lying. He'd be a good buffer between them today, the first time they'd been alone since she flew back to Hobart. Flew away from her out-of-control feelings for Sam. She'd said yes to coffee today with the intention of saying goodbye in person. Respectfully.

She hadn't expected the sledgehammer between the ribs on seeing him again, nor his obvious hurt at her farewell. A mountain of sadness sagged through her. 'I'm sorry you've been roped in, though, Tony.'

Those broad shoulders shrugged. 'Not a problem. I was visiting Sammy anyway. Might as well eat and talk.'

'You're staring, Aimee,' Sam murmured.

Heat chased up her neck as they stood to cross to a larger booth. She wished she could extricate herself right now and flee. 'I'm sorry. I'm just… You two are similar, but I'm just trying to pinpoint why.' There was a lot about them that wasn't alike—their eye colour, their individual features—yet the overall picture… 'It's very interesting.'

He and Tony slid into the booth in much the same way, and then addressed the waitress with the same tone, the same courteous head-tilt. They even laughed the same.

'Amoeba interesting,' Sam clarified for his brother. 'Aimee's a student of human nature.'

Tony stretched along the booth, one muscled arm lying across its back, and smiled at her across the table. 'Stare away. I have no problem being scrutinised by a beautiful woman.'

Awkwardness rushed in to displace the burbling curiosity. Her mouth fell shut. Tony's self-confidence should have been appealing—it clearly was to the waitress, who appeared with their coffees, got hers mixed up with Sam's in a daze, and then stood hovering for unnecessarily long—but Aimee couldn't rustle up more than a professional curiosity in the man sitting across from her.

Unlike the man at her side. Even without looking at him Aimee could feel Sam's presence. The way he studied them both. His badly disguised interest.

That made her frown.

She reached across and automatically swapped the short black in front of her for the decaf latte the waitress had mistakenly put down in front of Sam. He tossed her a sugar lump, then waited until she had stirred her coffee before using the same spoon to dissolve his one lump in the small, steaming cup of dark, fragrant goodness.

Tony's eyes followed every action.

In that moment everything got incredibly *real*. Having Sam's closest friend and brother here with them was only a half-step from having Melissa sitting here, watching. Drawing conclusions.

Judging.

She wanted to cry out that this was a goodbye meeting.

Both of them had been living in their personal little Sam/Aimee bubble—to the exclusion of anyone else—anyone to reflect back to them what they were doing. How they must appear.

It was a blissfully protected way to run a relationship.

She stiffened and faltered and pressed her hands down beneath the table. Not a relationship. *A friendship.* Not even that...

'So, Aimee...' Tony said, then paused to take a sip of his long macchiato. 'Sammy tells me he rescued you off a mountain a while back?'

She looked sideways at Sam who glared at his brother. For some reason that shocked her—that he would have mentioned her at all, let alone the details of her rescue. For so long those hours had been a private thing between the two of them. A special thing. Maybe it was better that it wasn't private any more. Maybe Tony was doing her a favour with his sharp eyes and interest.

She dragged her eyes back to him. 'Yes. A lucky day for me.'

In more ways than one.

'Don't get me wrong,' Tony said, striving for normalcy and doing his best to ignore his still glaring brother. 'It wasn't like he was gossiping. Sam has always…decompressed…with me after particularly nasty jobs. It helps him deal with it all.'

That drew her eyes back to Sam's. 'I was *particularly nasty*?' she asked, lost in his blue depths. For some reason the fact that he'd needed to talk to his brother about her touched her way deep down inside.

He met her intensity and as always her insides squirmed. 'Your situation was. You were easy.'

'In the nicest possible way,' Tony cut in, glaring at his brother's rudeness. Though a hint of speculation strained his voice.

That got Aimee's attention. Sam was a married man, and she was sitting here making cow eyes at him. In front of his brother. She forced her focus back onto Tony with a forced laugh. 'Thank you. You must be the chivalrous one of the family.'

That earned a smile from both brothers— though Sam's was still tight—and the awkward moment lurched past.

They chatted for a bit longer, until Aimee bent to rustle her mini-recorder from her handbag to start the interview she imagined Tony expected.

As she straightened she caught the tail-end of a meaningful look between the brothers. Sam didn't look all that happy.

'I've just…' He fumbled in his pocket for his phone, avoiding her eyes. 'Phone call. Won't be long.'

And without so much as a smile of apology he slid out of the booth and headed for the door.

Well, that had been slick. *Not.* And entirely unconvincing, judging by the confused frown on Aimee's face—and the amused smirk on his brother's—as he'd bolted out of there.

Sam threw a right into the service alley next to the restaurant and rested his back against the wall, pocketing his phone. He'd only thought this plan up late Sunday night, when he'd discovered Tony would be in town this week. Bad timing, given his trip with Aimee, but then again Melbourne had given him a few days to think about it—to change his mind three times and then change it back again.

But he wasn't used to this sort of thing—opportunism, artifice—that was why his exit from the café had been extra lame.

Maybe that was why the whole thing with Melissa was doing his head in, too. He just wasn't cut out for all this…subterfuge.

Ten days ago, wanting Aimee to meet his brother had been just an excuse to see her again. The whole book thing. He'd thought the cover was pretty brilliant. But midway through the Melbourne trip—right after the kite incident— he'd come up with a whole new reason for the visit.

Tony was his favourite brother—no matter the difficulties they'd had between them in the past or the occasional awkwardness of the present— and he wouldn't trust Aimee with anyone else. Not because his brother wouldn't make a move on her, but because when he did—and he absolutely would—Sam trusted she'd be in safe hands. Tony had made some bad choices as a younger man, but he was rock solid now. The sort of man you'd trust your daughter with. Or your best friend.

Or someone else.

His brother was smart. He'd know the book excuse was fabricated. He believed that he was simply being set up. He had no clue that he'd originally been an accomplice to Sam's attempts to see Aimee. But then he and his brother had always had the same taste in women.

They'd be good for each other. Tony was overdue for his own happy ending. He'd tried and failed with several women in the past decade, never quite finding the right one. Eventually he'd just given up. Aimee had *right one* written all over her in bright, talented letters.

Maybe right enough to sway his brother from his lonely path.

She was crying out for someone good in her life. Someone who'd treasure her but not smother

her. Support her. And love her the way she wanted to be loved.

Deserved to be.

Thrusting Aimee at Tony had churned his stomach, but it was kind of like controlling a climbing fall. You knew it was going to hurt, but if you did it the right way then you minimised the injury when you hit bottom. He had nothing to offer Aimee himself, but this way she'd remain in his life—albeit in the periphery.

Given what it seemed she'd come here today to say, it wasn't a moment too soon.

A deep sigh racked his tight body.

So why did it feel so wrong when his head knew it was a good plan? Why had he had to force himself from that booth to leave her alone with the man he trusted above all others? It was just an introduction, just a chance for them to talk, to find a connection with each other. For two outstanding people to meet. Tony would do the rest.

Yet his brain was the only part of his body not screaming at him to go back in, to undo what he'd just done. To grab Aimee's hand and haul her out of the booth, out of the restaurant, and get her the hell out of Tony's orbit. And maybe not stop hauling her until they found themselves a remote, lawless mountain somewhere. Far from Hobart. Far from his wedding vows. Far from his family. Far from society's expectations.

Far from the total mess he'd made of his life.

Where they could just...*be*. Together.

He fished his wedding band out from under his T-shirt and stared at it. *Yeah, and if the moon was a balloon...*

He pressed his lips together and glanced at his watch. Ten minutes was enough. If Tony hadn't caught her attention in that time then he was off his game and didn't deserve the chance.

He pushed away from the wall.

There was something so staged, so *un-Sam* about the way he'd just sprinted out of the restaurant. He was never awkward. Only ever infuriatingly collected.

Aimee turned her attention back to Tony and ran headlong into his best *How're you doin'?* smile.

A hard twist bit low in her gut deep inside, and her mortified eyes drifted shut.

This was a set-up.

The bite turned into a rancid ache and spread around to her lower back.

Sam was setting her up with his brother. *Sam.* The man she had such complex feelings for. This was his answer to the rogue attraction between them—throw another obstacle into the mix. She smiled tightly, and scrabbled around for something harmless to say, but inside her mind screamed.

Genius! If his wife wasn't enough to head off her feelings, what on earth made him think his brother would be? No matter how handsome.

Or was he stacking the deck on his side?

She slid the digital recorder into the centre of the table—firmly. The interview was pathetically paper-thin as excuses went, but she was going to cling to it to the end. It had served her so well until now. Tony might be here for a set-up, but she absolutely did not have to play.

'So… You grew up in a big family with Sam,' she started. 'What was that like?'

'Subtlety has never been his strong suit,' he said, leaning forward.

A cryptic kind of answer to her question, but Aimee didn't let that put her off. 'It's hard for me to imagine, coming from a one-child family.'

'He means well, Aimee.'

She frowned. Were they having the same conversation? 'Was he competitive as a child?'

'I'm no more interested in a hook-up than you are. No offence.'

That got her attention. She abandoned her pretence and braved Tony's direct gaze. 'Then why are you here?'

'Honestly? I was curious.'

'About what?'

'About this random woman that keeps popping up in his conversations. About why he'd try and set me up with one of his friends after all this time. About what made you so special.'

Her heart thumped. 'And now?'

His brown eyes darkened and he leaned forward even further. 'Now I'm even more curious. The two of you made coffee like an old married couple just then. Perfectly choreographed.'

She laughed and tried to make it light. 'We've shared a lot of coffees.'

'Obviously.'

The speculation in his eyes bothered her. And the judgement. She pressed her lips together. 'But that's all we've shared, if that's what you're getting at.' If you didn't count an ill-considered kiss and some sky-high kite action.

'I'm not getting at anything. I'm just trying to understand.'

The intense scrutiny burned. 'Would he try to set me up with you if there was something going on?'

Tony's face twisted. 'That's absolutely what he would do. He's Sam.'

The man had a point. 'Maybe he just thinks we'd…get along.'

'I guarantee you we would.' Speculation glittered in his eyes. 'But I don't think that's why he did it.'

The strangest tug-of-war—between liking Tony and disliking him—nagged at her. It made her already tight body ratchet up a notch. 'Then why?'

He crossed his arms on the table and leaned on them. 'Deflection. He may not even realise it.'

It was so close to what she'd just been thinking she couldn't think of a thing to say. Nothing that wasn't dangerous. But Tony changed direction first, leaning back into the leather of the booth, the picture of relaxation.

'You should be flattered. I'm his favourite

brother; if he's letting me have you he must have a super high opinion of you.'

The arch look she threw him then should have stripped his skin. '*Letting* you have me? I hope you're joking.' The idea of someone giving her as a gift like that was as abhorrent as the thought that Sam might want to.

Tony laughed. 'He said you took no prisoners.'

Tired of the game, and feeling way more defensive than she was comfortable with, Aimee tried to turn the tables. 'He's married, Tony.'

A shadow flattened his eyes. 'I know.'

'So he wouldn't care one way or another what I do or who I do it with.'

He studied her. 'Do you believe that?'

'Don't you?'

'No. I see how he is with you. He cares.'

'Right. Enough to foist me off on his brother. *No offence.*'

'None taken.' He pressed his lips together. 'Maybe it's a way of keeping you close? Subconsciously?'

Her head-shake was immediate. 'He wouldn't do that to Melissa.'

Brown eyes turned nearly black. 'He's done worse to her.' But then they lightened a hint. 'And she's reciprocated, to be fair.'

There had been no hint of that a few days ago. She shook her head. 'He loves her.'

His eyes grew instantly keen. 'Did he say that?'

'Well, yes…' *Except*… She frowned. 'Actually, no. Not outright.'

He shrugged, as if that proved his point.

He mind whirled. 'Why would they stay together if they weren't happy?' Not that it was any of her business.

His eyes seemed to agree with that, but he eventually answered. 'Because of what it cost them. Neither one of them wants to throw that away.'

'What do you mean? What cost?'

Tony stared at her long and hard, deciding. 'Sam and I didn't speak for several years a while back.'

Years? Two brothers as close as this? 'Why?'

'Because of Melissa.'

Aimee flopped back into her seat. 'You were the brother she was friends with?'

'A lot more than friends.'

She internalised her gasp, but barely. 'He stole her from you? *Sam?*'

Tony's nostrils flared. 'Hard to know whether I should be flattered by your confidence in me or hacked off at your disloyalty to Sam. You think he was pitching out of his league?'

She ignored his attempt to redirect her and leaned in to match his brutal stare. 'Sam would never betray you like that.'

No question. Absolutely none.

The answer seemed to satisfy him. He relaxed. 'You're right. There's only one betrayer in our family and it isn't Sammy.'

'You loved her.' Aimee had felt enough shame

in her life to recognise it on sight. She sagged back into her seat. 'What did you do?'

And just like that the accuser became confessor. Suddenly his dark eyes looked a whole lot more like Sam's blue ones. 'Cheated on her. Dumped her after four years together. Sam willingly stepped in to fill the breach.'

She sucked in a stunned breath. 'He married her because you broke up with her?'

'He *dated* her because I broke up with her. He'd been waiting for his chance since his voice broke. He adored Melissa.'

'And then he married her.'

Tony's eyes fell. 'I beat the hell out of him. Three days before his wedding.'

Aimee couldn't help her shocked gasp.

'He could have taken me—he was so nimble and fast. But he didn't.' His voice thickened. 'He just let me pound him.'

Her heart squeezed for a young Sam who had loved his brother enough to allow that. 'Why?' she whispered.

The eyes that lifted reminded her of Coraline's. Filled with old, live pain. 'Because I needed to.' He swallowed hard and cleared his throat. 'He brought her down here not long after that. So it would be easier on her.'

Empathy surged from her aching heart and reached out to him, recognising its twin in suffering. 'Or maybe on you?'

He snorted. 'Or maybe on him. It doesn't

matter. All of that is in the past now.' His eyes blazed. 'All of it.'

He stared at her, and she had the distinct impression that he was trying to convince himself. And that she was missing something obvious. But before she could question him Sam appeared behind them, soundlessly.

'So, are there any secrets left?'

How much had he heard? On some instinctive level she knew that Tony had breached a trust by confiding in her. Made an exception for her. She wouldn't betray that—even if she didn't yet understand why he'd done it.

She fixed a light smile to her face and threw up her hands. 'Who knew you were such an ordinary child?'

'Ha ha!' Sam laughed thinly and slid in beside her. She wondered how long it would take her to be able to sit in a café booth alone without thinking of him.

Nothing she'd heard today changed anything. Sam's marriage might not be all roses but it was still a marriage. And if he was offloading her on his brother then he'd obviously decided where his loyalties lay. She struggled against the tightening of her face.

Sam's wary glance went from her to his brother. 'Everything okay?'

Aimee reached for her recorder and clicked it off. 'Sure,' she said, sliding it—and all its secrets—back into her handbag. 'We've just been getting to know one another.'

'You weren't kidding when you said she was bright.' Tony turned an appreciative smile on her.

Sam's gaze grew worried and ping-ponged between them.

You set us up, Sam! she wanted to shout. He could hardly protest at them getting along. Instead, she took a measure of satisfaction from matching Tony's warmth.

'You're very easy to talk to,' she said. Uncomplicated. Unconflicted. And un all the things his younger brother was.

But she'd still trade a dozen conversations with Tony for just one with Sam.

'I should get going,' Tony finally said, his voice still strained. Sam stood and they clutched forearms in brotherly farewell. Tony gently clapped him around the back of the head with his other hand. 'I'll see you next visit, Sammy.'

Then he reached down and took Aimee's hand in his and kissed the back softly. 'Lovely to meet you,' he murmured politely as he shot her a glance packed full of hidden meaning. *Don't hurt him.*

She inclined her head. 'And you.' *Understood.*

Sam's keen eyes saw it all.

Moments later it was just the two of them again. Just as it had been before Tornado Tony and his funnel of churning, swirling, baffling secrets had cut through her favourite riverside coffee shop.

And the hard conversation he'd interrupted

still needed to be finished. But she'd have to work her way back up to it.

'How often does he come to Hobart?' she asked casually, and Sam's eyes narrowed.

'Every couple of months.'

'What brings him here?'

He shrugged. 'Business. Why? Wanting to clear your diary for his next trip?'

She met his eyes head-on. 'You wanted us to meet.'

'I thought the two of you would…get along.'

'And we did.' In a tense, circling warriors kind of way. But beneath it all Tony struck her as someone she might come to like very much. 'He's a good looking man.'

But not a patch on his brother.

They were so similar, with a dozen key mannerisms in common. Both bright. Both articulate. Both brutally honest. And Tony *was* gorgeous—in a broody, damaged kind of way. Just ask the still dreamy-eyed waitress. Yet she'd felt nothing but curiosity when she'd looked in his eyes, nothing but warm breath when he'd kissed her hand, nothing but compassion when he'd spilled the secrets from their past.

So her attraction to his little brother clearly wasn't genetic. Or generic.

It was very, very specific.

Sam-specific.

So she owed it to herself to try one more time. To ask one more question before opting out of his life for good. To give them both a chance. She took a deep breath and leaned forward.

'Why did you come back early from Melbourne, Sam?'

There could only be two reasonable answers to that.

For my wife or *for you*. Either way, at least she would know.

She had no right in this world to hope or expect the latter, but if she never asked she'd never, ever know. And, as much as she believed the evidence of her eyes down by the river, she'd also believed the sincerity in his brother's voice when he spoke of Sam and Melissa together.

Sam's gaze grew guarded. 'I didn't.'

Aimee frowned. 'You must have.' To have been back in Hobart by noon, when their original flight hadn't been due to leave Melbourne until then.

Sam looked at her as if she was cognitively impaired. 'I came back on the original flight. Mel picked me up from the airport just after two. Why?'

She blinked at him, a cold suspicion washing over her. *Because that means it wasn't you I saw with your wife.*

She looked at the empty doorway through which Tony had departed and swallowed her dread. *Because that means you're being betrayed.*

'No reason,' she said, forcing lightness. Hiding her distraction. Her mind was furiously whirring as she scrabbled to know what the right thing to do was. The universe had just handed her everything she needed to end Sam's marriage. Her heart thumped under the burden of responsibility. 'Just making conversation.'

Sam looked at her oddly before he started filling her in on his last day of work in Melbourne. But the words only whooshed and buzzed in her head.

Melissa was cheating on Sam.

And it was Aimee's fault.

Sam's marriage was slipping away from him because he was too busy worrying about *her*. About *their* relationship. Never mind that it might have been slipping before he scrabbled down the side of the A10 and into her life a year ago, Aimee had felt responsible for it since they had met. If she hadn't been around he'd have picked up some kind of clue about a secret affair between his wife and his brother. He'd be taking action to prevent it.

She tried to look interested in whatever Sam was saying while her mind spiralled wildly.

'There's only one betrayer in this family and it isn't Sammy,' Tony had said, with dark eyes.

Present tense.

'You loved her,' Aimee had answered.

But maybe she should have used present tense, too.

'Are you okay?'

Aimee's attention snapped back to Sam from

the place where it had been drifting, out of focus. 'Sorry? What?'

'You kind of...zoned out.'

'I'm just...' She shook her head and sat up straighter in her side of the booth, looking every bit as distracted as she sounded. 'Sorry. What were you saying?'

Nice. She was away with the fairies while he was eating his heart out over the fact that, with Tony's help or without it, Aimee was leaving him. Today. He struggled not to let that frustration leak out as anger. None of this was her fault.

But he felt it as a seething, dormant kind of pain.

'I wasn't.' He studied her closely. 'We've been sitting here in silence for a couple of minutes. I've been watching you think.'

A flush chased up her throat. 'You should have...'

'Woken you sooner?' His smiled to take the sting out of his words and slid his hand over the table to cover hers, one finger curling under her palm. It practically burned into his skin. 'What's going on, Aimee? Why are you so determined to end our friendship?'

She took a deep breath, stared at their entwined hands. And she carefully extracted hers. 'You need to talk to your wife...'

His chest tightened. How many ways could he say it? And re-say it. 'We don't talk like this—'

'You *should* talk like this. With her. Not with me. You two need to talk about a lot of things.'

No doubt! Defensive heat surged up his neck. 'We're getting there.'

'Not fast enough.'

His gut dropped. If there was a way he could have everything he wanted didn't she think he'd take it? He pressed his lips together. 'You want out. I get that.'

I don't like it...but I get it.

Intensity surged green. 'I'm not good for you, Sam.'

'You *are* good for me.' The words tumbled out before he could think about the wisdom of uttering them. 'Seeing you is the highlight of my week. I can breathe when I'm with you.'

Her frown increased one more pained millimetre and her voice grew tight. 'That's what I mean. It shouldn't be that way.'

Frustration and panic struggled for dominance in the thumping of his heart. He wasn't used to being unable to control his fear, but none of his techniques were working. Was she working up to goodbye? 'You didn't cause my marriage difficulties. How is me not seeing you going to make things magically better with Melissa?'

'It will force you to focus your energies on your wife. Where they should be focussed.' His heart pounded as she straightened, reinforcing her lungs. 'I distract you, Sam.'

'You *save* me.'

The other patrons in the café paused in their conversations, their sipping, their clanking, and stared across the restaurant as the truth burst out of him like an accusation.

Aimee's eyes flared wide and dismayed.

He barely recognised his own voice: raw, tight. But he recognised the truth when he felt it. It sliced through him like a high tension wire.

He'd been in denial. All this time.

He'd dismissed it as friendship, he'd attributed it to the bond they had forged during the rescue, he'd dressed it up as an intellectual connection. Hell, he'd even set her up with Tony rather than see her walk from his life for good. How desperate was that? Even if his brother *was* the only man in the world he'd entrust her to.

Her eyes bled green pain across the innocuous café table. 'Don't you see how wrong that is?'

Shouldn't he trust his gut to tell him what was right and wrong? She didn't feel wrong. She felt very right. Which was why her judgement stung so much.

'I made a commitment to Melissa in front of family and God. And I will honour that commitment. I *am* honouring it.'

She tossed her head back, and her eyes were as scathing as he'd ever seen them. As judgemental. 'My father was fond of semantics when he wanted to be, too,' she spat.

Now? *Now* she chose to open up about her life?

'He justified cheating on my mother because he chose to do it within the marriage rather than leave her. How he must have patted himself on the back. *"I'm staying with Lis and the kid, I'll honour my commitment to them."'* Her chest heaved. 'What he never understood was that he should have been honouring *her*. Not just his legal obligation.'

It was only a glimpse into her life but it was an ugly one, and it reflected their present situation so keenly. The hurt in her eyes told him exactly how she felt about that part of her childhood, and how she likened it to what they were doing.

A dark shade crossed through him. 'I am not cheating on my wife.'

'Not physically.'

She might as well have booted him in the guts.

He thought back to the kite incident, to the many excuses he'd made to touch Aimee legitimately, or fire her up, to the burning desire to knock on her hotel room door that he'd only just managed to quash. Or—and his body reacted just as freshly now—to that one desperate kiss so many months ago that he'd never, ever forgotten.

But he fought the rising discomfort as though he was gasping for air. 'Not in any way.'

She leaned forward, one eyebrow arched. 'Does she know I exist?'

He stared, a numb anger burbling.

'No?' she challenged. 'Why not?'

Defensive heat swilled up and through him. He had no good answer. The anger-guilt threatened to spill over. But this was Aimee—kind-hearted, enchanting Aimee—not some hostile stranger. He floundered in her penetrating stare, silent. If he opened his mouth something bad was going to come out.

Bad for him. Bad for his marriage.

So he sat, rigid and silent in defiance of her inquisition.

But then her accusation softened, and she begged him with eyes rapidly filling with heart-break, 'Why, Sam?'

Because it seemed wrong. It seemed like—

'Oh, my God…'

She pressed her hands flat on the table to steady them and blinked back tears. 'Do you understand?' she whispered.

The violent turbulence of long-ignored emotion raged inside him. He nodded. It was all he could manage past the painful wringing in his chest.

He wanted Aimee.

Not just physically—although he did. Not just emotionally—although he definitely did. He *wanted* her.

With him. Under him. Wrapped around him.

He'd betrayed Melissa in spirit, regardless of whether or not he'd touched another woman.

And he'd betrayed himself. The values he'd been raised with.

A smarter man would have recognised the signs. A stronger man would have walked away and stayed away. Smiled, shaken her hand and received his award, and then got the hell out of Aimee's orbit.

A better man would have seen this coming and done whatever it took to not let it happen.

'I won't be that woman, Sam.' *The other woman.* 'I watched my family be torn apart because my father couldn't honour my mother. I won't break up a marriage now.' He opened his mouth to protest but she raced on. 'And I won't be the woman that takes whatever emotional leftovers you can spare for me, either. I've done that my whole life.'

The moisture in her eyes wanted to spill over, but sheer willpower seemed to prevent it. Typical Aimee. A warm surge of admiration raced through him at her strength.

Don't appreciate it, Sam, a sardonic voice whispered. *She's walking out of your life.*

'I won't be the woman telling her life story to someone at eighty-five and bleeding pain on the page for the feelings she's kept hidden her whole lifetime. Or the woman who settles for near enough. I want it all, Sam. I'm worth it all.'

Determination blazed in her beautiful eyes, and it only emphasised those qualities of hers he felt such admiration for. Such a connection with. It only emphasised how much was missing from his marriage.

His gut tightened around a fist full of razorblades. 'Are you asking me to choose?'

Choosing Aimee would be an unforgivable betrayal of Melissa.

But choosing Melissa felt like an unforgivable betrayal of himself.

Her laugh dripped sorrow. *'I've* chosen, Sam. I'm walking away—'

'No…' His pulse practically shoved the word out of his mouth as it leapt into his throat. But of course she was. Of course she wouldn't hang around. She had too much dignity.

She clutched at her shirt-front. 'I'm worth more than pathetic grabs at whatever Sam-time I can get. Longing for something I'll never have. It hurts too much.'

Longing. Hurt. Those words spoke of so much more than just attraction. For the first time he looked inside her. Really looked. At the pain. At the dashed hope. At the—

He sucked in a breath and sat bolt upright.

She watched the moment the penny dropped with a furrowed brow. 'You moron,' she whispered, but it wasn't offensive. It reeked of self-derision and sorrow…and love.

And—finally—she laid herself bare before him.

Elation flooded his synapses, passed from blood-cell to blood-cell and pooled into his arid heart, shoving aside everything in its path. Melissa. His family. All the reasons he shouldn't be feeling like this. All the compromises and concessions he'd made over the past decade. None of that mattered.

Aimee Leigh loved him.

The best part of his world *loved him.*

But right behind the shot of pure adrenaline came a sobering chaser and his stomach twisted again. He'd been hurting her. She was hurting right now, under all that dignity and strength. He wanted more than life itself to be able to hold her hand. Ease her pain. Except that taking her hand would only cause her more pain.

Sorrow bled through him. How blind had he been not to understand that sooner?

Rational sense fled ahead of a surge of one-hundred-percent proof passion and gratitude and relief. He reached across the table and took her icy fingers in his, trusting the hurt would only be brief.

'Ask me.'

She lifted tired eyes. 'What?'

His whole future was concentrated in his intent gaze. 'Ask me to choose…'

He'd choose *her*. He recognised it like a light-ning-strike. He'd choose Aimee and he'd deal with whatever came. Melissa's broken heart. The condemnation of his family. He'd deserve it all, but he'd weather it with this woman by his side. This woman who filled him with joy and light. This woman who asked nothing of him but his kindness.

All these weeks, all these months since he'd first climbed into her car, she'd seeped into his soul like water soaking its way through a levy just before the whole thing exploded outwards from the subtle pressure, freeing a torrent into the valley below. *He* was that torrent, getting ready to burst.

Every part of him tightened up. 'Ask me now and I'm yours.'

She reeled back against the booth's cushioned supports and gave awful voice to a dry sob. It cracked out from between her ribs before she trapped it with a clenched fist to her lips.

People around them looked away awkwardly.

'No.' The word haemorrhaged out, tight and raw. 'I won't be the reason you end your marriage, or the reason you save it. I won't look into your eyes in ten years and see regret there for the decision of a heartbeat today, or wonder if you're working on a way to leave me, too.'

Shame sliced through him.

'I won't face your family knowing what they must think of me. Knowing what *I* think of me. Even if she—' She sucked her words back fast and thoroughly.

'Even if she what?'

Her eyes widened at whatever she wasn't saying. She took several deep breaths as he watched, waiting. 'You can't choose me. That's not who you are.'

Reality gnawed out from beneath all the euphoria and left him full of gaping ice-cold holes. No, he couldn't choose her—but not because he was a particularly good person.

Because *she* was.

His Aimee.

She leaned forward. 'Attend to your marriage, Sam. Save it or end it, but do it on your own terms. For your own reasons. Without me as a safety net or an excuse or a prize. Ask Melissa what *she* wants. You owe each other that.'

With all the dignity of a goddess, she scooped up her handbag, slid from the booth and walked away from him without a backward look.

He sat, his empty hands flaccid on the table, the sound of the cheerful little bell over the door taunting him as the woman of his heart walked out of his life without a further word.

And the levy broke.

Right. Left…

Getting her feet one in front of the other out through the door—out of Sam's life—was harder than walking across exposed nails. Every cell screamed at her to turn around, to run back into the coffee shop. But she pushed them onwards, ignoring the pain. Focussing on the pain.

She would keep putting right before left until she got to the car. Until she got home. While she packed her suitcase, loaded her laptop, locked her house, taxied to a travel agent and from there direct to the airport.

Because staying in Hobart was no longer an option.

Staying anywhere near Sam Gregory was not an option. She'd discovered hidden strengths that amazed her this year, but even those had their limit.

Ask me to choose.

Her chest compressed. The awful, excruciating irony.

She'd waited her whole life for a man who gave her options. Who asked instead of told. Who listened to her opinion rather than dictating what it should be. And the first time a man gave her the power over his choices…it was one she simply couldn't make.

Ask me to choose.

She never would. Because forcing Sam's hand like that would be unfair and wrong. But somewhere way deep down inside she so desperately wished he'd simply taken the initiative. That he'd made this one executive decision for her and demanded it rather than asking her to decide.

Because that was what *ask me to choose* really meant.

It meant *choose for me.*

And that was not a decision she was prepared to make. Even if—in the panic of that moment—he picked her. He wasn't free to. It wasn't practical for him to. He was committed to someone else, no matter how that someone else was treating him.

She reached the car park, crossed it, and fumbled her keys twice trying to get them into the lock. Just as she heard the *thunk* of her central locking deactivating she heard something else. A footfall right behind her.

'Aimee…'

She froze, her hand on her keys, her eyes falling shut, her back to him.

So close.

'You're right. I set this course years ago. I can't go back on it now.'

'I know.'

'She's a part of my family.'

'I understand.' Her eyes stared bleakly at the top of her car.

'And she's given me her life.'

Part of it. The temptation to tell him was so strong. She owed Melissa nothing. But she'd be destroying a brotherhood as well as a marriage if she did. And it would look for ever—to everyone—as if she'd done it to split them up. To get Sam for herself.

Loathing gnawed at her. Maybe that was what it was. Could she even trust her own motivation when she wanted him so very much?

So she just nodded her head once rather than risk speech.

'And you deserve more…' His breath practically heated her nape he was so close. Her skin prickled, aroused and desperate. She sucked in a tiny fraught breath and then held it to ward against him coming any closer. It felt like the last gasp she'd ever take.

'So much more than a man who isn't free to love you the way he wants to.'

Her chest tightened around the ball of pain that his words wrought and she braced her hands against the car for support. 'It's going to be hard,' she murmured, as a caution against either of them weakening.

He stepped an inch closer and she felt his chest

press against her back—as soft as a kiss yet as hard as tectonic force. 'It's going to be hell,' he murmured, right against her ear.

She swallowed against weakening, against leaning back into his strength, and curled her fingers around the rim of her car's roof to prevent her body from swaying unconsciously back into his.

It didn't work.

Between the beats of his heart and hers every part of her pressed into every part of him. Heartbreaking, sustaining, heaven. Hot, illicit torment. Then Sam was curling around her, twisting her in opposition, and he breathed a vow against her lips as they parted on a sob.

'If I'm going to hell, I'll go for a reason.'

The wet heat of his mouth forced a distressed gasp out of her.

So long. So very long between life-sustaining contacts.

His lips slid unrepentant and fatalistic across hers, coaxing them back to warmth. Back to existence. His arms tightened to steel bands and pressed her back into her open car door. But the discomfort barely registered as his mouth plundered hers. Forcing. Coaxing. Giving. Pleading silently for a response. Aimee's senses swam with delirious sensation and she sagged into his iron hold.

He deepened the kiss, lapping at her inside and out, breathing fire everywhere he roamed.

She dragged her hands upward, skirting over

the heat of his biceps, the hard curve of his shoulder, and then curled one around the base of his hot neck while the other anchored in his hair.

And she kissed him back.

Like champagne surging up the neck of a bottle, sensation rushed up her body and spurted out through the sensitive place where their mouths met. Her legs sagged and her inner muscles clenched. She'd been kissed before. Hard and fast. But nothing she'd ever experienced in her life had prepared her for a fully unleashed Sam. She hung onto him for dear life. The moment she reciprocated he ignited like a scrub-fire finding dry fuel, pressing her, worshipping her lips, drawing a moan from her throat. Echoing it and whispering in those bare moments that they sucked in a lungful of air.

'Aimee…'

He shifted and pressed into her from a new angle, the kiss softening, growing tender. Slower. As if he needed to ration the pleasure. He lapped at her lips, easing the kiss.

'Never forget this…' His murmured words seemed to come from his soul, not his vocal chords. Certainly that was where she registered them.

'You taste like for ever,' he breathed against her skin, and the beauty and awe in his voice helped her forgive him the fact he'd broken their last kiss to say it.

It *was* for ever.

That was how long it had to last them.

Sam pulled back so that he could stare down into her very heart and brushed a large thumb across her swollen lips. And then he whispered, 'Live your life, Aimee.'

He released her back against her car.

Then he turned and walked away. Without looking back. Without a goodbye. At least not a verbal one. Just as he had on the mountain.

The sight of those shoulders, hunched and hurt and hurrying stiffly away from her, would be the last she ever had of Sam Gregory. That and the feel of his mouth hot and blazing against hers. She surrendered to her weak legs and sagged down into her front seat, her trembling fingers going immediately to her mouth to trap the kiss there before it was lost.

'Live your life, Aimee.'

Her heart fractured in two pieces. He'd said that on the mountain, too. But back then she'd heard it as 'live *your* life' and she'd gone on to do that, to reinvent herself and make the beginnings of a new life outside the control of other people. She shuddered and sagged into her seat-back, the fabric pressing dangerously against the spikes of pain poking out of her. Could she do it again? She'd only had to push him out of her heart last time—now she needed to rend him completely from her soul. Visions of Cora and Dorothy and every other woman she'd interviewed floated before her. They had done it. In much harder circumstances than she was facing now.

'Live your life.' She'd heard Sam's words as

that this time. As in don't wait for him. Don't put her life on hold.

Live.

She could. She would. But how much of a life would it be without Sam to love?

She dropped her head forward onto the steering wheel of her car and tried very hard not to remember that that was how Sam had found her when he'd come into her life in the first place.

It was almost fitting that that was how he'd go out of it.

For ever.

CHAPTER TWELVE

As islands went, this one was pretty Australian. Aimee had thought about going overseas, somewhere tranquil and restorative like Bali, but in the end her need to put fast distance between Sam and her wavering conscience and her lack of current passport had made the decision easy. She'd searched instead for the furthest Australian point from Hobart. The north of the country technically qualified, but it was hot, humid country, and good girls from the south of Tasmania didn't do hot and humid, as a rule.

And so Perth it was—way over on the west coast of the country, perched on the edge of the Indian Ocean. But on arrival she'd discovered one place even further west than that—a tourist island about twenty kilometres offshore—and she'd made immediate arrangements to lease one of the very few long-stay tenancies available there. It was expensive, but what were savings for if not for funding sanctuary when you needed it most?

And sanctuary this most certainly was.

There were no private cars on Rottnest Island and only a handful of public ones. Everyone got around on bicycles or on foot or one of several lumbering buses circling the island, which made for a wonderfully slow and easy pace everywhere she went. There were more than sixty small bays on the island, and regardless of the fact it was the middle of winter Aimee visited a new one every day, slowly crossing them off like a geographic calendar to mark her time on the island.

Her old brick cottage with its wrap-around verandas sat high on a bluff and offered sweeping views to the mainland and over the hustling activity of the island's primary mooring and commercial centre. She'd built herself a pleasing ritual in the six weeks she'd been here: a wake-up coffee on the veranda first thing, then a slow stroll following her nose down to the old settlement and the bakery that pumped out the delicious aroma of freshly baked bread. She had a tray full of condiments to slap onto lavish, thick toast, after which she'd shower and then pick a bay to visit.

If it was on the blustery seaward side of the island she'd go in the morning and work in the afternoon, so that she didn't have to battle against the strong sea breeze on her rented bicycle. If it was on the less blowy west side she'd flip her schedule and work until lunch, then spend lazy hours exploring the new bay. Either way she'd then spend the long evenings working on her book.

She stood before her pinned-up map and tipped her head. Today…landward. She traced the long, skinny island's rocky shoreline with her index finger, looking for just the right bay. Her tracing halted on a tiny unnamed divot out at the southernmost point of the island, half hidden between two larger bays. Pleasingly inaccessible. The fourteen-kilometre round trip would be just taxing enough to give her a sense of achievement. She crossed it through with a black marker.

Twenty-two to go.

She'd promised herself she'd be recovered and ready to move on by the time she'd made her final cross on the map. And so far her soul was healing very nicely, thank you.

If scabbing over could be called healing.

This too shall pass. Coraline's last words to her had become her own personal anthem. Somewhere deep in her mind she'd decided that if she could just get through her time on the island she could move on and live her life without Sam. She just needed time.

The morning passed quickly as she finished transcribing the last of her recordings not related to Sam Gregory. She'd avoided those files, tucking them away safely on her laptop for another day. She'd even considered using a commercial transcription service to spare herself the pain, but knew that so much of the meaning was in the tone, in between the words, and that was the stuff that gave her oral histories their flavour.

That either made her highly professional or fatally masochistic.

But after lunch the tiny bay—and the hearty cycle out to it—did not disappoint. More rocks than anything, but despite the coolest day on Rottnest being a perfectly normal day in the south of Tasmania she wasn't interested in swimming, and so a good old-fashioned beachcomb through the rocks, dunes and crystal blue shore was a serene and restorative way to spend the afternoon.

So much so that as a squall came through in the evening she stoked up the fire in her trusty cottage, pulled a rug over her knees, filled a glass with a good Western Australian red wine and hovered her mouse over the folder called *'Sam 1.'*

She was ready.

It was time.

Her usual transcription process involved listening right the way through to get all the context and subtext locked away before she busied herself transcribing.

She clicked 'open.' And then 'play.' Then closed her eyes.

'So...'

Her own recorded voice was unnaturally loud in the silent little cottage, followed by the shuffling sounds of the digital recorder as she'd slid it across the table to Sam after the awards ceremony a lifetime ago.

'Tell me about your family. You're the oldest of...what was it...seven?'

She took a deep breath in the heartbeat that had passed between her asking and him answering. Then it came: his voice, rich and deep and relaxed.

'Eight. Second oldest.'

Her chest compressed immediately and her fingers tightened on the wine glass. It was like having him in the room with her. She could almost smell him. After so many weeks of absence her body reacted immediately—aching, hurting. She took a big swig of wine as she heard herself say casually, *'Big family.'*

Her mind saw the easy shrug of his shoulders as he'd answered. *'Lots of love to go around.'*

Sam talking about love was too excruciating. She missed whatever he said next as her heart rebelled and railed at her mind for putting it through such pain. The pride in his voice when he spoke of his family should have been a warning. A man with those kinds of family values would never leave his wife.

She took a series of deep breaths and tuned back in to her own voice asking him about his parents' example.

'Pretty tough act to follow?'

'I think we'd all consider it inspirational. Not demoralising.'

Except he considered it a whole lot more than inspirational. Their marriage was the bar against which he measured the success of his own. Two people for whom the marriage vows were more than just sacred, they were ingrained. Their values were Sam's. They were the reason he wouldn't leave Melissa, even if his for-better-or-worse was two parts worse to one part better.

'You're protective of her.'

'Of course I am. She's my wife.'

His defensiveness hit her as strongly now, as it had all those months before. He hadn't liked his protectiveness being challenged. His carefully built up defences.

'You love her.'

Again. *'She's my wife.'*

Aimee frowned. That wasn't a yes. She paused and ran the digital file back a bit, listened to it again with more volume. His voice had been strained and curt, but he hadn't said yes. In fact he'd never said it explicitly in all the recordings she'd made and all the conversations they'd had. He'd spoken of her intelligence, her goodness, her gentle nature and his reluctance to hurt her.

But never love.

Yet he'd clearly loved her at the beginning. Enough to marry her. Enough to leave his family.

That didn't change the fact that he'd chosen to stay with Melissa now. But it killed her to imagine that he was condemning himself to a passionless marriage. A man who had the heat of a volcano bubbling away inside him, just waiting for a chance to erupt.

Her heart squeezed harder.

The recording went on as she remembered it. Everything had got sticky right about then, and she'd ended up calling a halt and bolting from the café.

She looked at her glass, which was suspiciously empty. She never drank while working—never—but this was an exception. This was too hard without a measure of Dutch courage.

A really healthy measure!

She double-clicked the file labelled *'Sam 2'* before pushing to her feet and padding across the cold floor in her woollen socks to the kitchen and the waiting bottle of red. *'Sam 2'* was the file from the ill-fated kite flying day.

They'd both grasped at the sanctuary her book offered rather than keep swinging away at each other's emotions. Any port in a storm.

She knew how this conversation started. She'd asked him to talk about how he'd first come to work in Search and Rescue. It had seemed safe after the tumultuousness of the conversations that came before it. And the kite flying. Her cottage filled with the sounds of the digital recorder clunking awkwardly to life and the noise of the café they'd sat in to record it.

Yet another restaurant. Yet another safe public place.

Red liquid tumbled high into her glass.

'Aimee...'

She fumbled the glass and sloshed wine all down her hand. Then she froze with her back to the laptop, to the warmth of the fire, staring out of the kitchen window into the swallowing darkness. As afraid to turn around as if Sam truly stood there.

That wasn't her voice.

'I'm recording this while you're in the bathroom...' He sighed, and it was so like the little groan he did while kissing it nearly undid her. Her knuckles tightened around the counter- edge. She still didn't turn around.

'I wanted to apologise again for today. The kites. I've been thinking while we walked back about why today happened.'

Her eyes fell closed.

'I can't honestly explain it. I only know that you energise me. You make me want to control time so I can slow it down when we're together and make it last longer. You make me smile and frown and roll my eyes with exasperation all at the same time.' Another sigh. *'But I like that. I want to teach you all those things your parents never did. I want to teach you about the world so that you are equal to it. You should never be less than you are capable of.'*

Aimee's hands curled so hard into the counter one of her nail-tips fractured. She peeled it off with trembling fingers, opened her eyes and locked them onto the darkness outside.

'It's awkward, this thing we have, but it's not insurmountable. We respect each other. We appreciate each other's mind. We're friends, Aimee. And that's a lot.' Dishes clanked in the background. *'That's something worthy—something to protect. I wish that I could have this conversation*

with you in person, but I get...' The longest pause
yet. *'...cloudy when you're here. The things I try
to say don't come out straight. But I know that at
some point you'll hear this and maybe you'll understand me a little bit better. You'll believe that
I have nothing but the best intentions in my heart.
And maybe we can talk about it then.'*

A guttural whimper escaped her tight lips. She
heard a raucous laugh that she remembered hearing the first time, back in the café. Sam's voice
sped up.

*'You're coming back now. Whatever happens
in the future, Aimee...I want you to know you can
always count on me. I feel like I didn't finish rescuing you that day on the A10. I feel like there's
more I'm supposed to do.'* Pause. *'I hope you
smile when you hear this. At very least I hope
you don't cry. I'm yet to see you do that. I hope I
never do.'*

There was a clunk and a click and the recorder
went to the moment's silence it was programmed
to put between individual files. Then her own
voice filled the room again, bright and oblivious.

*'So, Sam... Tell me about how you came to be
involved with Search and Rescue...'*

But Aimee wasn't really listening. And she
certainly wasn't smiling. Sorrow too deep and
too perfect for tears surged through her body. She
stood half doubled over, clinging to the counter
as if it was the only thing holding her on earth.
Stopping her spiralling away into a vortex of
compounding pains. Was that what he'd meant

when he'd stood in the hallway in Melbourne and asked her if she was leaving because of what he'd said on the recorder? Did he think she'd listened to these words and never acknowledged them?

Let him pour out his heart and then just pretended they didn't exist?

'I feel like I didn't finish rescuing you that day on the A10.'

Her eyes squeezed shut.

Though she'd never heard them before, Sam's words summed up her own feelings so succinctly, so keenly, they cut her as surely as if they had been an actual blade. She'd worked hard on her independence—to own her actions and thoughts, to learn from her mistakes—yet here she was physically resonating with the truth of that simple statement.

Unless it was just plain old trembling?

Maybe there was no strength in being alone? Maybe true strength came from two people grasping each other? Like an arch. Immovable. Unbreakable. The strongest shape in nature.

But if they were the wrong two people… What then?

Sam's voice crooned on behind her, answering the questions she'd asked almost as a Band-Aid to the pain of earlier in the day, and his tone formed a reassuring blanket to drape over her hollowness. Still her knuckles whitened and the kitchen bench kept her from launching off into orbit and she determined not to move from that spot until she could be certain her legs would hold her.

CHAPTER THIRTEEN

TODAY was a no-work day. Sam's 'beyond the grave' message had thrown her so badly she'd tossed and turned and dreamed turbulent thoughts when she finally had got off to sleep.

The only silver lining was being up before the sun on what was the first really clear, warm day since the wet weather had set in. The glorious sunrise streaming in through her veranda doors made her think of fresh starts and new beginnings. It combined with the goodbye message from Sam—not that he'd meant it that way—and gave the beautiful day a strange kind of serenity. As if it was the first day of the rest of her life. An emotional turning point of sorts.

Not how she'd imagined or wished it would be, but not terrible either. Exactly as scary and exciting as the last time she'd done it, but definitely tinged with more sadness.

The strange mood made her restless. She picked the furthest bay to visit—a wild little point, far out to the blustery west of the island—

and on her return she still didn't feel like resuming work with her files. Or her book.

A day off. Something she'd not had since coming here.

And so here she was, as the afternoon wore on, curled up in a comfortable recliner in the window of a nearly empty coffee-house perched high on the edge of the island's main settlement, overlooking all the vacant moorings in the bay and the jetty where the ferries came and went like clockwork through the day.

She'd been sitting here long enough to see two come and go. And she knew from experience that the last ferry of the day would arrive at five p.m. and leave thirty minutes later. It was the off-season, so there wasn't a lot of traffic, but this late in the afternoon virtually all of it was outgoing. Tourists stretching their visit until the last possible moment and island staff heading home to their families on the mainland. Kids with bikes and surfers carrying their boards like guitar cases, families and couples, all waiting down on the jetty for the arriving passengers to disembark.

It didn't take long.

A group of five got off, all tiny in the distance. That was it. Her professional eye was drawn to the make-up of the group—a woman, two children and two men. Was it two families? One family and a friend?

The group paused after disembarking, turned, and the two largest of the speck-sized people shook hands. Then the family of four walked down the jetty towards their insignificant pile of luggage, leaving the other man standing there with his suitcase, lost.

Aimee stayed locked on the tiny speck as he wandered to the end of the pier and looked out to sea. Even the suitcase was incongruous. It branded him clearly as an out-of-stater. Locals bought backpacks, satchels, surfboards, boxes of food for their holiday. Few got off with suitcases. Even fewer on their own. On the last ferry of the day.

Then again, *she'd* disembarked alone. She'd had a suitcase.

Maybe this guy was as much an outsider as she?

The speck turned, looked up at all the businesses and accommodation lining the bluffs around the jetty, and started the long walk to shore and then up to the settlement. He carried his suitcase as if it was weightless.

Aimee's hand stilled on her coffee cup, halfway to her mouth, and hot liquid sloshed over the rim. His carriage. A man alone. Completely in opposition to the way people usually flowed on and off this island.

Sam?

She squinted and leaned closer to the glazed window. It could be. Or not. Maybe he was so firmly in her mind after the surprises and hurts of yesterday that she was seeing ghosts. Maybe he was just some random guy come to join his family after getting caught up at work?

But there was something about the sad way he strolled up the pier that hinted he had nowhere important to be. Or nowhere he was looking forward to going.

She stared as he got closer.

'Excuse me, miss?' A young waitress appeared beside her and held out a pair of binoculars. 'If you're looking for whales you'll need these. They most often surface around the southern corner of the island.' She pointed in the opposite direction.

Aimee wondered what the girl would think if she confessed she was watching a whole different kind of mammal. She took the binoculars and smiled. 'Thank you so much.'

As soon as the woman had returned to her work behind the counter Aimee swung around and pointed the glasses down to the jetty, searching amongst the trickle of people going out to the ferry for the only remaining passenger coming in.

And then she found him.

The breath she sucked in drew the attention of both staff behind the counter, and they glanced out of the window to the horizon to see what she'd seen. By the time they returned their focus to their work Aimee was on her feet, dropping the binoculars back onto the counter and heading for the door.

'Have a good day!' one of them called after her.

It was a long walk down to the jetty, even

at the pace she was going, but it gave her just enough time to moderate her instinctive flash of excitement, her mind-spinning amazement that he was here at all, her desperate panic that might miss him and then never find him again. It slowed her footsteps slightly.

She didn't want to look desperate. She didn't want to *feel* desperate. But since when did what she wanted ever have anything to do with reality?

She curved around the limestone retaining wall that raised the café high above the road sloping down to the jetty and darted her gaze left and right. Then she saw him, asking directions at the visitor centre on shore.

Her heart exploded into a painful thumping.
Sam.

She slowed her steps to nothing. Forced them to stop.

It suddenly seemed imperative that Sam's first sight of her should not be her rushing enthusiastically towards him. She'd done enough rushing towards him to last a lifetime. This time *he* had to come to *her.*

She stood, frozen, on the tarmac hill and waited for him to notice her.

His eyes were off to one side, studying the historic limestone buildings lining the shore, glancing up towards the bluff where her little cottage was dwarfed by one of the island's lighthouses.

Still she stood, unmoving.
See me.

His head whipped left as he swapped his case

to the other hand, looking down the long, clean beach that stretched until the island turned a corner, looking down towards the popular tavern on the shore, the rows of cottages the image of hers that lined the beachfront on the island's west end.

Still she didn't stir. Though it was one of the hardest things she'd ever not done.

See me, Sam.

He swung his gaze back to the roadway ahead and lurched to a standstill…and saw her.

He didn't move. Neither did she. Though her heart hammered wildly to be let out of its constricting cavity and fly to him. Then his feet started moving steadily, with purpose, and his eyes stayed locked on hers until she had to tilt her head to stare back into them.

The *thunk* could have been him dropping his suitcase at her feet, or it could have been the sound of her falling in love with him all over again. And undoing the good work of the past six weeks.

'Aimee.' Said with wonder. Said with pleasure. Said with infinite softness and sadness.

Sam.

He shook his head. 'I can't believe you're here.'

She frowned and her stomach sank. 'You weren't looking for me?'

His smile, so gentle and familiar, warmed the incredulous chill in her bones. 'I've flown to four different towns in the past two weeks looking for you. I meant I can't believe you're here, meeting me. How did you know?'

'I didn't know.' Or maybe she did. Maybe it was fate that had had her listen to that file last night. That had given her a spectacular day to force her outdoors and a spectacular dose of heartbreak to waste away the afternoon in this café. 'I was—' *spying on you with binoculars* '—passing. And then I saw you at the visitor centre.'

She could tell him the full truth later, once she'd discovered why he was here. If she was still able to speak to him.

'You saved me a difficult search. The island staff are particular about the privacy of their guests, it seems.'

Unlike her friends and family. 'Who told you where I was?'

'I flew up to your mother's place only to find you weren't there, then went back down to your father's. Your friend Danielle gave me a bum steer before finally taking pity on me and telling me where you actually were.'

Her lips tightened. So much for the solidarity of friends.

'Don't be angry, Aimee. She knew how hard I'd been trying. And she remembered me.'

'She's never met you.'

His eyes softened. 'She remembered me from your stories.'

Oh. She had been very effusive in her praise and appreciation after the accident.

'She said she owed me one for saving you that day. But now we're even.'

'How did you—?'

'I contacted every Danielle that the Department of Heritage has until I found her.' His lips twisted. 'There's fourteen, if you were wondering.'

She battled her body's instinctive reaction to his smile, the almost irresistible urge to lean into it.

'She also asked me to tell you that the McKinley tapes are ready.'

The McKinley tapes. Their workplace e-mail code whenever one of them wanted the other to call them urgently to talk. When something exciting was up. Yes, the McKinley tapes were almost certainly ready to burst!

'Thank you.'

The island reeled around her. That she was standing here, making such smalltalk with Sam...

Sam!

She shook her head at the inconceivability of it.

'Is there somewhere we can go to talk properly?' he asked, reading her expression.

Her eyes flicked up to the bluff, to her warm little cottage. But taking him into her space didn't feel like the best decision ever. It was hard enough having him in her house in spirit...

'There's a café just here.'

To their credit, and Aimee's undying gratitude,

the two staff masked their surprise at her return and treated her as if they hadn't seen her run out of there just a few minutes before. They showed her to the same table and took a speedy order.

Aimee tucked her hands under her thighs and lifted her eyes to his. 'Why are you here, Sam?'

'I came to find you.'

'Why?'

'Because I don't like how we left things. In Hobart. I didn't know you'd gone.'

The subtext was clear. *You should have told me.* Old sensitivities bristled. From way before Sam. 'I wasn't aware I had to lodge an itinerary with you.'

He winced. 'I was worried about you. You just disappeared.'

Even her shrug was defensive. 'I might have been ignoring your calls.'

'I'm sure you were. You blocked my e-mails.'

She dropped her eyes at that little bit of immaturity. She'd been so desperate to close off any avenue back to him. A self-preservation thing. She couldn't trust herself not to weaken.

'I went to your apartment,' he persisted. 'It was all locked up and your neighbours told me they were collecting your mail and watering your plants.'

'So clearly I wasn't dead.'

'I wasn't worried that you'd done something, Aimee. I was worried that you were alone somewhere. Toughing it out. And I couldn't help you.'

'How exactly did you imagine you appearing was going to help?' *Is* going to help.

'Things got…out of hand that day. I wanted to apologise. To make sure you were okay.'

'Chivalrous to the end. Well, you've found me.' She held her hands up and indicated around them. 'Happy in paradise.'

'You don't look very happy.'

'On the contrary. I've found a real…peace here. It's helped me to get a lot of things straight in my head.'

Creases appeared between those expressive brows. 'What kind of things?'

'My future. What I want from life.' She straightened. 'What I don't want.'

'Sounds like you've had a productive holiday.'

'This isn't a holiday. I'm working.'

'On the book?'

She nodded. 'Amongst other things.'

'How's it going?'

'You came all this way to talk about my book?'

He stared at her. Shook his head. 'Did I do this to you, Aimee?'

Her heart whomped hard. 'This?'

'This sarcasm. The defensiveness. It's not you.'

'Maybe this was always me. We didn't exactly part on the best of terms.' If you didn't count the public display of more than affection.

'No, but… Through everything you were always so…gentle.'

Her laugh was everything but. 'If I seem harsh it's because I'm protecting myself, Sam.

It's not easy seeing you.' He glanced out to sea and then dragged his eyes back, as though facing her pain like a man was the punishment he was due. 'You've had weeks to get used to the idea of seeing me. I've had minutes. Give me a break.'

'I'm sorry. You're right.'

He smiled as the waitress slid two steaming cups onto the table, though it was hollow. Pretty much exactly how Aimee felt. She was full of the joy of seeing him again but she wasn't letting any of it out.

'Drinking coffee is all we seem to do,' he said.

'We always were particularly talented at finding legitimate ways of spending time together.'

They fell to silence. It was a far cry from the comfortable ones they'd used to share.

Her mind made the obvious leap. 'How is Melissa?'

He frowned and seemed to pick his words carefully. 'She's good. Really good.'

That hurt—why wouldn't she be good? She had the best man in the world fighting for her—but she watched him closely for his next reaction. 'And Tony?'

He flicked his eyes up, surprised, but gave nothing else away. 'He hasn't been back since you met him. But he's well.'

So Tony was off the scene and things were 'good' with Melissa. It was what Sam wanted. But it was hard to be pleased for him. Even with the benefit of six weeks of emotional distance. Those weeks had counted for nothing the moment she saw him standing on the jetty.

Her eyes followed that thought. 'Your ferry's leaving.'

He didn't take his eyes off her. 'I don't care.'

'It's the last ferry of the day.'

'I'll sleep on the beach if I have to.'

'It's the middle of winter, Sam.'

He shrugged. 'I'm rugged. And survival trained.'

She glanced at her watch. If he didn't get a cottage then she'd have no option but to offer him her sofa. 'If we hurry we'll catch the visitor centre before it closes. There's plenty of empty cottages on the island.'

'This doesn't strike me as an island that hurries anything. Finish your coffee. Tell me what you've been doing for the past six weeks.'

She pressed her lips together and drank as fast as the heat of her coffee would allow, and tried not to get annoyed at how he took his time. 'You're stalling.'

'I'm relaxing. It's been a hard couple of weeks.'

Tell me about it.

But eventually he finished up and they paid, and walked back down to the waterside visitors' centre. Just in time to see the shutters going up.

Her eyes squeezed shut.

Great.

'Got a plan B?' Sam said casually.

'Closed at 5.30p.m.' There was an enormous

notice next to the counter that advised custom-
ers. Sam had to have seen it when he'd popped
his head in here before. An urge to be contrary
overwhelmed her. 'I'll give you an extra blanket.
You're going to need it down on the beach, GI
Joe.'

Sam smiled at her churlishness. 'Great. Let's
go get it. I'll walk with you.'

Aimee turned and stalked ahead of him back
up the road, then threw a right at the top and trod
the familiar path around the edge of the bluff.
Sam lagged, studying the barred heritage buildings from a century before when the island had
been a penal colony.

'This reminds me of Hobart,' he said, calling
ahead to her. 'Except warmer.'

Maybe that was why she felt so at home here.
She slowed and let him catch up. They walked
past the budget family accommodation, where
the smell of early dinners for children wafted
around them and bright, inviting lights blazed
in old fashioned windows. Eventually she was
wiping her feet on the doormat to her cottage as
Sam clunked up the timber steps behind her.

'I'll just get you that blanket.'

He fired his baby-blues at her. 'Seriously,
Aimee? You're not going to ask me in?'

Of course this had always been his plan, and
of course she'd seen it coming. But had it not occurred to him that this was the first time they'd
been together behind a closed door alone *ever?*

It sure as heck had occurred to her.

An isolated cottage high on the bluff of an island was neither public nor safe. And it really wasn't somewhere that a married man should be with the woman he'd kissed half to death the last time they saw each other. But she could hardly throw him out.

Ugh! She pushed through her front door and let it swing wide behind her.

Into the breach...

'Wow. Look at that view.' The lights of the expansive capital of Western Australia twinkled in the distance across twenty kilometres of darkening ocean as the winter sun slunk down over the island behind them. 'I can see why you call this paradise.'

'It *was*...' she muttered, and left it hanging. She crossed to the fireplace and started to lay her evening fire.

He didn't offer to help, he just helped. And he didn't take over, either, like every man she'd ever known would have. He just anticipated her fire-making process and was ready with what she needed next. Kindling. Rolled up newspaper. Firestarters. Matches.

Within minutes the house crackled with the pop and hiss of a young fire just getting going.

Aimee walked into the kitchen and yanked the cork from the bottle of red sitting on the counter, then poured a liberal dose into the waiting glass. She held up an empty one in his direction.

He shook his head. 'No, thank you.'

Suit yourself. 'What?' she finally said when she noticed his quizzical expression.

'I've just realised I've never seen you drink alcohol.'

'Worried you've driven me to it?'

His tiny smile hurt her heart. 'No. But it's a reminder of how little we actually know about each other.'

She took a deep breath to smother the bite of pain that statement generated. 'Just as well you're not staying, then.'

He leaned on the old timber fireplace surround and eyeballed her. 'If you want me to go, Aimee, just say the word. I didn't come here to upset you. I just wanted to say my piece.'

'It upsets me. Naturally it does. I came a long way to try and restore some equilibrium. You've shattered it.' She waved at the cosy cottage features around them. 'Even this place will now remind me of you. My sanctuary.'

He dropped his head.

'But done is done. Say your piece and go. I'll go back to rebuilding my life. Although I really can't think of anything we left unsaid the last time we spoke.'

She crossed her arms and leaned on the far counter, the timber kitchen island strategically positioned between them.

His eyes burned into hers even across the room. As if there was something he really wanted to say but couldn't bring himself to. 'Back in the car wreck last year, you told me a story about

Dorothy, the woman who came out here as a teen and moved to the gold fields with a man she barely knew. How she stayed when she was terrified and miserable because she wanted to honour her commitment.'

It was a question, even if it didn't sound like one. 'I remember.'

'The way you spoke that night, and things you've said since…about your father… They led me to believe that you rate personal integrity highly. That you feel honouring a commitment is a worthy trait.'

She nodded.

'So why do I feel like you're disappointed in me for honouring my commitment to Melissa and persevering with my marriage? Like you're condemning me for it?'

It didn't surprise her that he'd picked up on it. It was exactly the complicated paradox she struggled with daily. 'Respecting your values and liking them aren't the same thing.'

'Would you have me do less?'

Would she? A man like Sam being free and easy with someone else's emotions? She shook her head.

'Yet it's still there in your eyes—the disappointment. Even now.'

'It's not disappointment. It's—' She averted her eyes for fear of what else he might see in them and changed tack. 'It wasn't like I didn't have fair warning. You told me back on the mountainside that you never started something without finishing it. On principle. Your marriage is no different.' It hurt to say it but she owed him the truth. 'I do admire your determination to make your marriage work.'

'But?'

But I hate it. She risked a direct stare. 'But I think you've made a mistake.'

Not what he was expecting her to say, judging by the fold in his brow. 'How?'

Because Melissa isn't working nearly as hard to honour your marriage as you are. Could she tell him that? Could she trust her subconscious not to be spitting it up intentionally to come between Sam and his wife? She hedged. 'What if you're not meant to be together? What if that's what you were supposed to take from all of this?'

What if the lesson she was supposed to take from Cora's story was that she should be fighting for what she wanted rather than just walking away? It had only taken an hour back in his company for her to know—without any doubt at all—that a life with Sam was what she wanted. More than anything.

'Then my mistake was made ten years ago, marrying Mel. It wouldn't really be honour if I only called on it when things were going well.'

His words fitted almost perfectly with her own values. Yet she abhorred them. Her throat thickened. 'What if I'm the person you're supposed to be with?' It was tiny and raw and the most honest thing she'd ever said to him. Possibly to anyone—including herself.

The wind battered against the window frame and his body stiffened in front of her as if he expected it to burst in and start buffeting him, too.

'You think I haven't asked myself that?' he murmured over the noise of evening closing in. 'Every time we were together having such a good time? Every time we laughed at the same corny joke? That maybe Mel and I weren't supposed to be together? My own disloyalty made me sick even as I was craving more time with you.' He ran expressive fingers through his hair. 'But then I started in on the blame game. Maybe I'd choked my marriage in trying too hard to take care of her? Maybe our inability to talk was my fault? Maybe being drawn to a fresh, bright new toy was just the coward's way of ending the relationship? And I ended up doubting that I had any honour at all.'

She stared at him.

'I used you, Aimee. I drew you in to my problems and then set you up as an excuse to avoid dealing with them. I indulged the attraction between us and I made a hundred excuses for why. I kissed you when I knew a clean break would be easier for you.' He took a breath. 'I have no more excuses now. I'm just so very sorry. That's what I came here wanting to say.'

Her heart squeezed up into her tight throat. Had she honestly expected more? 'Why are you saying it now?'

'There are things I wasn't free to say before.'

Before... The stream of thick blood powering

her pulse pushed harder against her artery walls. Her eyes instinctively went to his hand before she remembered that was not where he wore his wedding ring. They flicked to the spot below his throat instead. Tan fingers flipped the top button of his shirt and drew out the leather thong.

Absent of ring.

'Melissa and I have split up.'

A hole torn open in the planet's atmosphere right above the cottage, and all the oxygen fled Aimee's cells in a rush. She gasped for air she was sure wasn't there. If not for the sturdy counter behind her, her legs would have crumpled under the force of her shock.

He was free.

Her mind spun with a wild mix of vertigo and delirium.

He was free and he was *here*.

Blind hope she didn't dare give voice to crashed headlong into a wounded kind of fury. She exhaled, and feared the crush of emotion would stop her being able to breathe in again. 'What? You were just hoarding that fact close to your chest, like a prize? You've been here an hour, Sam!'

He was with her in a heartbeat, gently removing the glass from her trembling fingers and steering her to the sofa in front of the barely warm fire. 'You seemed so strong. You said you were fine...at peace. I had to be sure, Aimee. The way we left things you'd have been well within your rights to throw me that blanket and slam the door in my face.'

Fury swilled around her. The hour he'd kept that secret felt as long and painful as the weeks that had gone before it. 'That's still an option,' she gritted.

He twisted on the sofa to face her. 'Your strength mocked me. It showed me what a coward I'd been in not addressing things with Melissa openly. I'd been so concerned about hurting her, about ripping her foundations out from under her…'

What did you do? The words swam around her mind but refused to get in order on her tongue.

'But I was doing it for me, too. She'd been a part of my family for so long—a beloved daughter. I couldn't bear to imagine the look on my family's face when I came home at Christmas without her. I was her connection to them.' His eyes greyed over. 'But turns out I was her connection to something else. Some*one* else.'

'Anthony.' She barely whispered the name.

He stared at her, disorientated. 'You knew?'

'I was terrified if I told you it would be because deep down I wanted to come between you. Or that you would think it was that.' She lifted her eyes. 'He loves her.'

Sam dropped his head. 'He always has.'

His distress showed in the several places on his face that he didn't quite master. Empathy washed through her. For no reason she thought of Charley McMahon. She'd spent so long thinking about how Cora had lost her Danny she hadn't thought about Charley losing his only brother, too. Was this the end of Sam's relationship with Tony as well as Melissa? How badly was he hurting right now?

'But so do you,' she whispered.

He pushed to his feet, crossed to the fire, prodded it to flame and then dropped a large piece of karri onto it. 'Not like he does.'

She stared at him, the blood slowly returning to her face in warm tingles. 'You married her.'

He turned back, let his tongue worry his lip for a moment, then met her confusion with steady eyes. 'Melissa had been with Tony since she was thirteen, and I'd had a thing for her for most of that. She was smart and gentle and so pretty— and I was just brimming over with undirected adolescent angst. I was enraged when he broke it off with her—for her, that he could be such an ass—and embarrassed that someone from my family had done that to her. So I took my chance.'

He sighed.

'We started hanging out, then making out, then going out…And she got to stay with the people who loved her. After a few years there was a lot of pressure on us both to make a decision. The idea of breaking up with her after so long…'

'You couldn't do it.'

'One Gregory had already trashed her heart. I couldn't do it twice. Plus I honestly believed I loved her. I didn't look hard at all the reasons it wasn't the best idea.' He sank down next to her on the sofa. 'That was a bad call. For both of us.'

'It wasn't love?'

'I adore Mel. She's a brilliant scientist and a wonderful woman. But…' His eyes dropped. 'She wasn't mine to rescue. All the passion in our relationship came from my elation at finally having her for myself, and that eventually waned. By then I'd stopped looking at the signs it wasn't working. I just became determined that it would. For her sake.'

'She didn't love you either?'

'She never stopped loving Tony.'

A rush of sensation raced across her skin. Just like Cora and Danny. But Sam might have been the younger brother destined to live his life with a woman who never really loved him.

'Why did she stay?'

He snorted. 'We were as deluded as each other. Melissa felt like she'd used me—like *she* owed *me* something. And I had nothing to compare it to until…'

His eyes narrowed with the struggle to verbalise something.

'Until?'

He twisted further on the sofa and took both her chilled hands in his furnace hot ones. 'Until some crazy lady in a Honda just about took out my eardrums with the horn of her car one freezing night on the A10.'

She clenched her fingers around his to stop their tremor.

'One night, Aimee. We had just those few hours together and yet the memory of you troubled me more than I could understand. The connection I couldn't fathom. It killed me to see the disdain on your face as you walked across that stage in Canberra—'

'I was angry. You had a wife. And you let me…' *Fall for you. Overnight.* She pressed her lips closed.

'It doesn't matter. But as I stood there in my too-tight suit and you slipped your arms around my neck…that was like going home for me. The most perfect thing I'd ever felt. And I knew right then that my marriage was over. I just didn't want to acknowledge it.'

'I never wanted to be the reason you split.'

'*I'm* the reason we split. And Mel. She'd stalled me for years on the subject of kids. Now I know why. When we finally spoke it was like a tsunami of repressed feelings—a decade's worth. All so misguided and pointless. If we'd gone on much longer they would have turned hostile.'

'Ten years is already a long time.'

'It was turning thirty that did it for her. She realised she was going to grow old and die with a man she didn't love. All because she didn't want to hurt him.'

Shades of Coraline again. 'She didn't love you? Not at all?'

He thought about that. 'We care for each other deeply. Enough to know when to call it a day.'

She stared, her heart beating stronger and faster. 'And she's with Tony now?'

'She always was in her heart.'

'Will that bother you? Them being together?'

The left side of his mouth twitched. 'Not nearly as much as it's going to bother him knowing I slept with his wife.'

The comic image of a simmering Tony sitting across the dinner table from an irascible Sam with Melissa in the room even made *her* smile. Just a little bit.

'They're getting married?'

'I hope so. As soon as the divorce is finalised.'

More silence fell.

'I won't lie to you, Aimee. It wasn't a fun few days. I had to face some stuff in my life that I… Things I've done that I'm not super proud of. My original withdrawal from our marriage hurt her. I was the connection to the people that she loved—to Tony—and I used that to keep her kind of an emotional hostage. I think, without knowing it, I was punishing her for not being…perfect. I wanted the perfect marriage. The perfect love.'

He'd called *her* perfect just a moment ago.

'Like your parents?' she said. His head barely bobbed. 'What do they think about all of this?'

'They want us to be happy. All of us. It's weird for them, of course, but they barely need to do anything more than change the labels on our Christmas stockings. I imagine we'll have some awkward name slip-ups for the first few months…'

She stared at him. For eternity. The log showered loud sparks in the fireplace. 'So you're free.'

His eyes practically glowed as they fixed on hers. 'I'm free.'

'What will you do?'

Blue fire blazed down onto her. 'That depends on you.'

'Are you assuming that your marriage status is the only thing stopping me from being with you?'

'Uh...' That halted the blue fire. His gaze grew guarded. 'I kind of was. Yes.'

'No. There's something missing.'

'Missing? Between us?'

Aimee took a deep breath. 'You've spent the last half-hour telling me about the love you *don't* feel for your wife, the love that she *does* feel for Tony...'

The bemusement on his face would have made her smile if this wasn't so serious. This was the rest of their lives.

'Right...?'

'What about me?'

He shifted closer, gave her *the look*. 'You know how I feel about you.'

'No, Sam. I don't. We've never been able to acknowledge it. I know you're attracted to me, but that's not enough to change our lives for.'

'You want the words?'

'That's all I've ever wanted.' And in a flash she realised that was true. 'I want a man with character and integrity. A man who's compassionate but fearless.' Her heart tightened into a fist. 'Someone who's confident enough in himself to let me be in charge sometimes.'

'That's quite a wish-list.'

'I met a man on a mountain once who had all of those qualities.'

His eyes darkened with confusion. 'Anything else?'

She'd come this far. She wasn't backing away now. 'Yes. A good man who loves and respects me and isn't afraid to say it publicly.'

He stared at her long and hard. Then he got up and walked out of the room.

Aimee blinked, stared at the door expectantly. Waited for the return that didn't come. Then on an angry curse she launched to her feet and shot off after him, grabbing her scarf on her way out through the door.

When she got outside he was halfway up the hill to the lighthouse at the tip of the bluff. Rapidly disappearing into the shadows.

A sick hollowness weighed her down, and she pulled the scarf tighter around her shoulders. Had she asked for too much? More than he was prepared to give? More than he was capable of giving?

But, no. Asking for what she wanted was not a bad thing in her new life. And expecting Sam's love was not unreasonable. If he couldn't offer that... Well, then she would be no worse off than she had been this morning, staring at the sunrise and thinking about the promise of a solo future ahead of her.

Except that she would. How could a future without Sam possibly be as bright as one with him? But she wouldn't run after him this time.

She stopped. Turned for the house.

And then she heard it. Muted and buffeted by the night winds.

'Sam Gregory loves Aimee Leigh.'

She froze. Frowned. Turned back to look up to the lighthouse.

A tall shadow stood at the base of the building, his arms stretched out to the endless black ocean, throwing his voice to the heavens. Throwing his heart open to the heavens.

'Sam Gregory loves and respects Aimee Leigh!' This time louder, clearer, as the wind dropped.

Her breath caught.

The shadow turned and jogged down off the lighthouse's paved base, across the turf and back onto the road leading to her cottage. He didn't stop until he got to her.

'I will never tire of saying it publicly,' Sam vowed. 'But let me say it privately...'

He snagged both ends of her scarf and pulled her into his body, twisting the fabric ends in his fists and holding her tight against him. 'I love you, Aimee. I've loved you since the moment you gave me your trust on that mountainside. So distracted by your courage and strength I made rookie mistakes all night. Not being able to acknowledge it, not being able to acknowledge *you*, is a hell I don't ever want to repeat.'

She stared up at him. 'You love me?'

'I honour you. And I *choose* you.'

Tears prickled and spilled over

'Aimee...' He wiped at them, both sides, with his thumbs, frowning. 'You never cry.'

She laughed, watery and sniffly. 'I do now.' She stretched up and wrapped her arms around his neck. 'I love you so much, Sam.'

And then his lips were on hers, gentle and questioning, as his large hands framed her face. She kissed him back fiercely, determined to show him that she wasn't just accepting him because he was offering, to show him how much she wanted him. How much she loved him.

How strong she was without him but how much stronger she was with him.

'Your nose is freezing,' he murmured, and she nuzzled it into the warmth of his beautiful neck, amazed and awed to know that she could do that every day for the rest of their lives if she wanted. And of course she did.

'Let's get you inside,' he said, tucking her under his arm. 'There's a sofa in front of a fire in there that I'm just dying to stretch out on.'

'You don't really have to sleep on the sofa.' She laughed.

He nudged her sideways as they walked, entwined, his voice rich with promise. 'I have no intention of sleeping on it.'

* * * * *

IMPRISONED
BY A VOW

ANNIE WEST

CHAPTER ONE

'MARRY A STRANGER!'

'Don't sound so surprised, girl. You can't expect me to support you for ever.'

Leila bit back a retort that her stepfather's pockets were lined with the fortune he'd acquired by marrying her mother. She'd had years to learn open defiance wasn't worth the savage retribution that followed. Now wasn't the time to let him know he hadn't broken her spirit despite his best efforts.

'As for marrying a stranger, you'll wed the man I choose and there's an end to it.'

'Of course, Stepfather. I understand.' She'd heard servants' gossip that Gamil had his eye on another bride. He wouldn't want an inconvenient stepdaughter, a reminder of his previous wife, on hand. 'It's generous of you to organise this when you have so many business matters to deal with.'

Gamil's eyebrows lowered. His eyes narrowed as if he detected the sarcasm she hid behind a calm façade.

Leila had become adept at concealing emotion: grief, fear, boredom, anger…particularly anger. It burned inside her now but she held it in check. Now was not the time.

But soon! It struck her that an arranged marriage to a foreigner who'd take her far away was the chance she'd prayed for. Her previous attempts to escape had met with humiliating defeat and ever-tighter restrictions. But what could Gamil do once she was married?

It was her chance for freedom.

A thrill of excitement raced down her spine and she had to work to keep her face expressionless. Looked at like that, marrying a man she didn't know in a cold-blooded business deal was a heaven-sent opportunity.

'It goes against the grain to let him see you like this.' Gamil waved disparagingly at her bare arms and legs, her new high heels and the delicate silk dress flown in especially from Paris.

Even without a mirror, Leila knew she looked as good as she ever would. She'd been bathed, waxed, coiffed, manicured, pedicured, scented and made up by experts.

A sacrificial virgin to Gamil's ambition, primped and polished for a stranger's approval!

Leila doused a furious surge of indignation. She'd learnt long ago life wasn't fair. And if this preposterous scheme meant escape and the chance to lead her own life…

'But it's what he'll expect. He can afford the best in everything, especially women.'

Trust Gamil to see women as commodities to be bought. He was a misogynist through and through. Worse, he was pathologically controlling, revelling in his power.

His cold eyes pinioned her and Leila's skin crawled at the hatred in them. One day she'd be free of this brute. Until then she'd do whatever it took to survive.

'You'll do nothing to disappoint him. You hear?'

'Of course not.'

'And watch your tongue! None of your clever remarks. Stay silent unless asked a direct question.'

Gamil needn't have worried. Leila didn't speak when Joss Carmody entered the formal sitting room.

Her breath snagged as her gaze climbed a big frame to his rugged face. His strong features weren't chiselled but hewn, all tanned angles and sharp edges, stark lines and deep grooves. His black hair, though brushed back, curled over-long at the collar. She had the impression of unruly wildness, combed into temporary decorum, till she met his eyes and realised this man was anything but lacking in control.

He surveyed her with the keen alertness a banker devoted to his financial reports.

Joss Carmody's eyes were indigo dark, like the desert sky just before the first stars winked awake. They held hers and she felt a curious squeezing sensation high in her chest. Her pulse sped as she stood, mesmerised.

Whatever she had expected it wasn't *this*.

A moment later he turned to discuss business with Gamil. Oil of course. What else would bring an Australian resources tycoon halfway around the world? Or make him consider marrying her?

The land she'd inherit on marriage held the region's last and largest untapped oil reserves—a unique holding Gamil used to further his own prestige.

She watched Joss Carmody sit down, cradling a cup of strong coffee, effortlessly dominating the room.

Surely even tycoons took more interest in their potential brides than this? His utter indifference rankled. Surprising how much it rankled. After years under her stepfather's brutish regime it shouldn't bother her.

Why should a stranger's indifference matter? She should be grateful he had no personal interest in her. She couldn't have gone through with this if he'd looked at her the way Gamil had once stared at her mother—with that hot, hungry possessiveness.

Joss Carmody didn't see *her*, just a parcel of arid, oil-rich land. *She'd be safe with him.*

Joss turned to the silent woman sitting opposite.

Her green-grey stare had surprised him when he arrived.

He'd sensed intelligence, curiosity and, could it be, a hint of disapproval in that gaze? The idea intrigued.

Now she lowered her eyes demurely to the cup in her hand. She was the epitome of Middle Eastern modesty melded with elegant Western sophistication. From her sleek, dark chignon to the high heels that had restricted her walk to a delicate, swaying glide, she was the real thing.

Class. She had it in spades.

He didn't need the opulent black pearl pendant or the matching bracelet of massive pearls to tell him she was accustomed to luxury. She wore them with a casual nonchalance only those born to an easy life of privilege could achieve.

For a split second something like envy stirred.

He repressed it as he did anything that resembled untoward emotion. Instead he appraised her.

She seemed suitable. Her ownership of those enormously rich oilfields made her eminently suitable. It was the only reason he considered marriage: to get his hands on what would be the key to his next major venture. Besides that she had connections and the right background to be useful. Yet Joss never left anything to chance.

'I'd like to know your daughter better,' he said as Gamil drew breath. 'Alone.'

There was a flash of something in the other man's eyes. Fear or speculation? Then Gamil nodded and departed with one last, warning look at his daughter.

Joss pondered that look. Surely the old man didn't fear he'd force himself on her? As if Joss hadn't women enough to satisfy every whim!

'You've been very quiet. You don't take an interest in the oilfields you own?'

Eyes cool and clear as a mountain stream lifted to his. 'There seemed little to add.' Her English was flawless with a subtle, barely there accent that proved curiously enticing.

'You and my stepfather were engrossed in your plans.' Her charming smile didn't reach her eyes.

'You disapprove?' Sixth sense warned that her smile concealed rather than revealed.

She shrugged and he watched, intrigued as the silk slid and moulded a pleasing, feminine figure. His chosen bride was rounded in the right places, despite the fragility of her throat and wrists.

She was a necessary part of the deal yet he hadn't expected to feel more than slight curiosity about her.

The stirring of male appreciation in his belly surprised him. He hadn't expected a beauty. He permitted himself a moment's satisfaction. At least being with her occasionally wouldn't be a hardship.

'The fields will be developed.' Her low voice had a husky edge that drew his skin taut with anticipation. 'You have the resources to do that and my stepfather maintains a very close interest in the family business.'

In other words she didn't bother her head with sordid details like where her wealth came from. Why wasn't he surprised? He'd met lots like her: privileged, pampered and eager to live off the hard work of others.

'You don't work in the industry yourself? Take a personal interest in your assets?'

A spark of something lit her eyes, darkening them to stormy green. Her nostrils flared. Then her lips curved in another of those small Madonna smiles and she leaned forward gracefully to put her cup down with a click on the alabaster table.

Joss had an impression of something rippling like an undercurrent beneath her calm expression. Something elemental that made the air between them thicken, heavy with contained energy.

She spread her manicured hands. 'My stepfather takes care of all that.' Yet there was something ever so slightly out of kilter, perhaps the way her tinted lips thinned a fraction too much.

Then the impression was gone, leaving Joss to wonder at his flight of fancy. An overactive imagination wasn't his style.

He was accustomed to brokering deals with men as hard as himself. A life in mining had made him rough around the edges, unused to dealing with delicate females, except on the most basic level. His groin tightened as he imagined his cool bride-to-be losing that superior air and growing hot and eager under his touch. Satisfaction filled him, till he remembered that wasn't what he wanted from this deal. She'd sidetracked him.

'You expect your husband to take care of business while you enjoy the fruits of his labour?'

She darted a glance at the door where Gamil had exited. 'Forgive me. Perhaps I jumped to the wrong conclusion. I was under the impression you wanted me as a silent partner while you make the business decisions.' Her eyes were bright with apparently innocent enquiry. 'Would you welcome my interference?'

Her fine dark brows arched in eloquent surprise. For the first time in over a decade he felt wrong-footed.

Joss stiffened. It was an illusion, of course. Far from being out of his depth, he was running this whole scheme, including the marriage arrangements, to suit himself.

He didn't want her amateur meddling. Bad enough that he had to put up with her stepfather's uninformed ideas until the deal was done.

'If you have expertise in the area I'd like to hear it.' The words were mere form. Joss worked alone. There was room for only one commander in his empire. 'And of course your connections to key figures across the region will be invaluable.'

'Of course.' The flat expression in her eyes, now dulling

to grey, told him she'd already lost interest. 'But I'm afraid I have no expertise in petrochemicals.'

'And where does your expertise lie?'

Again that darting glance to the door. If it weren't for her smooth serenity he'd almost believe she was worried about saying the wrong thing.

'I doubt they overlap with yours. Mine are more on the domestic scale.' She smoothed a hand over the green silk of her dress.

'Domestic as in shopping?' This desire to delve beneath her self-satisfied composure surprised him. Why the need to understand her? To label her in a box marked 'self-absorbed heiress'?

Because she was to be his wife.

After thirty-two years he was finally acquiring a spouse, if only to further his commercial interests.

Marrying went against every inclination. His life was a cautionary tale about its inherent dangers. But the commercial imperative decided him. She was a business asset.

'How did you guess I love to shop?' she cooed, stroking the pearls at her wrist. Yet the light in her eyes and that heightened spark of energy humming between them said something else went on inside that lovely head.

'Just so long as you're not under the impression I'm looking for someone to domesticate me.' He didn't want her thinking this was personal.

Her eyes rounded and a gurgle of delicious laughter broke across his senses, tightening his skin and circling his vitals. He straightened. But already she'd clamped her lips against the sound.

Domesticating Joss Carmody!

Who in their right mind would take on that challenge? He was a big, hard man, all sharp edges and steely determination. It would take someone foolishly besotted by his brooding aura of power and that sizzle of unashamed male sexuality. Someone stupid enough to believe he could ever truly care.

He wasn't the same as Gamil, she could already see that. Yet viewing those coolly calculating eyes, that formidable self-possession and monumental ego, Leila saw enough similarities.

Joss Carmody didn't have a softer side.

'Don't look so worried,' Leila said hurriedly, appalled that surprise had provoked a genuine response from her. 'The idea hadn't crossed my mind.'

'You're sure?' His straight eyebrows scrunched down in a scowl of disbelief.

Leila supposed he saw himself as a matrimonial prize. With his looks and obscene wealth women must flock to him.

Yet surely she wasn't the only one to see him for what he was: self-contained, dangerous and definitely not ready for domestication. Impatience at his all-conquering attitude blindsided her.

'Surprisingly enough, I am.' To her amazement Leila heard the rapier-sharp provocation in her tone. His expression told her he heard it too.

After years guarding every word, how could she trip herself up now? Where was her hard-won composure? Even Gamil at his worst couldn't provoke an outburst these days. It was vital she play to the Australian's expectations if the marriage was to go ahead.

'So what did you envisage, Leila?' His voice dropped half an octave, slowing on her name. He rolled it around his mouth, almost as if savouring it.

Fine hairs rose on her arms and nape. No man had ever said her name like that. A challenge and an invitation at the same time.

Heat flushed her throat as she realised she'd stepped into perilous waters. He didn't threaten like Gamil, but she sensed danger in his sultry invitation. Not the danger of physical punishment but of something more insidious.

Her lack of experience with men told against her now.

She blinked. Gamil was no doubt hidden beyond the doorway, sifting each word, ready to mete out punishment for errors.

The laugh had been a mistake. She'd read it in Joss's surprise. Yet she couldn't regret it. He deserved to be shocked from his insufferable self-satisfaction, even if her stepfather made her pay later.

'I thought you were interested in my inheritance, not me personally.' She kept her tone even, holding his gaze, refusing to reveal how much hinged on his response.

After a moment he nodded brusquely. 'I'm not after an heir and I have no interest in playing happy families.'

At least he didn't expect intimacy. Relief swelled.

She'd wondered whether, when it came down to it, she would be able to sell herself into an intimate relationship in order to escape. Had wondered too about the logistics of disappearing as soon as they were married to avoid giving herself physically to a man she didn't want. Now it seemed she wouldn't have to.

This was pure business. He'd gain the oil reserves, while Gamil gained income and status through his new son-in-law.

She was supposed to be thrilled by Joss Carmody's offer of matrimony. Though come to think of it there'd been no offer. It had been a deal done between power-hungry men.

She squashed instinctive outrage as a luxury she couldn't afford.

'I don't want a wife who will cling or make demands.'

'Of course not.' She couldn't imagine him accepting emotional ties. Nor did she want any.

'So tell me, Leila—' he leaned closer, his voice a deep thread of sound that shivered across her flesh '—why do you want to marry *me*?'

Her brain froze as she watched those firmly sculpted lips shaping her name, feeling again that tremulous shock of disturbance deep inside.

Then she breathed deeply, her mind clicking into gear, considering and discarding possibilities.

Tell him what he expects to hear and seal the deal.

'For what you can give me.' His almost-imperceptible nod confirmed she was on the right track, feeding him the response he expected. 'To see the world and live the life of a billionaire's wife. Bakhara is my homeland but it's rather… confining.' Wry laughter threatened at the understatement and she bit her cheek, using pain to counter weakness. It was a trick Gamil, if only he'd known it, had inadvertently taught her over the years, with his regime of punishments for imagined infringements. 'Married to you my life will change for ever.'

Dark eyes surveyed her so closely she saw the exact moment he made up his mind. His lips pursed and his eyes gleamed approvingly.

Joss Carmody knew what he wanted. A wife who wouldn't clutter his life. A woman who'd marry him for his wealth and prestige. A woman who would shop and amuse herself while he got on with what interested him: making even more billions of dollars. Money drove him. Nothing else.

What would he do if he realised he meant just one thing to her?

Escape.

'He's late!' Gamil paced the courtyard, his heavy tread careless of the exquisite mosaics Leila's ancestors had installed and the carefully nurtured grass by the long mirror pool, a lush green bed in a land of scarce rainfall and high temperatures.

'What did you say to him?' He spun round, spittle spraying Leila's cheek. 'It must have been you. Everything else was settled. There's no reason for him to cry off unless you put doubt in his mind.'

His angry countenance filled her vision but she stood steadfast, knowing better than to retreat before his fury.

'You heard all that passed between us,' she said levelly. Too much in fact. Her temerity in laughing at Joss Carmody's self-conceit had earned her weeks of punishment on bread and water. Fortunately her rations had been increased this week so she wouldn't be too weak to say her vows.

'That I did.' Ire mottled Gamil's complexion. He leaned forward, his stale breath hot on her face. 'I heard you play word games! Obviously that was enough to make him have second thoughts. And now...' Gamil gritted his teeth and turned away.

'How will I hold my head up if you're jilted by such a man? Think what it will do for my reputation, my prospects at court! I have plans...'

He stalked to the other end of the courtyard, muttering. His hands clenched and unclenched as if ready to throttle someone.

Her stepfather rarely resorted to physical violence, preferring more subtle methods. But she had no illusions she was safe if he felt himself goaded too far.

Leila pressed clammy hands together. If only Joss Carmody would thrust open the ornamental doors and stride into the courtyard.

Never had an unwanted bridegroom been so eagerly awaited.

Fear churned her stomach. Was Gamil right? Had the Australian cried off? What, then, of her plans for independence and the career she'd always wanted?

No! She couldn't think like that. There was still time, though he was ninety minutes late and the whispering guests had already been ushered into the salon for refreshments.

Heat filled the courtyard. Leila stiffened her weary spine against the frightening compulsion to admit defeat.

How many more years could she take? This last bout of solitary confinement had almost broken her.

Gamil had broken her mother, destroying her vibrant optimism and love of life. Leila had watched her change from an outgoing, charming beauty, interested in everyone and everything. In a few short years she'd transformed from a society hostess par excellence and an asset to her first husband's brilliant diplomatic career to a faded, downtrodden wraith, jumping at shadows. She'd lost the will to live long before illness had claimed her.

Leila tipped her head up, feeling the sun on her face. Who knew how long before she'd feel it again?

Despite the gossamer-fine silks, the lavish henna decorations on her hands and feet, the weight of traditional gold jewellery at her throat and ears, Leila was no pampered princess but a prisoner held against her will.

If Joss didn't show, standing here in the open air might be the closest she'd come to freedom till she came of age at twenty-five in another sixteen months.

'What are you doing outside in the heat?' The dark voice sidled through her thoughts and shock punched deep in her solar plexus.

He was here!

Her eyes snapped open. At the sight of his imposing frame, his don't-mess-with-me jaw and piercing eyes, Leila found herself smiling with relief. Her first genuine smile in years. It stretched stiff facial muscles till they hurt, the sensation strange in her world of guarded emotion.

Joss halted, struck anew by her curious combination of fragility and composure. That hint of steel in her delicate form. She looked thinner, her neat jaw more pronounced and her wrist narrow as she raised a hand and the weight of gold bangles jingled.

Her eyes opened, the pupils wide in clear grey depths. Then as he watched velvety shades of green appeared, turning her gaze bewitching.

She smiled. Not that tiny knowing smile of last month, but a broad grin that made something roll over in the pit of his stomach.

Ensnared, he drank in the sight of her, the warmth in her frank appraisal, the pleasure that drew him closer.

Heavy scent filled his nostrils, a dusky rose that clogged his senses. It wasn't right on her. But then this woman, decked in the traditional wedding finery of her land, seemed so different from the one whose verbal sparring had intrigued him weeks ago.

'I was waiting for you.' There was no rancour in her voice but her eyes held his as if awaiting his explanation.

A hot spurt of sensation warmed his skin. Guilt?

Gamil hadn't dared voice reproach when Joss arrived, knowing as countless others had before him that Joss lived by his own rules, at his own convenience. He didn't give a damn if his priorities didn't match anyone else's.

Business came first with him—always. The urgent calls he'd taken this morning had required immediate action whereas a wedding could be delayed.

Yet seeing her expression, Joss had the rare, uncomfortable feeling he'd disappointed. It evoked memories of childhood when nothing he did had lived up to expectations. His tough-as-nails father had wanted a clone of himself: utterly ruthless. His mother…just thinking of his mother made him break into a cold sweat. He shoved aside the dark memories.

'You waited out here? Couldn't you have waited in the cool? You look—' he bent closer, cataloguing her pallor and the damp sheen on her forehead and upper lip '—unwell.'

Her smile slid away and her gaze dropped. Instantly the heat in his belly eased.

'My stepfather made arrangements for the ceremony to take place here.' She gestured across to a fanciful silk canopy. Joss dragged his gaze from her. There were pots of heavy-scented roses, ornate gilded furniture, garlands of flowers, rich hand-woven rugs and gauzy hangings of spangled fabric.

'Clearly he's not familiar with the idea that less is more,' Joss murmured.

A choked laugh drew his attention, but Leila was already turning away in answer to a brusque command from her stepfather. Beneath the flowing silk of her robe, she was rigid. She paced slowly, as if reluctant.

Joss watched the interchange between them. One so decisive and bossy, the other unnaturally still. His hackles rose.

He stalked across the courtyard to join his affianced bride. For reasons he couldn't fathom, his pleasure at today's business coup faded. He felt out of sorts.

The wedding was almost over. The ceremony had been short, the gifts lavish and the feast massive, though Leila hadn't been able to indulge much. After short rations for so long, she felt queasy even smelling rich food and the room had spun if she'd moved too quickly.

She'd had to work to repress excitement. Soon she'd be out of her stepfather's house for good.

She'd be the wife of a man who wouldn't impose himself on her. He'd take her away from here, his only interest in the oilfields she'd inherited. They'd negotiate a suitable arrangement—separate residences and then eventually a discreet divorce. He'd keep the land and she'd be free to—

'Leila.' His deep voice curled around her and she turned to find him watching, his dark gaze intent. He held out a heavy goblet.

Obediently she sipped, repressing a cough at the heady traditional brew. A concoction designed, it was said, to heighten physical awareness and increase sexual potency.

Joss lifted the cup, drinking deeply, and the crowd roared its approval. When he looked at her again his gaze as it trawled her was different. Heat fired under her skin. It felt as if he caressed her: across her cheek, down her throat then lingering on her lips.

Something flared in his eyes. Speculation.

Sharply she sat back, fingers splayed on the chair's gilt arms as she braced herself against welling anxiety.

'You make a beautiful bride, Leila.' The words were trite but the warmth in his eyes was real.

'Thank you. You're a very attractive groom.' She'd never seen a man fill a suit with such panache or with that underlying hint of predatory power.

Joss's mouth stretched in a smile. A moment later a rumble of laughter filled the space between them. 'Such praise! Thank you, wife.'

She didn't know if it was the unexpected sound of his amusement or the velvet caress of his gaze but Leila felt an abrupt tumble of emotions.

Suddenly this marriage didn't seem so simple. She'd spent so long fretting about escape, focused on getting through the marriage ceremony. Now it hit her that perhaps he had other ideas on what happened after the wedding.

Leila shivered.

For the first time she realised Joss Carmody might be dangerous in ways she'd never considered.

CHAPTER TWO

'THERE'S BEEN A CHANGE of plan,' Joss said as the limousine surged forward. 'We're going straight to the airport. I need to be in London.'

He turned to his bride, surprised to find her attention fixed on the back of their driver's head. She didn't acknowledge the wedding guests clustered to see them off. She didn't even lift an arm to wave to her stepfather, standing at the ornate gates to the road.

With her gold-encrusted headscarf pulled forward, obscuring her profile, Joss only caught a glimpse of her straight, elegant nose.

'Leila?' He leaned forward. 'Did you hear me?'

Her hands were clasped in her lap, the knuckles white.

What now? He didn't have time for feminine games. He'd already given up a whole afternoon playing the attentive bridegroom.

'Leila, look at me.'

The command did the trick and she turned instantly. Her eyes were a smoky grey, wide and unfocused. Her lips were flattened and her skin pale.

Impatience flared. What was the problem? Something he'd have to deal with no doubt when all he wanted was to get back to business.

He should have known marriage would complicate his

plans! It had gone against every instinct to acquire a wife, though the business benefits had outweighed the negatives.

Yet with the impatience came an unfamiliar pinprick of concern. 'What is it, Leila? Are you unwell?'

'No.' The single word was husky, as if issued from a dry mouth. 'I'm never sick.' Her lips moved in a shadow of a smile.

Joss remained silent. Something was definitely amiss. He told himself that so long as it didn't affect him it didn't matter. He wasn't his wife's keeper. But curiosity stirred. More, he acknowledged a faint but real desire to ease what he guessed was pain behind those beautiful blank features.

'Would you like to stop the car?' After the interminable wedding, he couldn't believe he was offering to delay further. 'We could go back inside and—'

'No!' Her voice was strident, her face no longer blank but animated at last.

'No,' she repeated, her voice softer. 'That's not necessary. Let's just…go.'

Was it his imagination or was that a plea in her voice?

'As you wish.' He leaned forward and opened the limousine's bar fridge. Ignoring the foil-topped bottle of Cristal and gold-rimmed champagne flutes some romantically inclined staffer had placed there, Joss reached for bottled water. Unscrewing the cap, he passed it to her.

She took it but didn't make a move to drink. Was she waiting for a cut-crystal tumbler as well? He wouldn't be surprised, given the pampered life she'd led.

'Drink,' he ordered. 'Unless you'd prefer me to call a doctor?'

Instantly she raised the bottle and sipped. She paused and drank again, colour returning to her cheeks.

Now he thought about it, he couldn't remember her drinking at the reception, except when he'd raised the goblet to her lips. Nor had she done more than peck at her food.

'You need food.' He reached for the gourmet snacks beside the bar.

'No, please.' She shook her head. 'I'm not hungry. The water is fine.'

Joss's eyes narrowed on the sharp angle of her jaw revealed as she tipped her head back. Her slim throat worked as she took a long pull from the water bottle.

'I'm feeling much better now.' This time she almost convinced him. Her voice was steadier, her gaze direct. 'What were you saying about a change of plans?'

'We're not staying in Bakhara,' he responded, watching her narrowly. 'Something has come up. I need to be in London tonight.'

He could go alone. But he'd just acquired a hostess with impeccable breeding, social standing and poise who'd be a valuable asset in his new business dealings. He intended to make use of her.

Besides, he saw no point in sabotaging the polite fiction they were a couple. Leaving his bride on her wedding night would be inconvenient front-page news. If she was to be of use to him, it would be at his side.

'London? That's marvellous!'

Leila's incandescent smile hit him hard. It wasn't the polite, contained curve of the lips she'd treated him to before but a wide brilliant grin. It was like the one she'd turned on him when he'd arrived a few hours earlier.

Its impact set his pulse tumbling.

She wasn't beautiful. She was stunning.

How had he not realised? He'd thought of her as coolly elegant. Now her sheer dazzling exuberance rocked him.

With colour flushing her cheeks and throat, her lips parted in pleasure and her eyes dancing, she beguiled in a way no blatantly sexy supermodel ever could.

An unfamiliar sensation stirred in his chest and Joss was stunned to realise it was his lungs struggling to pump oxygen. Perhaps whatever ailed Leila was catching. His reaction to her was unprecedented.

'I'm glad you're so excited about a trip to London.' His voice was gruff.

Joss had never been overcome by attraction to a woman. It was the way he was made. *An emotional wasteland*, one mistress had accused in tears after he'd crushed her fanciful hopes of happily ever after.

He desired women. He enjoyed the pleasure they provided. But they never caused a ripple in his life.

As for emotions…he'd been cured of those in his youth.

Growing up in a dysfunctional family, learning early the destructive power of so-called 'love', Joss had never wanted anything like it again. No emotions. No entanglements. No dependants. His gut clenched at the very idea of kids and a clinging wife. Only a deal like this, based on sound business requirements and no emotional expectations, could convince him to marry.

Joss was a loner to the core.

'You've spent time in London, I believe?' He should know more about the woman who was to be his hostess.

She nodded, her smile barely abating. 'I was born there. Then we moved to Washington when my father took another diplomatic posting, then Paris and Cairo with short stints in between in Bakhara. We moved back to Britain again when I was twelve.'

'And you enjoyed it?' That much was obvious. 'You have friends to catch up with there?'

Her smile faded and her gaze swept from his. It struck Joss she'd had her eyes fixed firmly on him all through their conversation. He felt an odd…lack now she'd turned away.

She shrugged. 'Perhaps.'

'So it's the shopping you're looking forward to?'

'No, I…' She swung to face him, but this time her lashes veiled her eyes. Did she realise how sexy that heavy-lidded look was? No doubt it was one she'd practised. 'Well, of course, shopping is part of the London experience.' Her mouth curved in a smile but this time it didn't have the same wattage. Its impact didn't resonate inside his chest.

Good. That earlier response was an aberration. He had no intention of feeling anything for his wife other than satisfaction at the benefits she brought to his balance sheet: fuel resources to exploit and her personal connections in the region.

'I can see you'll enjoy yourself in London.' He'd wondered if he'd face an emotional plea to extend their stay in Bakhara after the wedding. It pleased him she was so reasonable. They'd deal perfectly together. 'The jet is fuelled and ready to go as soon as we reach the airport.'

'That's—' She stiffened and sucked in a gasp. 'My passport! I can't—'

'You can. Your passport is waiting at the plane.'

'Really?' She leaned forward, her eyes searching. 'You had no trouble getting it from…from the house?'

'My staff did it. I assume there was no difficulty.' Joss surveyed her curiously. He'd almost swear that was shock on her face. 'Is something wrong?'

'Wrong?' Her voice stretched high. 'Of course not. I just…' She shook her head. 'Everything's perfectly fine, thank you.' She turned away to watch the retreating city as the car sped towards the airfield. 'How long till we reach the plane?'

Joss leaned back in his seat, intrigued by the flicker of emotions he'd seen in his wife's face. He'd pegged her for a woman of unruffled sophistication, with the poise of a socialite who took world travel and privilege for granted.

It was a surprise to find there was more to Leila than he'd expected. If he had the inclination he'd almost be tempted to discover more.

Almost.

He had higher priorities than learning about his wife on anything other than a superficial level.

* * *

'We're almost there.'

His words were music to Leila's ears.

Escape, not only from her stepfather's home, but from Bakhara, seemed too good to be true. Though she loved her homeland, she wouldn't feel safe from Gamil till she was a continent away. She'd expected to stay in the country a few more weeks and had fretted over the possibility Gamil would find a way to convince Joss to leave her behind when he went.

The few times over the years when she'd succeeded in escaping the house she hadn't got far. Gamil's staff had found her and forcibly hauled her back, and each time the punishments had grown more severe. Gamil's money and legal power as her guardian gave him control over her till she married or turned twenty-five. He'd restricted her travel, education, friendships and money.

Even now she was married, she'd feared he'd find some way to stymie her escape. But now—freedom! She could taste it on her tongue, sweet and full of promise.

The thrill was almost enough to dispel the strange queasiness she felt.

It had been over twelve months since she'd been allowed out of the front door. The clenching spasm of stomach muscles, the panic that had grabbed her throat and made her heart race as she'd left the house, had hit out of nowhere. She hadn't even been able to wave farewell to the guests, every fibre concentrated on conquering that sudden tension.

As if she'd been *afraid* to step into freedom.

Ridiculous! For years she'd done nothing but plan how to get away.

It was just the rich food after sparse rations that had turned her stomach. The heavy scents clogging the air at the wedding feast and the buzz of conversation after months of monastic silence that made her dizzy.

Or maybe it was excitement at being so close to escape.

Fear that at the eleventh hour it would all go wrong. She knew firsthand how Gamil liked to toy with his victims—hold out the illusion of liberty then yank it away. She'd watched it happen to her mother too. Each time Leila had vowed not to let him best her. But she shuddered, remembering.

'Are you cold?'

'Not at all.'

Nothing could stop her boarding that plane. This was the first day of her new life away from the man who'd made her world, and her mother's, hell. Soon she'd put her plans into action. Set herself up with the money she got on marriage and see about resuming her studies. She'd build a new life without ever needing to ask anyone's permission again.

Joy flooded her. This was real. Joss had already secured her precious passport. How often had Gamil taunted her that he kept it under lock and key?

The limousine was ushered through a gate and onto the airfield. Moments later they drew up near a sleek jet. Staff waited to see them aboard.

'Ready?' The deep rumble of her husband's voice tickled Leila's spine, leaving her skin tingling. But, she reassured herself, he was husband on paper only. The instrument of her freedom.

'Ready.' Eagerly she pushed open the door before the chauffeur reached it.

Warm, desert-scented air wafted into the car as she slid from the seat. She nodded her thanks to the uniformed driver, turned to face the crew lined up at the base of the steps and grabbed the car door as her knees abruptly crumpled.

The world swooped around her: the sky vast, almost endless as it tilted and stretched towards a far distant horizon. It was so huge, so empty, as if it had the power to suck her up into its immense nothingness. Sick heat beat at her temples.

Her pulse raced as her heart catapulted against her rib cage. In her ears she heard the roar of pounding blood.

A nameless, dragging terror clawed at her. She knew it would press her down till that infinite space swamped her, expelling the last of the air from her labouring lungs.

Leila couldn't breathe. Yet she fought to stay on her feet. She saw the chauffeur say something then Joss was in front of her. His mouth moved. His brow pleated in a scowl.

He might have been behind glass. Everything was distant but for the heat, the weight of the very air pushing at her, and the tandem crashing thud of her heart and lungs as panic seized her and her stomach churned.

Adrenalin surged as she fought the impulse to fling herself back into the car. Into that small cocoon of safety that beckoned so tantalisingly.

She wouldn't do it.

She wasn't going back, no matter what!

Yet it was all she could do to keep her feet on the ground, her hands limpet-like on the door.

'Leila!' This time she heard Joss. There was concern in his brusque tone. 'What is it?'

She dragged in a deep breath and with furious effort straightened her shoulders. She lifted her chin, swallowing with difficulty, her throat as dry as the great inland desert.

Joss's dark gaze held hers, reminding her she was strong. She'd survived years with her dangerously controlling stepfather. She'd got through a farce of a wedding that was all about business, not love. Surely she could walk to the plane.

The thought of being taken back to the capital, perhaps to her old home and her stepfather's tender mercies, was a douche of ice water on overheated flesh.

'Sorry,' she said in an unfamiliar voice. 'My legs are stiff from sitting so long.' She tried to smile but it was more of a grimace. 'I'll be okay in a minute.' At least her voice was merely hoarse now, not wobbly.

For answer Joss turned and said something to his staff, who dispersed out of sight.

Leila drew another breath. Whatever this unnamed fear, it wasn't rational. It could be overcome. She took a tentative step, still holding the car door. Her legs were made of concrete, so heavy, yet shaking and weak as water.

She took a second step towards the jet. Only twenty paces to the stairs. She could manage that.

With a shuddering breath Leila forced her cramped fingers to release the door. Willing herself on, she paced towards the plane.

Out of nowhere strong arms wrapped round her, scooping her up. They hefted her against a solid body that smelled of soap and citrus and what could only be the spicy scent of male flesh. A thread of heat eddied through her, warming her frozen body.

The arms tightened and she felt the reassuring thud of Joss's heart against her: steady, calm. Reassuring.

In that moment her instinctive protest faded away.

It didn't matter that she hated the idea of needing help. Or that Joss acted simply because he couldn't leave his bride collapsing on the tarmac.

For the first time since her mother's death Leila knew the comfort of being held. The shock of it helped clear her pounding head.

'Relax,' Joss said in an even tone as if dealing with a half-fainting female didn't faze him. Perhaps he was used to women swooning at his feet! 'I'll have you somewhere quiet in a moment.'

'I can walk. I want to board the plane!' She jerked her head up and found herself with a close-up view of his solid jaw and a full lower lip, incongruous in such a harshly defined face yet somehow right. Midnight-blue eyes bored into her, alight with speculation. Straight eyebrows tilted high towards his hairline as if he registered her desperation.

Anxiety still jangled like a drug in her bloodstream but she met his scrutiny with all the dignity she could muster.

'Please, Joss.' It was the first time she'd said his name and it slipped out with an ease that surprised her. 'I'll be fine once I'm aboard.'

He hesitated and Leila's nerves stretched to breaking point. She watched his brow furrow as he scrutinised her minutely. 'Very well. The jet it is.'

Leila dragged in the breath to fill her empty lungs. 'Thank you.'

She shut her eyes and tried to regulate her ragged breathing, willing her pulse to slow. She sensed him move but didn't open her eyes. It was enough to feel those hard muscles holding her, the sense of safety seeping slowly into her taut body.

She didn't let herself question why she felt safe in the arms of a stranger.

'I'm sorry,' she whispered. 'I'm not usually given to...' What? What was wrong with her? 'Usually I can even walk and make conversation at the same time.'

A huff of laughter riffled the hair on her forehead. 'No doubt. Don't forget I've seen you play hostess, deal with an unfamiliar husband in front of hundreds of guests at a never-ending wedding and maintain your poise without batting an eyelid.'

Leila's eyes popped open at the note of wry humour in that deep suede voice. It...appealed to her.

She'd thought Joss Carmody too dour for humour. Too focused for sympathy, especially for a wife he didn't want. She'd been sure when he looked at her all he saw was a vast tract of land awaiting development.

'That was a short wedding celebration by Bakhari standards,' she murmured, concentrating on his face and not the vast sky beyond his shoulder as he ascended the stairs to the plane. 'We got off lightly.'

Gamil had been furious, wanting to display his wealth and important son-in-law to the cream of society. He'd surpassed himself in ostentatious displays of riches that would have made her parents cringe. No wonder she'd felt ill. It *must* have been the heavy food.

Leila felt a solid shoulder shrug against her as Joss stepped sideways through the door. Strange how she didn't mind in the least the alien sensation of being clasped so close to him.

'I had places to be. I couldn't stay feasting for day upon day.'

'Of course not. Very few people insist on such traditions any more.'

She took a deep breath of cool air and surveyed the luxurious private jet. Already she felt better. Maybe after years locked away she'd simply lost her ability to deal with the Bakhari heat. The explanation buoyed her.

'I can stand now. Thank you. I feel all right.'

Joss tilted a look from his superior height, scouring her face as if penetrating her secrets. His expression gave no hint of his thoughts. But then he was a self-made multibillionaire. He'd perfected the art of keeping his thoughts to himself.

A flicker of unease trembled under her skin. What did he see as he watched her? A business asset or something else?

Leila pushed her palm against his collarbone, trying to lever some distance between them. It didn't work, only making her aware of his unyielding strength. Held in his arms, she suddenly felt not so much protected as vulnerable. Puny against his formidable masculinity.

It made her uneasy.

His gaze dipped to her mouth and her lips tingled as if she'd eaten chilli.

'Joss! I said I can stand.' Suddenly it was imperative he release her. She'd felt light-headed before but this was different. Something she didn't want to explore. Something to do with *him*.

Smoothly he put her down, watching her intently.

Fortunately the strength had returned to her legs. She was

herself again, able to walk, spine straight and legs steady, to the lounge chair the stewardess indicated.

Sitting straight despite its encompassing luxury, Leila turned to the hovering stewardess.

'I'd like some water, please. And do you have anything for travel sickness?'

'Of course, madam.' The woman bustled away.

If Leila tried hard enough she might convince herself it was motion sickness she'd experienced out there after her first trip in a vehicle in ages. Or the effects of heat.

She watched Joss sit on the other side of the cabin. His gaze didn't leave her as she took the medication and a healthy slug of water.

His scrutiny made her uneasy. It wasn't like Gamil's, which had always made her flesh crawl. But Joss's steady regard seemed to strip her bare. Surely he couldn't see the tumble of elation and anxiety she strove to hide? Concealing what she felt had been a matter of survival under Gamil's cruel regime and she'd become adept.

Deliberately she put her head back and closed her eyes, reassured by the hum of the engines starting.

When finally she felt the plane take off she opened them to see Joss, head bent over a stack of papers, his pen slashing an annotation across the page.

Relief welled up inside her. He'd forgotten her, his curiosity had been temporary. Once they reached London he'd forget her entirely.

She turned to see Bakhara drop away and exhilaration filled her. Her new life had just begun.

CHAPTER THREE

'I SEE YOU'VE made yourself at home.'

Joss sauntered into the kitchen. The sight of his wife setting a kettle to boil made the huge, functional room seem domestic, almost cosy.

It was the last place he'd expected to find her. Given the number of servants in her old home he'd imagined her reclining in bed and summoning staff to wait on her.

Leila swung round, eyes wide, and he felt the impact of her clear gaze like a touch. Intriguing. Yesterday he'd put the sensation down to curiosity and a tinge of concern when she'd all but fainted at his feet.

'You surprised me,' she said in a husky voice that purred through his belly. 'I didn't expect to see you here.'

Joss shrugged. 'I've been known to make my own coffee occasionally.' Hell, he'd spent enough time batching in rough-and-ready outback accommodation to know his way around a kitchen. He could feed a whole shift of hungry miners if need be. Plain, hearty fare that stuck to the ribs, not the sort of fancy delicacies a society princess like Leila ate. She was like his mother had been—used to being waited on.

'I meant I didn't expect to see you in the apartment.' As his brows rose she added, 'Not at this time of day. It's only early afternoon.'

'And tycoons never take time off?' He watched her gaze skitter away across the gleaming floor before returning to his.

The connection ignited a tiny spark of sensation.

Joss ignored it. He was good at ignoring unimportant things. Things that didn't figure in his plans.

'I understand you're a self-made man. You can't have got where you are without working long hours.'

So, she'd been interested enough to find out that much.

'You're right.' He strolled across the room, peeled off his jacket and dropped it on a stool near the enormous island bench. 'My working hours are long.'

There was an understatement! He didn't bother explaining that he enjoyed the cut and thrust of expanding his empire. That he revelled in the challenges of business despite the highly efficient teams he employed.

Business was an end in itself, giving total satisfaction. His commercial success gave him a purpose nothing else could. There was always a new goal, inevitably harder, more satisfying than the last. Hence his move into new territories with this Bakhari deal and his recent mining acquisition in Africa.

'I'll be working tonight, video conferencing with Australia, and I leave tomorrow to deal with a crisis.' The rest of his London meetings would have to wait. An oil-rig accident took priority. 'In the meantime it's time for us to talk.'

'Good idea.' Leila nodded but her shoulders looked stiff.

Why was she tense? Because of him? Or was she ill again? He frowned.

Last night, arriving in Britain, she'd barely stirred when they landed, knocked out apparently by the medication she'd taken. He'd had to carry her to the car and again from the basement car park to the apartment.

He'd left it to his efficient housekeeper to get her to bed. Then he'd put in a couple of hours in his private gym and study before retiring in the early hours.

Yet instead of sleeping instantly as he'd trained himself to do, Joss had lain awake pondering the enigma that was his wife.

There'd been no mistaking her fragility as he'd held her in his arms. She'd weighed next to nothing when he'd scooped her up and onto his jet. He'd felt the bony jut of her hip and the outline of her ribs.

That had stirred long-buried memories. Of Joanna at fifteen—all skin and bone, turning in on herself rather than facing the selfish demands of their parents. Parents who'd never given a damn about either of their children, except as weapons in their vindictive, ongoing battle against each other.

Holding Leila, feeling the tremors running through her, evidence of the weakness she strove to hide, Joss had been hit by a surge of protectiveness he hadn't known since he was ten, wanting to save the big sister who had wasted away before his eyes.

But Leila wasn't Joanna. Leila wasn't some wounded teenager. She was a grown woman, well enough to sell herself for an easy life of wealth.

It was no concern of his if she'd overdone the pre-wedding dieting. Yet he found himself checking. 'You're better today?'

'Much better, thank you. The wedding preparations must have tired me more than I knew.'

The kettle boiled and clicked off. 'Would you like something? I'm making chamomile tea.' She favoured him with one of those small, polite smiles. The perfect hostess.

'Sounds appalling. I'll stick with coffee.' He strode to the door, ready to call his housekeeper, only to find her scurrying towards him.

'What can I get you, Mr Carmody?'

'Coffee and a sandwich. My wife will have chamomile tea and…?' He raised an interrogative brow.

'Nothing else, thanks. I'm not hungry.'

Joss surveyed the demure beige silk dress hanging loose on her. She'd lost weight since they first met. Then she'd been slim but rounded in all the right places. Now even the line of her jaw was stark, too pronounced.

His eyes narrowed. It wasn't just the weight loss that disturbed him. She looked...drab. He was no fashion expert but even he could see that shade leached the colour from her face. The dress was completely wrong, suited to an older woman rather than a young and pretty one.

At least her legs were as delectable as he recalled.

At their first meeting he'd been distracted, enjoying the counterpoint of her sexy legs and lush mouth with her composed, almost prim demeanour. Plus there'd been those tiny flashes of spirit that had reassured him she had the capacity to hold her own as the society hostess he required.

She was a fascinating combination of intellect, beauty and cool calm. Or she would be to a man who allowed himself to be fascinated.

Joss wasn't in that category. He had no intention of disrupting a sound business arrangement with anything like an intimate relationship.

He strictly separated his business and private lives. Though physical intimacy probably rated in the business side of his life: sex for mutual pleasure plus the expensive gifts and five-star luxury he provided to whatever woman he chose to warm his bed.

'Mr Carmody?'

Joss found his housekeeper surveying him curiously.

'I leave it to you, Mrs Draycott. Just bring a selection that will tempt my wife's appetite.'

Leila's stare sharpened. That look provoked a tiny sizzle of pleasure in his gut, like anticipation at the beginning of a new venture.

'Of course, sir.'

'We'll be in the small sitting room.'

Leila held his gaze unblinkingly. Then without a word she crossed the room, her head regally high, her walk slow, drawing attention to the undulation of her hips.

But Joss kept his gaze on her face, trying to read what lay

behind her calm countenance. For there was *something*. The frisson of energy that charged down his spine when his gaze locked with hers proved it.

He could almost hear the words she wasn't saying.

Almost, but infuriatingly not quite.

He followed her, stopping abruptly as she halted in the doorway.

Her scent invaded his nostrils, not the heavy attar of roses from the wedding, but something light and fresh, barely discernible as he tilted his head towards her neat chignon.

This close he felt it again as he had on the runway yesterday: tension crackling in the air as if she generated some unseen power that magnetised his skin.

What was it about Leila that drew him?

'Which is the small sitting room? You have several.'

'To the right,' he said. 'Third door along.'

Following, Joss allowed his gaze free rein, cataloguing each dip and sway as she moved. His wife didn't flaunt herself with an exaggerated strut. Yet with each slow step the slide of silk over her backside and flaring around her legs screamed 'woman' in a way that had all his attention.

Was his wife sending him an invitation?

The possibility intrigued him. Yet remembering her cool look in the kitchen it didn't seem likely.

Besides, this was a marriage of convenience. She'd be an excellent society hostess and her connections would be invaluable. For her part Leila would acquire prestige, an even more luxurious lifestyle and unprecedented spending power.

A win-win deal. Only a fool would mess with that for the sake of sex. It would complicate everything.

With a wife he couldn't cancel all calls or silence protestations of devotion with an expensive farewell gift. Nor did he intend to face a moody spouse, smarting over some apparent slight, when they hosted an important dinner.

Sex with his wife might raise her expectations of a family one day; though he'd made it clear children weren't on his agenda.

His flesh chilled. No, this arrangement would remain simple. Impersonal.

Yet Joss's gaze didn't shift from Leila as she entered the sitting room and took a seat, the picture of feminine grace. He had the unsettling suspicion he'd got more than he'd bargained for in this marriage of mutual convenience.

Leila chose a deep chair. The soft leather cocooned her and the frisson of disquiet she'd felt since Joss had arrived eased a fraction. She didn't feel ready to deal with him when there was so much else on her mind.

Waking disorientated in an apartment that was all minimalist luxury she'd felt a wave of relief, finding herself alone. No one else had shared the huge bed, and the wardrobe was devoid of Joss's clothes. Yet she'd barely had time to register thankfulness that he'd kept his word and his distance.

Too quickly her thoughts had turned to yesterday's suffocating fear at the airstrip.

It was something she'd never experienced before. When she'd stepped onto the airfield the vastness of the open air had pressed down as if squeezing the life out of her.

Was it something to do with the sudden change after being forcibly kept indoors, confined for long periods?

She could only hope yesterday had been a one-off. She had no intention of letting the past dictate her future.

'Your room is comfortable?' Joss sat, stretching his long legs with the assurance of a man supremely comfortable with their glamorous setting. The place screamed wealth from the stunning views down the Thames, to the original artworks and designer furniture that impressed rather than welcomed.

With his back to the window it was hard to read his expression but she'd bet it was satisfied.

'Very comfortable. Thank you.' Leila had grown up with

wealth, but nothing like this place. And the last few years she'd led a spartan existence, until her stepfather had pulled out all the stops to impress Joss Carmody.

Even the feel of silk against her skin was an unfamiliar sensual delight. As for wearing heels…she'd chosen stilettos today, hoping to get used to the feel of walking on stilts. She intended to take every opportunity to break with the past.

Silence descended. Did her husband have as little idea of what to say to his stranger-spouse as she did?

'Have you lived here long?'

Broad shoulders shrugged. 'I bought the penthouse a couple of years ago but I haven't been here much. I tend to move wherever business takes me.'

She nodded. Mrs Draycott had intimated it was a pleasure having people to look after. Leila understood it was rare for Joss to be on the premises.

That suited her. She'd rather be alone to take her time sorting out her new life.

'How long will you be here?'

His long fingers drummed on the armrest. 'We'll be here at least a month.'

No mistaking the subtle emphasis on the pronoun. Leila's heart skipped a beat. 'We?'

'Of course. We *are* just married, after all.'

Leila pushed aside panic at the thought of sharing even such spacious premises with Joss Carmody. Despite their agreement to pursue separate lives, her hackles rose defensively at the idea of being close to him for even a short time. He was powerful, self-satisfied and used to getting his own way. Characteristics that reminded her too forcefully of Gamil.

Yet she understood Joss wouldn't want to broadcast the fact their marriage was a paper one only. No doubt their separation would be arranged discreetly later.

She'd use the time to investigate her study options and find the perfect home. She longed for a house with a garden, but maybe a flat would be more practical till she found her feet.

But a whole month here? Surely that wouldn't be necessary. Once she had her money—

'Leila?' She looked up to find him staring. 'What is it? You don't like the penthouse?'

'On the contrary, it's very pleasant.'

'Pleasant?' One dark eyebrow shot up. 'I've heard it called many things but not that.'

'I'm sorry if I offended you,' Leila said slowly. 'The apartment is spectacular.' If you enjoyed cold modern minimalism that broadcast too ostentatiously that it cost the earth.

'Here you are, sir, madam.' Mrs Draycott entered with a vast tray. 'There are sandwiches and—' she shot a smiling glance at Leila '—Middle Eastern nut rolls in syrup and cakes flavoured with rosewater. I thought you might appreciate a little reminder of home, madam.'

'Thank you. That's very kind.' Even though memories of home were now fatally tainted.

Leila accepted a plate heaped with delicacies and smiled at the housekeeper as she left the room.

'These are good,' Joss said after polishing off one of the pastries and reaching for a second.

'You have a sweet tooth?' Leila put her plate down on a side table and reached for her tea. 'Did your mother make you sweet treats as a child?' Though they'd always had a cook, Leila remembered her mother's occasional baking as the best in the world.

'No.' The word seemed shorter than ever in that brusque tone. 'My mother didn't sully her hands with anything as mundane as cooking.'

'I see.' His tone didn't encourage further comment.

'I doubt it.' Joss's voice was cool but the fierce angle of his pinched eyebrows told of harnessed emotions.

'My mother abhorred anything that might interfere with

her girlish figure or delicate hands.' His gazed raked her and Leila's skin prickled as if he'd touched her. 'Plus she believed the world revolved around her. She had no inclination for anything *domestic* if it involved dirtying her hands. That's what other people were for.'

Leila frowned at his scathing assessment. Or perhaps it was the burn of ice-cold fury in his eyes.

She looked away, uncomfortable with the sudden seismic emotion surging beneath his composure.

They were strangers and she'd prefer they stayed that way. The trembling hint of sympathy she felt at what sounded like an uncomfortable home life wasn't something she wanted to pursue.

Instinctively she knew he wouldn't thank her for it.

Leila cast around for a response. 'Your mother must be very impressed at all this.' Her gesture took in the architect-designed penthouse in a building that was the last word in London exclusivity.

And maybe that explained the soulless feel of the place. Apparently Joss didn't have the time or inclination for anything as domestic as furnishing his home. This looked as if it had been decorated by a very chic, very talented designer who wanted to make a bold statement rather than a home.

'My mother isn't alive.' Joss's gaze grew hooded as he let the silence between them grow. 'I don't have a family.'

'I'm sorry.'

'The absence of relatives at the wedding didn't alert you?' His tone was abrupt and Leila cursed herself for not noticing. Given the number of Gamil's invitees, the imbalance should have been glaringly obvious. Except she'd been on tenterhooks wondering if she'd finally managed to escape his clutches. Most of the day had been a blur of fear and elation.

'No. I…'

Her words petered out in face of Joss's frown. From his

steely expression it was clear he considered her abominably self-absorbed.

'Nor do I want a family. I have no interest in continuing the family name.' His eyes bored into her, their intense glitter pinioning her. 'And I don't see any point bringing more children into a world that can't feed the mouths we've already got.'

He looked pointedly at her plate, still laden with Mrs Draycott's carefully prepared treats.

Leila's stomach cramped at the thought of all that intense cloying sweetness. After her recent meagre rations she hadn't a hope of eating all this rich food. That had to be part of the reason she'd felt unwell yesterday, trying to force down the elaborate wedding feast under Gamil's watchful glare.

But, short of revealing to Joss the real reason for her lack of appetite, there was nothing she could do but eat. Joss might not be cast in the same mould as Gamil but she'd take no chances. He was bossy, powerful and authoritarian. She'd learned to her cost that domineering men couldn't be trusted. There was no way she'd trust Joss with the story of Gamil's brutality and her own helplessness against him. Who knew how he might use that against her?

Besides, the memory filled her with shame. Logic told her she'd done all she could to withstand Gamil's abuse, but part of her cried out in self-disgust at the fact she'd been a victim.

Reluctantly she reached for a tiny cake. Inhaling its rich honeyed scent, she felt a wave of nausea hit her and she hesitated.

'I happen to know Mrs Draycott went to a lot of effort to make something special for you.'

Leila felt the weight of Joss's scrutiny as she bit into the delicacy.

Bittersweet memories drenched her with that first taste. Of a time when she'd taken happiness for granted. Her mother laughing in their Paris kitchen with their cook's enormous apron wrapped twice around her slim form. Leila's father, debonair in evening jacket, sneaking a cake from a cooling rack and having his hand smacked, so he wreaked his revenge with a loud kiss on his wife's lips. Memories of childhood birthday parties and smiles.

'It's good,' Leila murmured and risked another bite.

Too soon the memories were dislodged as bile rose in her throat. Her stomach churned in a sickening mix of distress and unsatisfied hunger.

She made to rise. 'Excuse me, I need—'

'The bathroom?' Joss's tone was rusty with anger and she swung her head up to find him scowling down at her. 'Why? So you can dislodge any trace of food from your system?'

Leila shook her head, stunned by his anger.

'I'm feeling a little unwell, that's all. I—'

'You're making yourself unwell, don't you mean?'

'No!' She surged to her feet. 'I don't mean that at all.' She was tired of having people put words into her mouth and overseeing her every move. She was weary and out of sorts and—

'Tell me, Leila.' His voice was lethally quiet as he stalked across to block her exit. 'Is it bulimia or anorexia?'

Joss was determined to sort this out *now*.

His fragile patience for pampered princesses grew threadbare. And somewhere, deep inside, was a thread of real fear, the knowledge of precisely how dangerous an eating disorder was.

It did no good to tell himself Leila wasn't his concern. He couldn't turn his back.

'It's neither!' Her head reared back in what looked like genuine shock. 'There's nothing wrong with my eating habits.'

He surveyed her slowly, pleased to see her sick pallor had abated, replaced by spots of high colour in her cheeks and fire in her eyes.

It struck him that his wife was beautiful when roused.

'Then why have I never seen you consume more than a bite? Why are you sick after eating?'

He stepped nearer, close enough to inhale her fresh scent, and she angled her head high. He'd give her this: she didn't back down from confrontation. His skin sizzled as she surveyed him. A pulse of something like desire beat hard in his belly.

If he'd known Leila could be so…animated, he might have thought twice about marriage. He'd wanted a demure, stylish hostess, not a spitfire. But the coiling heat in his lower body made a lie of the thought.

'Do you always jump to conclusions?' One fine eyebrow arched high on her smooth forehead, giving her a supercilious, touch-me-not air that made him want to level the barriers between them and give her a taste of raw, earthy pleasure. The force of that need shocked him.

'Do you always avoid questions for which you've no answer?'

Her nostrils flared as if she kept tight rein on a quick temper. Unbidden, interest stirred. He'd always liked passion in a woman—in bed, not emotionally.

The thought brought him up sharply.

Leila was his *wife*. He was not going to bed her. He was not going to risk the possibility of messy, emotional scenes with the woman he'd just tied himself to.

She folded her hands in a show of patience that might have fooled him but for the heat still simmering in those luminous eyes. Despite his better judgement he found himself enjoying the contrast.

'I haven't been eating rich meals lately. The food at the wedding feast was designed to impress but it wasn't to my taste.'

'You've been dieting? Didn't your father warn you about becoming underweight?' His mouth thinned at her stupidity. Didn't she value her health?

'*Step*father.' Instantly she pursed her lips as if regretting the correction. 'And no, he didn't have a problem with my diet.'

Again that puzzling flicker of almost-expression crossed her face, as if she suppressed something. Something Joss was determined to uncover.

'And now? You can't tell me the cakes aren't to your taste. I saw the look on your face when you took that first bite.' She'd closed her eyes as if overcome by bliss. The sight of such unadulterated sensual pleasure had been arresting, drawing him towards her and heating a coil of masculine anticipation low in his groin.

Leila shrugged. 'It was lovely but, as I said, my diet has been very plain, very…restricted. This was just too much of a good thing.'

Joss clamped down the surge of admonition on his tongue. He knew she hid something. But her shock at his accusation seemed genuine. For the moment he'd have to reserve judgement.

'And now? Do you still feel sick?'

She tilted her head, her eyes widening. 'You know…' she paused as if considering '…I don't!' She looked genuinely pleased.

'Good. You need to build up your appetite.'

'I do?'

He nodded, already resuming his seat and picking up his coffee. He was savvy enough to realise it would take a while to get to the bottom of whatever ailed Leila. 'I'm going away on business but when I return and we start entertaining you won't be able to run to the bathroom through every meal.'

Entertaining? Shock slammed her and her stomach knotted in dismay. Since when would a couple leading separate lives entertain guests?

Leila sank into her chair, her eyes fixed on Joss as he

drained his coffee then bit into another syrupy nut roll with strong white teeth. Dazed, she watched the rhythmic movement of his solid jaw. Clearly he was a man of healthy appetite, part of her brain registered, just as if she weren't reeling from his announcement.

'What do you mean, entertaining?'

'You'll assist when we have guests.' He shrugged. 'A lot of business is done, connections made, socially. One of the reasons I considered you a suitable bride is your pedigree: child of diplomats, brought up in the best circles, with links to many powerful families with whom I'll be doing business.' He sat back, clearly pleased with himself. 'You're a born hostess. It was one of the things I checked when we met.'

'Indeed.' The word emerged between gritted teeth. Her skin prickled as fury engulfed her.

He looked so smug that he'd deigned to *consider her suitable* as his wife. And he wanted her to be his hostess? As if *she* owed *him* something! He'd come to *her*, wanting her inheritance.

'That wasn't in our agreement,' she bit out.

'It wasn't?' His sculpted lower lip firmed. His eyes narrowed and abruptly the tension in the air thickened.

'No.' Leila refused to be cowed. 'You didn't mention us entertaining together.'

Slowly Joss crossed one leg over another. His fingers splayed over the arms of his chair. But Leila wasn't fooled into believing he was relaxed. There was an alertness about him that made her think of a predator, sizing up dinner.

'You think the mere fact of our marriage entitles you to be kept in the style to which you'd like to be accustomed? Without stirring yourself in any way?'

'You're a fine one to talk. You married me for my father's oil-rich land.' How dared he try to make her sound mercenary?

'So I did.' His smile had a hungry edge that tightened

every nerve. 'And in doing so I acquired a hostess to help me achieve my goals. At present that involves smoothing my dealings with the elite of European and Middle Eastern society. You're perfectly placed to assist me.'

Perfectly placed!

Leila pressed her lips together rather than let rip with a scathing retort.

'I'm afraid I have other plans.' She sat back and stared into sparking midnight-dark eyes.

She was safe now, out of Bakhara. Soon she'd have her own funds and in a country like England Joss couldn't impose his will as her stepfather had.

'Other plans?' Joss surveyed her critically, noting the mulish line of her lips. 'How can you have other plans when we've just married?'

He stifled a sigh. Wasn't this one of the reasons he'd avoided marriage? The contrariness of women? To marry and then tell him she had *other plans*!

If she thought to play him the way his mother had played everyone around her, Leila had plenty to learn.

Leila shrugged and her insouciance needled a spur of annoyance under his skin. 'You said this was a paper marriage. You made it clear we'd live separate lives.'

Why did her eagerness to be rid of him rankle? He didn't want a clinging vine. But he wasn't used to a woman trying to dump him. *He* always ended relationships.

'So we will. Except when we appear together for major social functions.' He knew her interest in his dividends. She'd sold herself without any pretence of emotional connection. That had been the clinching factor in his decision to marry her.

'Don't worry, I won't interfere in your private life so long as you're discreet.' He smiled, secure in the knowledge the penalty clause for pregnancy in their prenup meant she wouldn't try foisting another man's baby on him. 'But there *will* be times when I need your services as hostess.'

'And if I refuse?' Her voice was cool.

'Refuse?' The idea of anyone refusing Joss was so novel it took a moment for anger to kick in. 'Don't be absurd. Why would you refuse?' Surely she wasn't so lazy as to begrudge this small effort?

'It doesn't suit me. I intend to live my own life from now on.'

Joss fixed her with a glare. 'I think not, dear wife.' His words were silky, delivered in a tone under-performing managers on four continents dreaded. 'Remember the prenup you signed. You've already agreed to this. You have no choice.'

CHAPTER FOUR

THE AIR SQUEEZED from Leila's chest.

He wasn't kidding.

What sort of man specified such detail in a marriage agreement? Weren't they supposed to be about safeguarding wealth, not setting out wifely duties?

Though looking into his furious eyes, Leila realised Joss Carmody was the sort of man who crossed every t and dotted every i, especially in business. And this marriage was business.

Leila clung to that like a lifeline in a stormy sea. Business she could cope with, it was emotional games she couldn't face.

'You did *read* the prenup?' One ebony eyebrow shot up in disbelief.

How she hated his supercilious expression! She'd had enough of men who thought themselves superior.

Leila's hands curled into damp palms, her nails scoring her flesh.

She'd wanted to read the papers but her stepfather had covered them so all she'd seen was the bottom of each page where she'd initialled and the final page where she'd signed in full. She'd been furious and frustrated, but so desperate she'd signed. It had made her sick to the stomach but she'd forced herself to do it so she could get away.

'Leila?' Joss's terse voice demanded an instant response.

Had she escaped one tyrant only to fall under the yoke of another? Her heart plummeted at the possibility.

'I must have skimmed that section.'

Pride demanded she gloss over the truth. That was in the past. She refused to revisit it, especially in front of a man who viewed her as a tool to be used for his own ends.

Her stepfather had exploited any weakness. Leila had no intention of revealing weakness to any man again. Especially to her husband. *It was too dangerous.*

Dark eyes bored into hers. It felt like a daring luxury to meet his stare head-on and not look away as she'd trained herself to do with Gamil. Even something as small as that made her feel strong and intrepid.

How far her stepfather had eroded her life!

Leila was determined to start anew as she meant to go on. Now she was free, or almost, she'd never let a man bully her again.

'Ah, you concentrated on the financial rewards. Naturally.' Joss nodded. He didn't even sound sarcastic. He seriously believed money was all she cared about.

'You don't think much of women, do you?'

He looked surprised. 'I treat people as I find them, male or female.'

Which meant he had little respect for anyone.

What sort of man had she married? She knew of his ruthless reputation in business—that was something Gamil respected. But she'd assumed Joss would have a softer side, not with her, but with *someone.*

She pushed aside the memory of the competent way he'd handled her weakness yesterday. His unfussy sympathy that had eased her fear.

He'd dealt with the situation because he'd had to get to London. That was all there was to it. She'd be foolish to mistake necessity for caring.

Everything she learned about him confirmed he was a man she preferred not to know better.

'So the contract specifies my duties as hostess.' Leila forced her mind to the matter in hand. 'Is there anything else?' She was proud of the cool tone that hid galloping nerves. What else was included in those papers?

'I'll have a copy brought round so you can reacquaint yourself with it.' He shot a look at his custom-made watch, as if turning his mind to more important matters.

Damn him! *This* was important.

'Indulge me, Joss.' She crossed her legs and eased back nonchalantly though every tensed muscle protested. Instinctively she hid how desperate she was for details.

His gaze returned, travelling the length of her legs before skimming her dress to rest on her face. Leila's skin tingled where his look brushed her like a caress. Defiantly she angled her chin, pretending she felt nothing.

Something flickered in his hooded eyes. Her nape prickled as if she confronted danger.

Clearly Joss was used to calling the shots, not answering questions.

Strange how the flare of warning in his eyes spurred her on. As if she enjoyed her ability to provoke him. After years of feigned subservience it was wonderful to exercise her independence even in such a small way.

She stroked her mother's pearl pendant, projecting an air of casual interest. 'What else might I have missed?'

His stillness was unnerving. He was so completely focused on her, and, it appeared, on the massive pearl in her hand. Hurriedly she released the pendant, feeling it fall between her breasts.

Joss's eyes fixed on the spot where it rested and Leila's breath hissed in a rush of reaction as heat hazed her breasts and her pulse danced.

She wasn't used to being looked at like that.

'You should read the papers.' His tone suggested she wouldn't understand them. Annoyance shook her from the strange stasis his look had induced.

'I will.' Leila made her smile saccharine sweet. 'But in the meantime…?'

He exhaled audibly, his jaw tensing—an indication he wasn't totally in control. Her smile widened. She detested the idea he could simply dismiss her as his latest commercial acquisition.

'You agreed to act as my hostess, but don't worry, the work won't be hard. There'll be plenty of time for…' He waved a hand as if unsure what ordinary people did with their time.

'Shopping?' Her smile grew fixed. Her stepfather's obsessive need to control had deprived her of the right to make even the smallest decisions. Now she'd married a man who thought she wanted only to spend his money! It didn't occur to him that she might aspire to a career.

'Precisely.' He gestured again. 'Apart from that there are penalties if you embroil yourself in scandal. Penalties for divorce or pregnancy—'

'Penalties for *what*?' Her tone rose in disbelief.

'You heard me.' He drained his coffee as casually as if they discussed the weather. 'I specified no children in this marriage.'

'I remember.' How could she forget? She'd clung to the knowledge he didn't expect her to share his bed. 'But surely it takes two to—'

'It may very well take two to conceive a child but I won't be one of them.' The words shot out like rifle fire, biting into her. The warning glitter in his eyes chilled her to the marrow.

Finally she understood. He meant children with other men, other lovers.

'If you find yourself pregnant, don't come whining to me for support. You'd lose every benefit this marriage gives you.'

His tone was glacial, each syllable brittle with disdain. He looked every inch the tycoon, a man devoid of human warmth.

'Don't look so shocked, Leila. I'm sure you're too sensible to get pregnant.'

His distaste was unmistakeable. For the notion of a child? Or at the idea of getting her pregnant himself? It couldn't be at the possibility of his wife having sex with another man. Joss had told her she could do as she liked so long as she was 'discreet'. He virtually invited her to sleep around, so long as she didn't become pregnant!

Leila had experienced degradation at her stepfather's hands but Joss plumbed new depths. He'd managed to hurt a part of her Gamil had never touched. Pain scored her vitals and she sat straighter, every sinew taut with disgust.

This shouldn't hurt. She knew Joss had a low opinion of her. Yet his casual assumption about her morals felt like the final straw.

'Don't worry. I won't get pregnant.' When she eventually had children it would be with a man she loved. A man who loved her with his whole being, not a man fixated on contracts and profits. One day when this union was just a bad memory…

Her forced smile felt stiff but Joss's narrowed eyes told her it looked real. It prompted her to make her point.

'I have no intention of sleeping with any man, especially you.'

Joss put his cup down on the table with a precise click, his gaze fixed on her. 'Oh,' he murmured, his voice a low purr that fuzzed the sensitive skin of her neck and arms, 'I never *sleep* with women. My interest in them is rather more active than that. I always sleep alone.'

His lips curled in a smile of pure satisfaction that sent a warning jangling through her. Despite his despicably smug attitude, that smile was *dangerous*.

Fire seared Leila's face as he did that thing with his eyes, that sweeping glance that drew every nerve tight with thrumming awareness.

Whatever this strange sensation was she'd almost rather face the sick panic she'd experienced at the airport yesterday. Instinct warned her that the unfamiliar awareness deep inside put her at Joss's mercy.

Leila couldn't allow that to happen.

She'd be at no man's mercy ever again.

Deliberately she shifted her weight, settling more squarely in the seat and recrossing her legs, projecting an air of assurance. She lifted the pendant, reassured by its smooth solidity and the fact it had been her mother's. Gamil had kept it and the rest of her mother's jewellery locked away, begrudgingly giving this to her so she could dress the part to convince Joss she was a suitable fiancée.

'Excellent.' She paused to make sure she had Joss's full attention. 'It's reassuring to hear confirmation you don't expect intimacy.' She pitched her voice low. 'Just make sure you maintain your *fitness* regime elsewhere. Accidental meetings with your workout partners would be so tiresome.'

Joss's eyes widened fractionally, and then to her amazement he tipped his head back and laughed.

The sound was deep and rich, surprisingly inviting. Amusement cast his features in a younger, more approachable light. Yet she felt no inclination to join his mirth.

'Touché. Spoken like a true wife.'

'I'll do better next time,' she bit, annoyed at being the butt of his humour.

At his quizzical look she explained, 'It's not a real wife you want.'

'Of course not.'

The laugh died on Joss's lips. For an instant there, enjoying her sharp retort, he'd almost forgotten the need for distance between them. Getting close to his wife would complicate things unnecessarily.

He preferred curvaceous, accommodating blondes. Not underfed, sharp-tongued brunettes who questioned and prodded.

Yet heat danced in his belly as he watched her chin notch higher and her eyes flash emerald fire. The pendant throbbed with her every breath, drawing his gaze again to that demure bodice, which did such a poor job of concealing her firm, high breasts. Thank God she hadn't dieted hard enough to be skin and bone there.

Those breasts had pressed against him as he'd carried her, reminding him that despite what their contract said his wife was all woman.

'And if I decline to act as your hostess?' Her question ambushed him as he lingered over thoughts of how Leila's breasts would look minus the beige silk.

'Why would you?' He sat forward a fraction, intrigued despite himself. Why did she make so much of such a small thing, coming back to it yet again?

Most women would love helping him host exclusive parties or being escorted to A-list events.

Leila shrugged and played with her bracelet, exuding an air of nonchalance that almost fooled him, till he saw her other hand locked in a tight fist. Curiosity deepened.

'It's the one thing I want from you.' Apart from the land he'd secured. 'If you don't honour our agreement, I'll sever it. You'll return to Bakhara immediately.'

Her breath hissed. Stormy eyes clashed with his. He read emotion there, strong emotion. Then there was a clattering sound and she tore her gaze away, long lashes veiling her eyes.

Around her feet precious black pearls bounced and rolled. Yet Leila sat as if frozen, one hand fisted in her lap and the other grasping the broken catch of her bracelet so hard it shook.

'Leila?' Joss half rose to go to her, till he realised what he was doing and subsided.

She didn't notice, her gaze was fixed on the floor.

'Leila, what is it?'

Damn it! She infuriated him. One moment she was sassy and challenging and the next… He couldn't put his finger on it but the word 'vulnerable' came to mind.

Hah! She was as vulnerable as an icebreaker, cruising through life. Witness her casual attitude to reading important legal documents. She was used to stepdaddy looking out for her and no doubt bailing her out financially.

Leila had grown up with all the advantages of wealth. Gamil said she'd even finished her education privately rather than trouble herself attending classes with the hoi polloi.

'I don't know my own strength.' She gestured to the pearls spinning on the high-gloss wood floor. Her lips curved in a familiar cool smile that this time wasn't convincing.

To his amazement Joss realised her husky tone revealed stress. This wasn't a game after all. But what was it?

She shuffled forward in her seat as if to go down on her knees and collect the pearls.

'You don't want to go home?'

Instantly she stilled. She shrugged but tellingly didn't meet his eyes. 'I've lived all over the world. Bakhara isn't necessarily home.'

Did she think he hadn't noticed her evasion?

Did she take him for a fool?

He reminded himself it didn't matter what Leila's personal hang-ups were, so long as she fulfilled their bargain. He had more pressing matters to attend to. But he found himself persisting.

'You didn't answer me, Leila. Why don't you want to return to Bakhara?'

Her shoulders hunched high, her hands clenching in her lap. Then with a deep breath she deliberately opened her hands and placed them on the wide arms of her chair, sinking back as if at ease. She looked the epitome of relaxed nonchalance. Almost.

Joss could read people. In Leila he found a challenge, a woman who hid more than she revealed. But he saw tension cloak every line of her slim form.

'I've lived there for years. It's time for a change. I'm used to moving every few years.'

She waved a hand airily and a mark caught his eye. A bluish line ringing her slender arm. The double row of massive pearls at her wrist had concealed it today, and yesterday a fortune in gold bangles had hidden the spot. The intricate henna decoration on her hands and wrists obscured it, but the underside of her arm was definitely marked, and not in henna.

It was an encircling bruise.

Tension churned deep in his belly and with it sickening doubt.

He recalled the way she'd looked over her shoulder the day they'd first met, as if worried someone would overhear or seeking cues from a hidden bystander. He'd been so intent on pushing through the deal he hadn't bothered to consider what it meant. Now he did and the possibilities hollowed his gut.

Guilt, an emotion he barely remembered, surfaced.

Had she been coerced into marrying him?

Leila reeled from the discovery she was trapped. Horror filled her.

Gamil had already bragged of stealing the money her parents had left her. 'Investing' it, he'd said. Investing it in his own schemes for self-promotion! Without her money Leila had relied on the allowance she'd get from marriage to fund her independence.

Except that allowance was tied to her living with Joss! Unless she wanted to be packed off back to her stepfather.

She shuddered as her dreams crumbled around her. She'd do *anything* to avoid going back.

Joss surged to his feet. The violence of his movement made her flinch, the tang of fear sharp on her tongue, till she conquered the response instilled by years with Gamil and forced her muscles to relax.

Warily she looked up.

Joss didn't approach but stalked to the windows, tall and imposing against the late-afternoon light. She watched, fascinated by the restrained energy of his long-legged stride.

He looked as if he should be out conquering mountains or striding the deck of an oil rig, the wind in his hair and his eyes narrowed against the harsh sun. He was dynamic and strong. Even his business clothes couldn't hide the breadth of those shoulders or the power in his thighs.

Joss had a potent, masculine air of purpose she'd never seen in any man. Or was it just that she'd been cloistered too long? His sheer magnetism drew her gaze and did strange things to her insides.

She remembered him carrying her. How wonderfully secure she'd felt for the first time in years. She'd had to remind herself security came from independence, not a solid chest and strong arms.

'Tell me.' He swung round abruptly, his voice harsh. 'Were you forced into this marriage?'

Leila's eyes widened.

'Answer me!' His voice was terse, his stance rigid. Then, as if realising he'd barked the command, his tone softened. 'Leila?'

Stunned, she shook her head. 'Would you care if I was?' He'd wanted the marriage and what Joss Carmody wanted he got. Her agreement was a mere formality to the arrangements agreed between him and Gamil. That still galled her. She was sick of being manipulated.

'It's true, then?' Even with the light behind him, Leila saw he looked shaken. Gone was the expression of complete confidence. His strong features were stark with shock.

'No.' Annoyed though she was, Leila couldn't lie. 'It's not true.'

Joss took a stride towards her then stopped, lifting his hand to rub the back of his neck. For the first time since they'd met he looked uncertain.

'You can tell me if your stepfather forced you into marriage.' There was a note in his voice that sounded like sympathy, despite its gruff edge.

'What makes you think he did?' Leila blinked, wondering what she'd said to make him think so. Determined to put the past behind her, and with her expertise in concealing her thoughts, she couldn't believe she'd revealed Gamil's hold over her.

Joss paced closer, heedless of the pearls skidding from his polished shoes. He reached out and took her hand, his long fingers firm and warm against her flesh.

Fine wires of heat spun through her veins and drew her skin tight. Leila had never known anything like the gossamer net of warmth raying from his touch.

She tugged but instead of releasing her he turned her hand over.

There, on the pale underside of her arm, she saw telling marks. The imprint of Gamil's fingers.

It was rare for Gamil to touch her. If anything he'd always seemed to dislike physical contact. But his anger had reached fever pitch at what he had deemed Leila's insolence. Gamil had grabbed her while he spat his fury at her.

Shivering, she thrust the memory aside, focusing on the present. On her wrist. On the way Joss's bronzed hand cradled hers so gently.

The sight brought a skewed smile to her lips.

How long since she'd known gentleness?

Hard on the thought came the realisation it could be a ruse.

Her stepfather had been a master at mind games; waiting till the precise moment she was most vulnerable to wreak vengeance for supposed misdemeanours.

Was Joss luring her into dropping her defences?

A tiny protest rose—that Joss, for all his faults, wasn't Gamil. But how could she be sure? She didn't want to put it to the test.

'Leila?' His voice was low.

Slowly she raised her head to find he'd bent close. Those dark eyes remained unreadable yet his look sent warmth shuddering through her.

'Gamil got agitated about something and held me too tightly.' Pride, the need to keep her past weakness hidden, prevented her revealing what Gamil had done. The last thing she needed was for her new husband to learn she could be cowed and browbeaten. Even though she assured herself that here in Britain even a husband didn't have the power over her that her guardian had wielded in Bakhara.

'Did he hurt you often?' Joss's voice was a soft growl. His fingers tightened. Not painfully, but…supportively.

It felt so real. But was it?

Confusion filled her. The desire to trust warring with caution learned at the mercy of a vicious, dangerous brute.

Leila looked away. 'This is the only time he bruised me. It's not his way.' She drew a deep breath, knowing she should pull back but unable to sever the contact. The only friendly touch she'd known since her mother died was Joss's. It was all she could do not to curl her fingers around his and beg him to hold her as he had yesterday.

The wayward thought horrified her. How easily he breached her defences!

'I wasn't forced into marriage.' Leila kept her gaze on their hands. Hers slender and feminine with its temporary henna patterns of flowers and birds. His sinewy and squarish, with fingers long enough to wrap around her wrist. 'I agreed to the wedding. There was no coercion.'

Strange how those words sounded different when her hand rested in his. She was so *aware* of him, the spicy scent of his skin, his breath grazing her face, his frame, taller and broader, less than an arm's length away.

Would she react like this to any man?

'You're sure? Now is the time to tell me.'

'It's true. I *wanted* to marry you.' How could she not? Anything was preferable to the life she'd led.

'I'm pleased to hear it.'

Joss lifted her hand. Her gaze rose till she met eyes of deepest indigo.

To her amazement he lifted her hand to his mouth, his lips grazing a whisper-soft caress against her skin.

Leila's eyes widened. She'd never been kissed before. The contact sent sensation zinging through her. Dazedly she wondered how a kiss on the mouth felt.

As she watched Joss pressed his lips to the sensitive skin of her wrist, right over the fading bruise.

Leila's breath escaped in a whoosh of air. His lips caressed in a way that made her shiver as sensations she'd never known ran riot through her body. Her mouth dried and her nipples drew tight and hard.

Joss Carmody was dangerous. One touch, just a hint of gentleness, and she was completely out of her depth.

CHAPTER FIVE

HELL! WHAT HAD got into him?

Joss had been away almost two weeks, dealing with an oil-rig fire and its aftermath in the Timor Sea. Days of crisis management and too little sleep. Yet his thoughts had strayed continually to Leila. *His wife.* To the taste of her soft skin, the promise of delight in her dazed eyes and parted lips. To that hint of vulnerability, quickly hidden.

Since when had any woman created such havoc?

She was a business asset, no more. Acquired in a deal that allowed him the challenge of new enterprises—drilling for oil as well as developing the perfect site for a radical alternative power plant. The Sheikh of Bakhara himself was interested in that scheme, if Joss could bring it together.

Leila was a means to an end.

So why did she invade his thoughts when he should have been snatching precious sleep or, worse, when he was working?

Had this marriage been an error of judgement?

Joss didn't make errors of judgement. He sized up each situation, determined what needed to be done, then followed through: swiftly, effectively and unemotionally.

But this marriage of convenience wasn't as convenient as he'd thought.

Leila distracted him from his goals. Why this consuming curiosity to know more about her?

She evoked protective instincts he hadn't experienced since Joanna had succumbed to an illness that no one, least of all a ten-year-old brother, had been able to stop.

Joss told himself that was why Leila had snagged his interest. She roused fears of the same happening to her.

But it was more than that.

With her tantalising anomalies, contradictory hauteur and vulnerability, Leila disturbed his equilibrium. He told himself no one as grounded as she could be anorexic, but she'd definitely been far too thin. She was feisty yet reserved. She was bright but she hadn't bothered to read their prenup. Above all she was secretive.

Perhaps that was it. He didn't like not knowing what was going on. Once he understood her he could put her from his mind.

Soon, he hoped! He'd been back in London only a few hours, in the apartment just long enough to shower and change, and already he was eager to see her.

Joss wrenched off his bow tie and threw it down, annoyed that anticipation prickled his spine at the thought of seeing Leila again.

He grabbed a fresh tie and looped it round his neck, tying a perfect bow. His mouth twisted. His mother would have approved. She'd set such store by appearances. Wrangling formal dress was something he'd learned almost in infancy. His father, on the other hand, had taught him to look beyond the surface. To learn a man's weakness…and exploit it.

Joss grimaced at his reflection in the mirror. He'd rather do business in a boardroom or an outback shed than at a society party, but needs must.

He strode from the room.

Leila was waiting in the larger sitting room. The sight of her slammed him to a stop.

'What are you wearing?' Disbelief turned the question into a bark of accusation.

Slowly she turned from examining a modern sculpture. He had time to note the steel in her spine as well as the delicacy of her slender frame. At least she didn't look quite so underweight now.

Relief eased his muscles. He told himself it was purely impersonal. He needed her healthy enough to be at his side on demand. That was why he'd instructed Mrs Draycott to ensure Leila ate in his absence.

'Clearly that's a rhetorical question. Unless something has happened to your eyesight?'

The colour in her cheeks and the flash of temper in her eyes almost distracted him from the catastrophe of her clothes. They hinted that behind her poise and superior air lurked a woman of fire and passion, which piqued all sorts of inappropriate thoughts.

That annoyed him even more than what she'd chosen to wear for their first public appearance. Did she want to make a laughing-stock of him?

'Poor eyesight would be preferable.' He shook his head in disgust. 'What possessed you? I want my wife looking glamorous, not like a bag lady.'

Leila lifted her chin high in a move he realised now was characteristic. It bared her long, delicate throat and made him want to reach out and see if the flesh there was as exquisitely fine as it appeared.

'It's from a leading couture house.' Her eyes snapped but her voice was calm. 'I doubt they get many bag ladies.'

'I don't care where it's from.' Joss took in the fussy design that concealed her natural assets. 'That navy makes you look washed out and it hangs like a sack.' He shook his head, appalled. 'Take it off. Now!'

For a horrified moment Leila could only stare up into his dark scowl. Surely he didn't want her to strip for him?

Belatedly logic seeped into her brain and she drew a shaky

breath. That fire in Joss's eyes made her imagine the stupidest things. As if he'd want to see her naked!

She ignored as impossible the tiny splinter of disappointment that grazed her.

The shameful truth was that she was completely off balance. All because she feared she'd give herself away when the time came to leave the apartment. Every day she tried to go out, till a wave of panic engulfed her and sent her reeling, her head spinning and stomach heaving.

She had to get control of herself for her own sanity! She refused to be a prisoner in this plush apartment as she'd been Gamil's prisoner for so long. It was no consolation realising it was probably his maltreatment, the way he'd locked her up, that created her fear.

She was determined to conquer it. But she didn't want Joss witnessing her struggle.

'You want me to change?'

'Got it in one.' His laconic words sounded patronising to her sensitive ears, stiffening her spine. 'Something with colour. Something eye-catching.'

Leila doubted there was anything like that in her vast walk-in robe. She'd had no say in the clothes bought for her trousseau. Her only involvement had been to stand while her measurements were taken. But even that had been a pointless exercise as whoever had ordered the new wardrobe had chosen clothes a size too large.

Gamil's obsession with counteracting her supposedly loose morals and flawed character had obviously influenced the selection. Or was he just having the last laugh?

'Some time soon would be good.'

Leila jerked her head up to find Joss, arms crossed, looking the picture of masculine impatience. The fact that he looked gorgeous—if you liked bold, powerful features and raw testosterone—didn't help.

Her hackles rose. She was *not* his servant to be ordered

around. She'd spent too long dancing to her stepfather's tune to do it again. Indignation was a welcome change from anxiety and the self-doubt that dogged her.

'You're *so* persuasive when you ask nicely, Joss.' She purred his name coolly, putting one hand on her hip in a show of easy confidence. 'I bet women just queue up to get a taste of that charm.'

He didn't move an inch yet suddenly loomed larger than ever. His long fingers twitched then curled at his sides. His midnight eyes glittered and a sizzle shot down her spine that she felt all the way to her toes.

She refused to be cowed. His fury spurred her defiance.

Leila had grown up around men in formal clothes. She'd been a diplomat's daughter. Yet she couldn't remember one to match Joss for sheer impact. Magnificent tailoring complemented what she guessed was an equally magnificent body. But it was his potent power, the sense of barely restrained masculinity, that had shackled her attention from the moment he entered the room.

That and his anger.

Strange how it didn't scare her the way Gamil's cold fury had. But then her stepfather's emotions had been sickly distorted.

By comparison there was something almost reassuringly healthy about the simmering heat in her husband's expression.

Was that why she enjoyed provoking him?

'I'll go change.' She swung towards the door, appalled at her thoughts.

Nevertheless she rather enjoyed the undulating sway her high heels gave her. It made her feel feminine and...powerful. Something she hadn't felt in a long time.

Heat seared her. It should be impossible yet she was sure it was from the impact of his eyes on her. Leila felt his gaze as if he reached out and touched her. The sway of her hips

grew a touch more pronounced. She half turned her head.
'Formal, you said?'

'Formal,' he reiterated. 'I want you to look spectacular.'

Spectacular!

Leila's footsteps faltered and she almost tripped. She
hadn't a hope of achieving spectacular. Even on a good day
and in the loveliest of clothes.

It had taken hours of practice and multiple mistakes just to
get her make-up passable. It had been years since she'd worn
any and it had been no mean feat to replicate the work of the
beautician brought in for the wedding.

Nevertheless Leila held her shoulders straight, determined
not to let Joss see her doubts.

'I'll be back soon.'

Two minutes later Leila surveyed the racks of exquisitely
made clothes her stepfather had ordered. Apart from a couple
of casual dresses and a pair of black trousers that, miracu-
lously, fitted like a glove, the rest was a disaster.

Beige, navy, drab olive and a mustard that made her look
jaundiced. The worst colours for her. Leila flicked through
the clothes, spirits plummeting.

There was nothing spectacular. The best she could hope
for was neat and not over-sized.

With one fluid movement she unzipped the navy dress,
stepped out and hung it up. Then, hands on hips, stood pondering, hoping for inspiration. None came.

'Can't decide?'

The deep drawl from the doorway made her spin round,
her heart thudding high in her throat.

'You can't come in here!' Frantically she searched for a
wrap to throw round herself but everything was stowed away.

She raised her hands to cover herself, till she saw the quizzical tilt of one straight eyebrow and read the glint in his eye.
Heat shimmered under her skin. Her mouth dried and she

was sure the blush covered her whole body. Yet she forced her hands to her sides.

Instinct told her revealing her nerves at being half naked would give Joss a weapon to use against her later. That was how dominating men operated.

He'd see more on a beach any day, she assured herself. Her cream panties and bra were conservatively cut, plus she wore sheer stay-up stockings and stilettos. Yet she felt vulnerable. Whether from baring so much flesh after years of being covered or from the fact it was Joss who saw her, she didn't want to investigate.

Insouciance was beyond her. She settled for keeping her hands at her sides though it strained every muscle to breaking point.

'I can't come in?' He shook his head. 'But I just did.' He paced further into the room she'd once thought enormous. His presence filled it, drawing out all the air and leaving in its place prickling, static electricity. His subtle scent surrounded her.

And his eyes didn't leave her. Surely she imagined heat flaring in those dark irises?

Finally, thankfully, he turned to the clothes on the hangers. Leila put a hand to her chest as she gulped in air and her blood started to pump again.

He rifled through the first few outfits.

'Tell me you didn't choose this stuff.' Disbelief dripped from each word.

'I didn't.'

He didn't turn to face her. 'Then who—'

'My stepfather. It's complicated.'

Joss paused, then began shoving his way through the hangers again. Clearly he had no interest in the reasons for her sombre wardrobe. All he cared about was her appearance as a fitting companion. She had a precise function in his life and that was all that concerned him.

It should be a relief to remember that, but she was too agitated to feel anything like relief.

'What about this?' He held up a pair of trousers in some fluid black fabric. 'Do they fit?'

'Yes, but you said formal. They're not—'

'At this point I'll settle for anything vaguely acceptable.' He tossed the trousers to her, already turning to the large bank of drawers.

Leila opened her mouth to protest the invasion of privacy, but he'd already opened and closed a drawer full of panties and bras and was yanking open another one. His hand plunged into silk.

Disturbingly, as he sifted through camisoles and nightwear, Leila imagined the feel of his hand on *her*, his long fingers stroking then moving on.

She staggered back a pace, horrified and a little scared at the weird sensations bombarding her. She shot out a hand to brace herself against a cupboard. Her pulse thudded too fast and there was a curious stirring in her lower body as she watched him trawl through her things.

'How about this?' He turned, a camisole of sea-green silk in his hand.

'What about it?' Her brain was slow to chug into gear.

His brows lowered. 'How about wearing it with the black pants?'

She took the proffered camisole. The silk was so fine she'd be wearing the barest whisper of covering. Did she want to dress like that when she was with Joss—a man whose gaze already evoked the strangest reactions?

She had no choice. Besides, all day she'd fretted and worried about the challenge of merely leaving the apartment. What she wore would soon pale into insignificance beside that.

'I'll try them together.' She paused, taking in his waiting stance. 'When you've left.'

With one last, impenetrable stare Joss turned and walked out. 'I'll meet you in the foyer.'

Joss stood, hands clasped behind his back, surveying the city view. But he didn't take in the glittering vista.

It was Leila he saw in his mind's eye. Spunky, sassy Leila with her air of challenge and smart mouth. Berating him in his own house! Infuriating him as no one in recent memory had been able to do.

Nearly naked Leila wearing surprisingly decorous underwear and a full-body blush that made her look like a virginal innocent, even with sexy heels and even sexier stockings accentuating the long, slender line of her legs.

He shook his head, trying to banish the vision.

How could he think her sexy when he preferred ripe, voluptuous women? True, she wasn't as bone-thin as she'd felt when he carried her on their wedding day. *Thank God for that!* According to Mrs Draycott, Leila had been eating regularly, so hopefully her extreme dieting was a thing of the past.

In fact, he'd found her slim form with its lithe curves and high, pouting breasts surprisingly arousing.

Joss wondered how Leila's pert breasts would fit in his palms. Would her hair be as soft as he imagined? Long enough perhaps to bury his face in as he gave himself up to pleasure?

He'd had no trouble calculating exactly how those long, coltish legs of hers would feel wrapped around his waist. Blood pooled heavily in his groin as he remembered her half naked and delectable, staring defiantly down her neat nose at him.

Didn't she realise he was a man who always rose to a challenge?

He stalked into the sitting room where decanters sat on a sideboard. Reaching out to pour a slug of whisky, he paused. He rarely drank. He'd watched his father, a shrewdly calculating businessman with the scruples of a barracuda, use alcohol too often to soften weaker opponents. He'd seen them lose control.

Joss was nothing if not controlled. Discipline, determination and vision had got him where he was today.

Since when had he turned to alcohol when his feelings overcame him?

Since when had he experienced *feelings*?

He jerked his hand away, heart thudding as a premonition of danger punched hard in his gut.

Yet strengthening his will didn't prevent the insidious knowledge filling his brain. That the sight of Leila, defiant and desirable, had ignited a blaze of desire within him.

He'd like to ignore his plans to network at a charity gala and instead enjoy sparring verbally with his bride.

Or exploring the fine texture of her flesh. He'd taste her sulky pouting lips and lose himself in pleasure. The sort of pleasure logic decreed should be forbidden between them.

He spun on his heel and paced, frustration soaring.

Leila was mouthy. She didn't have the richly curvaceous shape he preferred.

She had eyes that gleamed provocatively and shadowed with secrets and intrigued him as if he were some callow youth lusting after his first woman.

Joss forked his hand through his hair in exasperation. For reasons he couldn't fathom his convenient bride upset his well-ordered existence.

'I'm ready.' The husky voice swept across his senses.

Joss turned and wished he'd taken that drink.

The black trousers accentuated her feminine shape, clinging to hips and thighs. The camisole matched her eyes, making them look bigger than ever. The silk was fragile, shifting with each breath she took and shimmering invitingly over the unfettered curves of her breasts.

Heat roared in his belly as he prowled across the room to

stand before her. Her eyes widened but she didn't budge. He liked the fact she stood up to him. Or perhaps she had no notion what was on his mind.

He wanted to touch her, possess what after all was his, bought in marriage.

The appealing, insidious thought set warning lights blazing in his head.

'That's better,' he murmured, despising the effort it cost him to sound casual. 'It suits you.'

Her mouth twisted. 'It's too simple, considering you're wearing a dinner jacket. We're mismatched.'

Joss shook his head. 'Far from it. But now you mention it, the chignon doesn't suit your new look. Take it down.'

As he said it a spark of anticipation ignited.

She stared, wide-eyed for a moment, then with a half-shrug reached up to release her hair. It uncoiled in a long, glossy swinging curtain. Not straight as he'd thought but softly waving, a gentle froth of mahogany across her shoulders and halfway down her back.

Lust jabbed his vitals.

In barely there silk and nothing beneath it, with her loose hair curling around her in gentle disarray, she looked as if she'd just risen from bed.

His lower body tightened and he fought the urge to haul her to him, determined to conquer this weakness.

'Much better,' he grated through choked vocal cords. 'Let's go.'

He didn't touch her but Leila was aware of his palm hovering at the small of her back as he ushered her into the foyer.

Her pulse still raced after that scene in her dressing room. Joss's presence, his glinting stare on her half-naked body, had stolen her breath and turned her into an incoherent idiot.

Hastily she donned her coat before he could help. Call her a coward, but she preferred not to meet his eyes or feel his touch. She needed all her willpower for the hurdle to come. The moment she'd alternately feared and prepared herself for all day. When she'd face the demon of fear that had prevented her going out and exploring the city.

Too soon the plush, mirrored lift arrived.

Leila took a step towards it and halted, heels squeaking in protest on the marble floor.

'Leila?' He stood aside so she could precede him.

She took another staccato step, only to stop on the threshold, her heart hammering out of control.

Was it the thought of leaving the apartment or the sight of that confined space that sent anxious fingers clawing at her lungs?

Leila had spent too long locked in a space not much bigger than that. Even today after weeks of trying she'd not managed to stay in the lift long enough to reach the foyer.

An off-key laugh escaped her lips.

She'd prided herself on the fact Gamil hadn't broken her will and she'd remained strong. Now had she developed a fear of wide-open spaces and small ones too?

It was preposterous. Absurd. Terrifying.

Fury as well as fear surged in her veins. At Gamil for bringing her to this. At herself for succumbing.

At Joss for being here to witness it.

'Have you forgotten something?'

Leila cast a quick glance upwards, seeing that firm chin and that lavishly sculpted lower lip. She swallowed an obstruction in her throat. Maybe if she concentrated on Joss…

'Leila?' His tone was impatient.

On a rush of determination she stepped over the threshold, her body chilling instantly as if she'd walked into a deep freeze.

She felt Joss enter behind her, his big hand at her waist. If she focused on the feel of his palm, maybe she could push aside the terror eating at her.

The sinister hiss of the doors closing almost stopped her breath. She swung round, her hand already raised to slam the control that would open the door.

Her hand hit a deep chest, a smooth lapel. Hard fingers wrapped around hers, pressing her palm to the rhythmic thud of Joss's heart.

'What is it, Leila?'

She shook her head, barely conscious of the unfamiliar caress of unbound hair on naked shoulders and arms. She pressed forward, swallowing convulsively, trying to move him, to reach the controls before the panic gnawing at her stomach got the better of her.

He didn't budge, just stood blocking her escape.

'I've changed my mind.' Her voice was raw. 'I don't want to go out.' Desperation drove her. This cramped lift was bad enough, but then she faced the vast space that was the city of London—huge and sprawling and as terrifying as the desert had been. Leila tried a shaky sidestep but Joss's hand clamped hers. His grasp tightened at her waist.

'It's too late for that!'

'I don't care…' The words clogged in her throat as her chest constricted.

A large hand tilted her chin. Blazing midnight-dark eyes held hers. She shoved at his chest, needing to make him open the door, even as the lift descended with a sudden slide that rearranged all her internal organs.

'Let me out!' Terror made the words a glacial command.

Hazily she saw his perplexed scowl and the flash of ire. One solid arm wrapped round her back and hard fingers angled her jaw up, his thumb hot on her frozen cheek.

'You really are some piece of work,' he mused. 'Is this a game to make me jump to your tune because I made you change? Your stepfather may have allowed you to play the spoiled princess but you're with me now, sweetheart.'

For the length of one heartbeat he stared. Then his lips

tilted into a grim smile. 'I won't be made a fool of, Leila. We play by my rules now.'

Then his head swooped down, blocking the light.

CHAPTER SIX

JOSS'S MOUTH SLAMMED into hers with a precision that spoke of furious control and deadly expertise. His arm at her waist lashed tight, securing her against his unforgiving frame. His hand on her face held her uncompromisingly still.

Not that there was anywhere to escape. Nowhere except the tiny, enclosed lift.

A tiny sob welled in her throat. A sob of frustration and despair that for all her vaunted strength she had no weapons to fight this new challenge. Not when the fear came from within.

How could she fight the weakness when it was inside her head?

Joss's mouth moved expertly on hers, shaping its contours, his head tilting overhead.

Heat, darkness, danger. She didn't know if she tasted them on his lips or absorbed them with the air she tried frantically to drag into her lungs.

The spice scent that had intrigued earlier filled her nostrils and she knew it for *his* scent. Not bottled, but the fragrance of his skin, unique and intrinsically masculine.

His mouth moved again and now it was different. His tongue thrust into her mouth: conquering, demanding and giving no quarter.

Leila shuddered as a riptide of unfamiliar sensations flooded her. There was no allowance for inexperience. No concession for the thrill of fear skimming her spine, only a demanding caress that felt like invasion.

Except that a tiny part of her responded to his uncompromising demand.

A tingle shot to her breasts, shivered lower still, at the sensations evoked by Joss's sweeping tongue. His mouth pressed like a challenge against her lips. Her eyes flickered closed on welcoming darkness.

His fingers splayed over her cheek, slipping into her hair.

Then somehow, without deciding to, Leila was kissing him back, ravenously, clumsily, as the dregs of fear morphed into angry hunger.

She wanted so much to *live. Experience. To be free.*

For years she'd been thwarted by her stepfather and now, on the brink of freedom, by fear and a husband who wouldn't let her be.

Gloriously, furiously angry, Leila clutched the satin lapels of Joss's dinner jacket. She stretched up, bringing the kiss to him, delving daringly into his hot velvet mouth. Pressing against him with a surging need for something: sensation, validation, pleasure, she didn't know which.

He tasted mysterious. Perilously addictive.

Part of her stunned brain, the minuscule part still working, catalogued that *this* was how a man tasted. How he felt. Joss's iron-hard frame against hers was more exciting than anything she'd known. Except the way their tongues thrust and tangled. Rivulets of molten sensation poured into her bloodstream. Sparking shards of fire cascaded through her.

She wanted more.

More of the luscious heat. The heady thrill of unleashed emotion in such delicious counterpoint to that leashed masculine power.

For, despite the ravaging intensity of the kiss, she sensed Joss restrained himself. He was rock solid, unmoving, except for his mouth and the hand caressing her scalp in seductively slow circles, drawing the fear and anger away. Yet it did nothing to lessen the tension building inside. A different sort of tension.

Pleasure ignited. It burned brighter than the fear that had crowded her or the fury born of frustration that had catapulted her into responding.

Her hands slid up Joss's chest, past the quick thud of his heart. Her fingers grazed the hot skin of his neck, his jaw, before tunnelling into thick locks of silk.

Leila heard a low growl. A growl of need and satisfaction, and had no idea if it came from her or him. She simply wanted more of this magic.

With her arms over his shoulders her body stretched against his. Hot shivers of delight racked her. Her breasts grazed silk and the heavy friction of Joss's chest, drawing her nipples into hard little nubs.

Could he feel them?

The thought excited her unbearably.

The arm around her slid up and a large palm curved round her, burrowing beneath her coat. She'd swear it branded her through the gossamer silk of her top. Long fingers swirled lazily at her side, skimmed higher, brushing the side of her breast in a teasing, deliberate move that sent a jolt of response through her.

Leila sagged, clutching Joss's thick hair, waiting for his next touch.

This time it was heavier, moulding to the side of her breast before sliding down to her waist.

She moaned, holding Joss's head in a fierce embrace as she poured out her need into a kiss that grew slow and lush despite the urgency escalating inside her. A pulse throbbed low between her legs.

His hand circled her waist then slid down her bottom, fingers splayed. With a jerk he tugged her close and high till she was pressed to the length of him. Solid thighs supported hers. She moulded to that broad chest and hard belly, and to the long, hot ridge of arousal that even a woman as inexperienced as Leila couldn't mistake.

She gasped at his blatant need. Fire poured through her, pooling low as she gave in to temptation and rubbed against him. He felt glorious.

Their kiss grew sumptuous, heavy with promise.

Ribbons of heat unravelled through her, weighting her limbs. Leila pressed closer.

Joss's hands clamped hard on her buttocks, drawing her higher so their bodies aligned perfectly.

Bliss beckoned.

Something vibrated against her chest. A low buzz of sound penetrated the syrupy haze of bliss.

There was stillness but for the beat of hearts pounding in unison and the heated pulse of Joss's breath in her mouth—and that low buzzing.

Then his hands were on her upper arms as his mouth lifted. She gasped for air, her breath raw and loud.

Did he realise she was in danger of slumping boneless at his feet? Was that why he held her so hard?

Dazed, she catalogued his rumpled hair and the smear of lipstick at the corner of his mouth.

She wanted to lean back in and taste his mouth again. Till she lifted her gaze and saw the glint in his eyes.

At last Leila found the presence of mind to stumble back, away from that knowing scrutiny. She grasped the rail on the lift wall to keep herself upright since her legs had dissolved into quivering jelly.

She blinked, taking in the fact the lift had stopped moving. They'd reached the basement without her realising!

Joss reached for his phone and Leila could only stare. She hadn't even connected the buzzing vibrations with anything as prosaic as a mobile phone. She'd been on another plane entirely.

A strange hollow ache engulfed her, as if Joss had scooped out her insides.

Her lips throbbed, tingling in the aftermath of that punishing kiss. No, not punishing, not after that first moment. Thrilling. Exciting. Soul-destroying.

Her fingers tightened on the rail as he turned away and spoke into the phone. Leila concentrated on deep breaths, trying to slow her galloping pulse. And all the while she felt as if she'd stepped off a precipice into a world she didn't recognise.

It was only as silence filled her ears that she realised she'd shut her eyes, trying to gather the tattered remnants of control.

Gathering her strength Leila opened her eyes. A crisp white shirt faced her. A tuxedo, unbuttoned. She lifted her gaze to a bow tie half undone and rakishly trailing.

She forced herself to look up past that firm chin, past compressed lips that mere moments ago had taken her by storm, to glittering midnight-blue eyes that seared straight into her soul.

Tension screamed through her as she fought for strength to deal with him. Leila's brows knitted as her brain supplied the words she'd been avoiding.

Her husband.

He was her husband and he'd kissed her as if there were no tomorrow! As if nothing mattered but the combustible desire that had engulfed them.

Where had that come from?

And more importantly, would he now expect—

'After you.'

Leila frowned, then saw he held the door open.

Automatically she stepped forward, careful not to brush against him lest that shocking heat, that need, swamp her again.

It was only much later that she realised she'd faced the cavernous underground car park then the open streets of London without a tremor of the fear that had haunted her since the wedding.

She'd been so wrapped in shock over her response to Joss Carmody's sizzling kiss, so aware of his even breathing, his tall frame so near, his seductive power, there'd been no room for anything else.

Leila stood out from the throng like a diamond of the first water among overbright imitations.

Joss had sensed it from the first—her innate class. Not class in the way his snobbish mother, granddaughter of an earl and weighed down by her expectation of privilege, had used the word. But class in the sense of unmistakeable quality.

Even underdressed by the standards around her, Leila shone. Joss had to force his gaze from the tempting high thrust of her breasts, naked beneath thin silk.

Knowing precisely how underdressed she was made the evening a trial. He had no time to be bored with the social flim-flam because most of his brain was engaged in remembering how she'd felt in his arms.

And imagining how she'd feel naked beneath him as he thrust between her lissom thighs.

Heat poured across his skin as it tightened in arousal.

This wasn't supposed to happen, not with *her*.

Joss wasn't interested in a relationship with any woman that lasted more than a night. He wouldn't destroy his peace, and his plans to use Leila to further his commercial interests, by having sex. She'd want more—of his time or attention or, God help him, his emotions. It had happened before. Women always wanted more of him, not understanding he had nothing more to give.

And they hadn't been married to him! How much higher Leila's expectations if he succumbed to the lure of carnal satisfaction that brewed potent and dark in his veins?

He gave a huff of self-disgust and tried to tune in to Leila charming Boris Tevchenko, key investor in a major consortium with interests in Bakhara.

Instead Joss's focus lingered on her lips, now turned up from their natural sultry pout into a smile.

Joss recognised it as the polite smile she wore as easily as make-up, part of her repertoire of charm. Not as breathtaking as the no-holds-barred grin she'd given him when he'd taken her onto his plane, but enough to bedazzle most men.

Boris looked dazzled.

Joss wondered at his surge of discontent. Leila had the Russian eating out of her palm. Wasn't that what he wanted?

Yet Joss felt edgy, aware of the buzz of interest Leila had stirred, not liking the hungry glances sent her way.

He'd never felt possessive of a woman.

He'd never been married before. That had to be it.

Joss slid his arm through Leila's, drawing her to him. Her start of surprise was natural since she hadn't seen him move closer. But the stiff way she held herself, as if repelling more intimacies, sent anger surging through him.

He was her husband and she'd have to get used to his touch in public.

'So, Boris, you're interested in my plans for the Bakhari plain?'

The other man shrugged, his eyes flicking back to Leila. 'Possibly. Though right now your lovely wife interests me more.'

Her laugh was light and musical. It was only the second time Joss had heard it, and it arrested him. Like some moonstruck kid! 'Boris, I appreciate the compliment—' she leaned in conspiratorially '—but you're an astute businessman. How could you not be interested in the last, vast untapped oil reserves in the Middle East?'

'How, indeed?' A harsh baritone made Joss turn to meet the shrewd eyes of Asad Murat as he joined them.

Excellent. London-based Murat was one of the men he'd come to meet and one of the reasons Leila would be valuable, because of her family connections with Murat. No doubt that was why Murat had approached after proving elusive earlier.

Everything was coming together nicely. Attending this function had been worth it after all.

'Tevchenko. Carmody.' The newcomer nodded to the men before flashing a glance at Leila, but to Joss's surprise offered her no greeting.

Beside him Leila stood rigid. Annoyance stirred as Joss felt tension hum through her. Clearly she disdained his touch.

How could she object to his hand on her arm after she'd wrapped herself around him an hour ago? She'd been all over him. They'd have had sex up against the lift wall if it hadn't been for that phone call.

Heat spiked and his groin tightened uncomfortably. He hadn't been thinking with his head when he'd kissed Leila.

Hadn't he known a wife would bring complications?

Murat turned to Joss. 'Aren't you concerned about over-extending yourself with this new venture? You've had oil-rig trouble and didn't I hear about unrest in that African gold mine? Labour problems?'

Leila lifted her glass of sparkling mineral water to parched lips. Casually she glanced around the room as if her heart hadn't dived at the sight of her stepfather Gamil's crony.

She had herself in hand now. When Asad Murat had looked at her as if she were some insect he planned to skewer with a pin, she'd wanted to dash her drink in his face.

She was proud she'd kept her poise. No matter that Murat had approved and encouraged Gamil's maltreatment of her. He'd been a regular visitor to the house and she'd seen enough to know he and Gamil were two of a kind.

He hated being ignored by her. Even now he darted curious glances her way while in discussion with Joss.

Leila had no intention of talking to her husband about the past. She wanted to believe Joss wasn't like Gamil. He was bossy and accustomed to getting what he wanted, but she hadn't seen a sadistic streak.

Yet she wouldn't put it to the test. Revealing how she'd been dominated in the past was revealing a weakness.

Her husband was dangerous enough. Look at the way he'd kissed her in the lift. The way he'd made her *feel*. She couldn't believe she'd unravelled in his arms. She didn't even *like* him.

A tremor rippled through her, arrowing between her thighs, as she remembered their bodies locked together.

As if he was responding to her thoughts, Joss's grip tightened and he drew her close.

Her traitorous body wanted to melt against him. Only the memory of that kiss stopped her. And the sight of Asad Murat watching through narrowed eyes.

Revulsion filled her. If this was the sort of man Joss associated with, she needed to be on her guard.

'I'll fetch Mrs Carmody to the phone, sir.'

'She's at home, then?'

'Oh, yes, sir.' His housekeeper paused. 'She's always home.'

Joss opened his mouth to query further, then realised it was no business of his what Leila did with her time. He wasn't interested. So long as she was discreet and fulfilled the function he required as his hostess.

Though the idea of Leila being *discreet* with another man gnawed at him. Maybe because the men at last night's reception had all but salivated over her.

He yanked at his tie as he waited for his wife to pick up. *His wife.*

Damn it. He'd spent last night trying not to think about her as his wife. That according to custom she should have spent the night in his bed, finishing what they'd begun with that kiss. That he wanted her more than he could remember wanting any woman.

After one taste!

'Joss?' Her voice was husky, making heat spool low in his groin.

He cleared his throat. 'Leila. I'm glad I caught you.'

'Yes?' Her tone was wary. Why? What had she been up to? Ruthlessly Joss crushed a surge of jealous curiosity.

'I have plans for tonight and thought I'd better warn you.' He paused but she said nothing.

What did he expect? That she'd gush and chatter? She'd been silent on the trip home last night, withdrawn in her corner of the limo and distant even as they made their way up to the penthouse. If he hadn't been busy calculating some new business connections, he'd have been annoyed at her abstraction. She hadn't even looked at him—had been lost in reverie.

'We're going to dinner tonight with some associates and then, if things go well, I'll continue the discussions in the penthouse over port and coffee. I thought you'd need notice to prepare.'

'To look the part of a tycoon's wife, you mean?' Was that a huff of amusement?

'Well, you can't wear anything currently in your wardrobe. I want you looking chic and sophisticated.' He paused but again she said nothing. He wished he could see her face and know what she was thinking. Then he caught the direction of his thoughts and annoyance stirred. 'You know how, I presume?'

'I told you, I didn't choose those clothes.' Was that anger in her voice? Why did her reaction, *any* reaction, feel like a victory?

'Yet you did nothing to replace them.'

'Because I didn't have the money.'

'What?'

'You heard me, Joss. I've been waiting for the first of the payments you're supposed to provide.'

He frowned. 'I've been away, you know that. Tied up.'

What did a week or so matter? He'd had more urgent matters on his mind than her allowance. 'Couldn't you have used your own money in the interim?' Was she trying to make him feel *guilty*?

'According to the prenuptial agreement that money *is* mine. I earned it when I married you, remember?'

He stiffened. She made it sound as if he were some undesirable who had to pay a woman to marry him! He recalled the number of women who'd angled for permanency in his life. It was ironic that the bride he'd tied himself to viewed him as a necessary burden.

'What are you laughing at?' Her voice was suspicious.

'Nothing. But I don't understand why you haven't been shopping. You've got all London at your disposal.'

'I told you.' This time her voice was low, as if the words were drawn out unwillingly. 'I don't have any money.'

'That's impossible!' Joss paused, waiting for her to contradict him. She said nothing. 'Leila? How is that possible?'

'I inherited land, not money. And you now have the land, remember?' Her clipped tone warned him off further questions.

Joss ignored it. 'What about the money you already had? Surely there was plenty to cover a new wardrobe?' She was an heiress. Her stepfather was wealthy in his own right and her family was one of Bakhara's oldest. 'Leila?'

'Do you really think I'd have dressed as I did last night if I'd had a choice?' His nape prickled as he heard bitterness lace her words.

She wasn't joking. Hell! How could it be?

His image of her, all his certainties, fractured.

He opened his mouth to demand an explanation, but stopped himself.

Did he want to embroil himself in the details of Leila's past? He'd spent too many hours already pondering his beautiful, enigmatic bride. She'd distracted him as he'd sought to network and his concentration this morning had been shot. *Because of her.*

'You should have told me.'

'You weren't here to tell.' She paused. 'I could have phoned your office and left a message but frankly the idea of explaining to a third party—'

'I'll have the arrangements made immediately.' Joss swiped a hand over his jaw, as if he could rub away the shard of guilt that pierced him. He supposed he should have given her his mobile number before he left. The fact that he was unused to being tied to anyone was no excuse.

'Someone will contact you within the hour with details of your new account and how to access it.'

He wouldn't give her cause to claim he'd reneged on their marriage bargain. Too much rode on it.

And as for his wife?

He set his jaw. He couldn't avoid it any longer. It was time he satisfied his curiosity about her.

CHAPTER SEVEN

LEILA PACED the sitting room, schooling herself not to twitch the slippery fabric of her new dress that clung and caressed in the most unfamiliar, sensual way.

Sophisticated, Joss had ordered in that offhand tone. *Chic.* And then he'd had the gall to ask her if she could manage that! His tone had reminded her again of her place in his world: mere window dressing for his schemes.

Pride smarting, Leila had aimed instead for *spectacular*.

She refused to be dismissed and ordered about by another arrogant man. She'd show Joss she was a thinking, feeling, capable woman who demanded respect!

She bit her lip and spun on one spindly heel, her heart diving. She felt like a sham.

How to convince him she was worthy of respect when she hadn't got the nerve to leave this apartment? The only time she'd left was last night, with him. When the emotions he aroused had eclipsed all else.

Today she'd tried again alone and been overwhelmed by wrenching nausea at the prospect of stepping outside.

Leila's nails dug into her palms, hating that even now Gamil had a hold over her. She had no doubt her imprisonment at his hands, and the stress of living with his unpredictable moods, had led to this…weakness.

Even this gorgeous new dress was courtesy of a personal

shopper who'd arrived at the penthouse, bringing a bewildering array of outfits for approval.

Joss had been as good as his word. She'd had money of her own within thirty minutes of their phone call. The first money of her own in years! That fact sent a tingle of excitement down her backbone. Money meant a level of independence that had been too long denied her.

No wonder she'd splurged on some extras as well as the clothing she needed. Leila surveyed the colourful scatter cushions enlivening the austere furniture and the bowls of fresh flowers, all ordered by phone or online.

And there was money enough to begin saving a nest egg. One day she'd find a way out of the legal agreement that kept her here at her husband's pleasure. Then she'd be truly free.

'Leila, you're ready.' The words cut across her thoughts and made her stiffen.

Joss stood just inside the doorway, handsome in a craggy, rough-around-the-edges way that oozed raw masculinity. Her breath snagged. He looked more vital, more potently alive than any man she'd ever seen.

Reluctantly Leila met his eyes. A sizzle of raw power arced across the room and sparks fizzed through her.

Her gaze dropped helplessly to his firm, sculpted mouth. She swallowed hard, remembering the taste of him on her lips, the feel of being swept hard into his embrace, of going up in flames against his body.

'Hello, Joss. How are you?' Her voice dropped to a throaty murmur when she'd intended to sound unaffected.

For a moment he seemed not to register her words. His stare had a fixed quality. Then he paced into the room. 'Well, thank you. And you?'

'Fine.' Her smile was perfunctory. She'd told herself the stress of last night had skewed her perceptions. That she'd imagined him more compelling and disturbing than he really was.

She'd been wrong. One look and her body came alive in ways she hadn't known till that kiss… No, she couldn't afford to think about that.

The glint in his eyes drew her skin tight. For a man who saw her as merely a social asset his gaze was incredibly intense.

'Sophisticated enough for you?' she asked finally, gesturing to the gown of sea-green silk shot with misty grey she'd loved at first sight.

Still no reply.

Her assurance cracked. Had she fooled herself into thinking this worked?

Gamil had removed the mirrors from the house years ago. Maybe she'd lost her discernment in that time?

Annoyed for letting doubt in, Leila reminded herself she didn't care what Joss thought. She liked the dress and that was what mattered. It made her feel good.

Setting her chin, she lifted her arms a fraction and turned on the spot with exaggerated slowness. Her mother's pearl pendant, with its platinum chain fully extended, swung gently against her bare back where the deep V of the dress, mirroring a shallower V at the front, revealed a daring amount of flesh.

She'd decided to wear the pendant that way in a flash of bravado, annoyed at Joss's brusque demand over the phone. She'd wanted to look eye-catching.

Now, with his gaze fixed on her, she wasn't so sure.

A ripple of sensation tensed her muscles as he closed in on her. Automatically her jaw angled higher lest he guess the strange jittering unsteadiness inside her.

'Perfect,' he murmured. 'You look gorgeous.'

Really? She was stunned at her surge of delight.

Her father had called her pretty but since his death no man had complimented her on her looks. Not that many had been given the chance!

Now she read appreciation in Joss's eyes. After years of

being berated and denigrated, a compliment was a shock. It did wonders for her bruised ego. But it also, like tenderness after years of abuse, threatened her composure.

Dismayed, she blinked and lowered her gaze a little, battling a sudden tightness in her chest.

'Thank you,' she said when she found her voice. 'You do too.'

Joss's mouth lifted on one side, driving a crease down his cheek. It emphasised the sexy curve of his mouth and the wholly masculine set of his chin.

Jerkily she reached for her purse. 'Shall we go?'

'After you.' He gestured for her to precede him.

'I hear you've had a visitor,' he said a moment later.

She shrugged, hypersensitive to the barely-there silk swishing around her with each step and the weight of the pearl heavy between her naked shoulder blades.

'I engaged a personal shopper.'

'Ah.' Joss drew out the monosyllable. 'And I gather there was a man too, several days ago.'

Leila slammed to a halt, glacial ice crackling down her spine. Even facing the daily frustration of her new-found fear of going out, Leila had believed herself free. She thought she'd left spies and coercion behind.

She swung round, meeting Joss's dark eyes with a blaze of fury. 'Is your staff spying on me?'

'Of course not.'

Her fingers bit the beaded softness of her bag. 'Then how do you know about my visitors?'

For what seemed an age Joss stood, watching her, his scrutiny sharp enough to take in her blush of rage and the pulse thundering in her throat.

'Mrs Draycott was worried.' He spoke slowly, almost gently. 'She said you seemed upset after he'd gone.'

With a hiss of air escaping from tight lungs, Leila's ire dissipated, leaving her off balance. She wasn't used to anyone worrying about her, had forgotten what it felt like.

'Leila? Who was he?' Amazingly she registered concern in Joss's voice. It stroked her like the brush of finest velvet, far more potent even than his admiration.

She was tempted to say it was none of his business who her visitor had been. But what was the point? 'A lawyer I consulted about the marriage contract. And as for being upset...' she shrugged '...I was just preoccupied.'

Worry about how she'd pay for that legal advice had been just an extra burden to add to the rest. She'd had no difficulty getting a private consultation—lawyers were used to visiting rich clients. But at the time Leila thought she'd have to sell her mother's jewellery to pay for the privilege if she didn't soon get the money to which she was entitled.

'I see.' Yet still Joss's frown lingered, as if he wanted to know more.

What was there to know? The contract was watertight. She abided by it or returned to Bakhara and Gamil's tender mercies. Stoically she repressed a shudder. She'd do anything rather than face that.

She turned and walked down the hall.

'Mrs Draycott also said you haven't left the apartment.'

Leila stiffened, but kept walking. 'Did she?'

'Yes.' He was so close she could swear she felt his warm breath on the back of her neck. Rills of sensation rayed out from the spot.

'I had a busy few weeks preparing for the wedding. I needed a rest.'

'You'll make yourself ill if you don't get some fresh air and exercise.'

Leila kept walking. 'Still afraid I'm anorexic?' She gritted her teeth. That accusation still rankled. 'Or did you hear my appetite's improved lately?'

Silence.

She'd been right! He *had* been checking on her. No doubt he wanted to make sure his shiny new trophy wife was fit for duty.

Impotent fury spurred her on as she entered the foyer, her heels clicking furiously on gleaming marble.

So much for being free! She was Joss's captive, though her cage was lavishly sumptuous.

The knowledge beat a heavy tattoo in her heart. She *would* find a way out of this.

'If you must know,' she said when the silence between them drew tight, 'I've been using the indoor pool to exercise.'

After her close confinement those laps had almost killed her to start with but she'd refused to give in. With her returning appetite and decent sleep, she was starting to build her strength. She felt better for it.

'I apologise.' His voice was gruff. 'I was…concerned.' Leila paused, caught by the note of something she couldn't read in his voice. Something that eased the fiery anger inside.

Beside her a long arm reached out and pressed the button for the lift. Immediately butterflies the size of kites dipped and whirled in her stomach. Her mouth dried.

The door swished open with a hiss like a venomous snake.

Leila stared at the mirrored wall at the back of the lift and stepped in before she could have second thoughts. She tried to focus on the reflection of her chic gown and Joss, tall and broodingly handsome behind her. But it was the small airless space that consumed her attention. And the fact that straight after this she'd face the wide-open streets of the city.

With each breath her pulse quickened.

'Leila?' Joss held the door open with one hand and she wanted to scream at him to shut the doors and get this over quickly.

'Yes?' Her voice echoed hollowly.

'Are you okay?'

'Just brilliant.' Her smile was a rictus grin but she couldn't prevent it. Her nails clawed the delicate purse.

'You don't look it.' Those penetrating eyes were fixed on her face as if they read every thought.

Tremors raced down Leila's spine, drawing her skin so she felt stretched on a rack of tension that screwed tighter with each slow motion moment. Her muscles ached with the force of fighting the impulse to flee straight back into the safety of the apartment.

It took everything she had to fight her fear.

Still he didn't move, just stood there, prolonging the agony.

With a suddenness that surprised him Leila lunged, grabbed him by the arm and hauled him inside. Her other hand slammed onto the control panel, sending the doors swishing shut.

This close he saw dampness bloom on her forehead and upper lip. She was pale, her features drawn.

Another punch of the controls set the lift plunging.

Leila's hand tightened like a talon on his arm and she stared fixedly at his shirt as if memorising every detail.

'Leila?' Her absolute concentration unnerved him. What was he missing?

'Yes?'

'Look at me.' She didn't move.

'Leila!' At his sharp tone her head swung up. His heart kicked hard against his ribs as shock smacked him. Her pupils had dilated so far her eyes looked black, only a tiny circle of crystalline green glittering at the edges.

Joss covered her hand with his, feeling her tremble.

She was afraid!

It was remarkable, inexplicable, but true.

He raised his hands to her cheeks. They were clammy. He tried to convince himself there was another explanation but none made sense.

His brain clicked in rapid replay.

Had it been fear earlier in the lift? When he'd taken her sudden change of mind for a spoiled woman's wilful games?

Fear too that day she'd half collapsed on the way to the plane?

And what about last night returning to the apartment when she'd sat statue-still in the far corner of the limo's wide back seat? He'd thought her lost in private reverie.

What if, instead, Leila had been frozen with fear?

Suddenly, appallingly, Mrs Draycott's comment about Leila not leaving the premises made awful sense. And the fact that instead of going out to meet friends or shop, she'd had visitors come to her.

Joss wanted to reject the mind-blowing suspicion, but couldn't. It fitted together too neatly.

Why hadn't he put it together before?

Because he'd had more important things on his mind than his bride.

A searing blade of guilt skewered him.

He, of all people, knew what happened to the weak when no one took time to notice and respond to their fears. Hadn't he told himself Joanna would still be alive if someone had taken a real interest in his sister?

Yet Leila wasn't weak. Even collapsing in his arms at the airport she'd been adamant about continuing the journey. The woman who'd just berated him for nosing about her private business was no weakling.

He looked into those unfocused eyes, remembering how she'd yanked him into the lift and slammed the button for the underground car park. She might be scared but she wasn't running. She faced fear head-on, with a reckless disregard for her well-being.

Joss's gut tightened at her valiant, confronting courage.

'Speak to me, Leila.'

'What do you want me to say?' She spoke slowly, the words thick on her tongue, as if she had trouble talking.

He couldn't believe this was the woman who moments before had tossed barbed comments at him.

'Tell me what you're scared of.' He had a pretty good idea, but he needed to hear it from her.

'I'm not scared of anything.' Yet her words were slurred, her eyes unfocused. Beneath his hands she shivered. Did he imagine her growing colder by the moment?

It was a lifetime since he'd worried about anyone, except in the impersonal way an employer took responsibility for his workers' safety. This didn't feel impersonal. It felt frighteningly *real*.

Joss's hold firmed as he recalled their kiss last time they descended his private lift. At least then she hadn't been frozen with terror. She'd been all vibrant, hot passion.

'Kiss me, Leila.' His voice was husky as he bent to meet her lips.

She jerked back, swaying till he caught her in a gentle grip. This was for her own good, he assured himself.

'No.' But her voice had lost its strength. Where were her sassy comebacks? That, more than anything, convinced him this was real, not a product of his imagination.

Joss threaded his fingers through her perfectly coiffed hair, tugging it loose. The fact she didn't stop him added to his alarm. He massaged her scalp and brushed his lips across hers as she stood perfectly still. Back again, feeling the soft swell of her bottom lip, the infinitesimal caress of warm air in his mouth as a sigh escaped her parted lips.

A thread of sensation unravelled in his belly as if in response to the most erotic lover's touch. The power of it took him by surprise.

And still she didn't move.

His lips firmed, slanting to cover hers as his tongue slid along those sultry lips. He reminded himself this wasn't about sex. It was about…what? Saving her from fear? That wasn't the whole truth.

His interest was personal.

Her mouth moved against his and a jolt of sensation speared him. Relief or pleasure?

Joss didn't analyse. He drew her closer, one arm wrapped around her, his palm pressed to her bare spine, capturing the pearl that had swayed so tantalisingly against her flawless skin as she sashayed in front of him to the lift.

Her skin was cool but it warmed to his touch as her mouth moved carefully under his, mirroring each gentle caress.

The sensation of her lips accommodating his, opening with a sigh at the lunge of his exploring tongue, was deliciously provocative. She tasted like desire and honeyed promise. Like the most luscious exotic fruit.

Dimly he heard the lift ping and the slide of the doors. Instead of moving, Joss gathered her in, wanting to prolong the almost innocent pleasure of her tentative response.

There was nothing innocent about the surge of possessive hunger that urged him to haul her back to the penthouse and into bed. Fire shot to Joss's groin and his embrace hardened. Her bare back was silken beneath his palm. Her mouth sweet distraction.

Even the touch of her palms, pressed flat to his jacket, heightened his carnal senses. He wanted those gentle fingers on his bare body, all over him.

Would she mark him with her nails in the throes of ecstasy? He'd wager she was as passionate in bed as she was when she fought him. Joss's skin tightened in a shiver of pure lust as he imagined Leila naked beneath him. Those pert breasts thrusting up into his palms, her throaty moans husky in his ears as he drove them both to a pinnacle of bliss.

Joss's hold tightened convulsively and suddenly Leila wasn't kissing him back.

With a wrench she broke free.

Disbelieving, Joss watched the rapid rise and fall of her breasts with dazed fascination.

'Don't look at me like that!'

He jerked his head up.

Huge eyes of cloudy emerald held his beneath heavy lids, as if she too had difficulty shaking off the erotic force of that kiss. Her hair was a mass of rich, dark waves around her shoulders, framing a face now flushed instead of pale. Her mouth was bare of lipstick and her lips looked plump and poutingly kissable.

Joss shoved his hands into his pockets before he could reach for her again.

'I'm not on tap for your pleasure.' Her eyes narrowed to slits of sizzling fire. Challenge vibrated in every taut line of her body.

Someone should warn her that he thrived on challenge. He had only one way of dealing with it: facing it head-on and winning. Every time.

It was all Joss could do not to haul her up against him and demonstrate how flimsy her outrage was. She'd kissed him back; there'd been no mistaking her shudder of pleasure as she'd leaned in.

'Did you hear me?'

'I heard you, Leila.' Even saying her name, after tasting her breath in his mouth, was a sensual experience. His eyes dropped to the jerky pulse at the base of her neck. Would her skin taste as delicious as her lips?

Suddenly he was ravenous with the need to find out.

He didn't need Leila's outraged expression to warn him he was on dangerous ground. He knew already. He'd been in treacherous territory all week as he spent hours pondering his intriguing wife instead of concentrating on work.

But even that didn't deter him.

Success was all about making plans then adapting them to suit emerging needs.

His lips twisted in a mirthless grin. What he felt for Leila was definitely an emerging need.

Was it possible he'd miscalculated, demanding this be a paper marriage only?

Would it be so very bad if he mixed a little personal pleasure with business after all?

'You can stop looking at me as if you'd like to…'

'Eat you all up?' Joss couldn't prevent his wolfish grin as anticipation weighted his lower body.

Leila's eyes widened, her mouth sagging a fraction before she snapped it shut.

Was that genuine shock? The idea intrigued Joss, and excited him. He was tired, he discovered suddenly, of women so experienced they were blasé about life and everything in it except money.

Leila would never be boring or predictable.

Even now she was primming her lips as if she'd like to punish him.

He'd enjoy watching her try.

'Don't put your hair up.' Already she was twisting it high at the back of her head in quick movements. He enjoyed seeing her long tresses around her shoulders. Last night he'd found one excuse after another to draw her close just to feel its softness and inhale its fragrance.

Leila shook her head curtly. 'Not with this dress.'

As she spoke she turned away, presenting him with a view of her sleek back, the graceful curve of her spine ridiculously alluring. The dress was completely decent, covering breasts, arms and most of her legs, yet something about that deep V of bare feminine flesh made his body prickle with renewed hunger.

His.

Leila was his.

The covetous thought filled his brain to the exclusion of all else.

Until he saw her stiffen as she faced the open door to the

vast underground car park. Her shoulders hunched and he heard her suck in her breath.

Belatedly his brain notched into gear and he remembered her anxiety. The fact that she didn't venture out, except last night when he'd given her no option.

He wanted to know more, to understand. But now wasn't the time.

Joss stepped close and slid his arm under hers, wrapped her hand over his and clamped it there, noting the way she held onto him as if fearing he'd let her go. It stirred a long-dormant protectiveness.

'This way.' He nodded towards the waiting limo he used in London. He preferred his driving off road and fast, not at a snail's pace in city streets.

He made to step forward but Leila stood her ground. She refused to go with him? Was she that scared?

He looked down and saw the determined angle of Leila's chin.

'I can walk alone.' She relaxed her grip, inviting him to release her. 'There's no need to act the doting husband.' Her tone was light and high as if her breathing was too shallow, but Joss couldn't mistake the fierce glitter of pride in her eyes.

So much for admitting she was anxious. She was toughing it out, pretending a calmness belied by the tiny tremors he felt racing through her body.

Something stirred deep inside him.

He liked that she was a fighter, refusing to give in. He could relate to that. Obstinacy was the quality that had helped him survive life with his self-absorbed parents and move on.

'Just getting in a little practice for our dinner guests.' He shrugged. 'I'm not used to being part of a couple. I need to get it right.'

Which was a lie. Few things had felt so instantly right as holding Leila.

'Very well.' She drew in a deep breath and Joss battled

to keep his gaze on her face. 'You can take my arm.' She sounded like a gracious monarch bestowing a concession. 'But let's get this clear. I don't appreciate being manhandled.'

Her gaze skimmed his face to rest at a point near his collar.

Not so brave after all. Was she afraid of what she might see in his face, or of herself? There'd been two of them kissing a moment ago.

'If you want kisses—' her voice was low '—find someone else to share them.'

'You're not interested?' he persisted, daring her to lie outright.

'Why should I be?' Leila lifted her eyes to his. He felt for an absurd moment as if he were drowning in a pure pool of deep mountain water. 'I kissed you yesterday out of curiosity.' She lifted her shoulders in a tight shrug. 'That doesn't mean I want to repeat it.'

'No?' She could have fooled him. Yesterday it had been more than curiosity driving her. But he'd cut her some slack. He'd seen her fear mere minutes ago. It hit him that he never wanted to see her like that again.

'No.' Gripping his hand firmly, Leila stepped out into the vast subterranean space, her attention locked on the car waiting for them. 'After all, it wasn't in our contract, was it?'

CHAPTER EIGHT

'I'D ALWAYS HEARD you were lucky as well as clever. Now I know it's true.'

Joss looked at the Russian beside him and raised his eyebrows. 'Really?' Tevchenko was one of Europe's wealthiest men. Joss's London apartment, though expensive and perfectly positioned, Joss had chosen it for convenience. It wouldn't draw accolades from a man who owned ex-imperial palaces in his own country.

'Really.' A chuckle of approval rumbled up from the other man's chest. 'Your wife.' He nodded across the wide sitting room. 'She's a jewel of the first water. A rare find.'

Joss read the appreciation in Tevchenko's dark eyes and felt a scimitar-sharp slice of jealousy.

He froze, his coffee halfway to his lips.

Jealousy? Impossible.

Slowly he turned. He knew exactly where to find Leila. All evening he'd been aware of her—had felt an undercurrent of electricity running under his skin, tugging him like metal towards his magnetic north.

Leila had understood without being asked that she was to look after the wives and partners while Joss focused on business. She'd done her job brilliantly, allowing him to pursue his discussions without interruption.

She was a born hostess. She'd charmed even the most difficult. The secret, he'd discovered, was her genuine warmth. She took an interest in everyone she met.

With the exception of her husband.

She evinced no interest in Joss, keeping him at arm's length all week since those kisses.

It was frustrating. His heavy schedule and her reticence meant he was no closer to uncovering those secrets she hid so well.

Joss's eyes raked her. Tonight she was dressed modestly. No bare back to distract him. Yet in a slim-fitting dress of aquamarine she looked like a sea nymph rather than anything as prosaic as a wife. She wore her hair up, accentuating those flawless, high-cut cheekbones and the fragility of her long neck.

Just looking at her drove pleasure through him.

Beside her the trophy wives with their plastered-on dresses and tanned flesh looked garish and cheap, though their gems were probably worth the GDP of a developing country.

By contrast Leila wore a simple pendant that drew the eye to the delectable curve of her ripe breasts.

Joss frowned, realising it was the same pendant she'd worn each time they'd gone out. Did she wear nothing else?

'You don't agree?' the Russian boomed in his ear. 'As a new bridegroom I thought you'd be aware of your wife's special assets.'

Surely Boris wasn't crass enough to appraise her body so blatantly? Joss swung round, fury welling, his hands tight fists.

'She puts everyone at ease.' Tevchenko nodded to the women on the other side of the room. 'Even those two cats who were spitting and snarling at each other earlier.' He sighed. 'With a woman like that at my side...' He shrugged and grinned. 'I repeat, my friend. You're a lucky man.'

He clapped his hand to Joss's shoulder and Joss relaxed. He'd overreacted.

'I know.' Who'd have guessed Leila would eclipse his expectations? She was a valuable asset indeed.

Despite the inconvenient lust she inspired.

And the way she distracted him.

And the annoying way she was pointedly avoiding him after that taste of raw, mind-blowing passion.

It chagrined him that it was he who chafed at the restrictions of a paper marriage. He wanted more than a polite goodnight and a closed door.

His blood steamed, remembering how she'd brushed him off. It was only the shadows in her eyes that had convinced him not to press further.

But soon. Anticipation stirred in his belly.

As Joss watched, a newcomer, Asad Murat, joined her and the other women melted away. Joss's brow knitted. Leila's stance spoke of sudden tension, though he'd swear she hadn't moved a muscle.

He turned to the Russian. 'You'll excuse me?'

'Of course. If I'd married a woman like that I'd keep her close too.'

Joss made his way through the knots of guests to the far side of the room, curiosity rising. Leila stood, glass in hand, head tilted towards their guest as if eager to hear his every word. Yet some preternatural sense warned something was wrong.

He lengthened his stride.

'Am I interrupting?'

Murat started and took a step back. It was only then that Joss realised how close the pair stood. Leila turned smoothly, her smile perfect. Only the sharp glitter in her eyes confirmed Joss had been right. Something was up.

He reached out and slipped his hand through her arm. She stood stiffly, the pulse at her wrist racing.

'Not at all.' Leila's crystal-clear diction reminded him of her tone when she argued with him: polite, calm and with an undercurrent of acid. 'We were just discussing the importance of discipline.'

'Discipline?' Joss frowned. 'Self-discipline?'

Leila shook her head. 'The lack of it in modern society.'

Joss looked from one to the other, wondering what he'd interrupted. Leila was wound so tight it was a wonder her smile didn't crack. 'For example?'

When she said nothing, Murat took the lead.

'Society today is full of do-gooders carping about the weak and disadvantaged. They don't understand the strong in society need to take a lead, set an example.' He paused. 'Like us.'

'Us?' Joss had learned enough about Murat in this week's preliminary discussions to realise they had little in common except wealth and large-scale mining interests.

'Leaders. Strong-minded men. Men who aren't afraid to take a stand for what's right.'

Beside him Leila stirred, standing taller.

'I'm sorry,' Joss murmured, his eyes on Leila's white-knuckled hand gripping the stem of her glass. 'You'll have to be more specific.'

'A man needs to rule his home fairly but with a rod of iron.' The other man darted a look at Leila. 'And in commerce too. Take those labour problems you're having in Africa.' He expounded his theory on how that should be handled. With each sentence he confirmed himself totally devoid of anything like a social conscience, much less a scrap of humanity.

'An interesting approach.' Joss cut him off, disgust pungent on his tongue as he eyed the other man in disbelief. 'But not mine. You'll read in the news tomorrow that the strike has been settled. The conditions at the mine under the previous owner were archaic and brutal. From now on, as many local workers will be engaged as possible, after a full health and safety review. There will be new equipment and appropriate training for everyone on site.'

Joss paused, letting his words sink in. 'I've also offered

a profit-sharing incentive scheme in addition to plans to improve the fresh-water access and education of the local villages.'

'Are you mad? What about your profits?'

Joss stared into the other man's shocked face and realised he'd conned himself thinking he could ever do business with him. Ruthless he didn't mind. Hell, he'd been labelled that more times than he could count. But to exploit workers as virtual slaves as Murat suggested? The guy made him sick.

'Decent conditions and respect for workers increases productivity.' He curled his lips in a smile that showed his teeth. 'I recommend you try it before you're forced into it.' He paused. 'It's only bullies who can't respect the rights of others.'

Murat huffed and muttered then stalked away. Joss didn't bother to watch him go.

'Did you mean that?' Leila's lustrous eyes were huge as she looked up at him.

'Of course I meant it. He gives mining a bad name. One day there'll be a major disaster at one of his sites—a preventable disaster.' Joss paused, watching her closely. 'I know he's a family friend of yours but there's a limit—'

'He's no friend of mine!' She all but spat the words. 'I've spent the last five minutes gritting my teeth rather than tell him to leave and never come back.' Her brow knitted. 'I thought he was important to your plans?'

'No one is indispensable, Leila. Especially not him. I won't be doing business with him after all.' It was a decision he'd been considering all week. Tonight had just been the final straw.

Joss threaded his fingers through hers, feeling the tension thrumming through her. 'What did he say to you?' The waves of anger that had built as he listened to the other man swamped him.

'Nothing important.' Her gaze slid away and he knew she lied.

'Leila.' Joss slipped a warning finger under her chin and lifted her face. 'What was it?'

If the bastard had insulted her—

'Nothing worth repeating. Really.' She tilted her head, looking straight into his eyes as if trying to read *him*. 'Was that true? About your plans for the mine?'

'Yes. The deal just went through today.' He watched her arrested expression, wishing yet again he understood what she was thinking. 'Does it matter?'

Gravely she nodded. 'It matters.'

The slow curve of her lips was tiny, the barest hint of a smile, but it warmed him like sunrise in the desert, spreading heat in places that hadn't felt warmth in a lifetime.

Hours later Leila turned away as Joss closed the door on the last guest.

Tiredness caught her between the shoulder blades. It had been a stressful evening. She loved meeting new people but she was badly out of practice.

Time spent poring over papers and the Net couldn't make up for years cut off from news. All evening she'd wondered when she'd make some obvious gaffe, revealing how little she knew about what had happened in the world these last years when she'd been locked away.

Then there was Murat. Leila rubbed her hands up her bare arms, remembering the feral heat in his eyes as he'd cornered her.

'I'm tired,' she said to Joss over her shoulder. 'I'll go to bed now. Goodnight.'

She was at the entrance to the bedroom wing when his voice reached her. 'Not yet, Leila. We need to talk.'

Turning, she saw his stubborn expression. It had been there as he'd questioned her about Murat. Couldn't he let that rest?

She didn't like Joss getting too close. He made her feel things she had no business feeling, especially for a man who kept her purely for business.

Even a man who'd proved he was nothing like Gamil or his crony Murat.

Pleasure sang in her heart as she remembered Joss tonight, looking down his superb nose as he called Murat a bully. As he deliberately excluded him from a multibillion-dollar deal.

Joss, she realised, would never behave brutally like her stepfather. Despite his formidable power and strong will, *he* wasn't a bully.

He'd cared enough to worry about her health. He'd instructed his housekeeper to provide her favourite meals. He treated her with respect in front of others.

And when they were alone…heat washed her. Even when they fought, or kissed, he hadn't tried to force her.

That said everything about him. He was a man she could respect, maybe even like. It undermined her resolve to keep her distance and made her wonder about that lightning strike of passion. She'd never experienced anything like it. Maybe that was why she felt off balance.

She had so much to think about. She needed to be alone.

'I'm sorry, Joss. I'm exhausted. We can talk tomorrow.' Leila didn't wait for him to insist but walked down the hall to her bedroom. She felt tightly strung and hadn't the strength to face his probing.

She'd almost made it to her door when long fingers wrapped around her elbow, halting her.

Leila refused to think about how that warm grip sent ripples of sensation up her arm. How Joss's subtle spice scent brought back those heady moments in the lift when he'd taken her to the gates of paradise with his kisses and the press of his powerful body.

Heat scalded her cheeks as she swung to face him.

'We haven't finished talking.'

She arched her eyebrows. 'I told you I'm tired. We can talk in the morning.'

Her heart thudded once, twice, as she met his stare. Her chest grew tight as she held her breath, willing him to release her. She told herself he made her uncomfortable, invading her space. Yet it wasn't discomfort throbbing through her body.

'What are you frightened of, Leila? You can tell me.' His voice was deep and low, thrumming across her taut nerves. How could a man's voice feel like the stroke of velvet across her nape and breasts? Her skin tightened, her nipples budding as if from cold. Yet it was heat she felt, insidious heat that burrowed deep, deep inside.

'I'm not frightened.'

'No?' His dark eyebrows pitched down in a look of pure disbelief. 'Not even of our guest, Murat?'

'Him?' Leila's lip curled. 'He's a dreadful man but I'm not frightened of him.' Oh, there'd been a moment when they'd met again that had brought back in painful vibrancy all her stepfather had done, how he'd tried to reduce her to a shell of her real self. But tonight she'd felt only loathing.

In the dimly lit hall Joss stared. Why was he so persistent? He was the one who insisted they lead separate lives.

'If not Murat, then what are you hiding from?'

'I'm not hiding. Your imagination is running away with you.' Even as she said it, Leila knew it to be a lie. She longed for the sanctuary of her suite, away from Joss's piercing gaze. She didn't understand the warring emotions he evoked. His interest annoyed yet excited her.

She tugged her hand but he held her easily.

'If you're not hiding and you're not afraid, then you won't mind strolling with me out on the roof garden.'

Leila's skin iced.

'There's a marvellous view across the Thames and the scent of blossoms on the night air is magic.' He scrutinised her carefully. 'Out in the open we can get a breath of fresh air after that crush of people.' He paused. 'I understand you haven't been out there yet. Allow me to show you. There's a wonderful feeling of space and openness.'

Leila bit her lip, trying to stem rising panic. Space and openness... She shuddered, remembering how the sky had pushed down on her that day at the airport. Even going out with Joss in London in the safety of the limo had taken every ounce of courage. And the distraction of his kisses.

Her heart gave a nervous jolt.

He was waiting and there was something in his eyes that told her he understood her fear.

Her chin jerked up. Had he guessed? How?

Damn the man! Why couldn't he leave her be?

'If it's so important to you,' she said at last, her voice husky from her suddenly dry throat, 'do show me your roof garden.' She pivoted on her heel, determined to get this over with as quickly as possible. Surely she could manage just a minute or two. Surely!

'This way.' Joss pushed open a door and led her across a wide, carpeted room towards full-length windows. Beyond it Leila saw the outline of potted trees, a pergola, the shimmer of a delicate trail of water cascading artfully to a pool.

Her pulse rose to a clumsy gallop as she looked beyond and up to the wide sky that seemed to store and reflect the city's light haze. She imagined standing out there, under the weight of that vastness, and stumbled, catching her heel in the deep carpet.

Joss caught her to him, his heart a solid beat under her palm as she steadied herself. He reached out and slid open one of the glass doors.

Leila sucked in her breath, her eyes fixed on the movement. Cool air wafted in, brushing her goose-pimpled flesh. The muted sound of an ambulance in the distance echoed in her ears, mingling with the ebb and flow of her breathing.

Gritting her teeth, Leila moved away from Joss and took a

careful step towards the opening. She wobbled on the threshold and had to grab the door.

'Obstinate woman!' The words were a growl in her ear as Joss's arm wrapped around her waist, drawing her close.

She swung to face him.

'What do you *want* from me, Joss?' She couldn't hide the plea in her voice. Instantly pride came to her rescue. 'I told you I'm not afraid.'

'No?' Even in the semi-darkness she discerned the glitter of his eyes in that scowling face. 'You're running scared, Leila.'

She drew herself up, determined to keep her weaknesses to herself. They revealed too much she needed to keep private.

'What am I supposed to be running from?' If she had to she'd walk right across his precious roof terrace and lean out over the street below, rather than have his pity.

Even in the gloom she saw his jaw set hard.

'This.' It was a hiss of sound that barely reached her ears before his head obliterated the light and his lips took hers.

This time as his mouth crushed hers, something inside rose up to meet him. Something instantaneous and eager, hungry and desperate. Some animal instinct in her morphed out of fear and anger and the need that had been growing ever since Joss had held the wedding goblet to her lips and claimed her as his wife. Ever since he'd taken her in his arms and obliterated nerves and doubt and disquiet with the reality of his big, hard body and tender touch.

Leila melted, her knees giving way as she grabbed his shoulders with hard fingers.

'I'm not scared,' she whispered, her words muffled against his lips.

It was true. He was huge, powerful and strong, a dominant male. But she knew deep inside that Joss Carmody was a man unlike the one she'd learnt to fear. She clung tighter to his hard frame, feeling a tremor quake through him.

Joss made her feel…he made her feel…

Thought spiralled into nothingness as her senses took over.

'You should be scared.' Joss hauled her close, lifting her till their bodies were perfectly aligned. His long fingers spread over her bottom, holding her high and tight as he dragged his mouth from hers and rained hot kisses across her throat. 'You make me want to lose control.'

Leila's neck arched back under the weight of those brief, hard kisses that brought her body to tingling restlessness. She felt hot all over, shivering with it, yet craving the warmth of his body against hers as if her life depended on it.

She burrowed her hands in his hair, revelling in the thick softness against her fingers, cradling his head as he dipped lower, following the line of her necklace down between her breasts.

Liquid desire swirled and pooled low in her body, shocking her. It wasn't Joss losing control, it was her!

She should hate it. She should fear it. Surely losing control at his hands was to let him dominate as she'd vowed never to let him do?

Yet this felt glorious. It felt like victory, pleasure and power.

Joss lowered his head further and licked the line of her cleavage right up to the pearl pendant. He did it again, this time following the edge of her bodice high over her breast. Leila gasped as raw delight tore through every barrier she'd erected between them.

'You're totally in control,' she whispered, her voice a husky protest. She wanted him as helpless in the face of these overwhelming sensations as she. But she didn't have the experience to do it. All she had was instinct to guide her and Joss's undeniable expertise.

He looked up and she gulped, dry-mouthed, watching his tongue swirl anew over the side of her breast, feeling sparks of pleasure wherever he touched. She'd never known anything so erotic.

'You want to see me lose control?' Another swipe of his tongue, this time across the fine fabric of her dress till he found her nipple and bit gently through the fabric.

Leila's fingers dug into his scalp as her whole body jolted. Her eyes widened in shock as a low moan escaped her lips. Brazen excitement hummed through her. No thought of modesty or hesitation. She wanted Joss's touch on her. *She needed it.*

Her breath hissed between clenched teeth as she realised she teetered on the brink of giving herself to a man she'd known mere weeks.

'You don't want sex with your wife. You said so!' Was that her voice, that uneven whisper? Leila scrambled to straighten her body and her thoughts. This couldn't be happening.

But he held her tight so her wriggles only brought them into more intimate contact. Clamped against his erection, each movement was an erotic caress.

She stilled, horrified at how much she wanted to move against him.

'Oh, believe me, Leila, I do.' He ended the sentence solemnly, slowly, as if repeating the marriage vows they'd shared just weeks ago.

Valiantly she strove for sense.

'It's not in our agreement,' she gasped, telling herself to break his hold even as her hands cradled his head.

'Agreement be damned.' His mouth was at her throat again, each word planted against flesh that quivered at his touch. One large hand cupped her breast and she sagged in his embrace.

He swung her up as if she weighed nothing and whirled her away from the door.

A soft mattress took her weight as he crushed her beneath him. For a moment something like panic flared as his supe-

rior strength imprisoned her. Then he drew back, one hand
going to her hair, the other tracing her lips so tenderly she
had to work to repress a sigh of delight.

He wasn't forcing her. He was seducing her.

Leila waited for dismay to strike. It didn't.

'We can change our agreement, Leila.' His lips against her
ear had her arching up from the bed, senses on overdrive at
the unfamiliar touch.

'I want you, Leila. You want me. It's that simple.'

'How do you know I want you?' She put her palm against
his chest and pushed till he lifted his head. The dark shadows
emphasised the harsh planes of his features, their strength and
arrogance. His eyes glowed avariciously as he surveyed her,
as if anticipating the act of possessing her body.

Leila swallowed hard as anxiety pierced her.

Then she looked down to his taut mouth, saw what looked
like pain there. She heard his ragged breathing, so like her
own, and realised his heavy burden in holding himself in
check.

'Don't you?' His words were raw but his touch, one finger feathering her cheek then brushing her parted lips, was
gentle. Leila trembled at its devastating tenderness.

He heaved a deep breath. 'There's nothing wrong with
lust, Leila. Simple, straightforward physical need.' His lips
curved in a tight smile. 'You can't deny it's here between us.
It needn't change anything else.' He stroked her mouth again
and something unravelled inside her.

'Why not accept it? Enjoy it?' His low voice was deliciously persuasive. 'It won't go away no matter how much
you want to hide. Not till we've sated it.' His touch feathered
delight through her senses and despite herself, Leila revelled
in the hot weight of him holding her down.

Was that what she was doing? Hiding?

Leila tried to marshal her thoughts but Joss's touch, his

body, his breath on her face and the spicy male scent of his skin every time she inhaled made logic impossible.

'Enjoy it while it lasts, Leila. Then move on.'

Move on. She grasped at the words. He was right. She wanted to move on. Her plans for the future depended on her breaking away from Joss and standing on her own two feet. How could she do that when desire caught her in its silken net?

She looked up into dark, knowing eyes and realised he, with all his experience, understood this…conflagration of need far better than she.

Maybe it was her very inexperience that caught her out. She'd never kissed a man before Joss. No wonder her hormones ran riot. He touched her, the merest brush of one finger, and she went up in flames like a powder keg primed to explode.

Would this need haunt her till she gave in to it? How could she concentrate on her future while she fought this terrible longing for the man she'd married?

One taste of passion. Why not? One taste to satisfy the gnawing hunger. Then she could move on.

It sounded deceptively easy but at the same time inevitable.

Tentatively Leila lifted her hand to cup Joss's jaw, feeling the unfamiliar tickle of emerging bristles against her palm. He felt foreign. Unfamiliar. Wickedly attractive.

She slipped her hand into his hair and pulled his head down to hers.

CHAPTER NINE

WHAT HE'D DONE to deserve Leila in his bed, Joss didn't know. He *did* know she was different. This thing between them was different—more intense than anything he'd experienced.

Every touch, every look, grazed through the layers of familiarity, even boredom, that had accumulated after so many easy lovers.

This wasn't easy. This was heart-poundingly raw and hard and unfamiliar. He felt passion so potent it caught his throat as he stripped her dress to reveal the woman who'd haunted his thoughts.

His wife.

Was that why this seemed profound? Some remnant of primitive male instinct to possess *his* woman? Was that what invested her sleek, alluring body with such fascination?

His wife. His woman.

Joss shook his head. He didn't want to own her, just possess her long enough to find the mutual pleasure that had teased for weeks. He had no interest in a lifelong partner.

As for the tremor in his hands as he ripped open his shirt—eagerness, that was all.

His gaze raked her body, bare but for an innocent-looking cream bra and panties. He'd been wrong to worry she was anorexic. Slim, yes, delicate in a supple way that hinted at hidden strength, ripe in all the right places.

His heart hammered.

'Take your hair down.' The words grated as he wrenched out of his jacket and shirt together. Even the weight of air on his bare torso was heavy on sensitised skin. How would it be when Leila caressed him?

His gaze dropped to her sultry mouth as she reached to undo her necklace. He imagined her lips on his flesh, and his body spasmed tight in anticipation.

She dropped the pendant on the bedside table, drawing his gaze, reminding him of the need to grab the protection he kept close.

Abruptly he levered himself up, his mouth tightening in a crooked smile at her instinctive protest.

'Just for a moment, sweetheart.' Standing, he bent to kiss her stomach. The taste of her was addictive, and her scent, like sandalwood and sunshine, sent blood rushing urgently through his veins. He paused, swirling his tongue in her navel, biting a line of gentle nips down her flat belly to the top of her panties. He couldn't resist cupping her there, through the fragile fabric. She was hot and wet, pushing up against his palm with gratifying urgency.

'Soon,' he promised, planting a kiss where his hand had been and feeling her quake in response.

Joss fumbled with the rest of his clothes and the condom, hands shaking in his urgency. When he turned, her hair was spread wide around her shoulders, a ripple of voluptuous satin. Her eyes were huge in the moonlight, flickering down to his groin then back to his face.

That hint of trepidation would have been gratifying if he weren't so painfully aroused.

As it was he barely had the patience to strip her underwear without tearing it from her body. Then she was naked beneath him and he stilled in awe.

'You're more beautiful than I could have imagined.' He didn't recognise his roughened voice.

Leila shook her head, reaching for his shoulders and drawing him down to lie on her soft skin and slippery silk tresses. All his senses rioted as he pressed against her. Each harsh breath created friction that sharpened the tension, and when she slid her hands over his body…

'Yes, like that,' he growled, his voice a guttural whisper. 'Touch me.'

She was taking him to heaven. No, to purgatory, with those long, stroking caresses that ended too abruptly. With fingers that fluttered tentatively, then grasped firmly as they moulded and explored.

Joss moved his weight to one side, taking the opportunity to thrust her legs wider and sink between them. Her roving hands stilled and he grabbed one, anchoring it around his rigid shaft, his hand covering hers.

Was that a gasp? His hearing was clogged with his pounding heartbeat.

Her fingers twitched around him and his breath seared from his lungs. The feel of her there was almost too much to bear. And when she slid her fingers up, exploring, lightning flickered at the edge of his vision. He held her still, then guided her lower, gritting his teeth against the need to surge hard and high against her touch.

Too soon, he told himself, even as his buttocks tightened and his hips tilted urgently.

'Later,' he whispered, drawing her hand away and kissing her palm. She shivered as he laved the erogenous point on her hand, reminding him of how delightfully responsive she was.

That gave him the focus he needed to pleasure her instead of himself. At this rate his pleasure would come in an instant.

'Tell me what you like, Leila.'

Leaning down, he tasted her tip-tilted breast and heard her gasp. Gently he blew on her nipple, watching it bead for him.

'Tell me,' he demanded.

Her fingers burrowed in his hair, tightening as if to keep him there. 'Yes. That. I like that.'

'And this?' He turned to her other breast, one stroke of the tongue and then he held still, waiting.

'Yes!' She moved restlessly beneath him, her hands trying to drag him down to her breast.

'Say it, Leila.'

Her eyes flashed in the darkness. 'Kiss me there. Please, Joss.'

He rewarded her with a kiss and then opened his mouth to suckle her hard, revelling as she writhed beneath him.

He caressed her throat, the taut skin over her ribs, the soft flesh at her hipbone, with Leila's words soft music in his ears. 'Yes. There. Like that. Please!'

Every caress elicited a sigh, a ripple of tight pleasure and answering caresses of her own. By the time Joss reached her belly he'd never been so aroused.

He let his hand swoop low to her feminine curls and she arched against him.

Game playing could wait. Joss's control was at an end. Pushing her thighs wide, he palmed her bottom, tilting her pelvis.

'Yes?' He paused, needing to make sure.

'Yes.' Her soft sigh was an invitation to heaven.

Seconds later Joss did what he'd been craving from the first, one long, sure thrust deep and hard that seated him at her very core.

His skin prickled at that taste of rapture, his eyelids lowering the better to concentrate on the inconceivable pleasure assailing him. In the darkness he felt tight heat draw him down. Leila's fingers at his shoulders were a sharp reinforcement of pleasure so exquisite it bordered on pain. Was it like that for her too?

With a deep breath he opened his eyes and looked down. Her teeth were sunk into her bottom lip, her eyes closed and brow furrowed. The better to concentrate on pleasure or, it hit him, to stop a cry of pain?

Joss frowned. 'Leila?'

She didn't hear him, was lost in her own world. That he could understand. Tentatively he withdrew then surged again, watching her breasts wobble invitingly. Automatically his hand closed over one, a delicious, perfect fit.

Again he moved and the tension in her face eased. Her mouth sagged open in a soundless O of surprise.

He had the rhythm now, gentle at first, watching her eyes open and find his in dazed delight. With each measured movement the tension ramped up between them.

Still he moved slowly, trying not to rush her. She grabbed him hard and he heard breathless gasps as if the onslaught of pleasure caught her by surprise. She shuddered around him, her movements racking her whole body as ecstasy consumed her, her gaze holding his as if afraid to let go.

She tipped him over the edge. He let the dam wall of control shatter and spilled himself into her with a roar of rapture as the darkness collided with a sunburst of heat and power and unbelievable pleasure.

When Joss came to his senses he was draped over her, pushing her into the bed. His dazed brain scrambled towards sanity. Regretfully he rolled to his side, drawing her limp form with him. Her hair slithered between them, making him shiver as if he weren't sated to the core.

'Leila?' He squeezed her shoulder.

'Hmm?' She burrowed against him, all languid satiation. Joss grinned, his moment of doubt forgotten.

'Nothing.' He brushed the back of her head, letting his hand trail down her hair, swooping the curve of her back and bottom.

Heat stirred again in his groin and Joss froze.

Already?

Then his lips curved in a smile of masculine appreciation. Leila would kill him with her tempting body if he wasn't careful, but what a way to go!

Carefully he pulled back, gritting his teeth against the exquisite sensations, and slid from the bed, hauling up a sheet to cover her.

He strode to the bathroom and switched on the light, whistling between his teeth in anticipation at the thought of joining Leila again. Then he looked down to remove the condom and saw a smear of blood.

His easy satisfaction stripped away in a heartbeat. Frowning, he thought back to Leila's look of shock as they'd joined. The excruciatingly pleasurable tightness he'd encountered. The way she'd bitten her lip as if to hold back a cry.

Joss's breath hissed from cramped lungs.

Suddenly bedding his wife wasn't nearly as straightforward as he'd thought.

Joss's departure roused Leila from her dreamy state. Her body still vibrated with the echoes of pleasure. She thought she'd understood, or guessed, but nothing had prepared her for the reality of making love with Joss Carmody.

Was it always like this? This bliss so profound it stupefied?

Remembering snippets of past gossip she doubted it. She could only be thankful Joss had taken the time to make it good for her—make it wonderful. He'd been generous in a way she guessed not all men were.

Another point in his favour.

Leila smiled into the pillow that smelled of Joss and heat and something unfamiliar. Sex?

Her smile died as reality intruded. It had been sex between them and she knew what he expected of his bed partner. No strings. Short relationships. She shook her head, amending that to no relationships.

He wouldn't want her mooning over him just because they'd shared themselves. He'd talked of sating this lust and then moving on. Wasn't that what she wanted too?

A moment's hesitation horrified her into realising she

wasn't ready to move on from the bliss she'd found in Joss's arms. Not just the climactic pleasure, but the sense of oneness. She'd been alone so long, so very alone. That feeling of incredible closeness with Joss held an allure that beckoned her greedy heart. It was balm to the soul after the wasteland her life had been.

But she'd had her taste of pleasure. She wouldn't beg for more. Joss would be aghast if he guessed how much their union, that sharing of power, bliss and tenderness, had meant to her.

The bathroom door opened and Joss stalked into the room, backlit by a shaft of light. Leila's breath clogged at the sight of him, long, solid and moving with the easy grace of an athletic male in his prime.

She swallowed and told herself it was okay to eat him up with her eyes. It would be the last time she'd see him like this.

Her heart dived at the realisation.

He strode towards the bed, but instead of scooping up his clothes he stood, arms akimbo, staring down at her. She felt a blush rise to the roots of her hair and was glad for the sheet covering her.

'Goodnight, Joss.' She had to get the words out before her throat closed completely.

'Goodnight?' His eyes narrowed and she felt his scrutiny on her flushed face.

She dropped her gaze to the fuzz of dark hair across solid pectoral muscles, preferring not to meet his gaze.

'You said you don't sleep with your…with women.' She swallowed hard, digesting the fact she was now one of Joss's women and striving to squash the flare of jealousy she felt towards those nameless others. 'So I'll say goodnight.'

She pasted a smile on her face and made a show of plumping her pillow before lying down. As if she said goodnight to a lover every night and lay naked between the sheets, ignoring the way every slight movement teased her flesh with memories of his touch.

He didn't move. She frowned, finally meeting his eyes. He scrutinised her as if he'd never seen her.

'What's wrong?'

He shook his head. 'Nothing. But…' He paused and for a moment something like discomfort flitted across his features. 'How are you? Are you okay?'

Did he know? Had he guessed she'd been totally innocent, not even adept at kissing? Her cheeks turned fiery at the idea of him comparing her to his other women and finding her wanting.

'Never better.' She paused and realised it was the truth. Despite some stiffness, she felt marvellous. 'I'm ready for sleep. Goodnight.' Determined, she closed her eyes and tried to slow her breathing as if exhausted.

'Are you sure?' For the first time since they'd met Joss sounded tentative. So, she'd been that obviously inexperienced? Leila shrank inside.

'Really, I don't want to talk any more. Goodnight.'

Silence. No sound of him moving away.

'There's only one complication.' His deep voice curled around her like a caress. 'You're in my bed.'

Her eyes shot open and she surveyed the room. Horror filled her as she realised her mistake. She hadn't even noticed. She'd been totally swept up in passion.

Leila gripped the sheets in tense fingers. Now she'd have to leave the sanctuary of the bed and find her clothes under Joss's scrutiny. He mightn't feel embarrassed about his nudity but she wasn't used to showing herself to anyone. She bit her lip, acknowledging that just a short time ago she'd gladly bared herself to Joss. But that was in the heat of passion. This was different.

Taking a deep breath, Leila slid to the side of the bed. 'I'll go.'

But before she could get out Joss took the sheet from her and climbed in. Instantly Leila scooted away across the king-sized mattress.

'What are you doing?'

'Joining you.' He lay down, head on the pillow where she'd lain.

'But...you don't sleep with—'

'I thought you didn't want to talk? But if you'd prefer to chat...' He propped himself up on one elbow, watching her expectantly.

'No!' She refused to participate in a postmortem of what they'd done.

'Then close your eyes and go to sleep.' His voice dropped to a gentle note that made sensation ripple deep in her stomach. Longing? If she wasn't careful she could get used to his tenderness.

To stay here or to brave the open air? Leila told herself she had the guts to walk away, naked as the day she was born. After what she'd endured in the past, a few moments' discomfort was nothing.

But she *wanted* to stay. Foolish maybe, but she wasn't ready to walk away from Joss yet.

A wedge of fear lodged under her ribs, a presentiment of trouble. Leila ignored it and for once chose the easy path.

Silently she rolled away from him, drawing the sheet high.

For long moments she lay stiff and taut, straining to discern any movement. Joss said nothing and at last she began to relax.

Then an arm slid around her bare waist and drew her back against him.

'What are you—'

'Hush.' He settled her in the curve of his body, his hot flesh blanketing her. His hairy thighs tickled the backs of her legs and his powerful chest rose and fell against her back.

Fizzing excitement rose in her blood, a jitter of awareness that they were close enough to—

'I don't think this is a good idea.' She made to pull away but his arm at her waist prevented her.

When he spoke his lips were in her hair, his breath warming her ear. 'Just relax, Leila. Don't worry, I don't expect a repeat performance tonight.'

The stirring hardness behind her told a different story.

Contrarily his statement didn't reassure her. Why didn't he want her again? Had it been so very unsatisfactory? Leila blinked, dry-eyed, into shadows.

Had it been a mistake, succumbing to her feelings for Joss? Had it complicated her already difficult situation?

Leila had an awful feeling Joss's logic about giving in to lust to sate it was flawed. She felt she'd unleashed a genie, a strong, hungry, demanding force, that would be impossible to push back into its bottle.

'Relax, Leila.' His words drifted to her, deep and soothing, like the rhythm of his breathing and the gentle caress of his broad hand at her waist. 'Sleep.'

Since she and her mother had gone to live with Gamil, Leila had been a light sleeper, ever alert for subtle changes in atmosphere that might herald one of her stepfather's extreme mood swings. She knew she was too wound up to sleep, that it would take her hours.

Yet somehow that thought was the last thing she remembered before falling into deep, refreshing slumber.

CHAPTER TEN

JOSS INSERTED THE KEY that gave basement access to his private lift and waited impatiently for it to descend to him.

He'd left the office after one meeting and rejigged his commitments so he could return to the apartment mere hours after he'd left it.

His mind filled with a vision of Leila, sleeping in his bed, and a groan of pleasure escaped him. She was the problem, the reason he'd cut his work short.

A vigorous, healthy male, he'd had his share of women. But nothing had prepared him for the intensity of pleasure he felt with Leila. He couldn't put his finger on any one reason for it—her lithe, luscious body, her husky voice urging him on, the rich veil of her long hair that made her look mysteriously sexy and innocent at the same time. Her combative spark that urged him to provoke her. The fact that, even when she panted for his touch, he'd had to work to convince her to have sex with him. The look of wonder in her eyes as he'd brought her to climax.

The fact he'd been her first lover.

The embers of lust that had warmed his belly all morning burst into flame as he lingered on that thought. He'd never considered a woman's virginity until now. But Leila's reckless abandonment in gifting hers to him, the sheer beauty of watching her come alive for the first time ever to his touch, stole his breath.

He wanted more.

He'd been semi-aroused all night, sleeping with her yet determined to restrain himself when she was no doubt sore and stiff.

Joss had waited for her to wake this morning, eager to tempt her gently into pleasure. To his chagrin she'd slept soundly as he showered, shaved and loitered over his dressing, till he had no excuse to delay.

He'd revelled in the fact their lovemaking had knocked her out so completely. Yet he'd alternated between the desire to yank back the sheets and concern.

Concern. He didn't do concern. It was too…personal.

Yet, and it worried him to admit it, he spent more and more time thinking about Leila. Not simply as his hostess or partner in sex. But as a person.

He yanked his tie open. It choked like a noose, constricting his breathing.

Joss didn't get entangled with women. He was hard-wired to avoid it. He'd spent a lifetime shunning emotional ties and it was impossible he'd start getting wrapped up in them now.

No, this wasn't emotional. It was simple desire. Pleasure.

A noise roused him and he realised he'd been staring blankly into the open lift. How long had it been there waiting for him to step in?

Setting his jaw, he strode in and hit the button for the top floor. His image in the smoky wall mirror was grim. Joss wasn't surprised. He pulled his tie off and stuffed it into his pocket, then prised open the top buttons on his shirt, feeling marginally better by the time he'd stripped off his jacket.

Even after years in a suit he preferred to work in jeans, with his sleeves rolled up, out of doors.

But he wasn't working now. He'd come home to be with Leila.

He'd changed his work habits because of her.

Joss waited for anger to rise. Nothing came, not even annoyance. Instead of inconvenience it was pleasure he felt.

Last night they'd entertained in the apartment instead of an exclusive restaurant solely because of his suspicion that Leila had a problem leaving the premises. If someone had told him three months ago that he'd alter his plans for any woman, he wouldn't have believed it.

But last night had been an unrivalled success, providing the one-on-one time he'd wanted with key players in a relaxed environment. Leila, with her warmth and natural charm, had been a vital part of that.

The lift opened and he walked through the foyer and into the main sitting room.

He stopped. It looked…different. The ultra-modern designer he'd hired had favoured greys and black. Now it struck him that the room looked warmer than he remembered. Welcoming.

His gaze roved a low bowl of vibrant blooms, cushions in burnt orange and rust that softened the sleek lines of the leather sofa. There was a rug he'd only half noticed before, a swirl of colour that warmed the darker furnishings. A small, exquisite Art Deco bronze sculpture stood on an occasional table, its reflection clear in a nearby wall mirror that enhanced the light.

On the arm of a chair he saw a book, face down. He went over and picked it up. A recent political biography. Under it was a newspaper open at a section on university programmes and beneath that a glossy gardening magazine.

Hastily Joss put them down, feeling absurdly as if he'd intruded on Leila's privacy. He surveyed the room and it hit him what felt different. It felt lived-in. Like a home.

He stood, caught between horror and something like longing.

He'd never had a home in the usual sense. As an adult he'd been on the move too much to put down roots. As a child…

His mouth flattened. The places he'd lived as a kid had had none of the welcome he felt here. They'd been the scenes of too many emotional battles.

Joss looked around, telling himself a few ornaments didn't make a difference. It was window dressing. An illusion.

He turned on his heel and went looking for his wife.

His bed had been made—smooth and pristine as if he hadn't experienced the most climactic night of pleasure there hours before. He quelled disappointment. He hadn't really expected to find Leila there, waiting.

Movement outside caught his attention and he went to the sliding glass door that gave onto the roof garden.

His pulse thudded as he spied her in the shadow of the pergola. She wore slim-fitting jeans, a shirt of bright scarlet, and her hair was down, rippling loose to her waist. Joss's hands twitched as he recalled the feel of it in his fingers, its scent in his nostrils. In the sunlight it shone dark mahogany shot through with glints of russet.

He went to meet her.

Leila stood, head slightly bent, apparently grasping the back of a chair. He quickened his pace. This was the first time he'd found her outdoors by her own choice.

'Leila?' He halted behind her. The stiff set of her body made him pause instead of reaching to touch her.

'Joss.' She straightened but didn't turn.

'What are you doing?' He frowned. Had he been wrong then about her not wanting to leave the apartment?

She laughed, a short, harsh sound that grooved deep through his belly. 'Getting some fresh air.'

He closed the space between them till a mere hand span separated them. Tension radiated off her in waves.

'How long have you been out here?'

'Nine minutes.'

Nine. Not ten. A precise nine. He peered over her shoulder and realised she was staring at her watch. Timing herself?

Her hands were white-knuckled. His heart kicked hard against his ribs.

Joss reached out and brushed his hand down the dark glory of her hair. It was soft and sun-warmed but beneath it she shivered.

Hell! He'd been right. A turbulent roil of anger and anxiety filled his belly.

'Come on. Let's get you inside.' He closed in on her, bending to lift her into his arms.

'No!' She turned, gifting him with a view of stark eyes. She swallowed hard. 'Why do you always think I need carrying? I can walk.'

Before he could stop her she stepped past him. She moved like an automaton, stiff and jerky, but she walked. Even as he reached for her, instinct intervened and he dropped his hand. She didn't need him to carry her. Even if he wanted to. Nevertheless he shadowed her, a pace behind till she walked through the door he'd left open.

She stopped a couple of steps inside, breathing deeply. Behind her Joss snicked the door closed.

'Are you going to tell me about it?' No matter how often he told himself theirs was a business arrangement, Leila stirred protective instincts that had lain dormant since Joanna. The need to safeguard her was so strong it made a mockery of all he knew about himself.

'There's nothing to tell.'

So she was going to play it like that. Stubborn, independent woman!

If she wouldn't talk about that there was plenty more on his mind.

'Why didn't you tell me you were a virgin?'

She speared him with a glare. 'Why? So you could lower your expectations accordingly?'

Joss stared as her luscious mouth flattened in a mutinous line and couldn't prevent a bark of laughter.

Leila's hands went to her hips.

'Was I that amusing?'

Joss shook his head and took her hand. She tried to tug free but he held her easily. 'Warn me, don't you mean, to pre-pare for the most potent sexual experience I've ever had?' His thumb stroked her pulse point and he felt tremors race through her.

'There's no need to pretend.'

'You truly have no idea, do you?' He closed in so she was flush against him. Predictably she stood her ground, tilting her chin so she could watch him. 'What we shared, Leila—it was…' he sought words '…spectacular. Memorable.'

That was why he'd been preoccupied all morning. He let his finger trail from her palm up the inside of her arm to her elbow and saw her eyes dilate. Good. She felt it too, this pow-erful undercurrent between them.

Her cheeks coloured. 'Yes, you're very good at sex.'

'No, Leila, *we* were good together. *The two of us.* The chemistry is…explosive.' He paused. 'I just wish I'd known it was your first time. I'd have taken it slower and made it better for you.'

Her blush deepened to a delectable rose madder and she looked away. 'There was no need. I…enjoyed it too.'

Joss bit down the bubble of laughter that rose at her un-derstatement. He'd watched her come apart beneath him, had ridden the lingering vibrations of her long climax and read the wonder in her eyes. 'Enjoyment' hardly covered what they'd shared. But he'd give her latitude since she was so in-experienced.

'I'm glad,' he murmured, lifting his hand to palm her cheek. Her skin was as soft as he remembered. His blood quickened. 'It will be even better next time.'

'Next time?' Leila's voice was unsteady. 'You said we'd get it out of our systems. Enjoy it then move on.'

It struck Joss that for all her fiery spirit and stellar social skills, Leila was incredibly naïve about what went on between a man and a woman. He drew a deep breath. He looked forward to teaching her.

Joss wrapped his other hand around her waist, drawing her up to feel his arousal. Surprise crossed her face and a fleeting instant of furtive feminine pleasure.

Oh, yes, he was going to enjoy this thoroughly.

'And so we will move on.' He lowered his mouth to her neck, inhaling the scent of sandalwood and sweetness. 'After we've had our fill.' He planted a kiss beneath her ear and revelled in her quiver of response. She lifted her hands to his chest and his heart pounded. 'But it will take some time to reach that point.'

'I see.' Her words were a soft exhale. Her hands crept up his shoulders and Joss smiled.

'Until we reach that point I suggest we enjoy it.'

Leila leaned back in his arms, her eyes more pewter than green as she surveyed him intently. 'But no strings?'

Joss frowned. *She* asked for no strings? That was a turn-around. It was usually him insisting on independence while women wanted more. For some reason that niggled at him.

'Absolutely.' His mouth hovered over hers. 'Simple mutual pleasure.' After all, he didn't know any other way.

Simple? There was nothing simple about what she shared with her husband.

Leila lay under his massive form. Her breath came in desperate gasps, aftershocks of bliss rippled through them and she knew with absolute certainty that sex had complicated their relationship.

But she couldn't regret it.

Her chest constricted on a surge of emotion as she palmed the damp luxury of his back and felt his growl of approval reverberate through her. She'd never known such wondrous pleasure. They were joined, were still one, and, no matter how hard she tried to deny it, the feelings that evoked were profound. Peace. Pleasure. Trust.

Would it be like that with another man? Was this what any woman felt with her first lover or was there something special about Joss? Without words, with the gift of his passion he'd reached deep inside her to emotions she'd repressed and drawn them to the surface.

In the last weeks Joss had ceased to be a stumbling block to her new life. He'd become vital to it.

That scared her. Her strength came from self-reliance. She couldn't afford to need anyone, especially not the man who'd chosen her for the commercial benefits she brought.

'Back in a moment,' he murmured and rolled away, heading for the bathroom.

Leila sighed, telling herself it was relief she felt being alone, not regret. Yet her arms were empty without him and the bed cold.

Annoyed with herself, she rolled away. She'd been caught up in the glamour of receiving Joss Carmody's full attention and the sensual onslaught of his lovemaking. She shivered and drew the sheet tight around her. He made her feel as if she were the only woman in the world, the only woman who mattered.

Did all his lovers feel that way or was that a sign of her inexperience?

For a moment there she'd felt something so profound it was hard to believe it wasn't real and permanent.

The bed shifted as he got in, reaching for her. Leila stiffened. She should move away, assert herself instead of succumbing to his touch. But her body had other ideas. Already she was snuggling close as he settled her against his shoulder.

'Are you going to tell me now?'

'Tell you what?' Her breath caught as his hand circled lazily along her ribs and grazed her breast.

'About the roof garden. What you were doing, timing your-self.'

'You said there'd be no strings.' Leila fought to inject power into her voice as her body softened like sun-warmed chocolate at his touch. 'I don't have to answer questions.'

'No, you don't. But I'm…' he paused so long she wondered if he'd continue '…concerned about you.'

There it was again, that fillip of sensation at the idea some-one cared. That *Joss* cared.

Did it take so little to winkle out the weakness she'd striven so hard to hide? A weakness revealed was a weakness to be exploited. She'd learned that from Gamil.

'There's no need to be concerned. I'm fine.'

'That doesn't answer my question.'

Leila braced herself against his chest, trying to rise. His arm wrapped around, holding her close. She tried not to enjoy the feel of his hot, bare chest beneath her cheek.

'Why do I have to tell you anything? You never tell me about yourself.'

Her curiosity about the man she'd married grew daily. In-stead of a brash, bossy, self-important tycoon, Joss had proven himself not only intelligent and with a keen nose for busi-ness but affable, sexy and *likeable*. Initially he'd angered her with his demands and the assumption she'd starved herself deliberately. But these past weeks she'd come to enjoy his company. Though she was a trophy wife he somehow made her feel *more*, as if he truly valued her, as if he cared for her well-being, even her opinions.

'All right, then. Answer a question of mine and I'll an-swer one of yours.' He stroked the underside of her breast and she shivered. She tried to summon anger that he used her response to his touch against her, but it was delight she felt, not annoyance.

'Tell me why you dislike Murat so much.'

The question took her by surprise. She'd expected him to

ask about her fear of going out. She was almost certain he'd guessed it.

'And then you'll answer my question?'

'Cross my heart.' Yet it was the upper slope of her breast that he crossed with his index finger. When he'd finished his hand trailed provocatively to her nipple, awaking every nerve in a clamour of sensual delight.

Leila grabbed his hand and clamped it at her waist. He wouldn't have this all his way.

'I dislike Murat because he reminds me of my stepfather. They're two of a kind and I despise them both.'

A charged silence followed her words. Leila could almost hear Joss digesting that and considering its ramifications.

She was breathing hard and fast, her grip on Joss's hand vice-like with the strength of her feelings. Deliberately she lifted her hand away but had nowhere to plant it but his broad chest. That was solid beneath her touch, wiry hair tickling her palm, the even thud of his heart calming after her rush of emotions.

Before he could question, Leila spoke again. 'Why do you want a business arrangement instead of a real marriage? A wife for show, not a real one? And no children, no family?' It had puzzled her ever since she had realised Joss wasn't the cold tycoon she'd imagined. 'Most people want love, belonging, children.' Leila paused, realising suddenly how much she asked. No doubt he'd avoid answering.

'Remind me to think twice about negotiating with you again.' His deep voice held reluctant admiration and humour. She imagined that sexy half-smile grooving his cheek.

'You won't tell me?' She ran her fingertip over his chest, watching his nipple harden intriguingly as she circled it. His hand caught hers, imprisoning it flat against his chest.

'I left myself wide open, didn't I?' His other hand stroked her hair and she tilted her head into his touch.

'How can you want something you've never known or

seen?' he said at last. 'I know there are people who swear their family life is wonderful, but I suspect they exaggerate.' He breathed deep. 'I'm not stupid enough to put myself in a vulnerable situation where some woman has the power to make a fool of me when I discover we're all wrong for each other.' He shrugged. 'Not that it would happen. No woman has ever tempted me to consider a long-term relationship.'

Leila digested that. 'You're scared to trust?'

His hand tightened on hers. 'Not scared. Just understandably doubtful.'

'Because you don't trust women?' He wasn't a misogynist. His attitude surprised her.

'Because I've seen how destructive families can be, especially for kids.' His voice was grim. It tugged something deep inside her and she turned her head, pressing her lips to his chest in a gesture of sympathy. Whatever had happened in his childhood it had scarred him.

'You don't need to feel sorry for me, Leila.' Yet his palm caressed the back of her head as if to keep her close. She breathed deeply of his intriguing, masculine scent.

'I know.' He was big and tough and in control of his life— well able to take care of himself.

Yet even she, after Gamil's brutal treatment, held out hope of trusting a man with her happiness one day. She had her parents' example as a model and not even the last years had extinguished her belief in the power of love.

What was it like not having hope to hang onto? She slid her arm around his torso, hugging him, and his hand settled in her hair.

'I'm sorry your childhood was hard,' she murmured.

'Yours wasn't?'

She shook her head. 'Oh, no. Mine was sunshine and laughter and lots of love. My parents adored each other and made me feel special every day of my life.' She'd never imag-

ined telling Joss any of this, but the words slipped out easily.
'I was very lucky.'

'You were.' His deep voice held a new note. 'My earliest
memory is of my mother screeching abuse and the sound of
china smashing.'

'She was violent?' Leila shuddered, burrowing closer.

'Only with breakables.' His tone was sardonic. 'My mother
made her point with maximum drama when she didn't get
her way. As her expectations exceeded her income and her
vanity, that was often. My father, on the other hand, special-
ised in aloof disapproval. He'd cut anyone down to size with
a few words.' He paused. 'One passionate, the other cold,
both focused on themselves. They should never have had a
child, much less two.'

'You have a sibling?'

The hand stroking her hair stilled and the fine hairs at her
nape prickled.

'Had. Joanna died when I was ten.'

'I'm sorry, Joss.' She hadn't meant to cause pain. 'An accident?'

'For someone who doesn't want to talk about herself, you
ask a lot of questions.'

It was true. The depth of her curiosity surprised her.

She lifted her head. His eyes glowed dark indigo and his
face was pared to stark, powerful planes. Deep lines brack-
eted his mouth. Fellow feeling welled up inside her. She
wanted to wipe his hurt away, give him ease.

'I'm sorry,' she said again.

'It's okay, Leila.' His lips quirked. 'Don't look so worried.
It's all in the past.'

She shook her head. 'Some things stay with you.'

His smile faded and he gathered her close.

'You're right. I'll never forget Joanna and what she went
through. Our parents made her life hell, pulling her between
them. Six months in England with our mother, being taught

society ways, then six in Australia, berated for being too delicate instead of athletic and academically gifted. Her life was a struggle to conform to what *they* wanted. They played out their feud using her as a pawn. Never once did they think about what *she* needed.'

Leila noticed he talked about his sister, not the impact his parents' feuding had on him.

'By the time she was thirteen she was depressed. At fourteen she was severely anorexic.'

Leila gasped. Now it made sense—his accusations about her weight loss. He hadn't just been crass, but genuinely worried. 'So that's why—'

'It seemed possible,' he said flatly. 'I'd seen it before.'

'What happened to her?' Leila's throat dried.

'She ran away at fifteen and I never saw her again.' His voice was empty. 'When my mother told me she'd died of her illness she tried to make me believe it was because Joanna had been selfishly wrapped up in herself rather than caring about *her* like a daughter should.'

Leila propped herself up. 'That's outrageous!' What a thing to say to a grieving little boy.

'That was my mother, generous to the bone.' He shrugged. 'I've seen too much of dysfunctional families to want another. I'm alone and that's how I like it. I'll never bring a child into this world to suffer because its parents grew to hate each other like my parents. Even on opposite sides of the world they fought their petty battles through us. The last thing I want is children. My family genes aren't something I want to pass on.'

His mouth tightened and she read grim intent.

Now the terms of their prenup made sense. No real marriage. A penalty for pregnancy. Joss used the law to cut himself off from any chance of a family.

Her heart went out to him. He had it all socially and financially yet she grieved for the vacuum at his heart where love should be. He'd probably call himself self-contained. She thought it tragic.

His gaze clashed with hers. 'I don't want sympathy. It's wasted. I didn't tell you so you'd feel sorry for me, but so you'd understand I'm serious about no long-term emotional involvement.' His gaze shifted, dropping from her face, and his expression took on a saturnine cast that skimmed something almost like fear through her.

'But there's something else you can give me.' He cupped her breast, not gentle this time, but purposeful. His fingers pinched her nipple and she gasped as pleasure teetering exquisitely close to pain shafted through her. Involuntarily her body curved into his.

His smile was wolfish, past hurt buried behind a visage of hungry lust.

'That's what I want, Leila. Sex. Simple physical pleasure. Can you give me that?'

His eyes glittered and she felt a tide of answering hunger engulf her. The passion they'd unleashed was primitive and unstoppable. Yet that didn't prevent her seeing the shadows in his eyes, the hurt buried deep. Her heart squeezed hard for all he'd endured.

So when he grabbed a condom then tipped her onto her back she didn't object. He pushed between her thighs, suckling hard at her breast and she gathered him close, giving herself up to his need. He touched her between her legs, probing her readiness, and she arched into his hand, eager to give him the sweet oblivion he craved.

When, moments later, he thrust in hard and sure, his hands unyielding on her hips, his face stern with the force of his need, Leila gave herself willingly. And when he shuddered to a climax that pumped on and on, his hoarse shout echoing in her ears, Leila tugged him to her, cradling him with all the tenderness that welled up inside her.

CHAPTER ELEVEN

AFTER THAT JOSS ASKED no more questions. Since revealing his troubled past he avoided anything personal.

Personal except for their ardent lovemaking every night and morning. And now he'd taken to coming back to the apartment for lunch.

The first day he'd arrived as Leila was finishing laps in the indoor pool. She still blushed to think of what they'd done on the wide lounger by the water. She'd been utterly abandoned, giving herself up to the spiralling whirlwind of desire that grew daily rather than abated.

A flicker of anxiety stirred. It didn't *feel* as if this was the way to get rid of her physical weakness for Joss.

If anything, she turned to him more, enjoying the evenings when, instead of working or entertaining, Joss joined her to listen to music or watch a DVD. Intimacy wasn't just about skin-to-skin contact, but precious shared peace.

That she'd found it with her husband of all men stunned her.

Perversely, the fact he no longer pressed her for information made her wonder if she should trust him with the truth.

He must have guessed some of it. Though he said nothing, every time they went out he gathered her to him in the lift and kissed her till her head spun and her nerves vanished. When the limo threaded busy city streets, Joss would clamp her to his side and distract her with conversation or, more

often, his marauding touch. Now she almost looked forward
to going out.

She'd given up worrying that she emerged from the car di-
shevelled. Joss declared he preferred her looking sultry and
hot rather than buttoned up and cool.

Maybe he was just boosting her ego. Unlike Gamil, who'd
made it his mission to destroy first her mother then her, Joss
made her feel good. He valued her contribution to his commercial schemes and said so. And when they were alone and
naked, the sound of his praise always filled her with delight.
He made her feel wonderful: sexy and strong.

Had he any idea how much that meant?

Leila slid a look at Joss beside her in the restaurant alcove.
Each day she expected to discover he'd diminished, that the
glamour that drew her to him wore off. If anything he looked
more charismatic and potently masculine.

As if attuned to her thoughts, Joss slid his hand to hers,
tracing a finger up her arm till he reached her sensitive inner
elbow and she shivered. Instantly he smiled, his hooded eyes
giving a glimpse of ravening hunger she knew no meal could
sate.

A trickle of excitement slid low as his smile widened.

Sex, that was what he was thinking about.

Yet he hadn't needed to bring her out to lunch every day
this week if he'd just wanted sex. She was so blatantly eager
for his touch they both knew she'd give him what he wanted
the moment he entered the apartment.

Nor was he here to network. They were seated away from
the windows in a quiet, exclusive corner.

Now she thought about, it they were always seated well
inside any venue. Deliberately?

Slowly Leila put her knife and fork down, reviewing the
past weeks. The occasional outings had become more fre-
quent. Her nerves had stretched that first time when the city
had seemed vast and threatening. Joss never gave her time

to worry or back out, simply appearing and announcing they were going to lunch. He kept her close, distracted by conversation and his blatantly sensual caresses.

Her eyes rounded as she digested details she'd not taken time to consider before.

Her progress in venturing out wasn't all down to Joss. She forced herself outdoors every day, starting with a few minutes on the roof garden and short expeditions to the building's foyer and onto the street.

But with Joss she'd managed to do so much. With Joss the fear faded into a mere prickling undercurrent.

'Leila? What is it?' The lustful glint in his eyes dimmed and concern replaced it.

That was when she knew.

Joss had no need to take her out. With his wealth he could bring in the best chefs to cook for him.

This was about *her*.

Leila's head spun.

'You've brought me out to lunch every day this week.'

Joss looked into green-grey eyes turned mysteriously smoky and wished again that he could read his wife better. Some things, like her desire for him, were easy. But always he sensed she hid so much.

It shouldn't matter. Yet he couldn't quench his need to know.

'You don't enjoy yourself?' He frowned. *He'd* enjoyed spending time with a woman who was every bit as fascinating as he'd suspected.

'Of course.' She gestured abruptly. 'But you're giving up your work time. You even come home early at night.'

Home. There it was again, that word filtered into his subconscious again and again when he was with Leila.

Returning to her felt like coming home.

Joss frowned and swallowed a mouthful of Chablis. His

gazed dipped to Leila's kissable mouth and his muscles tightened in ready arousal. He…appreciated Leila but that was as far as it went. He didn't need her.

'You're afraid I let my responsibilities slide?' He tried to tell himself she worried about whether that would impact his profits and her allowance, but it didn't work. Leila no longer convinced as a money-hungry gold-digger. That woman had been a mirage.

'I know what you're doing, Joss.'

His gaze rose to her eyes, lustrous and huge. When she looked at him that way his chest tightened and he had trouble marshalling his thoughts.

'What am I doing?' The words emerged gruffly. 'Spending time with my bride is hardly a crime.'

Yet he bluffed. Deep within he felt something akin to embarrassment at how much pleasure he took in her company. Never had he enjoyed a woman outside bed as much as he did in it. It was a first. One he preferred not to examine. Better to accept and enjoy the unexpected bonus marriage had brought then move on.

'You're not doing this just because you want to.'

Joss swallowed the betraying truth that his choice to be with her was utterly selfish. Just watching her lips move, hearing her husky tones, knowing soon she'd be in his arms, was pure pleasure.

'You know, don't you?'

Something in her voice dragged him out of his reverie. Leila looked—defeated.

He snagged his hand around hers where it rested on the table. Instantly a frisson of electric energy sizzled under his skin. Normally it disturbed him—that charge for which there was no rational explanation. Now he ignored it, too intent on Leila.

'What are you talking about?'

Her lips twisted in a travesty of a smile and she darted a look at the plate-glass windows across the room.

'That I'm…anxious about going out.' Her words were soft, as if she didn't want him to hear, but her chin tilted regally and she swung round to meet his gaze with a stoic pride that squeezed his chest.

Joss's fingers meshed with hers. 'I guessed.' At first it had been hard to believe—that a woman as sassy and strong as his bride should harbour such fear, but the evidence had built inexorably.

'You haven't asked about it.'

He shrugged. Of course he wanted to know. But after revisiting his own troubled past, his desire to push her into telling him had waned. Her desperate pride struck him as precious and hard won. Who was he to strip that away?

Carefully he weighed his words. 'I'm interested, of course.'

'Because you don't want a defective wife?' Her bite of self-derision told him how much she abhorred what she saw as a weakness.

He slid his fingers over hers, as if his touch could soothe. He, who had no skills in caring for anyone!

'I owe you an explanation, I suppose.'

She looked as if she faced a firing squad, drawn up tight and proud. A better man would assure her he didn't need to know her secrets.

But Joss had never thought himself a better man in anything other than wheeling and dealing, and getting whatever he wanted.

He wanted to understand.

Leila looked down at his hand covering hers. 'It happened first the day of the wedding.'

'Not before?' His gut clenched. She couldn't mean marrying him had caused her fear!

But already she was shaking her head. 'Never before.' She

paused and the taut silence stretched every nerve into jangling discord.

'When the car drew away from the house I was nauseous,
wobbly as if I'd eaten something that disagreed.' She swallowed convulsively. 'When we got to the airstrip…'

Leila shook her head. 'I'd never felt anything like it. It was
as if the weight of the sky crushed me, pushing the air from
my lungs so I couldn't breathe.' Her breasts rose and fell as
her breathing grew choppy. 'It all seemed so huge, so limitless, so frightening.' Her voice faded on a gasp that rattled
in her chest.

Joss wrapped his other arm round her and drew her to
him along the banquette seat. She sat stiffly. She didn't even
seem to register his touch and Joss wondered if he should
have deflected this discussion. But selfishly he waited for
enlightenment.

When she continued it was in a breathless voice that didn't
sound like the proud woman he knew.

'I thought myself strong. Even fighting a battle I couldn't
win I never gave up. But when the threat is on the inside…'
She swallowed hard, as if forcing down rough shards. 'These
last years, even on the worst days I refused to admit defeat.
But this—' She shook her head and a lock of hair tangled
over her shoulder, an unwinding skein of mahogany silk. Joss
chafed her hand, stunned at how it had chilled. 'I thought I
was going to die.'

'I wouldn't let you.' He didn't formulate the words. They
simply emerged. But they were true.

Her lips pulled in an uneven smile that spoke of pain. 'You
distracted me enough to stop me giving in to it. Thank you.'
Her eyes met his and again that electric spark hit him. This
time it jagged deep into his vitals.

'Why? Do you know what brought it on?'

Leila shifted straighter, tugging her hand from his. Inexplicably he felt…deprived.

'I—' Her tongue flicked out to moisten her lips as she stared towards the window and its view of bustling London. 'I suspect it's because I wasn't used to going out.'

Joss waited. The pressure of expectant silence would draw the truth better than any encouragement.

'My life before this wasn't…normal.'

Joss watched her skin draw tight over her finely moulded features and fought the urge to ask. She said this had started on their wedding day yet she'd spoken about the last few years as if they'd been a battle. Tension screwed every muscle. He had a dreadful pit-of-the-belly premonition he wasn't going to like what he heard.

'Didn't you ever wonder why I married you?' Her gaze flicked to him.

He shrugged, about to say he'd assumed it was for wealth and position—what women always wanted. He'd learned that early from his dear mother. But since coming to know Leila, he'd learnt neither of those topped her list of desires.

Why hadn't he bothered to find out?

Because he didn't want to delve too deeply?

Her eyes bored into his. 'I would have married *anyone* if it meant escaping. No matter how unappealing.'

Leila found him unappealing? She had a fine way of showing it. Yet the bone-shivering urgency in her voice extinguished Joss's instant outrage.

'Tell me.'

She held his gaze so long he wondered if she'd speak again. Finally she dipped her head to look at her hands, twisted together on the table.

'My mother was a beautiful woman. Not just pretty but vivacious, the sort who drew admiration without trying.'

It didn't surprise him. Her daughter was the same. Leila had a special quality, not mere beauty or charm or even spirit, but a combination of the three that spotlighted her in any crowded room. It tugged at him like an inexorable tide.

'After my father died Gamil courted her. He was always there, wherever she was. He was charming, eager to please and devoted.' Yet Leila's voice was flat as she spoke. 'Eventually my mother agreed to marry him. It wasn't a love match like her marriage to my father, but he seemed a good man and she wanted me to have someone other than herself to rely on.'

Leila bit her lip so hard Joss feared she'd draw blood. But as he reached out she spoke again. 'It turned out Gamil wasn't the model husband she'd thought. What he called love was really obsession. Once they married he grew increasingly possessive and controlling, needing to know where she went, who she saw. He was pathologically jealous.'

Eyes the colour of a storm cloud met his and any idea she exaggerated died at the wretchedness Joss read there.

'He called her a whore. Accused her of being unfaithful. Accused her of bringing me up to be the same—weak, corrupt and licentious.' Lightning flashed in her eyes. 'My mother was *nothing* like that!'

'Of course not.' If she had been, Leila would have been different, not the wife who bedazzled him with her spirit and unshakeable honesty. The memory of the night she'd given him her virginity still had the power to suck the air from his lungs.

Joss's skin prickled at the idea of her being at the mercy of such a man. He didn't question her story. His wife was secretive but she wasn't a liar.

'Gamil was unhinged. I'm sure to anyone outside the house he appeared normal. But inside it was different. The restrictions tightened one by one. First the Internet stopped working. Trouble with the connection, he said, but he'd cancelled it. Then the phone. There were limitations on where we went. My mother's servants were dismissed on various pretexts and replaced with his own—people who'd spy for him. People who'd tell him what he wanted to hear.' She drew a deep breath. 'By the time my mother succumbed to cancer he'd broken her spirit and her will to live.'

Joss's skin iced as the implications sank in. 'You were alone with him then?'

'Except for his servants.' Her bitter tone told him they'd been no protection.

'He hurt you?' Joss leaned forward, his hand hovering over her taut fists. He remembered the livid bruise on her wrist, and red mist rimmed his vision. If he'd known this when the bastard had toadied to him—

'Not physically.' Yet she rubbed her hand absently over her arm. 'He had other ways.' Again Leila looked towards the restaurant's full-length windows and her expression made his belly clench.

'Gamil kept me prisoner after Mum died. I'd started a university course but deferred it when she got ill. He informed the university I wouldn't return.'

'Why did you let him?' Disbelief rose in him. Leila always stood up for herself. It was one of the things he admired even though initially he'd found her feisty attitude annoying.

She laughed. He didn't like the humourless sound.

'In Bakhara a guardian has complete control over his daughter, or stepdaughter: where she lives, where she goes, who she sees. That lasts until she turns twenty-five.'

'Or until she marries.' It was a guess, but it explained why she'd marry a stranger when she needed neither wealth nor social standing. What she must have suffered! The thought of Leila so desperate and defenceless made him feel sick with thwarted fury. How he wished Gamil were here right now.

Her eyes lifted and her lips curved in a tight smile. 'I always knew you were clever.'

Something sliced through his belly like a hot blade. Horror at her story? Regret that she'd come to him out of desperation? Guilt that he'd married her without bothering to find out why?

What sort of man was he, so self-important that he'd accepted without question that any woman would want him?

He looked at her wry smile, her proud chin and shadowed

eyes and knew she was strong in ways he'd never had to be. He felt pride, pleasure and gratitude that she was his…for now.

'You couldn't get away?'

Her mouth pursed. 'I tried. Several times. But I didn't get far. The law was on his side and I had no money, nothing but the clothes I stood up in. I couldn't go to my friends for help. Those would be the first places he'd look. He even brought the police in to search—saying I'd been kidnapped!'

'So he kept you in the house.' No wonder she'd called herself a prisoner. He'd seen the house. It was old and rambling, with several courtyards, but he couldn't imagine being locked up there. 'How long?'

She shrugged. 'Two years, more or less.'

'Two years?' Shock reverberated in his voice. 'Surely…' He shook his head, trying to process that it was possible in this day and age.

'I know.' Her voice grew husky and her gaze slid away. 'I should have found a way to escape for good, even with his guards and the police on his side. But each time it got harder, the punishments harsher.'

'I thought you said he didn't hurt you?' Joss's hand clenched on the back of the seat but he resisted the urge to embrace her. She sat rigidly as if there were a 'Do Not Touch' sign emblazoned across her.

'Not physical violence. But one by one he removed what he called my *privileges*. There was no phone or Net. I couldn't go out and there were no visitors, not even my few distant family members. Finally he cancelled the newspapers and removed the books.' Her eyes lifted to his. 'We had a library of books, some hundreds of years old, collected by my family. They vanished overnight.'

Her hollow tone tore at Joss. He thought he'd known dysfunctional relationships, but Gamil could have taught even his parents.

'All the servants changed, even the cook who'd been with us for years. No mirrors—'

'No mirrors?'

'They encourage vanity and licentiousness.' Leila gave him a straight look. 'I told you he was unhinged. My mother's jewels disappeared. He only gave me back the pearls so I could impress you and he kept the money that should have been mine.'

Joss swallowed hard. He remembered how she wore that pendant again and again. She'd clutched the pearl bracelet the day he'd threatened to return her to Bakhara if she reneged on their agreement. Ice slid down his spine as he recalled the pearls scattering across the floor as shock froze her face.

Why hadn't she *told* him?

Even as he thought it the answer came. After years of abuse why should she trust a stranger? A male stranger. One who had done business with her dreaded stepfather. Joss reviewed his actions from Leila's perspective and his pride shrivelled. Had she thought him as odious as Gamil?

He felt physically ill, rejecting the comparison with every cell in his body.

Whatever her first impressions, Leila trusted him now. She'd trusted him with herself, with her virginity. It struck him that she opened herself to him now with an honesty beyond anything he'd experienced with anyone.

Her trust and strength humbled him.

'After my last escape I was confined with bread and water in a storage room. That was what scared me most.'

'That's why you were so thin at the wedding?' The truth hit him with a crippling blow. 'You'd been starved?'

'Shh.' Leila looked around the restaurant but it was late and they were seated far from the rest of the diners. The staff kept their distance, respecting Joss's earlier request for privacy.

'Leila—tell me.' He grabbed her hand, feeling the supple warmth of her grip, assuring himself she was recovered.

'Not quite starved.' Her tone was bitter. 'I had to be well

enough to marry. Gamil is ambitious and wants to leverage his position at court using your status.'

'I played into his hands.' It didn't matter that the deal they'd struck gave Joss everything he'd wanted. He felt dirty, knowing he'd aided Gamil's schemes.

'It doesn't matter.' Her fingers threaded his. 'Because of you I got away. I escaped.'

At what price? Married to a man she'd never wanted. Terrified to go out.

'Don't look like that,' she whispered. 'You'll scare the waiters.'

He looked into her bright eyes and wondered how she'd endured without giving up. 'Tell me about the room where you were kept.' He had to know it all.

She blinked but didn't look away. 'It was small. Just large enough to lie down. It had a high window that let light in but had no view.' She paused. 'It was a little bigger than the lift to your apartment.'

Joss's breath hissed from his lungs. He'd been right about her terror. But he'd never imagined anything like this.

'No wonder you didn't want to go out.'

Her taut smile tugged at his heart.

'Pathetic, isn't it? The day I left home in Bakhara it suddenly struck me how big and dangerous the outside world was. How safe I was inside. Safe!' She shook her head. 'If it wasn't funny it would be heartbreaking.'

Joss saw the self-disgust in her face and knew it *was* heartbreaking. That Leila had had to endure this. That even now she seemed to blame herself in some way.

He'd never felt such a connection, an awareness of another's vulnerability, since Joanna. Yet this was different. It was more than pity and fear. There was admiration and much more—emotions he couldn't name. They churned inside like a curling wave smashing down on the shore.

'You're a remarkable woman, Leila.'

Startled, her eyes rounded. 'A freak, you mean?'

Joss wasn't having any of that. He wrapped his arm round her and dragged her up against him, where she belonged.

'I'd have gone crazy within weeks, locked up as you were.' It was the truth. He revelled in open spaces and pitting himself against the elements. It was one of the reasons he'd taken to geology. That and the need to prove himself to his father. 'I'd have been a gibbering wreck.'

He lifted his hand to her mouth, tracing the sultry shape of her natural pout, revelling this time in the tiny dart of electricity sparking from that touch.

'You're a survivor, Leila. You should be proud.'

What courage had it taken to survive? To walk away and embrace a new life with a man she didn't know?

Joss wanted to wrap her close and not release her. Assure himself he had her safe where he wanted her—with him. But he forced himself to ease his hold. She'd had coercion enough.

'What now, Leila? What do you want now you're away from all that?'

He waited for her to say she'd take up her studies again or pursue the money Gamil had stolen from her. Obviously she'd want revenge on her stepfather. Who wouldn't?

Yet the tension swarming in his belly had nothing to do with those things. It struck him that, now the truth was out, Leila might demand a release from their marriage.

He wasn't ready to let her go. His whole body stiffened in rejection.

She tilted her head, her sudden smile stealing his breath.

'Since you ask…' she paused and his heart plunged to his toes '…I want to learn to drive.'

CHAPTER TWELVE

'CLUTCH.' THE INSTRUCTION was automatic but unnecessary. Already Leila had her foot on the clutch, changing gears with only a mild grate of the gearbox and a tiny judder of the powerful engine.

Joss watched her tongue slick her bottom lip, her brow crinkle in concentration, and felt an urge to stop the car and pull her into his embrace. To make love to her here despite the bucket seats, gear stick and restricted space in the sports car.

He had it bad when teaching a woman to drive aroused him. Once he'd have scorned the idea of teaching a lover to drive. His connection to the women who passed through his life was fleeting and based solely on pleasure.

Yet this was pleasure too.

Being with Leila, watching her grow in confidence with every turn of the wheel on the deserted estate road. Sharing her excitement at what must be a dazzling taste of freedom after the horrors she'd endured.

Joss wouldn't have missed it for anything.

The idea of another man sharing this moment gouged a hole through his belly. He didn't want to think of her with anyone else. He wanted her with him. Not just for sex, nor her social skills and connections.

He rubbed his chin, puzzling over that.

She'd thanked him profusely when he offered to teach her

on a friend's country estate. As if he bestowed an impossibly precious favour.

He felt a fraud. It was nothing to bring her here. He was the one who basked in the warmth of her radiant smile. Who had the pleasure of watching her excitement and confidence grow. Who'd reap the rewards of that excitement later.

'Sorry.' She grimaced as she changed down for a bend and grated the gearbox again. 'I shouldn't be driving anything so expensive.'

'It's a car, Leila. That's all. It can be repaired or replaced like any other.' His ego had never been caught up in owning status-symbol vehicles. He used four-wheel drives chosen for reliability on his site visits. This top-of-the-range sports model was purely to indulge his love of speed out of the city.

'I suppose I should have waited and organised something more sedate for you.' Had he been selfishly eager to treat her?

Leila shook her head, flyaway strands of mahogany hair catching his shirt as she manoeuvred around a curve and the breeze caught her hair. The scent of it, rich with sunshine and exotic flowers, tingled in his nostrils.

'No! I love it. I love the way it responds to my touch with such power.' Her husky laugh set anticipation bubbling in his bloodstream. Joss thought of the way Leila responded to *his* touch—with eager passion and an innocent generosity that belied the trauma she'd been through.

She was indomitable and resilient.

He'd never known a woman like her.

It struck him that his need to look after her was far removed from the brotherly concern he'd felt for Joanna. Poor Joanna hadn't had the resources to fight the pressures she'd faced. But Leila, despite the panic attacks she seemed to be outgrowing, had an inner strength that shone through. He did no more than give her the chance to be herself.

Her resilience meant she'd be okay when the time came

to part. She didn't *need* him. She wouldn't cling, as so many had before.

Joss frowned, disconcerted that that knowledge brought no satisfaction.

Leila stared up at the canopy of the willow. Sunlight filtered in translucent beams of soft green, giving this shady bower an otherworldly quality. Trailing branches stirred gently in the breeze, brushing the emerald turf. Water chuckled by in a narrow brook at the boundary of their secret picnic spot.

She watched Joss unpacking a hamper and knew he'd chosen this spot especially. Not just for its beauty but because it blended the outdoors with a sense of enclosure—perfect for a woman who until recently had suffered panic attacks leaving the apartment.

Joss's was a practical sympathy—he just got on and *did* things for her without fuss. Wonderful things, like kissing away her anxiety in a lift, even yesterday in an unfamiliar building with strangers present. Her toes curled thinking of that kiss. It felt as if he'd welcomed her *home* when he'd opened his arms and drawn her close.

Afterwards she'd felt dazed and disoriented from what had been only a gentle caress. Yet it had twined ropes of longing round her, binding her to him.

She gulped down a clot of emotion.

'Leila?' Sharp as ever, he noticed. 'Are you okay?'

'How can you ask?' She smiled. Her hands still trembled from the effort of controlling that growling, gorgeously sexy beast of a car. 'I felt like I was flying.'

He shook his head, his one-sided smile plucking at something deep in her chest. 'You weren't going fast enough to get out of fourth gear.'

Leila shrugged. She'd spent so much time behind high walls. Controlling that powerful vehicle, steering it where *she* chose, was stunningly liberating. As was the fact Joss trusted her to manage it.

'But I drove it. I did it myself.'

His smile faded. He nodded, his gaze holding hers so she felt its intensity.

'That you did, Leila.' He turned to the hamper. 'We'd better organise proper lessons so you're not dependent on me finding time to teach you.'

Leila bit back an instant protest. She wanted Joss to teach her. Not because she felt safe with him—that went without saying—but because today had been special, so special she wanted to do it again and again.

The thought stopped her voicing her protest. It was unreasonable to expect him to do this regularly. He ran a multinational corporation! He had back-to-back meetings scheduled for months.

Yet Joss had made it seem natural he should teach her to drive his designer sports car then picnic on a private estate. Just as he made it seem normal they spent so much time together, not just at charity galas and business dinners. They spent quiet evenings reading or watching films and lunched at superb restaurants that somehow stayed off the paparazzi radar.

Leila had got used to being with Joss, relaxing with him, enjoying his company.

Was she too dependent on him?

Surely not. If she'd learned one thing it was independence. She relied on no one but herself.

'What is it?' Joss looked up to see her watching. 'I can't have food on my face—we haven't eaten.'

He drew his hand across his gold-tanned jaw and Leila was sucked into memory. Of her kissing that jaw in the dawn light. Of his bristles teasing her lips. Of the earthy, clean scent of aroused male in her nostrils and the texture of hot silk skin over hard muscles. Pungent pleasure swamped her and desire eddied, a familiar swirl, dragging at her abdomen.

'Nothing.' Why did she have to sound breathless? 'I was just thinking.' Leila blinked and saw his look change from curiosity to heavy-lidded awareness.

Instantly she plunged back into that heady place where nothing mattered except being with Joss. Why did he affect her this way? He'd assured her they'd go their separate ways when they'd sated this need for each other. But it grew stronger, not weaker.

Weeks it had been and she was no closer to pursuing her goals. She hadn't even chosen a course to enrol in. As long as she could remember she'd wanted to be a diplomat, but now the urgency for that career had faded. She drifted, happy to share Joss's life, interested in the snippets he revealed about his business. She'd even wondered about taking a role in managing the land she'd inherited, despite her lack of experience.

Was she in danger of giving up her goals just for the pleasure of being with Joss?

Or had her goals changed? Had her plans been out of loyalty to her father? It struck her that Gamil's disapproval had cemented them because she knew he hated the notion.

What was it she really wanted?

Her heart thudded a tattoo as Joss stood, his eyes on hers as he stretched to his full, imposing height.

His expression told her he'd lost interest in food.

He watched her as if seeking a sign.

Leila drank in the sight of him, solidly muscled and uncompromisingly male. She read desire in those sin-dark eyes and strength in those massive hands. She remembered his tenderness as he kissed her, his generosity as he'd given her free rein with his ruinously expensive car. His teasing as he'd distracted her from fear and supported her growing confidence.

Anticipation welled as Joss strode to her.

He dropped to his knees where she sat, his hand anchoring

her hair from her face. She loved the feel of him massaging her scalp. Pleasure speared every erogenous zone.

'We'll eat later,' he murmured, his mouth a kiss away.

Leila looked into his eyes and her soul shivered at the depth of what she felt. He was…he was…

She couldn't put it into words. Instead she cupped his jaw, felt a tremor of response and pressed her lips to his. Sweet pleasure unfurled.

She'd live for the moment and worry about the future later.

'You'll be fine,' Joss murmured. 'These are your people.'

It wasn't what he said but the way his voice feathered the bare skin of her neck that sent a tide of delight rippling through her.

'And you look stunning.' He touched her wrist, brushing the opal-and-diamond bracelet he'd given her. Between her breasts hung a matching pendant of green opal shot with scarlet fire. It was magnificent, worthy of a queen, and Joss had given it to *her*, saying it reminded him of the fire in her eyes when they argued. And when they made love. He made her feel precious.

Her hand slid down the heavy peacock silk of her designer gown. 'I know what you're doing, Joss. You're trying to distract me.'

Though the Bakhari Embassy in London had been home territory once, a lifetime had passed since then. The imposing mosaic-and-marble reception hall with its crystal chandeliers and glittering throng was a far cry from her memories. She was as nervous as a child playing dress up, summoned to a reception to meet the new sheikh and his bride.

Last time she'd been on Bakhari territory it had been her wedding day. Before that she'd spent years under the tyranny of a man who by Bakhari law had had ultimate power over her. Her love of her homeland was soured by bad memories.

'Am I succeeding?' Joss's mouth curled in a smile that

told her he planned something deliciously wicked for later. Her heart jolted. In his dinner jacket and bow tie he was the most potently attractive man she'd ever seen.

'You always succeed.' She let herself fall into the glorious inky depths of his knowing eyes.

How could she resist? He made her feel life was a secret to which he alone knew the answer. He offered it to her as he gathered her close.

The evening passed in a blur. The pleasure of speaking her native language mixed with bittersweet joy as she renewed acquaintances severed by years of isolation at Gamil's hands. He'd stolen her freedom and self-confidence, but also family friends who'd thought she'd chosen to drift away rather than stay in contact. Meeting people who'd known her parents brought joy leavened with anger.

'Leila.' Joss's voice cut across her thoughts. 'It's our turn.' They'd made their way to the inner sanctum where the sheikh and his wife received guests.

Sheikh Zahir of Bakhara was a commanding figure, tall and broad–shouldered in traditional robes. Only the heavy gleam of gold on his ring finger and the intricately inlaid scabbard at his belt relieved the austerity of his garb. That face—shrewd, proud and determined—didn't need adornment. He looked as if he'd stepped straight from the desert into the reception.

His wife, abundantly pregnant and beautiful in dark violet, smiled warmly and nodded at Leila. She placed a hand on her husband's arm and instantly his features softened as he inclined his head.

Something sharp jabbed Leila under the ribs. At the sight of that powerful man so attuned to his wife? Because of the tenderness in Queen Soraya's eyes as she looked up at her husband?

It was the impression of an instant yet the powerful connection between them hit Leila with the impact of a force field.

Longing welled up inside her. For what they had. For love, for permanence.

For the things she'd hoped for since she was little and shared the warmth of her parents' love. Since she'd seen beyond her marriage of convenience to the man beneath the drive and hard-nosed business acumen. Joss was tender and patient. He was strong enough not to be threatened by her strength of character. He cared.

What would it be like carrying Joss's child, as Queen Soraya carried the sheikh's? Leila's breath hitched as warmth flooded her. Joss's child…

The sheikh's gaze turned to her. She read curiosity and something that sent anxiety plunging through her.

She grasped Joss's hand and he covered it with his.

Stupid to fear. Her marriage had saved her from Gamil's influence, even if he'd used it to climb the greasy pole of court influence.

She was safe. She was free. Nothing could harm her.

'Joss, it's good to see you.' The sheikh stretched out an arm and Leila watched, perplexed, as they shook hands. Joss knew the sheikh? He'd never mentioned it.

'Your Highness.' Joss drew her forward and introduced her.

To her relief the royal couple were friendly, despite the sheikh's penetrating gaze. Soon they were discussing the recent upgrade of the embassy buildings and plans to renovate the Paris embassy. From there the queen steered discussion to Paris, her favourite city, and Leila found herself sharing reminiscences of the city.

By the time the ambassador called the assembly to quiet, Leila was enjoying herself.

It was only as she surveyed the silent crowd that she saw a familiar face—Gamil.

The blood drained from her face in a rush that chilled to her toes. Her breath hissed between her teeth and she had to work to keep her composure. Why was he in London?

Leila couldn't stop a shudder of hatred and—though she was loath to admit it—fear, at the sight of him.

Joss tightened his grip, his thumb caressing the pulse at her wrist. His gaze was fixed on the far side of the room too. Feeling his strength, Leila realised that whatever came next she could face it.

She wasn't alone any more.

Of the opening speeches Leila heard little. Her head filled with the urgent thrum of blood as her stepfather pushed to a more prominent position. He was opposite, watching the sheikh with an excitement that made her stomach dip in premonition.

There was a pause, a ripple of anticipation across the crowd, and Leila realised the sheikh spoke about the ambassador's retirement and his successor.

Gamil straightened, his hand smoothing his sleeve in a familiar gesture that revealed nervous excitement.

Bile rose in her throat. Gamil had destroyed her mother and tried to destroy her. How could she listen silently to the news he was being elevated to that prestigious position?

The sheikh spoke again and applause thundered. All eyes turned to a distinguished man on the other side of the sheikh: a career diplomat and friend of Leila's father.

Leila clapped the news of his promotion to ambassador but her attention was riveted on Gamil, whose eyes flashed shock and whose jaw worked with suppressed emotion.

'As we are all friends gathered here,' the sheikh continued, 'I'd also like to take this opportunity to acknowledge one of our own.' He gestured across the room at Gamil, addressing him by his full name.

Leila stiffened. What royal honour was he about to bestow? Gamil preened, chest puffed out and smile self-satisfied.

'It's come to my notice that, due to personal family matters—' the sheikh's voice dropped to a steely note '—our advisor Gamil is forced to withdraw from public life.' He paused. 'Permanently.'

Stunned, Leila watched as Gamil opened and shut his mouth as if seeking the nerve to protest the royal announcement. But the Sheikh's grimly carved expression left no doubt this was a royal decree. A decree of exile from the positions Gamil had schemed to make his own.

Gamil turned a sickly colour and Leila realised he'd known nothing of this. He'd expected promotion and instead received the equivalent of banishment.

Her heart pounded as she realised the implications.

Power was Gamil's reason for being and he'd been robbed of it. Publicly. Irrevocably. The sheikh's word was law—there would be no negotiation.

'And on the same subject…' The sheikh gestured to Joss, standing close.

What was happening? Leila looked from one to another, her mind spinning in dazed circles.

'Thank you, Your Highness. Ladies and Gentlemen.' Joss's baritone carried effortlessly.

He paused and flashed a look at Leila. His eyes were bright with something she couldn't name. Something that warmed her to her soul. His fingers threaded hers.

Joss turned back to the reception. 'In view of His Highness's news, and given the widespread interest in my Bakhari enterprise, I have an announcement. As Gamil is retiring to private life, his position on my new company board will be ably taken by his stepdaughter, my wife, Leila Carmody.'

Leila started, eyes widening as Joss turned. She saw satisfaction and a hard, triumphant glitter in his gaze. Applause welled. Dazed, she caught approving looks from familiar faces.

'But I—' She shook her head, trying to take it in. 'I don't have the experience,' she whispered.

'I have faith in you, Leila.' The sincerity in Joss's voice eased the tension clamping her stomach. 'Just one more challenge.' His smile reminded her that he'd been beside her through so many recent challenges.

Would he be beside her now? Surely taking her onto his board wasn't the action of a man planning to say goodbye any time soon. Had he changed his mind about not wanting a permanent relationship?

She barely had time to digest the idea when the sheikh spoke. 'I'm pleased to see another capable woman contributing to our economic future.'

Heat rose in Leila's cheeks. 'Thank you, Your Highness.' She had no idea why he thought her *capable*. She had no business expertise. Then she saw Sheikh Zahir and Joss exchange a look and suddenly so much tumbled into place. This was Joss's doing. Not just the position in his company but what had happened to Gamil.

Her breath stalled in her lungs.

Joss had done that for *her*.

How much had he told the sheikh? She cringed from the idea of anyone else knowing her past, yet turning to find Joss's gaze warm on her, full of tenderness and pride, she knew he'd have shared only what was necessary. And she couldn't regret the outcome.

'Congratulations.' Queen Soraya shook her hand, beaming. 'This means we can pursue our acquaintance. I have an interest in this enterprise too.'

Leila returned her smile, her brain buzzing as excitement fluttered in her stomach. Was she imagining this heralded a new stage in her relationship with Joss?

She was the centre of a congratulatory throng. Old acquaintances and new wished her well. And all the while Joss stood beside her. She was glad of his presence, overcome by what had happened.

She'd wanted to be involved in developing her family's land. Despite the enormous learning curve ahead, this was the opportunity she'd sought. A chance to make her mark. The news was crazy, scary, exhilarating. Yet, she realised, it was exactly what she wanted.

Joss shifted abruptly. She sensed tension in his rangy frame and turned.

Gamil approached, his face mottled with choler, his eyes flat and hard.

'I'll deal with this,' Joss muttered.

'No.' Leila put her hand on his arm, feeling taut muscles flex. 'I will.' She'd face this battle alone.

The rest of the room faded as she paced towards the man who'd made her life hell. The man whose cruelty had turned her world into a prison. She waited for hatred to surface. For that snap and sizzle of defiance. Instead, seeing him defeated and deprived of his grandiose dreams she felt nothing. He was a shadow of the puffed-up figure he'd been.

Leila stopped before him, waiting for his vitriol to spill out, knowing it couldn't harm her. She'd moved on. The knowledge gave her a strength she'd never imagined. She felt ready to take on the world.

Gamil opened his mouth, then, after one burning glare, spun away and barged towards the exit.

Still Leila felt nothing. Till she turned and found Joss watching. The heat of his gaze was a caress of welcome. Of homecoming.

Knowledge slammed into her. Knowledge that had hovered on the edge of her consciousness for weeks.

It was so momentous that the blaze from the chandeliers dipped as the world slid into a blur then back into sharper focus, each detail more vivid than before.

Leila sucked in a stunned breath.

No wonder Gamil had no power over her now.

She had everything she wanted. She had Joss.

CHAPTER THIRTEEN

LEILA STROKED the damp contours of Joss's chest, luxuriating in the aftermath of his loving. He'd barely walked in the door after a morning of meetings before she was in his arms then in his bed.

She stretched, arching her spine as his hand slid down her back then rose to tangle in her hair. She adored the way he touched her—those powerful hands gentle as if she were precious and breakable. Almost as much as she adored the times passion eclipsed gentleness and he took her with fierce urgency, times when it seemed their souls were one.

'We didn't even make it to lunch.' His voice rumbled beneath her as she lay across him.

'Hmm.' She had so much on her mind, food didn't feature.

Excitement stirred as she leaned over to press a kiss to his collarbone. All morning she'd seesawed between delight and trepidation. But after Joss's tender loving she told herself there was no need for nerves. Everything would turn out right. More, it would be *perfect*. She could see herself growing old with this man. Bearing his children.

'What are you smiling about?'

'Can't a woman be happy to see her husband?' She feathered her fingers down his torso and across his ribs to the sensitive spot that always made him shiver. Inevitably he captured her hand.

'How happy?' His voice dropped to a gravelly scratch

that scraped deliciously through her. 'Happy enough to delay lunch a little longer?'

Her smile turned to a knowing grin. 'I could be persuaded.'

Her heart was so full of joy she couldn't keep it to herself any longer. Leila thrust aside the tiny voice of warning that she couldn't quite banish.

She pressed another kiss to his skin, inhaling his salty spice tang. Remembering all he'd done for her, how he *cared*, gave her courage to admit the truth. She didn't want secrets between them.

'I love you, Joss.' Suddenly shy, she didn't meet his eyes, but waited, heart thudding in anticipation.

His chest rose as he took a huge breath. His fingers tightened around hers.

'What brought this on?'

Leila frowned. He didn't sound pleased. His voice had a sharp edge she hadn't heard in ages.

'What do you mean?' Mesmerised, she watched his chest rise again as part of her brain screamed that this wasn't going how she'd hoped. Far from being delighted, Joss sounded suspiciously out of sorts. Had that warning voice been right after all?

Leila shoved the idea aside. She *knew* Joss. He wasn't the cold, emotionally isolated man she'd once thought him. She raised her head. He was staring at the ceiling, brow lined by a ferocious scowl.

Her insides dipped like a swooping roller coaster.

'What led to this announcement?'

He kept his gaze on the ceiling as Leila surveyed his taut features. His mouth was flat, pulled tight. His nose was pinched and lines carved deep around his mouth, giving him an uncompromising air.

Joy turned to wariness. Where was the man who seconds ago had burned hot with desire, who'd held her against his heart? He *was* real. She hadn't imagined the changes in Joss since their marriage. They'd been profound. Enough to make her risk revealing her own fragile hopes.

'I realised how I felt about you.' Too late to rescind the words. She was committed now.

'When?' Still he stared unblinkingly at the ceiling. Leila was tempted to wave her hand over his face to grab his attention. Yet the taut flex of his muscles beneath her, his whole body stiffening, told her he was totally focused. 'Last night, when I gave you a seat on the board?'

Leila frowned. He sounded…almost sarcastic.

'Over a period of time.' Not for the life of her would she admit he was right. The knowledge had struck like a lightning bolt as she'd met his eyes and felt that overwhelming sense of belonging, just after he and Sheikh Zahir had broken their news.

'You don't have to do this.' His mouth twisted. 'I don't expect more from you.'

'Do what?' She shook her head, her hair sliding around them both. She watched it slip across his broad shoulder.

'Pretend to feel more. I know you're grateful about Gamil but it's unnecessary.'

'Grateful.' The word sank like a stone in still water. 'You think I'm grateful?'

'Aren't you?' Finally he turned, skewering her with a glittering stare that should have sizzled her blood. Instead she felt hoarfrost crackle across her skin.

This had been the happiest day of her life and suddenly, inexplicably, it was going completely awry. She knew of his emotional scars but had told herself they'd begun to heal. Surely a man as caring and generous as Joss deserved love.

Had she fooled herself into thinking he was ready for that?

Fear engulfed her.

Joss looked into smoky green eyes and felt a pang of loss so keenly it stole his breath.

Everything had been so good—too good, he realised now. He should have known it wouldn't last.

Hadn't he had moments of premonition these past months? Moments of pleasure so exquisite he knew they must be fleeting? Because they were all tied up with Leila.

Because happiness that centred on another person was a mistake.

Because everyone left eventually. Or betrayed. Or used you till they'd eaten you up like acid eating skin, scouring till there was nothing left to feel.

He turned away from her intent gaze, back to the ceiling. Smooth, white, perfectly blank, it should have soothed.

His gut twisted in a searing knot that sent bile up to burn his throat.

Nothing soothed. Not now.

It was too late.

He'd let himself pretend this wasn't dangerous. That they could go on as they were.

He should have known better.

I love you, Joss.

Even now he felt a desperate urge to cling to Leila's words. To forget all he'd learned about love and loss and take a chance on the mirage being real this time.

He swiped his hand across his face.

Hell! He hadn't wanted to believe so badly since he was ten. Since Joanna had run away and left him, despite her supposed love for him. Since he'd failed her and proved himself unworthy.

I love you, Joss. How often had his mother said that? Used the words to tie her children to her, only to reject them whenever they behaved like normal kids rather than extensions of her ego?

I love you, Joss. How many times had some woman simpered those words, clutching tight, hoping for more of the material riches he could give?

I love you, Joss.

They were a death knell to the happiness he and Leila had shared.

He gulped swirling nausea, skin crawling at the notion she might have deliberately set out to ensnare him with that supposedly magic formula.

Yet even worse was the suspicion Leila meant it. That she'd become emotionally invested in an illusion. That she believed him capable of returning…love.

Joss put a hand to her shoulder and moved her aside as he jackknifed to sit on the edge of the bed. He gulped huge draughts of air yet couldn't fill his lungs. His ears buzzed and he thought he was going to black out. He leaned forward, elbows on knees, trying to calm the writhing knot of pain where his belly and his heart had been.

'Joss. Say something!'

His mouth twisted. What was there to say?

Her hand closed on his shoulder, clutching. As if she knew she'd lost him?

Damn it. He wasn't ready for this to end. Not yet. Selfishly he wanted the pleasure to last. Pleasure with no complications.

He surged from the bed and stood facing the windows.

'We said no strings. Remember?' His voice wasn't his own, rasping like flint on stone.

'Things have changed.' She sounded bewildered. Joss raked his hand through his hair, telling himself it wasn't real. It couldn't be love. He didn't inspire such affection. She offered what she thought he wanted to hear.

'You don't owe me. Last night—' He hand slashed the air. 'Last night was about setting things right, that's all. You don't need to feel…obligated.'

For long seconds she said nothing.

'I'm grateful for what you did with Gamil,' she said finally. 'But that's not why I love you.'

Her words taunted him. Words he'd once craved but finally

learnt to despise. They dragged through his dark soul, dredging the depths as if seeking the needy boy he'd once been.

Joss swung to face her, blocking out the emotion that rose unbidden at those lethal words. He wasn't a naive kid any more. He wasn't vulnerable.

'*Don't*…say that. I told you it's not necessary.' The more she said it, the further they slipped into a no-win situation.

She clutched the sheet to her breasts and he knew it was too late. The damage was done. There was no going back. Inside him a raw howl of loss rose, a wordless tearing roar of rage at her naivety in ending what they'd had. It had been glorious, spectacular. Addictive.

He read her hurt and knew she'd never forgive him for what he had to do.

Even so, he wanted selfishly to buy more time. He wasn't ready to release her. He had to try to make her see.

'It's okay, Leila. I know you didn't mean it.' Joss spread his hands wide.

Leila stared at the man she loved, wondering at the change in him. His face was grim and pale beneath his tan and he refused to meet her gaze.

Why wouldn't he look at her?

Why this farce that she didn't know her own mind?

'I do mean it.' The words spilled out, and she recognised his expression now—anger. So fierce it shrivelled the tender bud of joy she'd nursed all morning.

It was like watching Dr Jekyll transform into Mr Hyde, seeing Joss's expression shut down into stark lines of disapproval.

'Don't, Leila.' Was that desperation in his voice? Leila leaned forward, looking for signs of the man who'd made love to her passionately such a short time ago. 'You'll regret it later.'

She sat straighter. She regretted it now. She'd been so sure of Joss's feelings. But far from reciprocating what she felt, he acted as if she'd done something terrible.

'We'll go on as before,' he said, pacing the floor. His nakedness only reinforced his aura of formidable strength. 'We can forget about this.' He waved his hand dismissively as if her announcement was a mere nothing.

Through her confusion anger drilled down.

'I don't want to forget it.' Couldn't he see how vital this was to both of them? Couldn't he *feel* it?

Joss swung round, his gaze pinioning her with a force that sucked the air from her lungs. He looked…savage. Desperate. Furious.

'It's the only way.'

Leila wrapped the sheet tighter. Despite the room's temperature control she was chilled to the marrow. 'What do you mean?'

He'd stopped pacing and stood, arms akimbo and jaw thrust forward, the image of male aggression. 'We had an understanding, remember?'

'If you mean the no-sex rule, I didn't see you complaining about breaking that.' Indignation bubbled inside her.

'Of course not. That was mutually agreed. I'm talking about no strings attached. No emotional entanglement.' He wrapped his palm around the back of his neck and for a moment looked like a man out of his depth, wrestling with forces beyond his control.

Before her sympathy could stir, he went on. 'You're breaking our agreement.'

Agreement? Joss was concerned about an *agreement*?

What about the fact she'd fallen in love with him? That she'd bared her feelings and been rejected? Had he any concept of how much she hurt right now?

'You don't love me?' Her voice was brittle, barely penetrating the thickened atmosphere clogging the room.

But he heard. She could tell by the way he stiffened.

'I don't do love. I made that clear in the beginning.'

Pain scythed through her and she wrapped one arm across her belly as if to ward off a physical blow. She hunched forward, her breath coming in short, hard gasps. He sounded cold as ice. Not the warm, generous, caring man she'd fallen for.

Had he been a mirage?

She'd heard his pain when he spoke of his family and the need to be alone. But everything he'd done, the tenderness he'd shown, had convinced her to hope.

'We had an agreement.' He stood before her, arms folded. 'I give you money and you act as my hostess. Beyond that—sex for mutual pleasure, that's all.' His gaze bore into her. 'I'm willing to overlook this morning and continue as we were.'

Leila couldn't believe what she was hearing. She swung her legs off the bed but didn't stand. She had a horrible feeling her legs wouldn't support her.

'You're happy for us to live together, and have sex of course—' her voice dripped disdain '—as long as there aren't messy emotions like love.' Her voice quivered on the last word, echoing the shuddering pain in her heart.

He raised his eyebrows. 'Don't look surprised. That's what we agreed.' He paced closer, his expression grim. 'We do this my way, take it or leave it. That's the deal—it always has been.'

Leila gasped. Revulsion swirled through her.

Deal! He had the temerity to talk of deals after what they'd shared?

Looking up at Joss's adamant face, his ferocious scowl and narrowed eyes, she was reminded suddenly of Gamil. Of how he'd demanded and ordered—always imposing his will, never considering anyone else.

Could she have been so wrong about Joss? Right now he was every bit as domineering and unreasonable as her step-father—the epitome of everything she'd learned to loathe.

She couldn't believe it. Yet surely now, if ever, was the time for him to show his true colours.

Had she let love blind her to his selfishness? Had passion skewed her judgement so badly? She was inexperienced about men and lust—had she confused the situation?

No! Surely not.

Desperately she sought some sign of the Joss she knew in the steely-eyed man before her. Just a hint of softening.

Disappointment crushed her as he stared back, showing no tenderness or understanding. One thing was clear. There was no softness in him, only selfish demands and disapproval.

He didn't love her.

Suddenly Leila felt aged beyond her years. Even breathing took more effort than she could manage. Was this how her mother had felt when she realised Gamil had duped her? When she realised he didn't truly love her? That he didn't have the capacity to care for anyone but himself?

Everything in Leila revolted at the idea. Not Joss! But the man before her stood solid and accusing.

Shakily Leila got to her feet, hauling the sheet up.

'You don't want a wife.' She drew an uneven breath. 'You want a woman who'll share her body and ask for nothing but money.' Bile rose. 'You want a whore.'

Joss's head jerked back as if she'd slapped him but he didn't move. 'I told you at the beginning, Leila. I never wanted a real wife. No emotions, no kids, no complications.'

Leila swayed as the cold, hard clarity of his words struck deeply in her wounded heart.

How had she ever imagined he'd cared? It had been convenient for him to help her overcome her fear of going out. It made her a more useful companion. Perhaps he'd even banked on gratitude making her more amenable to sex. She swallowed convulsively.

As for what he'd done to Gamil, maybe it wasn't about her

after all. Maybe it was easier having an inexperienced, compliant wife on the board than her wily stepfather.

No man who truly cared would treat her this way.

Leila's head swam as she tried and failed to make sense of this nightmare.

One thing remained constant—the arrogance carved on Joss's face as he waited for her response.

'No emotions, no kids, no complications.' She repeated his words in a scratchy whisper. Her lips curved in a grim smile that held no humour. 'Too bad, Joss. It's too late.'

'Just because you said—'

Leila lifted an imperious hand. 'Forget that.' She shied from going there. The pain was too raw. 'There are other complications.' She drew a slow breath, wondering how this morning's incandescent joy had turned sour so quickly. 'I found out this morning—we're expecting a baby.'

The last of the colour drained from Joss's face, leaving it sickly pale. He staggered back, grabbing at the wall as if needing support.

'You're lying.' His whisper was hoarse with shock and, could it be—revulsion?

If she'd needed anything to convince her she'd deceived herself, seeing stark horror on Joss's face did it. Her skin prickled and drew tight.

She slipped a hand protectively across her stomach.

'I don't lie, Joss.'

How she found her voice she didn't know. Her body kept functioning even when he'd dealt her heart a lethal blow.

He opened his mouth as if to speak but no sound emerged. The pulse at his temple pounded out of control and the tendons in his neck and shoulders stood out rigidly.

Leila waited. Waited because even now she couldn't believe it could end like this. She waited for Joss to haul her into his arms and apologise. To say he loved her. That he was ecstatic at her news.

She'd wait a lifetime, she realised finally. Because she'd been mistaken in him. She'd taken casual generosity for real caring. Sex for true passion and love.

'Don't bother asking,' she said through gritted teeth, despising herself for even now wanting more. 'Mother and baby are both healthy.'

With one final sweeping glance at the man who'd taken her heart and ripped it apart, she stalked out the door.

When Leila emerged from her room hours later, it was to the news Joss had packed his bags and left. Urgent negotiations overseas, the housekeeper said.

'When is he due back?' Leila didn't know whether to be relieved she didn't need to face him or furious he'd gone. They had things to sort out.

Her blood sizzled in renewed fury that almost eclipsed the hurt gouging at her heart.

'I'm sorry, madam.' Mrs Draycott's gaze skittered away. 'I had the impression… That is, I…' She wiped her hands down her skirt. 'I believe he'll be gone quite some time. He didn't talk about returning.'

Leila read the woman's discomfort and a chill descended that froze her to the spot.

Even after hours of digesting today's scene, she hadn't quite been able to believe it was the end of all she'd held so dear. Belief in the man she loved. Her dream that they'd build a life together, raise and love the child they'd created between them.

She understood some of Joss's reaction had been the product of shock. She'd convinced herself that when he thought things through he wouldn't be so adamant. Whatever his hang-ups about family, he couldn't throw away what they had.

It seemed he could.

He'd left without a backward glance. Without a murmur of regret or apology.

Leila told herself she didn't care. She and her child were better off alone than with a man like that. Yet it took a superhuman effort to ignore the shudder of pain that hit her and walk carefully back to her room.

She had plans to make.

CHAPTER FOURTEEN

JOSS SWITCHED OFF the engine and stared at the house across the quiet street. Rambling, set back from the road in its own garden, it looked solid and comfortable.

Perhaps it was the sunlight glinting off the large windows or the mellow warmth of old brick that gave the illusion. Perhaps the ornamented chimneys or budding roses around the door. No matter how illogical that bricks and mortar should convey anything so sentimental, the place looked like *home*. A warm, welcoming home such as he'd never known. The sort of home he could imagine Leila living in. Leila and their child.

He caught his breath as white-hot pain seared his chest.

He had no right to be here. He'd given up that right when he'd turned his back on Leila and what she thought was her love for him.

The pain twisted hard and sharp, skewering his sternum.

He grimaced, telling himself he wasn't surprised Leila had opted for comfort rather than a trendy apartment. He recalled her gardening magazines and how she'd reminisced about her childhood, the importance of a home.

This would be a real home. Not because it was charming and reassuringly solid, but because Leila would make it so. Leila with her warmth and determination and optimism.

What right had he to barge in? It was her sanctuary. She deserved it after what she'd been through.

What right had he, who knew nothing of homes or love, to intrude?

Joss looked again. This time the roses around the door and either side of the gate looked like thorned sentinels, keeping out unwanted visitors. The very warmth of the old house was a reminder of why he had no place here. He'd only brought her misery.

He reached for the thick wad of papers on the passenger seat, the envelope crackling in his grasp. Opening the door and striding across that road was the hardest thing he'd ever done.

Leila hummed as she knelt over the garden bed, weeding. That was why she didn't hear anything. The first hint she wasn't alone was when a shadow blocked the sun and she looked up to see feet coming to a stop on the gravel path. Large feet wearing hand-stitched loafers.

Emotion trembled through her. An instantaneous recognition she fought to douse.

It wasn't him. It would never be him. Hadn't she learned that after two months' silence? She'd left Joss's apartment, left his life, and heard not a word from him.

Nevertheless it took Leila a moment to harness her wayward emotions and don a calm expression.

'Can I help you?' She looked up, past long, long legs covered in washed denim, over a flat male belly, past a casual jacket and white shirt to wide, straight shoulders and a jaw honed from steel.

Her heart gave a great leap and lodged somewhere near her throat. She thrust out a hand to keep her balance as she swayed backwards.

'Leila!' He lunged towards her then froze as if recalling he had no right to touch her.

Her eyes widened as she took him in. He was as spectacular as ever—more so; the casual clothes suited him, as did the curl of dark hair brushing his collar. In the clear spring sunshine he looked like everything she'd secretly dreamed of for so long.

The realisation stiffened her sinews and finally engaged her brain. Jerkily she got to her feet, backing from the path till she realised she was retreating and planted her feet.

'Are you all right?'

Leila teetered on the brink of believing that was concern in his voice. But she'd learned better.

His gaze swept her. Did she imagine it lingered on her belly? She stifled the urge to slip her hand protectively over her baby.

'Joss.' Her tone was flat. 'What are you doing here?'

He swallowed hard, his mouth firming, as if he didn't like being challenged.

Leila took off her soil-encrusted gloves and dropped them at her feet. Bad enough to be caught on her knees, but did he have to find her in gardening clothes?

She'd wanted, if she ever saw him again, to look cool and sophisticated, calmly unimpressed by his presence. Yet heat rose in her cheeks at his scrutiny and her breath came in uneven little pants. Valiantly she strove to calm herself. He'd be gone soon. He wouldn't linger.

'You're looking well.'

She opened her mouth to respond then closed her lips. She refused to bandy polite greetings. Though now she looked more closely he appeared tired, the hollows around his eyes and in his lean cheeks more pronounced. Obviously devoting himself to his business empire was demanding.

When she said nothing his eyes narrowed as if trying to read her thoughts.

'Aren't you going to invite me in?' He gestured to the house behind her. She'd bought it with the funds she'd earned by signing his precious agreement and marrying him. That house was her sanctuary and her hope for the future.

'No!' Her vehemence surprised him. She saw it in his raised eyebrows. But she didn't want him on her territory. It would be harder than ever to eradicate memories of Joss once she'd let him into her house. 'That's not necessary. We can talk here.' She folded her arms.

On tenterhooks she watched him breathe deeply, his nostrils flaring. Would he try to force her hand?

'How are you, Leila?'

It was the last thing she'd expected. What was more, his voice held that soft gravel note she'd learnt to heed because it signalled deep emotion.

Her fingers dug into her arms through her shirt. Who was she kidding? She'd thought she'd known Joss but she'd been wrong. So wrong it would be laughable if it weren't tragic.

'I'm well.' She didn't ask how he was. She told herself it was because she didn't care but she feared it was because she cared too much. She didn't trust him, didn't like him, but remnants of her feelings for him still lingered.

That was why she had to get rid of him.

'And the baby?' His voice dropped, rolling right through her belly to where their child nestled. This time she couldn't prevent her instinctive gesture, palm to abdomen, as if to shield it from danger.

Anger surged within her. At him for having the gall to ask. At herself because she'd longed for him to acknowledge their child, though she knew it was pointless.

She opened her mouth to sneer that it was none of his business, but stopped.

'The baby is fine.' She dragged in a sharp breath as pain, jagged and raw, sliced through her. Then words she hadn't been aware of forming spilled out. 'Were you hoping it was all a mistake? Or that maybe I'd miscarried and you wouldn't have to worry about *complications*? Is that it?'

Once before she'd seen shock pare his features to the bone and colour ebb from his face. She saw it again now and it cut her to the quick. There was no mistaking his reaction as anything but genuine.

Shame surfaced. What had she come to that she was so vitriolic?

'I'm sorry,' she whispered, appalled. The surge of emotion ebbed abruptly, leaving her feeling wobbly. Her shoulders sagged; the weariness she'd fought for weeks dragged at her so suddenly she felt light-headed.

'Leila?' This time when the world tilted he didn't pull back. His hand was hot through her sleeve, his touch firm and sustaining. 'You need to sit.'

Eyes the colour of twilight locked with hers and she felt something shift in her chest. Leila squeezed her eyes shut, trying to keep it out, but already she felt warmth flowing through her. From his touch, his concern.

What a fool! There was nothing between them, there never had been. Yet still she longed…

'This way.' His tone and his touch were gentle enough to soothe her shredded nerves. She opened her eyes and let him lead her to a garden seat.

'I'm sorry.' Her voice stretched thin as she lowered herself to the seat. She felt like an old, old woman, weary beyond her years. 'That was uncalled for.' She blinked hot eyes and brushed at a smear of soil on her loose shirt.

'I deserved it.'

Leila's head jerked up and she met his gaze as he stood before her. Had she heard right?

'But believe me,' he continued, 'I want nothing more than for you and the baby to thrive. I want only good for you both.'

Staring up at him, she almost believed he cared, *really* cared. Except he'd left her in no doubt that was impossible. Her heart cracked.

'Why are you here, Joss?'

He took a breath as if about to say something momentous.

Yet no words came. His eyes held a shuttered look she hadn't a hope of reading. At his side one big hand curled into a fist.

If she didn't know better she'd think him nervous.

'Because of that?' She gestured to the large envelope in his other hand. She hadn't wanted to acknowledge it, guessing it contained divorce documents.

She wished she could be blasé about ending what was simply a legal contract. But she wasn't her parents' daughter for nothing. She believed in love and family. She craved them. She craved Joss, with a silent fervour that defied logic.

Except the Joss she craved was a figment of her imagination, a man she'd invented based on a little kindness and a whole lot of sexual magnetism.

He wasn't real.

That knowledge gave her the strength to reach out for the envelope he crushed in his fist.

'Is this for me?' Finally he opened his hand. Her pulse skipped as she took the envelope and ice slithered down her spine despite the sunshine. She suppressed a silent keening wail. This was so far from what she'd dreamed.

But she'd deal with it. She'd be strong and face this as she faced everything else.

'You want me to send it back when I've signed it?' Leila was proud of her even tone.

Joss blinked, his brow furrowing. 'They're for you. Reading material for the board meeting that's coming up.'

Board meeting? Joss had come to give her agenda papers for a meeting? She sagged back in her seat, her heart thrumming out of rhythm.

Nothing about this meeting made sense, least of all Joss, who stood looking as poleaxed as she felt.

'Joss?' She tried to collect herself. 'Why are you here? Your staff could have sent the papers.'

His eyes burned into hers. She felt the impact right to her

toes curling tight in her gardening boots. He only had to look at her and she wanted to believe—

'I had to see you. I needed to make sure you were all right.' His voice was a harsh riptide of sound that undercut her determination.

'Why? You don't want complications, remember?' Weariness rather than bitterness laced her words. She'd been bitter so long. Now, looking at his taut features, she felt regret and pain. And that welling of emotion she hadn't been able to crush.

She looked away. She needed to be alone. Needed never to see him again. Maybe then she'd convince herself this would work out for the best.

Leila blinked as he dropped to his knees before her. Large hands gathered hers.

She tried to pull back but his hold was firm. And—dreadful to admit—part of her revelled in his touch.

This would be the last time he held her.

'Because you were hurting so much. Because when I finally got past my posturing and my fear, I realised how cruel I'd been.'

Fear? Joss didn't do fear. Just as he didn't do emotional entanglements.

'I told you, I'm okay.' Yet she couldn't gather the strength to tug her hands free. She bit her lip, hating her weakness.

Slowly he shook his head. 'No, you're not. And that's my fault.' He nodded at the envelope on the seat beside her. 'The papers were an excuse. I needed to see you and apologise.' He drew in a ragged breath. 'I was a louse, a complete bastard. I deserve for you to hate me but I had to see if there was anything I could do, to make things easier.'

'Easier?' Her voice was scratchy as she strove to process his words.

His hold tightened. 'You...cared for me, Leila. I threw that in your face.' He shook his head. 'I shouldn't have taken out my fears on you. I know I can't fix things but I wanted to apologise and—'

'What fears? I don't understand.' Joss was powerful and determined, the strongest individual she knew. She'd leaned on his strength time and again. 'Joss?'

His mouth tugged up at one side in what might pass for a smile if she hadn't see the agony in his eyes. Leila's heart pounded hard in sympathy, even as she told herself she shouldn't get dragged in. She was well rid of the man who'd hurt her so devastatingly.

'I was scared, Leila, petrified.' His voice was low and she had to lean forward to catch it. 'I still *am*. That's why I turned on you.'

'Don't talk in riddles.' She tried to tug her hands free, wondering if this was some convoluted scheme to dupe her. But why?

Joss released one of her hands but planted the other over his chest, pressed to his heart. Heat spread from the point of contact. His heart beat to the same frantic rhythm as hers.

It didn't mean anything. Yet the look in his eyes dragged at her resistance.

'I told you I don't do emotions. I *can't* do emotions.'

Leila opened her mouth to disagree but his ravaged expression stopped her.

'I've never had love.' He wasn't looking at her now, but over her shoulder, into the distance. 'That's no excuse, just an explanation. Every time someone told me they loved me, I got hurt, till I steeled myself never to be hurt again. My parents claimed to love me but they only cared about their egos. Love was a blackmail weapon, using us to play their sordid games to best each other. All my life, whenever someone claimed to love me it was about what they could get. Even my sister—' He sucked in a deep breath. 'I loved her but I couldn't protect her and when she left I knew she hadn't cared enough about me to stay.'

Leila's hand moved convulsively against him and he grimaced.

'I know. I was as selfish as my parents, believing that. I was a kid and didn't know better. But deep down I *did* know I wasn't cut out for love. I don't inspire deep feelings in anyone. And as the years went by I realised I wasn't able to love anyone either. I lacked the capacity.'

'Joss, that's absurd.' She'd known he'd been damaged by his past, but to believe he wasn't capable of love!

His eyes cut to her and the force of what she read there dried her protests.

'It's true. I got accustomed to using people and being used—life was a series of barters. Sex for a few trinkets and some good times. The closest I came to love as an adult was when a woman claimed to love me in the hope I'd set her up financially.'

'That's horrible!' It was no more than she'd expected, but hearing it put so brutally was shocking.

He shrugged. 'It's what I expected. Until you.'

Joss stroked his thumb over the back of her hand where it rested on his chest. She told herself she should yank her hand away but there was a disconnect between thought and action. She couldn't do it.

'With you I felt…things I'd never experienced. When you said you loved me I desperately wanted it to be true. But I didn't dare believe it.' He shook his head. 'It was easier to believe you were mistaken or lying than that you loved me.'

'Oh, Joss.' Leila's heart rolled over as she read his pain. Guilt struck her. She should have tried harder to convince him, not given up so easily.

'I'm not after sympathy. I just need to explain why I turned on you and apologise.'

'You already have.'

He looked surprised. 'It's not enough.'

'No, it's not.' Mixed with her sympathy was anger. Anger

that a man so intelligent should have put them through all this because he couldn't comprehend anything as straightforward and wonderfully simple as love. 'You talk as if there's a wall around you, cutting you off from love. All you have to do is reach out and trust your feelings.'

He hesitated. 'I see now that it's possible—in theory.'

At her puzzled look he continued, 'After you left—' his voice dipped '—I couldn't work. I couldn't function. Nothing held my attention. I wanted…' He shook his head. 'I couldn't have what I wanted so I found something else to occupy my time. I traced my sister Joanna's movements. I thought finding her grave might help put the past behind me.'

Leila wanted to ask what it was he wanted, but he continued.

'Eventually I found her.' Emotion flickered in his gaze. 'She hadn't died at fifteen as I'd been told, she just disappeared.'

At Leila's gasp he nodded. 'I guess I was told she died to keep me quiet. I was asking about her all the time.' He rubbed his jaw with his free hand. 'So for weeks I've had investigators searching.'

'You found her?' Leila's heart was in her mouth.

'I did.' The quiet satisfaction in his smile was balm to her shredded nerves. 'She's alive and living in the wilds of Yorkshire with her farmer husband and three kids.'

'And she'd never thought to contact you?' Anger stirred within her at the thought of all those wasted years when Joss had had no one.

His smile died. 'Apparently she tried once, a few years after she left. She was living on the streets and our mother told her she couldn't come back into our lives until she'd cleaned up her act. Joanna was told as far as I was concerned she was dead and it was better that way.'

'That's appalling.' Leila reached out and stroked his hair

from his forehead, needing the connection, needing to comfort him.

'I warned you—my mother *was* appalling.' He captured her hand in his and she welcomed his touch—so familiar. 'But she's gone and Joanna—she's happier than I ever remember. And she's living proof that I was wrong. That our family *can* find love.'

His eyes glittered fiercely and she could have sworn heat arced between them.

'You thought it was a family curse?' Leila was breathless.

'I thought it likely, given my experiences.'

'Joss Carmody, for an intelligent man, sometimes you can be totally stupid!'

He nodded and tugged her closer so she leaned forwards in her seat. 'I know. I've been a fool in all sorts of ways. Worse, I've been a coward. I wanted your love but I was too scared I'd get hurt.'

Leila's heart jumped and her airways jammed at the expression in his eyes. A flicker of excitement stirred.

'What are you saying, Joss?'

'I…fell in love with you, Leila.' His hands tightened and she revelled in his touch. 'I know it's too late, that I've destroyed what you felt, but I had to let you know. And tell you I'm here whenever you need me. Whenever either of you need me. You or the baby.'

The world stood still around them. Even the clouds stopped moving and the drone of a distant car faded as she read the emotion blazing in his face. Hope rose, a trembling, fragile bud.

Did she have the courage to reach out and grasp it?

Could it be true? She wanted to believe it with every atom of her being.

'When did you fall in love, Joss?'

'I don't know. It was a bit at a time. When you kissed me

in the lift that first time and I thought I'd died and gone to heaven.'

Heat crept up her throat as she remembered the no-holds-barred passion of that kiss.

'When you stood up to me, whenever I tried to get my own way without compromise. When I learned how brave you'd been with Gamil.'

Leila shook her head. 'I wasn't brave. I—' His index finger on her lips stopped her words. She tasted salt and Joss and had to fight the instinct to suck his finger into her mouth and taste him better. Hunger slammed into her. It thrilled and appalled her.

'When you drove my Ferrari that first time and managed not to crash it.'

'You're such a *man*!'

His broad shoulders lifted in a shrug and his smile made her heart flip over. 'So sue me.'

Then his grin faded. 'You deserve to know, Leila. I had to apologise and tell you how I felt.'

She looked into his stern face and felt again that throb of impatience.

'And that's all?'

He looked genuinely perplexed.

Slowly her anger faded. It struck her anew that he really was completely inexperienced when it came to love.

It was up to her to educate him.

Leila surged to her feet and paced away.

'Much as I enjoy having you on your knees apologising, I prefer a man who stands up for himself.'

An instant later he stood before her, potently masculine, puzzled and ever so slightly challenging.

'I want a man who believes me when I say I'm in love and doesn't think that will change just because of harsh words or a misunderstanding, no matter how severe.' She raised her brows. 'I want a man who understands when I love it's not negotiable, not put aside easily or lightly.'

'I see.' His deep voice curled tight around her and she shivered.

'I need a man whose love is like that too. Not a fair-weather lover who's only around in the good times.'

'Someone who's there through thick and thin.' Joss nodded and took a pace closer, blocking her exit.

'Precisely.' She swallowed, noting a gleam in his eyes that hadn't been there before. 'I want a man who will be with me and my child for ever.'

Her words hung between them, like a fragile ribbon extended over a yawning void.

'It's a big ask.' His voice was sombre, his face stern.

She lifted her chin. 'My child deserves a father who will love her and support her always.'

'Her?' Joss stepped closer, the heat of his body encompassing her.

'Or him.'

'Or both,' he whispered, trailing his fingertips across her jaw and down her throat, till her senses rioted and her hormones surged. She shivered under his caress.

'Oh,' she breathed. The heat in Joss's eyes needed no interpretation. Leila felt a shimmy of answering arousal deep in her womb.

He lowered his head towards her, but stopped a kiss away, eyes locked with hers. Hope, fear and profound excitement melded within her.

'Leila Carmody, can you forgive me for being such a fool and hurting you so badly?'

'I can.' She watched his eyes squeeze shut for a moment on a sigh of relief and knew she'd been right after all. The man she'd fallen for was no mirage.

'Will you consider staying as my wife, the love of my life, always?'

Words failed as emotion swamped her.

'Could you trust me to love and honour you and be true to you always? Could you help me try to be a good father, the sort of father I always wanted?'

She reached out and squeezed his arm. 'You'll be a wonderful father.' The thought of his patience, his tenderness and encouragement, made her heart swell.

'Does that mean you will?' Joss's voice was unsteady. His hesitancy cut her to the core.

'I think I could.' Her heart pounded a rough tattoo.

'You think?' One dark eyebrow rose.

'I could be persuaded.'

'Could you indeed?' In one swift move he swept her up into his embrace. 'I've a good mind not to let you go until you say yes.' Leila wanted to stay there for ever in his arms. This close she read his fierce possessiveness.

'So much for humility.'

His grin tugged at her heartstrings.

'It didn't suit me. Anyway, I thought you wanted a man who'd stand up for himself.'

Leila smiled, relieved to see her own Joss back.

'Seriously, Leila. You're sure? This isn't just about the baby? I'll be there for our child whether we're together or not.'

Leila punched him lightly on the arm, her heart singing as she realised he took this every bit as seriously as she did. 'I'm absolutely sure, Mr Carmody. We come as a package deal, take it or leave it.'

'Oh, I'll take it, Mrs Carmody. Believe me, I'll take it.'

His kiss was swift and possessive and over too soon. But Leila didn't complain because he strode up the steps to the house and shouldered open the front door.

They had come home.

* * * * *

THE MILLIONAIRE
AND THE MAID

MICHELLE DOUGLAS

To Laurie Johnson for her enthusiasm, insight…
and for introducing me to mojitos.
It was a joy to work with you.

CHAPTER ONE

MAC PRESSED THE heels of his hands to his eyes and counted to five before pulling them away and focussing on the computer screen again. He reread what he'd written of the recipe so far and fisted his hands. *What came next?*

This steamed mussels dish was complicated, but he must have made it a hundred times. He ground his teeth together. The words blurred and danced across the screen. Why couldn't he remember what came next?

Was it coconut milk?

He shook his head. That came later.

With a curse, he leapt up, paced across the room and tried to imagine making the dish. He visualised himself in a kitchen, with all the ingredients arrayed around him. He imagined speaking directly to a rolling camera to explain what he was doing—the necessity of each ingredient and the importance of the sequence. His chest swelled and then cramped. He dragged a hand back through his hair. To be cooking…to be back at work… A black well of longing rose through him, drowning him with a need so great he thought the darkness would swallow him whole.

It'd be a blessing if it did.

Except he had work to do.

He kicked out at a pile of dirty washing bunched in the corner of the room before striding back to his desk and reaching for the bottle of bourbon on the floor beside it. It helped to blunt the pain. For a little while. He lifted it to his mouth and then halted. The heavy curtains drawn at the full-length windows blocked the sunlight from the room, and while his body had no idea—it was in a seemingly permanent state of jet lag—his brain told him it was morning.

Grinding his teeth, he screwed the cap back on the bottle.

Finish the damn recipe. Then you can drink yourself into oblivion and sleep.

Finish the recipe? That was what he had to do, but he couldn't seem to turn from where he stood, staring at the closed curtains, picturing the day just beyond them, the sun and the light and the cool of the fresh air…the smell of the sea.

He kept himself shut away from all that temptation.

But it didn't stop him from being able to imagine it.

A ping from his computer broke the spell. Dragging a hand down his face, he turned back to the desk and forced himself into the chair.

A message. From Russ. Of course. It was always Russ. Just for a moment he rested his head in his hands.

Hey Bro, don't forget Jo arrives today.

He swore. He didn't need a housekeeper. He needed peace and quiet so he could finish this damn cookbook.

If the rotten woman hadn't saved his brother's life he'd send her off with a flea in her ear.

Scrubbing a hand through his hair, he shook that thought off. He understood the need to retreat from the world. He wouldn't begrudge that to someone else. He and this housekeeper—they wouldn't have to spend any time in each other's company. In fact they wouldn't even need to come face to face. He'd left her a set of written instructions on the kitchen table. As for the rest she could please herself.

He planted himself more solidly in his chair, switched off

his internet connection, and shut the siren call of sunshine, fresh air and living from his mind. He stared at the screen.

Add the chilli purée and clam broth and reduce by a half. Then add…

What the hell came next?

Jo pushed out of her car and tried to decide what to look at first—the view or the house. She'd had to negotiate for two rather hairy minutes over a deeply rutted driveway. It had made her grateful that her car was a four-wheel drive, equipped to deal with rough terrain, rather than the sports car her soul secretly hungered for. After five hours on the road she was glad to have reached her destination. Still, five hours in a sports car would have been more fun.

She shook out her arms and legs. *'You can't put her in that! She's too big-boned.'* Her great-aunt's voice sounded through her mind. She half laughed. True, she'd probably look ridiculous in a sport car. Besides, what were the odds that she wouldn't even fit into one? As ever, though, her grandmother's voice piped up. *'I think she looks pretty and I don't care what anyone else thinks.'*

With a shake of her head, Jo shut out the duelling voices. She'd work out a plan of attack for Grandma and Great-Aunt Edith later. Instead, she moved out further onto the bluff to stare at the view. In front of her the land descended sharply to a grassy field that levelled out before coming to a halt at low, flower-covered sand dunes. Beyond that stretched a long crescent of deserted beach, glittering white-gold in the mild winter sunlight.

A sigh eased out of her. There must be at least six or seven kilometres of it—two to the left and four or five to the right—and not a soul to be seen. All the way along it perfect blue-green breakers rolled up to the shore in a froth of white.

She sucked a breath of salt-laced air into her lungs and some of the tension slipped out of her. With such a vast expanse of ocean in front of her, her own troubles seemed suddenly less significant. Not that she had troubles as such. Just a few things she needed to sort out.

She dragged in another breath. The rhythmic whooshing of the waves and the cries of two seagulls cruising overhead eased the knots five hours in the car had conspired to create. The green of each wave as it crested made her inhalations come more easily, as if the push and pull of the Pacific Ocean had attuned her breathing to a more natural pattern.

The breeze held a chill she found cleansing. Last week the weather would have been warm enough to swim, and maybe it'd be warm enough for that again next week. Having spent the last eight years working in the Outback, she hadn't realised how much she'd missed the coast and the beach.

She finally turned to survey the house. A two-storey weatherboard with a deep veranda and an upstairs balcony greeted her. A lovely breezy home that—

She frowned at all the closed windows and drawn curtains, the shut front door. Heavens, Mac MacCallum *was* still here, wasn't he? Russ would have told her if his brother had returned to the city.

She sucked her bottom lip into her mouth and then folded her arms. Mac would be in there. Russ had warned her that his brother might prove difficult. He'd also had no doubt in her ability to handle difficult.

'Jeez, you save someone's life and suddenly they think you're Superwoman.'

But she'd smiled as she'd said it—though whether in affection at her dear friend and former boss, or at the thought of wearing a superhero outfit she wasn't sure. Though if she burst in wearing a spangly leotard and cape it might make Mac reconsider the soundness of locking himself away like this.

She planted her hands on her hips.

Painted a sleek grey, each weatherboard sat in perfect alignment with its neighbour—and, considering the battering the place must take from sand, salt, sun and wind, that was a testament to the superior materials used and to whoever had built it. The best that money could buy, no doubt. The galvanised tin roof shone in the sunlight. There was even a chimney, which must mean there was an open fire. *Nice!* Winter might be relatively mild here on the mid-north coast of New South Wales, but she didn't doubt the nights could be chilly.

She pulled her cardigan about her more tightly. Still, shut up as it was, the house looked cold and unwelcoming even in all this glorious sunshine.

There's only one way to change that.

Casting a final longing glance back behind her, she set her shoulders and strode towards the house, mounting the six steps to the veranda two at a time.

A piece of paper, stark white against the grey wood, was taped to the door with *'Ms Anderson'* slashed across it in a dark felt-tipped pen. Jo peeled the note away. Was Mac out? And was he going to insist on the formality of 'Ms Anderson' and 'Mr MacCallum'?

Ms Anderson
I don't like to be disturbed while I'm working so let yourself in. Your room is on the ground floor beyond the kitchen. There should be absolutely no need for you to venture up onto the first floor.

She let out a low laugh. Oh, so that was what he thought, huh?

He finished with:

*I eat at seven. Please leave a tray on the table at
the bottom of the stairs and I'll collect it when I take
a break from my work.*

She folded the note and shoved it in her pocket. She
opened the front door and propped a cast-iron rooster that
she assumed to be the doorstop against it, and then latched
the screen door back against the house before going to the
car and collecting her cases. And then she strode into the
house as if she owned it—head high, shoulders back, spine
straight.

Malcolm 'Mac' MacCallum had another think coming
if he thought they were going to spend the next two months
or so communicating via notes.

She dropped her suitcases in the hallway, wrinkling her
nose at the musty scent of old air and neglect. A large reception room lay to her right. She strode in and flung open
the curtains at the three large windows to let light spill into
the room. She turned and blew out a breath.

Look at all this gorgeous furniture.

Antiques mingled with newer pieces, creating an elegant warmth that reminded her again of Mac's success. She
glared at a gorgeous leather chair. What use was success if
it made you forget the people who loved you? Mac hadn't
visited Russ once since Russ's heart attack. She transferred
her glare to the ceiling, before shaking herself and glancing around the room again. It was all in serious need of
spit and polish.

She grimaced. Tomorrow.

She turned her back on it to open the windows. The
sound of the sea entered first, and then its scent. She
straightened. That was better.

She found her room at the back of the house. Someone
had made a half-hearted effort at cleaning it. Mac, she supposed. According to Russ, the last cleaning lady had left

over a month ago. It would do for now. She'd tackle that to-morrow as well.

Her window looked out over an unkempt lawn to a ga-rage. She lifted the window higher. She might not have a room with a view, but she could still hear the ocean. She leant against the windowsill, reaching out to touch a bank-sia flower on the nearby tree.

A moment later she drew her hand back, a breath shud-dering out of her as she thought back to that stupid note stuck to the door. Perhaps this wasn't such a good idea. Turning her life upside down like this was probably fool-hardy, irresponsible—even insane. After all, geology wasn't so bad and—

It's not so good either.

She bit her lip and then straightened. She'd gone into ge-ology to please her father. For all the good it had done her. She wasn't concerned with pleasing him any longer.

She'd remained in the field to keep the peace. She didn't want just to keep the peace any more—she wanted to create a new world where peace reigned…at least in her little part of it. She'd stayed where she was because she was fright-ened of change. Well, Russ's heart attack had taught her that there were worse things than fear of change.

Fear of regret and fear of wasting her life were two of those things. She couldn't afford to lose heart now. She wanted a future she could look forward to. She wanted a future that would make her proud. She wanted a future that mattered. That was what she was doing here. That wasn't foolhardy, irresponsible or insane. On the contrary.

But…what about Mac? What was she going to do? Fol-low instructions today and then try to corner him tomor-row? Or—?

Her phone buzzed in her pocket. She glanced at the caller ID before lifting it to her ear. 'Hey, Russ.'

'Are you there yet?'

'Yep.'

'How's Mac?'

She swallowed. *Or not follow instructions?*

'I've only just this very minute arrived, so I haven't clapped eyes on him yet, but let me tell you the view here is amazing. Your brother has found the perfect place to…'

What? Recuperate? He'd had enough time to recuperate. Work without distractions? Hole up?

'The perfect place to hide away from the world.' Russell sighed.

Russ was fifty-two and recovering from a heart attack. He was scheduled for bypass surgery in a few weeks. She wasn't adding to his stress if she could help it.

'The perfect place for inspiration,' she countered. 'The scenery is gorgeous. Wait until you see it and then you'll know what I mean. I'll send you photos.'

'Does a body need inspiration to write a cookbook?'

She had no idea. 'Cooking and making up recipes are creative endeavours, aren't they? And isn't there some theory that creativity is boosted by the negative ions of moving water? Anyway, there's lots of deserted beach to walk and rolling hills to climb. It's a good place to come and get strong—away from prying eyes.'

'You think so?'

'Absolutely. Give me an hour, Russ, and I'll call you back when I have something concrete to tell you, okay?'

'I can't thank you enough for doing this, Jo.'

'We both know that in this instance it's you who's doing me the favour.'

It wasn't wholly a lie.

She'd known Russ for eight years. They'd hit if off from the first day she'd walked into the mining company's Outback office, with her brand-new soil sample kit and her work boots that still held a shine. Their teasing, easy rapport had developed into a genuine friendship. He'd been her boss, her mentor, and one of the best friends she'd ever had—but in all that time she'd never met his brother.

After his heart attack she'd confided in Russ—told him she wanted out of geology and away from the Outback. She grimaced. She'd also told him she couldn't go back to Sydney until she'd developed a plan. Her jobless situation would only provide Grandma and Great-Aunt Edith with more ammunition to continue their silly feud. Battle lines would be drawn and Jo would find herself smack-bang in the middle of them. She was already smack-bang in the middle of them! No more. She was tired of living her life to meet other people's expectations.

She pulled in a breath. When she was working in a job she loved and doing things that made her happy, the people who loved her—Grandma and Great-Aunt Edith—would be happy for her too. She squinted out of the window. If only she could figure out what it was that would make her happy.

She chafed her arms, suddenly cold. All she knew was that another twenty years down the track she didn't want to look back and feel she'd wasted her life.

When Russ had found all that out he'd laughed and rubbed his hands together. 'Jo,' he'd said, 'I've just the job for you.'

And here she was.

She glanced around, her nose wrinkling.

She loved Russ dearly. She enjoyed his twisted sense of humour, admired the values he upheld, and she respected the man he was. She did not, however, hold out the same hopes for his brother.

She planted her hands on her hips. A brother did not desert his family when they needed him. Russ had been there for Mac every step of the way, but Mac had been nowhere to be found when Russ had needed him. But here she was, all the same. Mac's hired help. She didn't even know what her official job title was—cook, cleaner, housekeeper? Russ had dared her to don a French maid's outfit. Not in this lifetime!

Russ needed someone to make sure Mac was getting three square meals a day and not living in squalor—someone who could be trusted not to go racing to the press. At heart, though, Jo knew Russ just wanted to make sure his little brother was okay.

Cue Jo. Still, this job would provide her with the peace and quiet to work out where she wanted to go from here.

She pulled Mac's note from her pocket and stared at it.

There should be absolutely no reason for you to venture onto the first floor.

Oh, yes, there was.

Without giving herself too much time to think, she headed straight for the stairs.

There were five doors on the first floor, if she didn't count the door to the linen closet. Four of them stood wide open—a bathroom and three bedrooms. Mind you, all the curtains in each of those rooms were drawn, so it was dark as Hades up here. The fourth door stood resolutely closed. *Do Not Disturb* vibes radiated from it in powerful waves.

'Guess which one the prize is behind?' she murmured under her breath, striding up to it.

She lifted her hand and knocked. *Rat-tat-tat!* The noise bounced up and down the hallway. No answer. Nothing.

She knocked again, even louder. 'Mac, are you in there?'

To hell with calling him Mr MacCallum. Every Tuesday night for the last five years she'd sat with Russ, watching Mac on the television. For eight years she'd listened to Russ talk about his brother. He would be Mac to her forever.

She suddenly stiffened. What if he was hurt or sick?

'Go away!'

She rolled her eyes. '"There was movement at the station."'

'Can't you follow instructions?'

Ooh, that was a veritable growl. 'I'm afraid not. I'm coming in.'

She pushed the door open.

'What the hell?' The single light at the desk was immediately clicked off. 'Get out! I told you I didn't want to be disturbed.'

'Correction. An anonymous note informed me that someone didn't want to be disturbed.' It took a moment for her eyes to adjust to the darkness. She focussed on that rather than the snarl in his voice. 'Anyone could've left that note. For all I knew you could've been slain while you slept.'

He threw his arms out. 'Not slain. See? Now, get out.'

'I'd like nothing better,' she said, strolling across the room.

'What the hell do you think you're—?'

He broke off when she flung the curtains back. She pulled in a breath, staring at the newly revealed balcony and the magnificent view beyond. 'Getting a good look at you,' she said, before turning around.

The sight that met her shocked her to the core. She had no hope of hiding it. She reached out a hand to steady herself against the glass doors.

'Happy?'

His lips twisted in a snarl that made her want to flee. She swallowed and shook her head. 'No.' How could she be happy? He was going to break his brother's heart.

'Shocked?' he mocked with an ugly twist of his lips.

The left side of his face and neck were red, tight and raw with the post-burn scarring from his accident. His too-long blond hair had clumped in greasy unbrushed strands. Dark circles rimmed red eyes. The grey pallor of his skin made her stomach churn.

'To the marrow,' she choked out.

And in her mind the first lines of that Banjo Paterson poem went round and round in her head.

There was movement at the station,
for the word had passed around
That the colt from old Regret had got away

Regret. Got away. She suddenly wished with everything inside her that *she* could get away. Leave.

And go where? What would she tell Russ?

She swallowed and straightened. 'It smells dreadful in here.'

Too close and sour and hot. She slid the door open, letting the sea breeze dance over her. She filled her lungs with it even though his scowl deepened.

'I promised Russ I'd clap eyes on you, as no one else seems to have done so in months.'

'He sent you here as a spy?'

'He sent me here as a favour.'

'I don't need any favours!'

Not a favour for you. But she didn't say that out loud. 'No. I suspect what you really need is a psychiatrist.'

His jaw dropped.

She pulled herself up to her full height of six feet and folded her arms. 'Is that what you *really* want me to report back to Russ? That you're in a deep depression and possibly suicidal?'

His lips drew together tightly over his teeth. 'I am neither suicidal nor depressed.'

'Right.' She drew the word out, injecting as much disbelief into her voice as she could. 'For the last four months you've sat shut up in this dark house, refusing to see a soul. I suspect you barely sleep and barely eat.' She wrinkled her nose. 'And when was the last time you had a shower?'

His head rocked back.

'These are not the actions of a reasonable or rational adult. What interpretation would you put on them if you were coming in from the outside? What conclusion do you think Russ would come to?'

For a moment she thought he might have paled at her words—except he was already so pale it was impossible to tell. She rubbed a hand across her chest. She understood that one had to guard against sunburn on burn scars, but avoiding the light completely was ludicrous.

He said nothing. He just stared at her as if seeing her for the first time. Which just went to show how preoccupied he must have been. When most people saw her for the first time they usually performed a comical kind of double-take at her sheer size. Not that she'd ever found anything remotely humorous about it. So what? She was tall. And, no, she wasn't dainty. It didn't make her a circus freak.

'Damn you, Mac!' She found herself shouting at him, and she didn't know where it came from but it refused to be suppressed. 'How can you be so selfish? Russell is recovering from a heart attack. He needs bypass surgery. He needs calm and peace and…' Her heart dropped with a sickening thud. 'And now I'm going to have to tell him…' She faltered, not wanting to put into words Mac's pitiable condition. She didn't have the heart for it.

Mac still didn't speak, even though the ferocity and outrage had drained from his face. She shook her head and made for the door.

'At least I didn't waste any time unpacking.'

It wasn't until the woman— What was her name again? Jo Anderson? It wasn't until she'd disappeared through his bedroom door that he realised what she meant to do.

She meant to leave.

She meant to leave and tell Russ that Mac needed to be

sectioned or something daft. Hell, the press would have a field-day with *that*! But she was right about one thing—Russ didn't need the added stress of worrying about Mac. Mac had enough guilt on that head as it was, and he wasn't adding to it.

'Wait!' he hollered.

He bolted after her, hurling himself down the stairs, knocking into walls and stumbling, his body heavy and unfamiliar as if it didn't belong to him any more. By the time he reached the bottom he was breathing hard.

He'd used to jog five kilometres without breaking a sweat.

When was the last time he'd jogged?

When was the last time you had a shower?

He dragged a hand down his face. God help him.

He shook himself back into action and surged forward, reaching the front door just as she lugged her cases down the front steps. Sunlight. Sea air. He pulled up as both pounded at him, caressing him, mocking him. He didn't want to notice how good they felt. But they felt better than good.

And they'd both distract him from his work. *Work you won't get a chance to complete if Jo Anderson walks away.*

He forced himself forward, through the door. 'Please, Ms Anderson—wait.'

She didn't stop. The woman was built like an Amazon—tall and regal. It hurt him to witness the fluid grace and elegance of her movements. In the same way the sunlight and the sea breeze hurt him. It hurt him to witness her strength and the tilt of her chin and the dark glossiness of her hair.

Jo Anderson was, quite simply, stunning. Like the sunlight and the sea breeze. There was something just as elemental about her, and it made him not want to mess with her, but he had to get her to stop. And that meant messing with her.

With his heart thumping, he forced himself across the

veranda until he stood fully in the sun. His face started to burn. The burning wasn't real, but being outside made him feel exposed and vulnerable. He forced himself down the steps.

'Jo, please don't leave.'

She stopped at his use of her first name.

Say something that will make her lower her cases to the ground.

His heart hammered and his mouth dried as the breeze seared across his skin. It took all his strength not to flinch as the sun warmed his face. He dragged a breath of air into his lungs—fresh sea air—and it provided him with the answer he needed.

'I'm sorry.'

He sent up a prayer of thanks when she lowered her cases and turned. 'Are you really? I suspect you're merely sorry someone's called you on whatever game it is you've been playing.'

Game? *Game!* He closed his eyes and reined in his temper. He couldn't afford to alienate her further.

'Please don't take tales back to Russ that will cause him worry. He…he needs… He doesn't need the stress.'

She stared at him. She had eyes the colour of sage. He briefly wondered if sage was the elusive ingredient he'd been searching for all morning, before shaking the thought away.

Jo tilted her chin and narrowed her eyes. 'I don't take anyone's wellbeing or health for granted, Mac. Not any more. And—'

'This is *my* life we're talking about,' he cut in. 'Don't I get any say in the matter?'

'I'd treat you like an adult if you'd been acting like one.'

'You can't make that judgement based on five minutes' acquaintance. I've been having a *very* bad day.' He widened his stance. 'What do I need to do to convince you that I am, in fact, neither depressed nor suicidal?'

He would not let her go worrying Russ with this. He would *not* be responsible for physically harming yet another person.

She folded her arms and stuck out a hip—a rather lush, curvaceous hip—and a pulse started up deep inside him.

'What do you need to do to convince me? Oh, Mac, that's going to take some doing.'

Her voice washed over him like warm honey. It was a warmth that didn't sting.

For no reason at all his pulse kicked up a notch. He envied her vigour and conviction. She stalked up to him to peer into his face. To try to read his motives, he suspected. She was only an inch or two shorter than him, and she smelt like freshly baked bread. His mouth watered.

Then he recalled the look in her eyes when she'd recovered from her first sight of him and he angled the left side of his face away from her. Her horror hadn't dissolved into pity—which was something, he supposed. It had been scorn. Her charge of selfishness had cut through to his very marrow, slicing through the hard shell of his guilt and anger.

'Stay for a week,' he found himself pleading.

His mouth twisted. Once upon a time he'd been able to wrap any woman around his little finger. He'd flash a slow smile or a cheeky grin and don the charm. He suspected that wouldn't work on this woman. Not now. And not back then, when he'd still been pretty, either.

Mind you, it seemed he'd lost his charm at about the same time he'd lost his looks. Now he looked like a monster.

It doesn't mean you have to act like one, though.

Her low laugh drizzled over him like the syrup for his Greek lemon cake.

'I believe you're serious...'

Yeah? Well, at the very least it'd buy Russ another week of rest and—

What the hell? This woman didn't know him from Adam. She had no idea what he was capable of. He pulled himself upright—fully upright—and the stretch felt good.

'Name your price.'

He wasn't sure if it was more scorn or humour that flitted through her eyes. She straightened too, but he still had a good two inches on her. She could try and push him around all she wanted. He—

He grimaced. Yeah, well, if he didn't want her worrying Russ she *could* push him around. Whoever happened to be bigger in this particular scenario didn't make a scrap of difference.

He thrust out his chin. Still, he *was* bigger.

'Name my price?'

He swallowed. She had a voice made for radio—a kind of solid-gold croon that would soothe any angry beast.

'Well, for a start I'd want to see you exercising daily.'

It took a moment for the import of her words rather than their sound to reach him.

Risk being seen in public? *No!* He—

'During daylight hours,' she continued remorselessly. 'You need vitamin D and to lose that awful pallor.'

'You do know I've been ill, don't you?' he demanded. 'That I've been in hospital?'

'You haven't been in hospital for months. Do you have *any* idea how much you've let yourself go? You used to have a strong, lean body and lovely broad shoulders.'

Which were still broader than hers. Though he didn't point that out.

'And you used to move with a lanky, easy saunter. Now…? Now you look about fifty.'

He glared. He was only forty.

'And not a good fifty either. You look as if I could snap you in half.'

He narrowed his eyes. 'I wouldn't advise you to try that.'

She blinked and something chased itself across her face, as if she'd suddenly realised he was a man—a living, breathing man—rather than a job or a problem she had to solve.

Not that it meant she fancied him or anything stupid like that. How could anyone fancy him now? But…

For the first time since the fire he suddenly *felt* like a living, breathing man.

'If you want me to change my mind about you, Mac, I want to see you walk down to the beach and back every day. It's all your own property, so you don't need to be worried about bumping into strangers if you're that jealous of your privacy.'

'The beach is public land.' He had neighbours who walked on it every day.

'I didn't say you had to walk *along* it—just down to it.'

'The land that adjoins my property to the north—' he gestured to the left '—is all national park.' There'd be the occasional hiker.

'So walk along that side of your land, then.' She gestured to the right and then folded her arms. 'I'm simply answering your question. If you find daily exercise too difficult, then I've probably made my point.'

He clenched his jaw, breathed in for the count of five and then unclenched it to ask, 'What else?'

'I'd like you to separate your work and sleep areas. A defined routine to your day will help me believe you have a handle on things. Hence a workspace that's separate from your bedroom.'

He glared at her. 'Fine—whatever. And…?'

'I'd also want you to give up alcohol. Or at least drinking bourbon in your room on your own.'

She'd seen the bottle. *Damn!*

'Finally, I'd want you to take your evening meal in the dining room with me.'

So she could keep an eye on him—assess his mental state. He could feel his nostrils flare as he dragged in a breath. He was tempted to tell her to go to hell, except...

Except he might have given up caring about himself, but he hadn't given up caring about Russ. His brother might be eleven and a half years older than Mac, but they'd always been close. Russ had always looked out for him. The least Mac could do now was look out for Russ in whatever limited capacity he could. With Russ's health so tenuous Mac couldn't risk adding to his stress levels.

Jo's phone rang. She pulled it from the back pocket of her jeans. He stared at that hip and something stirred inside him. And then desire hit him—hot and hard. He blinked. He turned away to hide the evidence, adjusting his jeans as he pretended an interest in the horizon.

What on earth...? He liked his women slim and compact, polished and poised. Jo Anderson might be poised, but as for the rest of it...

He dragged a hand back through his hair. There was no denying, though, that his body reacted to her like a bee to honey. He swallowed. It was probably to be expected, right? He'd been cooped up here away from all human contact for four months. This was just a natural male reaction to the female form.

'I don't know, Russ.'

That snapped him back.

'Yeah...' She flicked a glance in his direction. 'I've seen him.'

Mac winced at her tone.

'You have yourself a deal.' He pitched his words low, so they wouldn't carry down the phone to Russ, but they still came out savage. He couldn't help it. He held up one finger. 'Give me one week.'

'Hmm… Well, he's looking a little peaky—as if he's had the flu or a tummy bug.'

He seized her free hand. Startled sage eyes met his. 'Please,' he whispered.

The softness and warmth of her hand seeped into him and almost made him groan, and then her hand tightened about his and his mouth went dry in a millisecond.

When she shook herself free of him a moment later he let out a breath he hadn't even realised he'd been holding.

'I expect it's nothing that a bit of rest, gentle exercise, home-cooked food and sun won't put to rights in a week or two.'

He closed his eyes and gave thanks.

'Nah, I promise. I won't take any risks. I'll call a doctor in if he hasn't picked up in a few days. Here—you want to talk to him?'

And before Mac could shake his head and back away he found the phone thrust out to him.

He swallowed the bile that rose in his throat and took it. 'Hey, Russ, how you doing?'

'Better than you, by the sounds of it. Though it explains why you haven't answered my last two calls.'

He winced. 'It's all I've been able to do to keep up with my email.' *I'm sorry, bro.* He hadn't been good for anyone. Least of all his brother.

'Well, you listen to Jo, okay? She's got a good head on her shoulders.'

He glanced at said head and noticed how the wavy dark hair gleamed in the sun, and how cute little freckles sprinkled a path across the bridge of her nose. She had a rather cute nose. She cocked an eyebrow and he cleared his throat.

'Will do,' he forced himself to say.

'Good. I want you in the best of health when I come to visit.'

He choked back a cough. Russ was coming to visit?

'Give my love to Jo.'

With that, Russ hung up. Mac stared at Jo. 'When is he coming to visit?'

She shrugged and plucked her phone from his fingers.

'Why is he coming?'

'Oh, that one's easy. Because he loves you. He wants to see you before he goes under the knife.' She met his gaze. 'In case he doesn't wake up after the operation.'

'That's crazy.'

'Is it?'

'Russ is going to be just fine!' His brother didn't need to exert himself in any fashion until he was a hundred per cent fit again.

She stared at him for a long moment. 'Are you familiar with the Banjo Paterson poem "The Man From Snowy River"?'

Her question threw him. 'Sure.'

'Can you remember what comes after the first couple of lines? "There was movement at the station, for the word had passed around that the colt from old Regret had got away…"'

'"And had joined the wild bush horses—he was worth a thousand pound, So all the cracks had gathered to the fray",' he recited. His class had memorised that in the third grade.

'Wild… Worth… Fray…' she murmured in that honeyed liquid sunshine voice of hers.

'Why?'

She shook herself. 'No reason. Just an earworm.'

She seized her suitcases and strode back towards the house with them, and he couldn't help feeling his fate had just been sealed by a poem.

And then it hit him.

Honey! The ingredient he'd been searching for was honey.

CHAPTER TWO

JO TOOK A couple of deep breaths before spooning spaghetti and meatballs onto two plates. If Mac said something cutting about her efforts in the kitchen she'd—

She'd dump the contents of his plate in his lap?

She let out a slow breath. It was a nice fantasy, but she wouldn't. She'd just act calm and unconcerned, as she always did, and pretend the slings and arrows didn't touch her.

Seizing the plates, she strode into the dining room. She set one in front of Mac and the other at her place opposite. He didn't so much as glance at the food, but he did glare at her. Was he going to spend the entire week sulking?

What fun.

She stared back, refusing to let him cow her. She'd expected the shouting and the outrage. After all, he wasn't known as 'Mad Mac'—television's most notorious and demanding celebrity chef—for nothing. The tabloids had gone to town on him after the accident, claiming it would never have happened if 'Mad Mac' hadn't been so intimidating.

She bit back a sigh. It was all nonsense, of course. She'd had the inside scoop on Mac from Russ. She knew all of that onscreen TV shouting had been a front—a ploy to send the ratings skyrocketing. It had worked too. So it hadn't surprised her that he'd donned that persona when she'd stormed in on him earlier. But the sulking threw her.

'What?' he bit out when she continued to stare.

She shook herself. 'For what we are about to receive, may the Lord make us truly thankful. Amen.' She picked up her cutlery and sliced into a meatball.

'You're religious?'

'No.' The prayer had just seemed a convenient way to handle an awkward silence. 'I mean, I do believe in something bigger than us—whatever that may be.'

Mac didn't say anything. He didn't even move to pick up his cutlery.

She forged on. 'One of the guys on the mineral exploration camps was a Christian and we all got into the habit of saying Grace. It's nice. It doesn't hurt to remember the things we should be grateful for.'

His frown deepened to a scowl. 'You really think that's going to work? You really think you can make my life seem okay just by—?'

She slammed her knife and fork down. 'Not everything is about you, Mac.' She forced her eyes wide. 'Some of it might even be about me.' Couldn't he at least look at his food? He needn't think it would taste any better cold. 'Your attitude sucks. You know that? Frankly, I don't care if you've decided to self-destruct or not, but you can darn well wait until after Russ has recovered from his bypass surgery to do it.'

'You're not exactly polite company, are you?'

'Neither are you. Besides, I refuse to put any effort into being good company for as long as you sulk. I'm not your mother. It's not my job to cajole you into a better temper.'

His jaw dropped.

And he still hadn't touched his food.

'Eat something, Mac. If we're busy eating we can abandon any pretence at small talk.'

A laugh choked out of him and just for a moment it transformed him. Oh, the burn scars on the left side of his face and neck were still as angry and livid as ever, but his

mouth hooked up and his eyes momentarily brightened and
he held his head at an angle she remembered from his television show.

It was why she was still here. Earlier this afternoon he'd
fired up—not with humour, but with intensity and passion.
He'd become the man she'd recognised from the TV, but
also from Russ's descriptions. *That* was a man she could
work with.

Finally he did as she bade and forked a small mouthful
of meatball and sauce into his mouth. When he didn't gag,
a knot of tension eased out of her.

'This isn't bad.' He ate some more and frowned. 'In fact,
it's pretty good.'

Yeah, right. He was just trying to butter her up, frightened of what she might tell Russ.

'Actually, it's very good—considering the state of the
pantry.'

She almost believed him. Almost. 'I'll need to shop for
groceries tomorrow. I understand we're halfway between
Forster and Taree here. Any suggestions for where I should
go?'

'No.'

When he didn't add anything she shook her head and
set to eating. It had been a long day and she was tired and
hungry. She halted with half a meatball practically in her
mouth when she realised he'd stopped eating and was staring at her.

'What?'

'I wasn't being rude. It's just that I haven't been to either town. I was getting groceries delivered from a super-
market in Forster.'

'Was?'

He scowled. 'The delivery man couldn't follow instructions.'

Ah. Said delivery man had probably encroached on

Mac's precious privacy. 'Right. Well, I'll try my luck in Forster, then.' She'd seen signposts for the town before turning off to Mac's property.

He got back to work on the plate in front of him with… She blinked. With *gusto*? Heat spread through her stomach. *Oh, don't be ridiculous!* He'd had his own TV show. He was a consummate actor. But the heat didn't dissipate.

She pulled in a breath. 'I'm hoping Russ warned you that I'm not much of a cook.'

He froze. Very slowly he lowered his cutlery. 'Russ said you were a good plain cook. On this evening's evidence I'd agree with him.' His face turned opaque. 'You're feeling intimidated cooking for a…?'

'World-renowned chef?' she finished for him. 'Yes, a little. I just want you to keep your expectations within that realm of plain, please.'

She bit back a sigh. Plain—what a boring word. *Beauty is as beauty does.* The old adage sounded through her mind. *Yeah, yeah, whatever.*

'I promise not to criticise your cooking. I will simply be…' he grimaced '…grateful for whatever you serve up. You don't need to worry that I'll be secretly judging your technique.'

'I expect there'd be nothing secret about it. I think you'd be more than happy to share your opinions on the matter.'

His lips twitched.

'Is there anything you don't eat?' she rushed on, not wanting to dwell on those lips for too long.

He shook his head.

'Is there anything in particular you'd like me to serve?'

He shook his head again.

There was something else she'd meant to ask him… *Oh, that's right.* 'You have a garage…'

They both reached for the plate of garlic bread at the same time. He waited for her to take a slice first. He had nice hands. She remembered admiring them when she'd watched him on TV. Lean, long-fingered hands that looked strong and—

'The garage?'

She shook herself. 'Would there be room for me to park my car in there? I expect this sea air is pretty tough on a car's bodywork.'

'Feel free.'

'Thank you.'

They both crunched garlic bread. He watched her from the corner of his eye. She chewed and swallowed, wondering what he made of her. She sure as heck wasn't like the women he was forever being photographed with in the papers. For starters she was as tall as a lot of men, and more athletic than most.

Not Mac, though. Even in his current out-of-form condition he was still taller and broader than her—though she might give him a run for his money in an arm wrestle at the moment.

Her stomach tightened. He was probably wondering what god he'd cheesed off to have a woman like *her* landing on his doorstep. Mac was a golden boy. Beautiful. And she was the opposite. Not that *that* had anything to do with anything. What he thought of her physically made no difference whatsoever.

Except, of course, it did. It always mattered.

'You've shown a lot of concern for Russ.'

Her head came up. 'Yes?'

He scowled at her. 'Are you in love with him? He's too old for you, you know.'

It surprised her so much she laughed. 'You're kidding, right?' She swept her garlic bread through the leftover sauce on her plate.

His frown deepened. 'No.'

'I love your brother as a friend, but I'm not in love with

him. Lord, what a nightmare *that* would be.' She sat back and wiped her fingers on a serviette.

'Why?'

'I'm not a masochist. You and your brother have similar tastes in women. You both date petite, perfectly made-up blondes who wear killer heels and flirty dresses.' She hadn't packed a dress. She didn't even own a pair of heels.

He pushed his plate away, his face darkening. 'How the hell do *you* know what type I like?' He turned sideways in his chair to cross his legs. It hid his scarring from her view.

'It's true I'm basing my assumption on who you've been snapped with in the tabloids and what Russ has told me.'

'You make us sound shallow.'

If the shoe fits...

'But I can assure you that the women you just described wouldn't look twice at me now.'

'Only if they were superficial.'

His head jerked up.

'And beauty and superficiality don't necessarily go hand in hand.'

No more than plain and stupid, or plain and thick-skinned.

He opened his mouth, but she continued on over the top of him. 'Anyway, you're not going to get any sympathy from me on that. I've never been what people consider beautiful. I've learned to value other things. You think people will no longer find you beautiful—

'I *know* they won't!'

He was wrong, but... 'So welcome to the club.'

His jaw dropped.

'It's not the end of the world, you know?'

He stared at her for a long moment and then leaned across the table. 'What the hell are you *really* doing here, Jo Anderson?'

She stared back at him, and inside she started to weep—

because she wanted to ask this man to teach her to cook and he was so damaged and angry that she knew he would toss her request on the rubbish heap and not give it so much as the time of day.

Something in his eyes gentled. 'Jo?'

Now wasn't the time to raise the subject. It was becoming abundantly clear that there might never be a good time.

She waved a hand in the air. 'The answer is twofold.' It wasn't a lie. 'I'm here to make sure you don't undo all the hard work I've put into Russ.'

He sat back. 'Hard work?'

She should rise and clear away their plates, clean the kitchen, but he deserved some answers. 'Do you know how hard, how physically demanding, it is to perform CPR for five straight minutes?' Which was what she'd done for Russ.

He shook his head, his eyes darkening.

'It's really hard. And all the while your mind is screaming in panic and making deals with the universe.'

'Deals?'

'Please let Russ live and I'll never say another mean word about anyone ever again. Please let Russ live and I promise to be a better granddaughter and great-niece. Please let Russ live and I'll do whatever you ask, will face my worst fears… Blah, blah, blah.' She pushed her hair back off her face. 'You know—the usual promises that are nearly impossible to keep.' She stared down at her glass of water. 'It was the longest five minutes of my life.'

'But Russ did live. You did save his life. It's an extraordinary thing.'

'Yes.'

'And now you want to make sure that I don't harm his recovery?'

'Something like that.'

'Which is why you're here—to check up on me so you can ease Russ's mind?'

'He was going to come himself, and that didn't seem wise.'

Mac turned grey.

'But you don't have it quite right. Russ is doing me a favour, organising this job for me.'

He remained silent, not pressing her, and she was grateful for that.

'You see, Russ's heart attack and my fear that he was going to die brought me face to face with my own mortality.'

He flinched and she bit back a curse. What did she know about mortality compared to this man? She reached across to clasp his hand in a sign of automatic sympathy, but he froze. A bad taste rose in her mouth and she pulled her hand back into her lap. Her heart pounded. He wouldn't welcome her touch. Of course he wouldn't.

'I expect you know what I'm talking about.'

Mac's accident had left him with serious burns, but it had left a young apprentice fighting for his life. She remembered Russ's relief when the young man had finally been taken off the critical list.

'What I'm trying to say is that it's made me reassess my life. It's forced me to admit I wasn't very happy, that I didn't really like my job. I don't want to spend the next twenty years feeling like that.'

She blew out a breath.

'So when Russ found out you needed a housekeeper and mentioned it to me I jumped at the chance. It'll give me two or three months to come up with a game plan.'

Mac stared at her. 'You're changing careers?'

'Uh-huh.' She looked a bit green.

'To do what?'

She turned greener. 'I have absolutely no idea.'

He knew that feeling.

Mac didn't want to be touched by her story—he didn't

want to be touched by anything—but he was. Maybe it was the sheer simplicity of the telling, the lack of fanfare. Or maybe it was because he understood that sense of dissatisfaction she described. He'd stalled out here in his isolation and his self-pity while she was determined to surge forward.

Maybe if he watched her he'd learn—

He cut that thought off. He didn't deserve the chance to move forward. He'd ruined a man's life. He deserved to spend the rest of his life making amends.

But not at the expense of other people. Like Russ. Or Jo.

'You're wrong, you know?'

She glanced up. 'About…?'

'You seem to think you're plain—invisible, even.' *Not beautiful.*

'Invisible?' She snorted. 'I'm six feet tall with a build some charitably call generous. Invisible is the one thing I'm not.'

'Generous' was the perfect word to describe her. She had glorious curves in all the right places. A fact that his male hormones acknowledged and appreciated even while his brain told him to leave that well enough alone.

He leaned back, careful to keep the good side of his face to her. 'You're a very striking woman.' *Don't drool.* 'So what if you're tall? You're in proportion.' She looked strong, athletic and full of life. 'You have lovely eyes, your hair is shiny, and you have skin that most women would kill for. You may not fit in with conventional magazine cover ideals of beauty, but it doesn't mean you aren't beautiful. Stop selling yourself short. I can assure you that you're not plain.'

She gaped at him. It made him scowl and shuffle back in his seat. 'Well, you're not.'

She snapped her mouth shut. She wiped her hands down the front of her shirt, which only proved to him how truly womanly she happened to be. The colour in her cheeks deepened as if she'd read that thought in his face.

'There's another reason I'm here,' she blurted out.

The hurried confession and the way her words tripped over themselves, the fact that she looked cute when flustered, all conspired to make him want to grin. He couldn't remember the last time he'd smiled, let alone grinned. He resisted the urge now too. In the end, grinning... Well, it would just make things harder, in the same way the sunlight and the sea breeze did.

But he did take pity on her. 'Another reason?' he prompted.

She moistened her lips. Like the rest of her they were generous, and full of promise.

'Mac, one of the reasons I came out here was to ask if you would teach me to cook.' She grimaced. 'Well, if we're being completely accurate, if you'd teach me to make a *macaron* tower.'

His every muscle froze. His nerve-endings started to scream. For a moment all he could see in his mind was fire—all red and heat. A lump the size of a saucepan wedged in his throat. It took three goes to swallow it.

'No.' The word croaked out of him.

He closed his eyes to force air into protesting lungs and then opened them again, his skin growing slick with perspiration.

'No.' The single word came out cold and clear. 'That's out of the question. I don't cook any more.'

'But—'

'Ever.' He pinned her with his gaze and knew it must be pitiless when she shivered. 'It's absolutely out of the question.'

He rose.

'Now if you don't mind. I'm going to do a bit of work

before I retire for the night. I'll move my sleeping quarters to the end bedroom tomorrow.'

She seemed to gather herself. 'I'll clean it first thing.'

That reminded him that she meant to do a grocery shop tomorrow too. 'There's housekeeping money in the tin on the mantel in the kitchen.'

'Right.'

He hated the way she surveyed him. Turning his back, he left, forcing knees that trembled to carry him up the stairs and into his room. He lowered himself to the chair at his desk and dropped his head to his hands, did what he could to quieten the scream stretching through his brain.

Teach Jo to cook?

Impossible.

His chest pounded in time with his temples. Blood surged in his ears, deafening him. He didn't know how long it took for the pounding to slow, for his chest to unclench, and for his breathing to regain a more natural rhythm. It felt like a lifetime.

Eventually he lifted his head. He couldn't teach her to cook. She'd saved his brother's life and he owed her, but he couldn't teach her to cook.

He rose and went to the double glass doors. With the curtains pushed back they stood open to the moonlight. Below, starlight dappled navy water. He couldn't teach her to cook, but he could do everything else she'd asked of him. He could ensure that Russ didn't have one thing to worry about on Mac's account.

One week of halfway human behaviour? He could manage that.

He thought back to the way he'd just left the dining room and dragged a hand through his hair. She must think him a madman. Hauling in a breath, he rested his forehead against cool glass. He might not be able to help her on the cooking front, but could he help her in her search for a new vocation?

The sooner she found a new direction the sooner she'd go, leaving him in peace again. A low, savage laugh scraped from his throat. He would never find peace. He didn't deserve it. But he could have her gone. He'd settle for that.

Mac had been awake for over an hour before he heard Jo's firm tread on the stairs. She moved past his door and on to the bedroom at the end. No doubt to clean it, as she'd promised. The need for caffeine pounded through him. So far he'd resisted it—not ready to face Jo yet.

He blamed the light pouring in at the windows. It had disorientated him.

Liar. It wasn't the light but a particular woman he found disorientating.

He could bolt down to the kitchen now, while she was busy up here.

Yeah, like *that* would convince her to tell Russ all was fine and dandy. He flung the covers back, pulled on a clean pair of jeans and a sweater, and stomped into the en-suite bathroom to splash water on his face. He stood by his bedroom door, counted to three, dragging in a breath on each count before opening it.

'Morning, Jo,' he called out. Amazingly his voice didn't emerge all hoarse and croaky as he'd expected.

She appeared at the end of the hallway. 'Good morning. Sleep well?'

Surprisingly, he had. 'Yeah, thanks.' He remembered his manners. 'And you?'

'No.'

She didn't add any further explanation. He took a step towards her, careful to keep the right side of his face to her. With all the curtains on this level now open there was a lot of light to contend with.

'Is there something wrong with your room? The bed? The mattress?'

She laughed and something inside him unhitched. 'I never sleep well in a new place the first night. Plus, I did a lot of driving yesterday and that always makes me feel unsettled. I'll sleep like a dream tonight.'

He rolled his shoulders. 'How long did you drive for?'

'Five hours.'

Five hours? And she'd arrived to… His stomach churned. She'd arrived to his bitterness, resentment and utter rudeness.

'Mac, we need to talk about my duties.'

That snapped him to.

'I mean, do you want me to make you a full cooked breakfast each morning? What about lunch?'

He noticed she didn't give him any quarter as far as dinner went. 'I'll help myself for breakfast and lunch.'

'Not a breakfast person, huh?'

He wasn't. He opened his mouth. He closed it again and waited for a lecture.

'Me neither,' she confessed. 'Most important meal of the day, blah, blah, blah.' She rolled her eyes. 'Just give me a coffee before I kill you.'

He laughed, but he was still careful to keep his good side to her. She hadn't flinched at his scars last night or so far this morning. But he knew what they looked like. He could at least spare her when he could.

One thing was for sure—she didn't treat him like an invalid, and he was grateful for it.

'There's a pot of freshly brewed coffee on the hob.'

He didn't need any further encouragement, and turned in the direction of the kitchen.

He swung back before he reached the stairs. 'Jo?'

Her head appeared in the bedroom doorway again.

'Don't bust a gut trying to get the house shipshape all at once, will you?' He'd long since dismissed his army of hired help. 'I've…uh…let it get away from me a bit.' At her raised eyebrow he amended that to 'A lot.'

She merely saluted him and went back to work. He made his way down to the kitchen, wondering if he'd passed the *don't worry Russ* test so far this morning. He poured himself a coffee, took a sip and closed his eyes. Man, the woman could make a fine brew.

Mac clocked the exact moment Jo returned from her shopping expedition.

His first instinct was to continue hiding out in his room. He stared at the half-written recipe on his computer screen and pushed to his feet. If he walked away and did something else for half an hour he might remember if he reduced the recipe's required infusion by a third or a quarter.

If he could just see it in the saucepan and smell it he'd have the answer in an instant and—

He cut the thought off with a curse and went to help Jo unpack the car. She'd only given him a week. He'd better make the most of it.

She glanced up when he strode out onto the veranda, and in the light of her grace and vigour he suddenly felt awkward and ungainly.

He scowled, unable to dredge up a single piece of small talk. 'I thought I'd help unpack the car.'

She pursed her lips and he realised he was still scowling. He did what he could to smooth his face out—the parts of his face he *could* smooth out.

'You have any trouble finding the shops?'

Heck. Scintillating conversation.

'None at all. You feeling okay, Mac?'

'I'm fine.' Striding to the car, he seized as many bags as he could and stalked back into the house with them.

It took them two trips.

He wasn't quite sure what to do after that, so he leant

against the sink and pretended to drink a glass of water as he watched her unpack the groceries. There were the expected trays of meat—hamburger mince, sausages, steak and diced beef. And then there was the unexpected and to be deplored—frozen pies and frozen pizza. Fish fingers, for heaven's sake!

He flicked a disparaging finger at the boxes. 'What are those?'

'I'm assuming you're not asking the question literally?'

She'd donned one of those mock patient voices used on troublesome children and it set his teeth on edge. 'Is this to punish me for refusing to teach you to cook?'

She turned from stowing stuff in the freezer, hands on hips. 'You told me you weren't a fussy eater.'

'This isn't *food*. It's processed pap!'

'You're free to refuse to eat anything I serve up.'

'But if I do you'll go running to Russ to tell tales?'

She grinned, and her relish both irked and amused him. She lifted one hand. 'Rock.' She lifted the other. 'Hard place.'

Which described his situation perfectly.

She grinned again and his mouth watered. She seized a packet of frozen pies and waved them at him. 'Pies, mash, peas and gravy is one of my all-time favourite, walk-over-hot-coals-to-get-it meals, and I'm not giving it up—not even for your high-falutin' standards. And before you ask—no, I haven't mastered the trick to pastry.' She shook her head. 'Life's too short to fuss with pastry. Or to stuff a mushroom.'

She was wrong. A perfect buttery pastry, light and delicate, was one of life's adventures. And mushroom-stuffing shouldn't be sneezed at. But why on earth would she ask him to teach her to cook if that was the way she felt?

'And I'll have you know that fish fingers on a fresh bun with a dollop of tartare sauce makes the best lunch.'

'I will *never* eat fish fingers.'

'All the more for me, then.'

He scowled at the pizza boxes.

'Also,' her lips twitched, 'as far as I'm concerned, there's no such thing as a bad slice of pizza.'

'That's ludicrous!'

'Don't be such a snob. Besides, all of this food is better than whatever it is you've been living on for the last heaven only knows how long. Which, as far as I can tell, has been tinned baked beans, crackers and breakfast cereal.'

She had a point. It didn't matter what he ate. In fact the more cardboard-like and tasteless the better. It had been his search for excellence and his ambition that had caused the fire that had almost claimed a young man's life and—

His chest cramped. He reached out an unsteady hand and lowered himself into a chair at the table. He had to remember what was important. He wanted to do all he could to set Russ's mind at rest, but he couldn't lose sight of what was important—and that was paying off his debts.

A warm hand on his shoulder brought him back to himself. 'Mac, are you okay?'

He nodded.

'Don't lie to me. Do you need a doctor?'

'No.'

'Russell told me you were physically recovered.'

'I am.' He pulled in a breath. 'It's just that I don't like talking about food or cooking.'

Realisation dawned in those sage-green eyes of hers. 'Because it reminds you of the accident?'

It reminded him of all he'd had. And all he'd lost.

CHAPTER THREE

MAC TENSED BENEATH her touch and Jo snatched her hand back, suddenly and searingly aware that while Mac wasn't in peak physical condition he was still a man. He still had broader shoulders than most men she knew, and beneath the thin cotton of his sweater his body pulsed hot and vibrant.

But at this moment he looked so bowed and defeated she wanted to wrap her arms around him and tell him it would all be okay, that it would work itself out.

She grimaced. She could just imagine the way he'd flinch from her if she did. Besides, she didn't know if it *would* be all right. She didn't know if it would work itself out or not.

She moved away to the other side of the kitchen. 'I can make you one promise, Mac.'

He glanced up.

'I promise to never feed you fish fingers.'

He didn't laugh. He didn't even smile. But something inside him unhitched a fraction and his colour started to return. 'I suppose I should give thanks for small mercies.'

'Absolutely. Have you had lunch yet?'

He shook his head.

She seized an apple from the newly replenished fruit bowl and tossed it to him.

This time she'd have sworn he'd laugh, but he didn't.

'I can see I'm going to get nothing but the very best care while you're here.'

'Top-notch,' she agreed. She grabbed her car keys from the bench. 'I'm going to put The Beast in the garage.'

Mac didn't say anything. He just bit into his apple.

The moment she was out of sight Jo's shoulders sagged. If Mac looked like that—so sick and grey and full of despair—just at the thought of the accident, at the thought of cooking…

She had no hope of getting him to give her cooking lessons. None at all. She twisted her fingers together. It was obvious now that it had been insensitive and unkind to have asked.

Why do you never think, Jo?

With a sigh, she started up her car and drove it around to the garage. It didn't solve her problem. She needed to make a *macaron* tower and she had just over two months to learn how to do it.

She pushed her shoulders back. Fine. She had a whole two months. She'd just teach herself. There'd be recipes online, and videos. What else was she going to do out here? Keeping house and cooking dinner would take—what?— three or four hours a day tops? Probably less once she had the house in order.

A *macaron* tower? How hard could it be?

'Don't say that,' she murmured, leaping out of her car to lift the roller door to one of the garage's two bays. The bay she'd chosen stood empty. Out of curiosity she lifted the second door too.

She had a French cookbook Great-Aunt Edith had given her. Maybe there was something in there—

Her thoughts slammed to a halt. She stood there, hands still attached to the roller door, and gaped at the vision of loveliness that had appeared in front of her.

Eventually she lowered her hands, wiped them down the sides of her jeans. Oh. My. Word.

Oh.

Dear.

Lord.

The sky-blue classic eighties sports car was her very own fantasy car brought to life and it was all she could do to not drop to her knees and kiss it.

'Oh, my God, you are the most beautiful car ever,' she whispered, daring to trail a finger across the bodywork as she completed a full circle around it, admiring the front curves, the fat spoiler, its gloss, its clean lines and its shape. What wouldn't she do to test drive this car?

What wouldn't she do just to sit in one!

She tried the driver's door. Locked.

With a jump, she spun around and closed the garage door. One needed to protect a piece of perfection like this from damaging elements. She parked The Beast in the bay beside the sleek machine.

Beauty and The Beast.

She cast one more longing look at Mac's beautiful car before closing the second roller door and racing into the house. Mac was still in the kitchen—eating a sandwich now, rather than the apple.

He glanced up when she clattered in. 'I take it I'm allowed to help myself to the provisions?'

'You have my dream car in your garage!'

'Is that a yes?'

How could he be so cool? She gaped at him and then mentally kicked herself. She spread her arms wide. 'Of course! You can help yourself to anything.'

He stared at her and his eyes darkened. He licked his lips and she had a sudden feeling he wasn't thinking about food, but an altogether different primal need. She pulled her arms back to her sides, heat flooding her veins. *Don't be ridiculous.* Men like Mac didn't find women like her attractive.

Mac turned away from her on his chair as if he'd just

come to the same conclusion. She dragged a hand back through her hair to rub her nape.

'You said something about my car?'

She swallowed back the request that he let her drive it—just once. She swallowed back asking him if he'd just let her sit in it. For all she knew that might be as insensitive as asking him to teach her to cook.

'I… It's beautiful.'

He glanced at her, raised an eyebrow, and she shrugged, unsure what to say, unsure what constituted a safe topic—because she never wanted to witness that look of defeat and despair on his face again. So she shrugged again and filled the jug. She measured out tea leaves.

'Feel free to take it for a spin any time you want.'

The jug wobbled precariously as she poured boiling water into the teapot.

Mac leapt up. 'Don't burn yourself!'

She concentrated on setting the jug back in its place. 'I didn't spill a drop.' Her heart thump-thumped. 'I'm fine.' She set the teapot and two mugs onto the table. 'But I gotta tell you, Mac, you shouldn't offer a girl her heart's desire while she's pouring out boiling water—and for future reference probably not while she's wielding sharp implements either.'

She smiled as she said it. Mac didn't smile back. He just stared at the jug with haunted eyes, the pulse in his throat pounding.

She sat down as if nothing in the world was amiss. 'Would you truly let me take your car out for a drive?'

He sat too. He wiped a hand down his face before lifting one negligent shoulder. 'Sure.' But he reached out to pour the tea before she could. 'It could use a run. I turn it over a couple of times a week, but I don't take it out.'

She gaped at him. 'You'd let me drive it? Just like that?'

That same slow lift of his shoulder. 'Why not?'

It took an effort of will to drag her gaze from that broad sweep of corded muscle. 'I…uh… What if I pranged it?'

'The insurance would cover it. Jo, it's just a car.'

'No, it's not. It's…' She reached out to try and pluck the appropriate description from the air. 'It's a gem, a jewel—a thing of beauty. It's—'

'Just a car.'

'A piece of precision German engineering.'

She almost asked how he could not want to drive it, but choked the question back at the last moment. That *would* be tactless. He'd been in the most dreadful accident, had suffered a long and painful recovery, and would bear the scars for the rest of his life. He'd been hounded by the media. She could see how fast cars might have lost their appeal.

So why hadn't he sold it?

She stared at him and pursed her lips. Maybe Mac hadn't given up on life as completely as he thought.

He glared. 'What?'

'You wouldn't consider selling it, would you?'

He blinked. 'Could you afford it?'

'I've been working in the Outback for the last eight years, making decent money but having very little to spend it on.'

He scratched a hand through his hair. 'But you're not earning a decent wage now.'

She was earning enough to cover her needs.

He jabbed a finger at her. 'And you may, in fact, be training for a new job shortly.'

'I suppose it wouldn't be the most practical of moves.'

He glared. 'You can say that again.'

He didn't want to sell it! She bit back a grin. There was still some life in Mac after all.

He settled back in his seat with a *harrumph*. 'But the offer stands. You can take it for a spin any time you want.'

'Lord, don't say that,' she groaned, 'or your house will never get cleaned.'

He laughed. It made his eyes dance, it softened his lips, and Jo couldn't drag her gaze away. 'You…uh…' She moistened her lips. 'You wouldn't want to come along for a spin?'

His face was immediately shuttered, closed, and she could have kicked herself. 'Well, no, I guess not. You're busy writing up your recipes and stuff.'

'Speaking of which…' He rose, evidently intent on getting back to work.

She surveyed his retreating back with a sinking heart. *Well done, Jo.*

In the next moment he returned. He poured himself a second cup of tea before unhitching a set of keys from the wall and setting them in front of her. 'Ms Anderson, you brew a mighty fine pot of coffee and not a bad cup of tea. Reward yourself and take the car for a spin.'

She shook her head. 'Not until I have your house looking spotless.' It would be a nice treat to spur her on. 'Maybe the day after tomorrow.'

He merely shrugged and left the keys on the table.

After lunch, two days later, Jo made a pot of tea and poured a mug for both her and Mac. Mac reached across to rattle the keys to his car. For the last two days those keys had sat on the table, where they'd tempted, teased and cajoled Jo mercilessly. Neither she nor Mac had put them back on the hook

'Does the house pass muster?' he asked.

Yes, it did. And so did the driveway since she'd found a pile of blue metal gravel out behind the garage. She'd used it to fill in the worst of the potholes along the driveway.

'You can retract your offer any time,' she told him.

'I'm not going to retract the offer, Jo. Go take the car for a spin and enjoy yourself.'

He tossed her the keys. She stared down at them, and then at him. 'I won't be gone long—maybe twenty or thirty minutes tops.'

He shrugged as if he didn't care how long she'd be gone. 'Just don't get a speeding ticket,' he tossed over his shoulder, before taking his mug and heading back upstairs to his mysterious work.

She wondered how on earth he could write recipes if he didn't cook them first.

She wondered how he could bear not to take his beautiful car out for a drive.

She drained her tea and then headed straight out to the garage. Would she even fit into the low-slung sports car? She planted her hands on her hips. If Mac did then she would too. She folded herself into it and sat for a long time, revelling in the moment and familiarising herself with the dashboard, the gears, the fact the indicator was on the left of the steering wheel rather than the right.

She started it up and gave a purr of delight at the throaty sound of the turbo engine. Would the reality of driving this car live up to the fantasy?

She negotiated the driveway with ludicrous care. She had no intention of bringing this car back in anything but perfect condition. When she finally reached the open road she let out a yell of pure delight, relishing the perfect handling, the smooth ride and the responsive power of the car. A body could get addicted to the sheer exhilaration!

After her first initial experimentation with the accelerator she made sure to stick to the speed limit. Instead of speed she savoured the way the car handled the twists and turns of these old country roads.

Oh, how could Mac stand to leave this amazing car in his garage and not use it?

She explored the roads that branched off from Mac's property, along with a couple of others that it seemed justifiable to explore, and discovered two tiny hamlets—Diamond Beach and Hallidays Point—both of which had tiny general stores if she needed to pop out for bread or milk. She also discovered more glorious coastal scenery.

Mac had certainly chosen a beautiful part of the world for his exile. Odd, then, that he didn't seem to spend much time appreciating it, that he'd taken such pains to shut it out from his sight.

It was grief, she supposed. Grief at having lost the life he'd had. There was no denying that until six months ago it had been a charmed life. Maybe when his grief had had time to abate he'd see a way forward again. Perhaps he'd realise his old life wasn't irrevocably lost to him forever.

Not if he refuses to cook.

She sighed, but a signpost pointing down another winding road had her slowing. *'Dog Shelter'.* A grin built through her and on impulse she turned down the road.

Mac will freak!

So what?

It's his house.

Nothing had been said about not being allowed a pet.

She turned into the signposted driveway. She wasn't the only person at the dog shelter. An elderly man emerged from the back of a small sedan as she pulled up beside it. A border collie leapt out behind him.

A woman dressed in overalls strode up from a nearby dog run. 'Mr Cole? And I expect this is Bandit?' She nodded to tell Jo she'd be with her shortly.

Mr Cole's hand dropped to Bandit's head and tears filled his eyes. 'It breaks my heart to leave him.'

Jo's throat thickened.

The woman glanced at the younger couple who had remained in the car. 'Your family can't take him?'

He shook his head and Jo had a feeling that *won't* rather than 'can't' was the operative word on that.

'Please find a good home for him. He's such a good boy

and has been such a good pal. If I wasn't going into a nursing home I'd…'

Jo couldn't stand it any more. She leapt forward. 'Oh, please let me take him. He's beautiful and I promise to love him.'

And then she was on her knees in front of Bandit, who obligingly licked her face. As she ran her hands through his fur she realised what a spectacle she must look. She rose, aware of how much she towered over Mr Cole and Bandit—not to mention the dog shelter lady.

'I was driving past and saw the sign and…well, it suddenly occurred to me that I'm at a point in my life where I can offer a dog a good home.'

Did that make her sound like a stark raving lunatic? Or a responsible, prospective dog owner?

'Maybe…' She swallowed. 'Maybe, Mr Cole, I could bring Bandit to visit you in your new home?'

Mac paced back and forth along the veranda. Jo had been gone for over an hour.

An hour!

Anything could have happened to her. His stomach churned. She could be lying in a ditch somewhere. Or wrapped around a tree. What had he been thinking to let her go driving off like that on her own? Had she even driven a performance car before? Why hadn't he gone with her?

He closed his eyes. He'd have enjoyed it too much. His hands fisted. If he didn't keep fighting the distractions this cookbook would never get written.

And he had to finish it.

He gripped the railing and stared out to sea. Jo was capable. She'd be fine. He drew air into his lungs. Of course she'd be fine. She'd just be caught up in the experience.

He knew exactly what that felt like.

He started pacing again. He hadn't done any real maintenance on the car since he'd buried himself out here. What if it had broken down? What if she was stuck on the side of the road somewhere? Did she have her phone with her?

He dug out his own phone to check for messages.

Nothing.

At that exact moment he heard the low rumble of the car's engine and he had to lower himself to the top step as relief punched through him. He closed his eyes and gave thanks. Jo was his responsibility, and—

Since when?

She was an employee, and that made her his responsibility.

Responsibility *and* a thorn in his side.

Nonetheless, when she parked the car in front of the house it took all his strength to remain where he was rather than leap down the stairs, haul her from the car and hug her. Those would be the actions of a crazy man. And, despite her first impressions of him, Mac wasn't crazy.

She bounced out of the car with a grin that held a hint of trepidation and, thorn in his side or not, he silently acknowledged how glad he was to see her.

'Have fun?' he managed.

'I didn't mean to be gone so long. I hope I didn't worry you?' She sent him a wary glance. 'The car is amazing.'

He tried to tamp down on the rising wave of enthusiasm he felt for the car too. 'I'm glad it lived up to expectations.'

'Oh, it exceeded them.'

He closed his eyes and refused to ask her how she'd felt as she'd swept around a wide bend in the road, or what she thought of the vehicle's magnificent acceleration.

'But I got a bit distracted.'

He snapped his eyes open and leapt to his feet. Had she scratched his car?

'What do you mean—?'

And he found a dog sitting at her feet. His jaw dropped.

'You put a *dog* in my car?'

'I… We made sure to use a blanket so Bandit, here, wouldn't damage the upholstery.'

He stared at her. 'You put a flea-ridden mutt in my car?'

She grimaced, shifting from one foot to the other.

Get over it, pal, he told himself.

Get over it? That car was his most treasured possession! It—

He suddenly flashed to Ethan, in the burns unit at the hospital, and had to lower himself back to the step. He'd give the car up in a heartbeat if it would turn the clock back, if it would change things. But it wouldn't.

Nothing he could do would achieve that. What did a bit of dog hair matter in the grand scheme of things?

She moved to sit on the step below him. The dog remained where he was. 'I know it's scandalous, Mac—a dog in your precious car. But…'

'What are we doing with a dog, Jo?'

Her gaze drifted to his scar. He turned that side of his face away from her and pretended to stare out to sea.

'Is this some underhand attempt to provide me with pet therapy?'

She huffed out a breath. 'No.' She patted her knee. 'Come on, Bandit.' The dog remained sitting by the car. 'I… He's for me, not you, but I don't think he likes me very much.'

He glanced at her to find her frowning at the dog.

'Bandit's is a sad story…' She told it to him, and then said, 'So, you see, when Mr Cole's face lit up so much at my promise to bring Bandit to visit him *and* he started crying I had to take Bandit then and there. Mr Cole would've fretted and thought me no fit carer for Bandit if I'd insisted on getting The Beast rather than letting him ride in Beauty.'

She'd dubbed his car *Beauty*?

It certainly suited the car. And it suited the woman who'd just driven it.

'You do see that, don't you?'

He let out a breath and nodded.

She reached forward and clasped his hand briefly. 'Thank you.' She turned to survey the dog again.

He stared at the hand she'd clasped. He closed it to a fist and tried to stave off the warmth threatening to flood him.

'Do you think he doesn't like me because I'm so big?'

'You're not big!'

Astonished sage eyes stared into his.

He clicked his fingers. 'Bandit.'

The dog immediately rose and leapt up the steps to sit at Mac's feet. 'See—I'm bigger than you and he's fine with it.'

'But you're a man, and I'm big for a woman. I expect animals sense those kinds of things.'

'Nonsense.'

'He likes you.'

Her crestfallen face told him that she had indeed bought the dog for herself, and not some attempt to lure him out of whatever dark pit of depression she imagined him in.

'His previous owner was a man, so it only stands to reason that he's used to men.'

'I guess…'

'Besides, he'll be missing this Mr Cole of his and not understanding what's happening.'

'Oh, yes, the poor thing.' She reached out and gave the dog a gentle hug and a kiss to the top of his head.

Mac's heart started to thump when he imagined—

Don't imagine!

He cleared his throat and tried to clear his mind. 'Once he works out that you're the person who feeds him you'll win both his undying love and his loyalty.'

'Are dogs really that simple?' She gave a funny little grimace. 'I've never had one before.'

'Feed them and treat them with kindness and they'll love you. End of story. You just need to give him some adjustment time. I'd suggest you set him up a bed in the kitchen or the laundry, so he doesn't try and wander off at night to find his old home.' He shrugged at her questioning glance. 'Russ and I had dogs when we were growing up.'

'Thank you.'

She suddenly leaned away from him and it made him realise he'd been talking to her, facing her, with his scar in full view.

'What are you doing outside anyway? Were you waiting for me to get back? Oh, I didn't worry you, did I? I didn't mean to be longer than twenty or thirty minutes but then—'

'Not at all.' His heart pounded. Hard. 'I was just going for a walk.' People went to hell for lying as well as he did.

She pressed a hand to her chest. Her lovely, generous chest.

'That's a relief. I was worried you'd think I'd made off with your fabulous car.' She bit her lip. 'I don't suppose Bandit and I could come on that walk too?'

What could he say to that? He glanced out at the beckoning sea, the field of winter grass and wild native flowers, noted the way the breeze rippled through it all and how the sun shone with winter mildness and tried not to let it filter into him, relax him…gladden him.

'Sure.'

'I suspect, though, that you should wear a sunhat to protect you…' She touched the left side of her face to indicate that she meant his burn scar. 'From sunburn.'

He should.

'You go get a hat and I'll put Beauty in the garage.'

They both rose. Bandit looked at Mac expectantly. Her face fell almost comically.

'You're not taking that fleabag in my car again,' he said to mediate her disappointment at the dog's reaction.

'So much for "It's just a car, Jo",' she muttered, but her

lips twitched as she said it. She patted Bandit on the head. 'You be a good boy. I'll be back soon.'

She folded herself into the car and her face broke into the biggest grin when she started it up again. She touched the accelerator just for fun and the car roared in instant response.

He turned on his heel and strode through the house to hide his sudden laughter. 'Bandit, I hope one day your new mistress gets herself her dream car. She'll know exactly how to enjoy it.'

Bandit wagged his tail, following Mac all the way through the house and up to his bedroom.

Mac rifled through drawers, looking for a hat. 'Don't look at me like that, dog. I'm not your master. *She* is.'

Bandit just wagged his tail harder. Mac shook his head and slathered sunscreen across his face. What on earth did Jo think she was going to do with a dog?

She was waiting on the veranda when he finally returned. She wore a basketball cap. 'I always have one in The Beast,' she explained when he glanced at it. 'Sunstroke is no laughing matter on a survey camp.'

'It's not a laughing matter anywhere, is it?'

She shrugged and pulled her hand from behind her back to reveal a tennis ball. Bandit started to bark.

'He came amply provided for.'

With that, she threw the ball and Bandit hurtled after it. She set off after him, turning back after four or five strides.

'Well? Aren't you coming?'

The previous two days he'd walked the property line behind the house and away from the sea. With an internal curse he kicked himself into action, trying not to let the holiday spirit infect him. But when Bandit came back and dropped the ball at Mac's feet and Jo gave a snort of disgust all he could do was laugh.

'Shut up and throw the ball for the ungrateful bag of bones.'

So he did.

They walked down a steeply inclined field, and then across level ground, and the whole time Mac tried to ignore the scent of the sea and the tug of the breeze caressing his face and the feeling of ease that tried to invade him. He hadn't realised it but he'd grown cramped in the house these last few weeks, and moving now was like releasing a pent-up sigh.

He didn't deserve to enjoy any of it.

He slammed to a halt. But it was going to prove necessary if he was to remain healthy. Jo was right about that. And he had to remain healthy. He had a debt to pay off.

'Are you okay?'

That warm honey voice flowed over him, somehow intensifying the sun's warmth and the silk of the breeze.

'Not tired out already, are you?'

He kicked forward again. 'Of course not.' That wasn't to say that the hill on the way back wasn't going to give him a run for his money. 'I'm just…'

'Yes?'

'I'm just trying to figure out the best way to apologise for my behaviour on Monday, when you arrived.'

'Ah.' She marched up a low sand dune.

He didn't want to go onto the beach. He hadn't guarded his privacy so fiercely to blow his cover now. As if sensing his reluctance, she found a flat patch of sand amongst a riot of purple pigface and sat to watch as Bandit raced down to the water's edge to chase waves. After a moment's hesitation he sat beside her. He kept his right side towards her.

'You *were* expecting me on Monday, weren't you?'

'Yes.'

'Then why the foul temper? You didn't seriously expect to live under the same roof as someone and manage to avoid them completely, did you?'

Had he? He wasn't sure, but he could see now what a ludicrous notion that was. 'I've obviously fallen into bad habits. It wasn't deliberate, and it certainly wasn't the object of the exercise.'

'By *exercise* I suppose you're referring to holing up out here in royal isolation? What's the object?'

'The object is to write this darn cookbook, and I was having a particularly rough day with it on Monday.'

She let out a breath. 'And I waltzed in like a…'

'Like a cyclone.'

'Wreaking havoc and destruction.'

'And letting in the fresh air.'

She turned to stare at him. His mouth went dry but he forced himself to continue. 'You were right. I've been shutting myself up for days on end, hardly setting foot outside, and some days barely eating. If you hadn't shown up and shaken me up I'd have been in grave danger of falling ill. And I can assure you that's *not* what I want.'

He wasn't on a suicide mission.

He readied himself for a grilling—did he mean what he said or was he trying to manipulate her for Russ's benefit, et cetera, et cetera?

Instead she turned to him, her gaze steady. 'Why is the cookbook so important?'

CHAPTER FOUR

WAS THE COOKBOOK a way for Mac to take his mind off the fact he no longer had a television show? No longer had a job? His fisted hands and clenched jaw told her it consumed him, and not necessarily in a good way.

When he didn't answer she tried again. 'What's the big deal with the cookbook, Mac?'

He finally turned to look at her. 'Money.'

'You have a deal with a publisher?'

He gave a single nod before he turned back to stare at the sea.

'If you hate it that much—' and she was pretty certain he did '—can't you just…?' She shrugged. She didn't know how these things worked. 'Change your mind? Apologise and pay back the advance?'

'You don't understand.'

Obviously not.

'I *need* the money.'

She had no hope of hiding her surprise, but she did what she could to haul her jaw back into place in super-quick time. 'But you must've made a truckload of money from your TV show.'

Not to mention all those guest appearances and endorsements. Still, if he'd gone around buying expensive cars willy-nilly she supposed he might have burned through it pretty quickly. Not that it was any of her business. And it wasn't any of Russ's business either.

'I… Sorry, I just thought you were rolling in it.'

'I was.'

So what on earth had he done with it all?

She had no intention of asking, but possibilities circled through her mind—bad investments, gambling, living the high life with no thought for the future.

'It's all gone on medical bills.'

That had her swinging back. 'Yours was a workplace accident.' It had occurred during the filming of one of his TV episodes. 'Insurance should've taken care of the medical expenses.'

'Not *my* medical bills, Jo. The money hasn't gone on *my* medical bills.'

A world of weariness stretched through his voice. And then it hit her. That young apprentice who'd also been involved in the fire. 'Ethan?' she whispered.

He didn't respond with either a yea or a nay.

She rubbed a hand across her forehead, readjusted her cap. 'But the insurance should've covered his medical expenses too. I—'

He swung to her, his eyes blazing. 'He's still in hospital! He still has to wear a bodysuit. His family wanted to move him to a private facility, where he'd get the best of care, but they couldn't afford the fees.'

Living the high life with no thought for tomorrow? Oh, how wrong she'd been!

She reached out to clasp his arm. 'Oh, Mac…' He'd taken on so much.

He shook her off and leapt to his feet. She pulled her hands into her lap, stung. A man like Mac would resent the sympathy of a woman like her.

Striking, huh? *Yeah, right.*

He spun to her, lips twisting. 'Who should pay but me? *I'm* the reason he's lying in a hospital bed with second- and third-degree burns to sixty per cent of his body. I've ruined that young man's life. I'm the guilty party. So the least I can do is—'

'What a load of codswallop!' She shot to her feet too. 'If we want to take this right down to brass tacks it's the producers and directors of your television show who should be paying in blood.'

Kitchen Encounters, as Mac's television show had been called, had followed the day-to-day dramas of Mac's catering team as they'd gone from event to event—a charity dinner with minor royalty one week, a wedding the next, then perhaps a gala awards night for some prestigious sporting event. Throughout it all Mac had been portrayed as loud, sweary and exacting—an over-the-top, demanding perfectionist. So over the top that even if Jo hadn't had the inside line from Russ she'd have known it was all for show—for the ratings, for the spectacle it created.

That wasn't how the press had portrayed it after the accident, though. They'd condemned Mac's behaviour and claimed the *Kitchen Encounters* set had been an accident waiting to happen. All nonsense. But such nonsense sold newspapers in the same way that conflict and drama sold TV shows.

Mac remained silent. He fell back to the sand, his shoulders slumping in a way that made her heart twist. Standing above him like this made her conscious of her height. She sat again, but a little further away this time, in the hope she wouldn't do something stupid like reach out and touch him again.

She moistened her lips. 'Russ told me that the persona you adopted for the show was fake—that it was what the producers demanded. He also said everyone on the show was schooled in their reactions too.'

Conflicts carefully orchestrated, as in any fictional show or movie, to create drama, to create good guys and bad guys.

Some weeks Mac had played the darling and others the villain. It had led to compulsive viewing.

'The accident wasn't your fault. You were playing the role you were assigned. You weren't the person who dropped a tray of oysters and ice into a pot of hot oil.' That had been Ethan. 'It was an accident.' A terrible, tragic accident.

'For God's sake, Jo, I was yelling at him—bellowing at him to hurry up. He was nineteen years old, it was only his second time on the show, and he was petrified.'

He didn't yell or bellow now. He spoke quietly, but there was a savage edge to his words that she suspected veiled a wealth of pain.

'He was acting. Just like you were.'

'No.'

He turned and those eyes lasered through her. Blond hair the colour of sand, blue eyes the colour of the sea, and olive skin that was still too pale. His beauty hit her squarely in the chest, making it hard to breathe.

'He was truly petrified. I just didn't realise until it was too late.'

She gripped her hands tightly in her lap to stop them from straying. 'From all accounts if you hadn't acted so quickly to smother the fire Ethan would be dead.' The other actors on the set had labelled Mac a hero.

'He hasn't thanked me for that, Jo.'

It took a moment for her to realise what he meant. She stared out to sea and blinked hard, swallowing the lump that was doing its best to lodge in her throat.

'Do you know how painful his treatment is? It's like torture.'

'He's young,' she managed to whisper. 'One day this will all be behind him.'

'And he'll be disfigured for life. All because I played the game the TV producers wanted—all because I was hungry for ratings and success and acclaim. At any time I could've said no. I could've demanded that we remain true to the "reality" part of our so-called reality show. I could've demanded that everyone on set be treated with courtesy and respect.'

If he had, she suspected the show wouldn't have lasted beyond a single season.

'I didn't. I chose not to.'

There was nothing wrong with wanting to be successful, with wanting praise and applause for a job well done. If anyone took a poll she'd bet ninety-nine per cent of the population wanted those things too.

'My pursuit of ratings has ruined a boy's life.'

And now he was doing all he could to make amends, to make Ethan's life as comfortable as he could. She shuddered to think how expensive those medical bills must be. She didn't believe for a moment that Mac should hold himself responsible, but neither did she believe she had any hope of changing his mind on that.

What a mess!

One thing seemed certain, though. If he didn't ease up he'd become ill. At least he seemed to recognise that fact now.

Or was that just a clever manipulation on his behalf so she wouldn't go telling tales to Russ?

She glanced at Mac from the corner of her eye as Bandit came racing up from the beach, tongue lolling out and fur wet from the surf. He collapsed at Mac's feet, looking the epitome of happy, satisfied dog. If only she could get a similarly contented expression on Mac's face her job here would be done.

Unbidden, an image punched through her, so raunchy that she started to choke. That *wasn't* what she'd meant! She leapt to her feet and strode a few steps away. Mac would laugh his head off if he could read her mind at the moment.

Laughter is good for the soul.

Yeah, well, in this instance it would shrivel hers.

She put the image out of her mind, pulled in a breath and turned to face him. His gaze was fixed on her hips. He stared for another two beats before he started. Colour slashed high across his cheekbones.

Had he been checking out her butt?

She wiped her hands down her jeans. Ridiculous notion.

But he couldn't meet her gaze, and then she couldn't meet his. She stared up at the sky. 'So what's the problem you've been having with your recipes?'

'They're complicated.'

'Naturally. It's one of the reasons your show was so gripping. There seemed to be so many things that could go wrong with each individual dish.'

'I promised the publisher a troubleshooting section for each recipe.'

That sounded challenging.

'I'm not a writer!' He dragged both hands back through his hair. 'This stuff—the explanations—doesn't come naturally to me. I don't know if they're coherent, let alone if a lay person could follow them.'

And if he refused to actually cook the dishes then how much harder was he making this on himself? He'd always proclaimed himself an instinctive chef. Just getting the order right of when to do what must be a nightmare.

It hit her then. How she could help him. And how he could help her.

She moistened her lips. 'Why don't you give me the drafts of your recipes and we'll see if I can make them? See if they make sense to me?'

She shifted her gaze to Bandit—it was easier than looking at Mac—but she couldn't help but notice how Mac's feet stilled where they'd been rubbing against Bandit's back.

'You'd do that?'

Forcing in a breath, she met his gaze. His eyes held hope,

and something else she couldn't decipher. 'I'll try, but you have to understand that I'm no cook.'

'You're the perfect demographic.'

She was?

'A plain cook who wants to branch out and try her hand at something new—something more complicated and exotic.'

That wasn't her at all. She just wanted to learn how to make a *macaron* tower.

'This would help me out. A lot.'

And her too, she hoped. He might refuse to stand side by side with her in a kitchen and show her how to make fiddly little *macarons*, but he might be worked on to create a sensible, within the realms of possible, *macaron* recipe for her.

'If you're sure?' he added.

So much for the demanding, overbearing kitchen tyrant. Russ had always chortled at Mac's on-air tantrums. She was starting to see why.

'As long as you're prepared to eat the odd disaster for dinner if things don't always work out.'

'What the heck? We've always got fish fingers to fall back on.'

She laughed.

'What if I give you the first recipe tomorrow?'

She nodded. And then glanced around at the lengthening shadows and shivered a little. The warmth quickly leached from the air as the afternoon closed in.

'Speaking of dinner, I'll need to get back and start it soon.' The beef stew she'd planned needed to simmer for at least an hour and a half.

'And I should get a bit more work done.'

He moved to get up and she started to offer him her hand, and then snatched it back, remembering the way he'd shaken off her touch earlier.

Mac's gaze narrowed and he leant back on his hands,

peering up at her from beneath the brim of his hat. 'Did my lascivious gaze earlier embarrass you?'

She almost swallowed her tongue. His *what*? So he *had* been…? Was he saying…? Surely not!

'Of course not,' she lied.

He rose to his feet in one smooth motion. Bandit immediately leapt to his feet too. 'I did tell you that you were a striking woman.'

She snorted and turned towards the house. 'You've been stuck out here on your own for too long.'

Without warning, cool, firm fingers gripped the suddenly overheated flesh of her forearm, pulling her to a halt. 'And you're selling yourself short.'

No, she wasn't. She just knew what she was. And she wasn't the kind of woman who turned men's heads. Mac was just trying to charm her, manipulate her.

'I should put your mind at rest, though.' He stroked her skin with his index finger before releasing her. 'I want to assure you that you're perfectly safe from unwanted attention. I have no intention of thrusting myself on you. I do mean to act like a perfect gentleman towards you, Jo.'

She wished he hadn't used the term *thrusting*.

She drew herself up to her full height but he still towered over her. 'No other scenario occurred to me, I assure you.'

'Good.' His eyes twinkled for a moment. 'It doesn't mean I can't enjoy looking at you, though.'

Jo stumbled. Mac laughed. Bandit barked and raced off towards the house.

Mac paced back and forth outside the kitchen door.

Jo peered around the doorway. 'You *can* come in and watch, you know. You could sit at the table.'

If he did that he'd bark instructions at her the moment she started. He'd make her nervous and she'd have an accident and burn herself. His stomach churned at the thought. If he sat in the kitchen he wouldn't be able to resist the temptation to take over.

He didn't deserve to indulge his passion when a boy lay in a hospital bed, suffering because of that passion.

'So, all I'm doing at the moment is infusing these few ingredients for the béarnaise sauce I'm to make tonight, right?

'That's right.'

'And—'

'No questions,' he ordered. 'I need to know if you can follow the recipe.'

'Okay—gotcha.'

He couldn't have said why, but her earnest expression made him want to kiss her.

He could just imagine how she'd recoil from *that*. He grimaced, and tried to push the thought from his mind, but it didn't stop the itch and burn that coursed through his body.

'If you're not going to watch then you best go somewhere else to pace. You're making me nervous.'

Go where? Do what? He didn't have a hope of settling to work at the moment. What if she didn't understand an instruction? What if—?

'Go toss a ball for Bandit.'

With a nod, he barrelled outside. The dog had a seemingly boundless reserve of energy.

Mac threw the ball three times. When Bandit brought it back the third time he gave the border collie an absent-minded scratch behind the ears. 'How do you think she's getting on in there, boy?'

He glanced back towards the house. It wasn't as if she had to do anything difficult—just measure out a few ingredients, chop up a tablespoon of onion. Simple, right?

He sprang up the steps and moved soundlessly across to the door. He breathed in deeply but couldn't smell anything. He straightened, ran a hand back through his hair. He should at least smell the vinegar being brought to the boil by now, surely? She should be reducing the mixture and...

Maybe she hadn't started the reduction yet.

He reached for the door handle.

Bandit barked.

With a curse, Mac wheeled away and clattered back down the steps. He threw the ball until his arm grew tired and then he switched arms. Bandit didn't show any signs of tiring. All the while Mac kept his attention cocked for any sign of sound and movement behind him.

Finally Jo emerged from the front door, bearing a plate of sandwiches, a jug of water and two glasses. 'Hungry?' she called out.

Not a bit—but he moved to where she'd set the things on the wooden table that stood at one end of the veranda and poured them both glasses of water. He drank his in an effort to appear nonchalant.

'Run into any problems?'

She settled on the bench that sat between the living room windows, bit into a sandwich and lifted one shoulder.

He peered at her sandwich and blinked. 'Is that peanut butter and honey?'

'Yup.'

He stared.

'What?' She glared. 'I *like* peanut butter and honey. You don't have to eat one. I made you roast beef and pickles.'

He obeyed the unspoken demand in her voice and selected a sandwich. 'What did the shrug mean?' He promptly bit into the sandwich to stop himself pressing her further.

She licked a drizzle of honey from her fingers. It was unconsciously sensuous and very seductive. The fact that she didn't mean it to be didn't make a scrap of difference. He forced his gaze away and concentrated on chewing and swallowing.

'I think I should probably tell you that I'm not up on a lot of cooking terminology. The very first time a recipe told me to *"cream the butter and sugar"* I thought it was directing me to add cream to the butter and sugar.'

He'd been leaning with a hip against the railing but he surged upright at her words. 'This recipe didn't ask you to cream anything.'

She waved a hand through the air. 'That's just an example. But…you know…*"reduce the mixture by a third"* isn't the kind of thing I read every day.'

'Do you think I need to add an explanation to describe what reducing means?'

She pursed her lips. 'No, I figured it out, but…'

He leaned towards her. 'Yes?'

'Why go to all the trouble of reducing at all? Why not just add less vinegar, water and onion to begin with?'

'Simmering the ingredients together infuses the flavours to provide a base for the sauce.'

She sat back and stared. 'Now *that's* interesting.' She pointed a finger at him. 'That should go in the cookbook.'

Really?

'But, you know, I want you to realise that I might be more clueless than your real demographic, so—'

'No, you're perfect.'

She glanced up, obviously startled at this statement. Their gazes locked for a moment. They both glanced away at the same time.

Mac's heart surged against his ribs. Why did this woman have to affect him like this? He'd known beautiful women in the past who had left him cold. Why couldn't Jo leave him cold?

Oh, no, not her. She threatened to ignite him. And for the first time in months the thought of heat and fire didn't fill his soul with dread. He glanced back at her. The pulse at the base of her throat fluttered madly. Unlike him, though, it wouldn't be desire but fear that had sent the blood surging through her veins. Fear that he would touch her.

It left a bad taste in his mouth.

'So…' She cleared her throat. 'My reduction is cooling and infusing, and I'll strain it later when I'm ready to make the sauce. Feel free to go and check it out.'

He started for the door.

'But…'

He turned back.

'I didn't know what tarragon vinegar was.'

He strode back to where she sat, one eyebrow raised.

'So I just used plain old white vinegar.'

He let out a breath.

'I briefly flirted with the idea of adding a herb to the mixture—like rosemary.'

He grimaced. It wouldn't be the end of the world, but—

'Though in the end I decided not to risk it.'

'It sounds as if you've done a great job.'

She didn't look convinced. 'I have another request to make. I've no idea what a double saucepan is.'

She needed to use one when adding butter—bit by tiny bit—to the reduction later, to create the sauce.

'I'm not asking you to tell me what it is, but can I bring my laptop into the kitchen with me? I would if I were cooking at home.'

'Of course you can.'

'And the final thing,' she said before he could walk away again. 'This recipe is Steak with Béarnaise Sauce, but you haven't said what you want served with it.'

'New potatoes and green beans.'

'Then you might want to include that at the end of the recipe too.'

Good point.

She suddenly laughed. 'I can see you're itching to check

it out, so go. But wash your hands first. I don't want dog hair in my reduction.'

He raced into the kitchen. He washed and dried his hands and then moved to the small saucepan sitting on the stovetop. He could tell at a glance that she'd used too much onion. He lifted the saucepan to his nose and sniffed. It was a pity about the tarragon vinegar—if she was happy to continue this experiment of theirs then they'd need to stock up on some of the more exotic ingredients—but all in all she'd done okay. The tension bled out of his shoulders.

She glanced up when he stepped back out onto the veranda. 'Well?'

'You've done a fine job. It's not exactly how I'd want it, which tells me what parts of my instructions I need to fine-tune.'

Elation suddenly coursed through him. He could make this work. He *could*! Then there'd be enough money for Ethan's hospital bills for the foreseeable future.

And after that?

He pushed that thought away. He had every intention of making sure Ethan was looked after for the rest of his life. Maybe he could do a whole series of cookbooks if this one sold well?

'This was a brilliant idea of yours, Jo. I can't thank you enough.'

She waved that away.

'If there's anything I can do in return…?'

She glanced up. The sage in her eyes deepened for a moment. 'I believe you mean that.'

'I *do* mean it.' He'd have sat on the bench beside her, but that would mean sitting with the left side of his face towards her. He leant against the railing again instead.

'Hold that thought.'

She disappeared into the house. She returned a moment later with a picture. His heart sank when she handed it to him. It was that damned *macaron* tower she'd already mentioned.

'*Macarons* are tricky.'

'Yes, but could you write me a recipe telling me how to make them—how to make that?'

He blew out a breath. 'This is an advanced recipe.'

'But practice makes perfect, right? I have plenty of time on my hands. I'll just keep practising.'

'Why do you want to make a *macaron* tower?' He could name a hundred tastier desserts.

He handed her back the picture. She took it, but a bad taste stretched through him when he realised how careful she was not to touch him.

She stared down at the picture before folding it in half. 'My grandmother turns eighty-five in two months, one week, four days and—what?—eleven hours twenty minutes? I've promised to make her one of these.'

Wow.

'I want to do something nice for her.'

'Nice' would be taking her flowers, or treating her to lunch at a decent restaurant. *Or making her a* macaron *tower.*

'Please, Mac, don't look like that! This *has* to be possible. I'm not that much of a klutz in the kitchen. This is something I can build up to.'

'Of course you can.'

'He says with fake jollity,' she said, so drily he had to laugh.

'I didn't mean that you can't do it. I'm just blown away by the fact you *want* to.'

'I love my grandmother. I want to do something that will make her happy. She's as fit as a horse, and as sharp as a tack, but she's still coming up to eighty-five.'

She rose and seized the other half of her peanut butter and honey sandwich and came to lean beside him on the railing, on his left side. He turned to stare out to sea, giving her his right side instead.

'My grandmother and my great-aunt raised me. Their relationship has always been tempestuous. My grandmother always praised me and indulged me. My great-aunt always thought it in my best interests to…um…not to do that.'

He stilled and glanced at her, but he couldn't read her face.

'There's an ongoing dispute over the rightful ownership of my great-grandmother's pearl necklace. My great-aunt scoffed at the idea of my making that *macaron* tower and I'm afraid my grandmother has staked the pearl necklace on the fact that I can.'

His jaw dropped.

'I believe my so-called *womanly* qualities have always been in dispute, and I'm afraid my great-aunt is now convinced that the necklace is hers.'

He straightened. 'What exactly does she mean by *womanly* qualities?' As far as he could see Jo's 'womanly qualities' were exemplary. 'You mean the domestic arts?'

She pointed what was left of her sandwich at him. 'Exactly.'

He reached around her for another sandwich. It brought him in close. She smelled faintly of onions, vinegar and honey. His mouth watered. He ached to reach across, touch his lips to her cheek to see what she tasted like.

Jo polished off the rest of her sandwich and pushed away from the railing to amble down the veranda a little way before turning. 'I don't mean to give up without a fight.'

He turned to face the house again, presenting her with his good side. 'I can understand that.' But didn't she resent being piggy in the middle between the two older women?

'Why do you keep doing that?'

A chill fluttered through him. 'Doing what?'

'Keeping the right side of your face towards me? Isn't it tiring?'

CHAPTER FIVE

IT WAS REALLY starting to bug her, the way Mac tried to hide his scar. Jo understood physical self-consciousness all too well, but Mac couldn't spend the rest of his life trying to hide one side of his face. It just wouldn't work.

'The way you're going, you'll give yourself whiplash.'

'I have no idea what you're talking about.'

How cold he could sound when he wanted—but she knew better. Mac wasn't cold. He was… Well, he was hot. But that wasn't what she meant.

He was devoting his life to making Ethan Devlin's life better. Those weren't the actions of a cold man.

'Really?' she said, walking around to his left side and deliberately surveying his scars. She'd noticed them before, of course, but scars didn't make the man, and she'd had other issues with Mac that had nothing to do with what he looked like.

The scars were red and angry. She sucked in a breath. Heck, they must hurt!

The pulse at the base of his jaw pounded. He held his body taut, as if it were taking all his strength to remain where he stood, and let her look at him.

He finally turned to glare at her, eyes flashing and lips pressed into a thin line. 'Satisfied?'

She stared back at him and had to swallow. Mac, when he was riled like this, was pretty virile. She had a feeling that the glare, the set of those shoulders and the angle of his jaw were all supposed to have her shaking in her boots. *Uh, no.* Though it certainly had her pulse racing. She moistened her lips. What it really made her want to do was run *to* him—not away from him.

Lord, wouldn't he laugh if he knew?

'I don't precisely know what you mean by *satisfied*, Mac.'

He swung away to stare out to sea, presenting her with his 'good' side again. 'Satisfied,' he growled, 'as in have you had your fill of looking at it?'

Oh.

He kept his gaze firmly fixed in front of him, but she had a feeling he didn't see the glorious view—the cobalt sky, the indigo and aquamarine of the sea, the white foam of the surf and the golden beach, all at their most vivid at this time of the year before the sun bleached everything pale with summer intensity.

'Doesn't it sicken you to look at it?'

Her head rocked back. 'Of course not.'

He turned to glare, a blast of arctic chill from frigid eyes. 'When you first arrived you said these scars shocked you to the core. Those were your exact words.'

She drew herself upright. 'I wasn't referring to your scars, you stupid—' She bit back something rude and vulgar. 'I was referring to how much you'd let yourself go!'

His jaw dropped.

She reached out and poked him in the shoulder. 'Don't you *dare* accuse me of being so shallow.'

His shoulders unbent.

She frowned and adjusted her stance. 'Does it sicken *you* whenever you look in a mirror?'

One of those lovely shoulders lifted. 'I'm used to it.'

'But what? You don't think anyone else can get used to it? You don't think anyone else can see past it?'

He didn't say anything.

'I've met beautiful people who've proved to be spiteful or

selfish or snobs, and suddenly I find their allure loses most of its gloss. I have friends who may not fit society's rigid ideal of beautiful, but they have such good hearts I think them the most beautiful people in the world.'

'Jo, I—'

'No! You listen to what I have to say! If you value yourself and others only through physical beauty then you deserve to suffer every torment imaginable at the thought of losing your so-called pretty face. But, as far as your face is concerned, I think it's as pretty as it ever was.'

He stilled. He stared at her for a long moment. 'You really mean that?'

She did.

He dragged in a breath and then turned to lean against the railing, his left side towards her. 'I'm sorry I insinuated...' He glanced at her. 'That you were shallow. I didn't mean to.' He paused. 'I agree that a person's attractiveness is more than how they look, but...'

She tried not to focus on the languid line of his body. 'But...?'

'There's no denying looks have an impact on how a person is perceived.'

'If a person is repelled by your scars they're not worth the time of day.' She folded her arms. 'You know, it could prove a useful filtering device.'

He gave a bark of laughter. 'You can't say that.'

'Don't let anyone know you feel self-conscious about it, Mac. That's my best advice. They'll see it as a weakness, and there are people in the world who pounce on others' weaknesses in an effort to build themselves up.'

He turned to her more fully. 'That sounds like the voice of experience.'

She shrugged and tried to walk the walk she'd just talked. 'Look at me.' She gestured down at herself.

'I've been doing my very best not to do that, Jo. I promised you gentlemanly behaviour, but when I look at you…'

She rolled her eyes. '*Do* be serious.'

Mac moved to trap her against the veranda post and the side of the house. He planted one hand on the weatherboards by her head, the other on the railing near her waist. Her mouth dried. Her heart thudded so hard she found it impossible to catch her breath.

'What on earth do you think you're—?'

'Shut up or I'll kiss you.'

She almost swallowed her tongue.

'You have the nerve to give me a lecture about shallowness, beauty and an individual's true worth, and then you want to carry on with *you're not attractive*?'

She opened her mouth. His eyes suddenly gleamed, fixing on her mouth with a hunger that had to be feigned! But she remembered his threat and snapped her mouth shut.

'What a shame,' he murmured, and in his eyes was a mixture of laughter and regret.

She wanted to call him a liar, but she didn't dare.

'When I said you were a striking woman I meant that in every positive way there is. I meant that I find you attractive. I meant that it takes a Herculean effort on my part whenever I look at you to conceal my desire.'

She choked.

'And it's not because I've been isolated for the last four months.'

Again, she was tempted to call him a liar. She was tempted to say anything that would make him kiss her. Warmth threaded through her stomach at the thought, her thighs softened and her breasts grew heavy.

But if he kissed her she wouldn't be able to help it. She'd kiss him back and then he'd know how much she wanted him, how attractive she found him, and it would make her vulnerable. She swallowed. She didn't want to be vulnerable around this man.

'You seem to think you're too tall for a woman...'

He moved in closer, his heat swamping her, though he still didn't touch her. He smelled of soap and freshly ironed cotton...and very faintly of dog. She really wished that last would put her off, but it didn't.

'I don't think you're too tall. I think you and I would fit perfectly.'

They might not be touching, but this close to him she felt dwarfed.

'I could stare into your eyes all day. They're so clear, and the colour changes depending on your emotion. I find myself wanting to learn what each shade means.'

That voice of his, its low intimate tone and the words he uttered, could weave a spell around a woman.

He eased back a fraction and she managed to draw air into her lungs again. Until she realised what he was doing and the breath jammed in her throat again.

'You have the most intriguingly womanly shape—all dips and curves.'

He was staring at her body the same way she'd stared at his face a short while ago. Had *he* felt this exposed? For heaven's sake, she was fully clothed, but Mac's eyes were practically undressing her—as if he was imagining what she'd look like without said clothes—and his eyes started to gleam and he actually licked his lips. She swallowed a moan and sagged against the wall, her pulse racing, bustling, jumping.

'Your body is lush and strong, and I'd be a liar if I said I wasn't aching to explore it. Thoroughly and intensely.'

The words scraped out of him, a hoarse whisper, and Jo's head fell back against the house as she struggled to draw air into her lungs.

'But that's just the outside packaging. The woman I'm

getting to know is passionate, she gives no quarter, but she is remarkably generous.'

His gaze burned fiercely down into hers. She couldn't have uttered a word if her life had depended on it.

'And all of that makes me ache that much more to make love with you.'

How on earth had the morning descended to this? For years she'd worked among teams of men in remote locations in the Outback and she'd always managed to keep things on a professional footing.

This was only her fifth day with Mac, and the air was charged with so much blatant sensuality it would melt anyone foolish enough to stumble into its path.

'But I promised to be gentlemanly, so I won't, but I'm sick to death of this ridiculous belief of yours that you're not attractive. You're a beautiful and very desirable woman.'

It frightened her. *He* frightened her. Because she wanted to believe him. Yet in her heart she knew it was all lies.

Mac eased away and she tossed her head. 'I know my worth, Mac, make no mistake. I'm smart and strong and I'm a good friend. But let's make one thing very clear. Boys like you do *not* kiss girls like me.' Not unless it was for a bet or a dare, or they were trying to manipulate them in some way. 'It's a fact of life.' A fact she had no intention of forgetting.

He'd started to turn away, but now he turned back, a flare of anger darkening his face. And then a slow, satisfied gleam lit his eyes, his mouth, even his shoulders—though she couldn't have explained how.

'Perfect…' he crooned.

And then he moved in.

She raised her hands. 'Don't you—'

He claimed her lips swiftly, pushing her back against the house, taking his time exploring every inch of her mouth. She tried to turn her head to the side, but he followed her, his hands cupping her face. He crowded her completely, pressing every inch of his rock-hard self against her. His chest flattened her breasts—breasts that strained to get closer. He thrust a leg between her thighs, pressing against her most sensitive spot in the most irresistible way. It made her gasp. With a purr of satisfaction his tongue plundered her mouth.

Stop! Stop! Stop!

But he didn't stop kissing her, savouring her, pressing against her, making her feel desired, making her feel beautiful, and with a moan scraping from the back of her throat she curled her hands into the soft cotton of his sweater and kissed him back. She wanted to know him, taste him. She wanted to savour him in the same way he savoured her. Her hands explored his shoulders and dived into the thickness of his hair. But she wanted more—so much more.

One of his arms went around her waist—he spanned it effortlessly—and hauled her closer as if she weighed nothing. It sent shivers of delight spiralling through her. Their kisses went from tasting and savouring to a deepening hunger. Held in his arms like this, dwarfed by his height and breadth, Jo felt almost dainty, utterly feminine and beautiful.

When his hand slid beneath her shirt to cup her breast his moan made her shake. He was moaning for *her*. He wanted *her*!

His thumb flicked across her nipple through the nylon of her bra. Desire spiked from her nipple to the core deep at the centre of her. She shifted against him, restless for more, seeking relief…seeking release and—

If they kept this up there was only one way it would end. She stilled. So did he. He didn't remove his hand from her breast and his heat branded her, tormented her. She didn't remove her arms from around his neck.

They both breathed hard, as if they'd run a race.

'I beg to differ.'

She blinked up at him blankly.

'Guys like me most certainly *do* kiss women like you. And what's more, Jo, they enjoy every moment of it.'

One kiss couldn't erase a lifetime of taunts, a lifetime of feeling she'd never measured up. A lifetime of never feeling beautiful.

She swallowed. Mac had kissed her as if he found her beautiful, but she still wasn't convinced he wasn't playing some deeper game. She removed her arms from around his neck. With the wall of his house behind her, she had nowhere to move to.

'Let me go, Mac.'

He did immediately.

Regardless of any of his reasons for kissing her, regardless of how much her body clamoured otherwise, this couldn't go any further.

'I've known you for five days.' Not even five full days. 'I don't jump into bed with men I've known for such a short time.' Was that his style?

He moved down to the next veranda post, leaving a whole span of veranda railing between them. 'I'm forty years old, Jo. The days when I thought one-night stands and flings were fun are long behind me.'

She'd never thought one-night stands or flings fun. Sharing her body with a man had always been a fraught experience and not one she'd ever raced into.

And yet today she'd almost…

She bent at the waist to lean her forearms along the railing, unconsciously mimicking Mac's posture.

'That kiss became a whole lot more a whole lot quicker than I meant it to,' he said.

She winced at the apology, glanced at him from the corner of her eye and found him staring stolidly out to sea. She grimaced, shuffled, and finally gave in, huffing out a breath. 'Yeah, well, it takes two to tango. It was just as much my fault as yours.'

He straightened and surveyed her. She tried not to picture what he must see—a clumsy giant of a woman. She remained in what she desperately hoped was a nonchalant, casual pose—a pose that proclaimed a kiss like that *hadn't* rocked her world. That kisses like that happened to her all the time and she was used to them.

Ha! If kisses like that happened to her all the time she'd be...

A very satisfied woman.

You mean a nervous wreck.

'I don't want to give you the wrong signals, Jo.'

She turned her head to stare at him. *Oh, right. Here it comes.* Inside, she started to shrivel.

'I'm not in the market for a fling. At twenty I thought such things could be uncomplicated, but I don't believe that any more. And I'm not in the market for a relationship. My life is already too complicated. A relationship would be one complication too many.' He swallowed and shuffled his feet. 'I...uh...hope you're okay with that.'

Men really were the most arrogant creatures. She straightened. 'Well, it might surprise you to hear that I'm not in the market for a relationship either—and I can't possibly imagine what gave you the idea that I was.'

He glared. 'You decided you had room in your life for a dog. It seems only logical a boyfriend would be next.'

Her jaw dropped. She hauled it back into place. She opened her mouth, then with a shake of her head snapped it shut. She moved to the door instead. 'I'm sure there's cleaning I should be doing.'

'So, we're okay?' Mac asked as she reached the door.

She folded her arms and turned. 'I don't know what *we* you're referring to, but I can tell you one thing—if I *were* in the market for a boyfriend, Mac, it wouldn't be with a man like you.'

His eyes practically bugged from his head. All his life

he'd probably had women falling over themselves for him. She had no intention of being one of them.

'This—' she gestured to the view and their surroundings '—is beyond beautiful. It's glorious. But you don't even seem to notice it, let alone appreciate it. You hide from life.' She'd had enough of hiding. 'Life's too short. I mean to live my life to the full and I'm not giving that up for any man.'

Not even for one as pretty as Mac.

'Then what the hell are you doing out here?'

'I'm having a breather—but I'm not hiding.' She flung out an arm. 'I relish that view every single moment I can. I'm learning to cook fancy French food. I'm adopting homeless dogs and driving fast cars. I suspect I've lived more in the last three days than you have in the last three months.'

He gaped at her.

There didn't seem to be much more to say so she whirled into the house and didn't stop until she came to the kitchen. And then she didn't know what to do. She'd already cleaned it after making that reduction.

She put the jars of honey and peanut butter that still stood on the table back into the pantry. She slammed her hands to her hips. She'd left the plate of sandwiches on the veranda, along with their glasses. She didn't feel like going back out there and facing him yet.

She could spout off all she liked about how she didn't want a relationship and she didn't do flings, but one look at the broad span of his shoulders and her blood surged, her thighs weakened and her resolve threatened to dissolve.

Almost against her will she tiptoed back down the hallway to the front door. She peered out through the screen door, but Mac was nowhere to be seen. With a sigh of relief she retrieved the dishes, spying Mac and Bandit halfway across the field leading down to the sand dunes and beach.

He moved with an unconscious grace and—

Argh! She stomped back into the house and then jumped when the hall phone—an ancient contraption—rang.

Russ, no doubt. She set the dishes on the floor and picked up the receiver. 'Hello?'

A quick intake of breath greeted her. 'Who are *you*?'

Jo blinked. Not Russ, then, but an angry female. It hadn't occurred to her but, despite Mac's protestations, was there some woman waiting for him in the wings? Some woman he was dangling until—?

She shook her head. She might only have known him for a few days but that seemed seriously unlikely.

She cleared her throat. 'May I ask who's speaking, please?'

'This is Mrs Devlin.'

Jo rested back against the wall, her stomach twisting.

'You may have heard of my son, Ethan Devlin?'

The apprentice burned in the accident.

Jo closed her eyes. 'Yes, of course. I'm terribly sorry about what happened to your son, Mrs Devlin.'

'Put that low-life swine Mac on the phone.'

Mrs Devlin's bitterness threatened to burn a hole right through the receiver. Jo managed to swallow. 'I'm sorry, but he's not available at the moment. Can I take a message?'

'What do you mean, he's not there? He should be *working*! And who the hell are *you*, my girl? His fancy woman?'

Wow. Just…*wow*! 'My name is Jo Anderson and I'm Mac's housekeeper—*not* his girlfriend. I don't appreciate the insinuation and nor do I deserve your rudeness.'

The sudden silence almost deafened her. 'He doesn't deserve the luxury of a housekeeper,' Mrs Devlin said, though her voice had lost the worst of its edge. 'He doesn't deserve a moment of peace.'

Jo dragged a hand through her hair. If Mac had been bearing the brunt of this woman's bitterness then no wonder he'd been driving himself so hard. She saw it then, in that moment—Mac was punishing himself. He refused to notice the glorious views, he refused to engage in physical activity he found pleasurable, he shut himself off from the things he loved, like his car, his brother…his cooking.

Oh, Mac.

'He needs to send more money. Tell him that. Where is he anyway?'

'He's out walking the dog.' Not that it was any of her business.

'He has a *dog*?' Outrage laced her words.

'It's my dog. And, Mrs Devlin?' she said, before the other woman hung up. 'I… Look, Mac is working so hard he's in danger of becoming ill.'

'He *should* suffer!' the other woman yelled down the line. 'He should suffer the way he's made other people suffer!'

Such venom. She understood Mrs Devlin's fear and concern for her son. She understood her fighting for the very best care he could get. But to blame Mac like this? It was wrong. So wrong.

To say as much would be pointless. Mrs Devlin didn't want to listen to reason. Not yet. But what if she was to become afraid that the cash cow might dry up?

Jo hauled in a breath, wishing her stomach would stop churning. 'If Mac does become ill, Mrs Devlin, the money for Ethan's care will dry up.'

'How dare you—?'

'All I'm doing is stating facts. You want Mac to suffer—that much is clear—but if he does get sick he won't be able to earn money.' Certainly not the kind of money they were talking about here. 'My job is to make sure he eats three square meals a day and gets out into the fresh air for some exercise. Basically, I just nag him. I doubt he enjoys it.'

But even after only a few days of this routine Mac was starting to look better.

'What are you trying to say to me?' the other woman asked stiffly.

'What I'm saying is that, for the moment at least, you need to choose between your desire for revenge and your son's care. If you choose the latter then I suggest you ease up on the venom for a bit.'

The phone was slammed down.

'Well…' She grimaced at the receiver before setting it back in place. 'That went well.'

Mac stomped across the fields. What on earth had possessed him to kiss Jo? From the first moment he'd clapped eyes on her he'd sensed that she'd be dynamite, that given half a chance she'd blow his life apart.

He clenched his hands to fists. That couldn't happen from a single kiss.

Except it hadn't been a single kiss but a full-on necking session that had hurtled him back to his teenage years, when he'd first discovered girls and sex. Kissing Jo had shaken him to his absolute foundations.

Bandit barked and spun in a circle—first one way and then the other. 'Okay, okay,' he grumbled, moving towards the sand dunes. 'Go for a swim, then.'

Bandit didn't need any further encouragement. Mac settled at the same spot where he and Jo had sat yesterday and raked both hands back through his hair. Okay, so those kisses had rocked his foundations, but they hadn't toppled them. As long as he didn't kiss her again he'd be fine.

He gave a low laugh. Kiss her again? The look she'd flung at him before she'd flounced into the house had told him she'd squash him like a bug if he so much as tried. Man, how he'd like to take up that challenge—to make her sheath her claws, to stroke her until she purred and—

He swore. She made him want all the things he'd turned his back on—all the things he couldn't have.

Bandit, damp and sandy, raced up the beach to fling himself at Mac, leaping onto his lap and covering his face in sloppy dog kisses. The show of affection took Mac off guard, but he put his arms around the dog and held him close. It was a warm body, and at that moment Mac found he needed a warm body.

Eventually the dog settled beside him.

'So you've decided to love someone else, huh?' Mac scratched Bandit's back and the dog groaned his pleasure. 'You should've chosen Jo, you know? She's a much better proposition.'

How would she take it when she realised the dog had chosen *him* as his new owner? He suspected some part of her had already realised, but…

He folded his arms across his knees and rested his chin on them. She'd take it as more proof that she wasn't good enough, that she'd been overlooked once again.

He lifted his head and glared at the glorious breakers rolling in. Why on earth couldn't she see how gorgeous she was? She'd mentioned something about her grandmother and great-aunt having a challenging relationship. Did that extend to her as well? Did they make her feel she hadn't measured up? A scowl lowered through him. Or had some jerk made her doubt her own loveliness?

So what if she wasn't one of those little stick figures who paraded around in tiny dresses and squealed that a carrot stick would make them gain weight? It was no fun cooking for those women. It would be fun to cook for Jo, though.

If he still cooked.

He blew out a breath. If he'd met Jo before all this had happened…

But he hadn't.

He clenched a handful of sand in his fist before releasing it. He couldn't imagine going through his entire life believing he was completely unattractive to the opposite sex.

He'd been lucky. Until the accident. Now he could definitely relate. No woman would look twice at him—

He froze.

Jo had. In fact Jo had kissed him with so much unbridled hunger and joy that… Well, it meant he'd been mistaken. There was at least one beautiful woman who found him desirable enough to kiss. He scowled. Even if she had discounted the possibility of something deeper and more permanent with him.

You discounted it first.

He swallowed. He'd kissed her and she'd given him an unexpected gift. She'd made him realise that other people might see beyond his scars too.

Which was a moot point if he never left this place. But if he ever did manage to pay off his debts? Well, it would matter then. Either way, it had lightened something inside him.

Could he make her realise she was beautiful too?

How? Not by kissing her, that was for sure. That would lead to too much trouble and too much heartbreak. Until he could guarantee Ethan would be looked after for the rest of his life Mac wasn't free to offer any woman his heart.

But it didn't stop him from liking the way she looked. He loved her height, her stature, and the way she held herself. She was strong and powerful—a force to be reckoned with. And she'd fitted into his arms as if she'd been designed to be there.

He turned to Bandit. 'How can I prove to her that she's gorgeous?'

Bandit merely rolled onto his back, presenting his belly for a rub. Mac stared. 'Bandit! You're not a boy dog!' He ran his hand over the fur of Bandit's tummy. 'You're a girl dog.'

He ran both hands gently over Bandit's tummy and started to laugh.

'You're a girl dog who I *think* is expecting puppies.'

CHAPTER SIX

MAC FOUND JO in the kitchen and opened his mouth to give her the news about Bandit, eager to get things on an easy footing between them again and hoping this latest news would push the memory of their kiss—kisses—to the nether regions of their minds, where it would never see the light of day again.

Jo beat him to the punch, though. 'You had a phone call,' she said, without preamble.

She didn't smile, and his nape and his top lip both prickled with sudden perspiration. There was only one person who called the house phone. Russ and his friends had his mobile number, though they usually resorted to email.

'Mrs Devlin,' she said—unnecessarily, though she couldn't know that.

'How…?' He swallowed. 'How's Ethan doing?'

'She didn't say.'

A weight settled across his shoulders. He pulled out the nearest chair and fell into it. 'Did she want me to ring her back?' Which was a ridiculous question. Of course she'd want him to return her call.

'She didn't say.'

He stared at her and she finally turned from where she was rinsing a few dishes and shrugged.

'She hung up on me.'

He closed his eyes. He could imagine the conclusion Diana Devlin had come to upon hearing a woman's voice at the end of his phone—especially a voice as rich and honeyed as Jo's.

When he opened his eyes he found a glass of water sitting in front of him. He drained it.

'She's a cheery soul, isn't she?'

'Jo, she's spent the last few months in fear for her son's life and now she fears for his future. There isn't much in her life to feel cheerful about.'

'Garbage.' She dried a plate. 'Her son's alive, isn't he? That's something to be grateful for. His recovery is coming along nicely, isn't it? Another thing to be grateful for.'

'He'll bear the scars from this accident for the rest of his life.'

'Oh, for heaven's sake—we're not going to have this argument again. Ethan's mother will love him no matter what he looks like.'

She bent down to place the plate in a cupboard and Mac got an eyeful of the curve of her hips. His heart started to pound. Jo had the kind of hips that could make a man salivate. He dragged his gaze to the glass he twirled between his fingers. He lifted it to his lips and managed to find another drop or two, but they did nothing to ease the thirst coursing through him.

Jo turned around. He kept his gaze on the glass.

'All I can say,' she said, 'is that I wouldn't want her in *my* sick room.'

Slowly he lifted his head to stare at her. She squeezed out the dishcloth and wiped down the table, not meeting his eyes. As far as he could tell the table was perfectly clean as it was, but he lifted both the glass and his arms out of her way and did his best not to draw the scent of her into his lungs.

'She's his mum. She'll be his best source of support…' He trailed off. He hadn't thought about it before. Not in that context. Ethan *was* doing okay, wasn't he?

For the first time he wished he hadn't so comprehensively cut himself off from his colleagues on the show.

He rose. 'I'll…um…' For heaven's sake—he didn't have to justify his every movement to her.

Turning on his heel, he strode out of the kitchen and headed upstairs. Seizing his mobile from the desk he punched in Mrs Devlin's number. As he waited for her to answer he glanced at the curtains. He moved to close them, to shut out the day, and then stopped. He didn't have the heart for it. What difference would a bit of sunlight make? Even if Mrs Devlin cared, she'd never have to know.

'Malcolm,' she said, obviously having checked her caller ID before answering. She never called him Mac. She never said hello. She just said Malcolm.

'How are you, Mrs Devlin?'

She didn't answer him. She usually made some sarcastic comment—*How did he think she was, sitting at her son's sick bed day in day out?*

While he welcomed the silence he forced himself to push on. 'I understand you rang earlier?'

He waited for her to demand to know who Jo was and what she was doing in his house. He could imagine her sarcasm when he told her Jo was his temporary house-keeper. It would be something along the lines of *It's nice for some.*

'I wanted to tell you that this quarter's bills have come in.'

He closed his eyes. This lot would just about clean him out. To receive a much-needed portion of his advance he had to get something substantial to his publisher. *Soon.* That would cover the next quarter's costs. After that… He swallowed. If necessary he'd sell the car, his Sydney apartment. And then this house.

And if Ethan's treatment needed to continue after that… He rested his forehead against the glass sliding door, welcoming its coolness against his skin. They'd better hope this cookbook did well. *Really* well.

'Malcolm?'

It hit him that her voice lacked its usual stridence, though it could by no means be considered friendly.

'Please send the bills to my lawyer. I'll take care of them.' His heart pounded. 'How's Ethan?'

'He's doing as well as can be expected.'

It was her standard line whenever he asked. And he always asked. He didn't ask her to send his best to the younger man. She'd made it clear that Ethan wanted nothing to do with him.

'How...?' She cleared her throat. 'How are *you*?'

He nearly dropped the phone. He coughed and swallowed back his automatic reply—*fine*. That would seem a mockery, considering Ethan's condition. 'I...I'm working hard at wrestling this cookbook into shape.' She knew he meant all its profits to go to Ethan.

'Right. Goodbye, Malcolm.'

'Uh...goodbye.'

He stared at the phone. Normally she hung up without so much as a by-your-leave. What on earth was going on?

He threw the phone back to the desk and dragged a hand through his hair. Was everything really okay with Ethan? Had he suffered some setback? He paced across the room. Could Diana have said something to Jo? Who knew? Maybe they'd had a moment of woman-to-woman bonding. Maybe—

'She's a cheery soul, isn't she?'

Hell.

He clattered back down the stairs. Jo wasn't in the kitchen. She wasn't in the living or dining rooms either, but as he walked through the house he couldn't help noticing how light and airy it all seemed. The curtains were pulled back and sunlight poured in at freshly cleaned windows. The heavy wooden furniture gleamed, the rugs were plush underfoot, and plump scatter cushions invited him to recline on the sofa. Not that he spent any time in this part of the house any more.

Why not?

He ground his teeth together. His life consisted of eat, sleep and work. It didn't leave room for loafing on the sofa in front of the television.

He pushed out to the veranda and strode halfway down the steps to survey the view in front of him. But there was no sign of a tall, lush woman striding down that field of native grass, or along the beach with Bandit. Maybe she was pegging laundry on the line. He turned back.

'Are you looking for me?'

He started at the voice to his left and found Jo on her knees, pulling weeds from a garden bed. He was pretty sure that wasn't part of her job description.

He nodded towards the few spindly rose bushes. 'I'm not sure you need to worry about those.'

'I want to.'

Whatever... He planted his legs. 'What did you say to Mrs Devlin?'

'Ah.' She went back to digging. 'I told her to wake up to herself.'

He choked. 'You *what*?' He dropped to the bottom step, head in hands. 'Hell, Jo, the poor woman has been worried half out of her wits and—'

'I said it in a nice way.'

He lifted his head.

'I didn't say the actual words, *Wake up to yourself.*'

That had been her message, though.

'She had a big go at me for being here. I didn't like her insinuation, so I set her straight.'

He opened his mouth. After a moment he shut it again. He deserved everything Diana threw at him, but Jo didn't. She'd had every right to defend herself, to demand respect.

'When she started mouthing off that you didn't deserve the luxury of a housekeeper I…' She shrugged.

'You what?'

'I told her you were working so hard you were in danger of falling ill. And I made it clear that if that happened you wouldn't be able to earn. And that, therefore, her cash cow would dry up.'

'Tell me you put it nicer than that?'

'I expect I did.' She dusted off her hands and rested back on her heels. 'Like you, she's been focussing on all the wrong things.'

His mouth dried. What else had Jo said to the poor woman?

'I told her she needed to choose between her desire for revenge on you and what was best for her son.'

He clenched his jaw so hard he thought he might crack a tooth. 'I wish you'd kept your mouth shut.'

She rose and planted her hands on her hips, towering over him. Her chest rose and fell, her eyes flashed, but even when she was angry her voice washed over him like a balm.

'She's turned you into her whipping boy. What's worse is that you've let her.'

He shot to his feet. 'I owe that family!'

'Codswallop!' She glared. 'Next you're going to tell me you're responsible for the national debt and world hunger.'

'Don't be ridiculous.'

'What did you do that was so bad, huh? You yelled at an apprentice. Even if it hadn't been scripted, we've all been hauled over the coals by our bosses before. In the view of things that you're taking one could equally accuse Ethan of being a spineless little ninny. I mean *he's* the clumsy clod who dropped a tray of cold food into hot oil.'

He couldn't believe what he was hearing.

'I'm yelling at you now, but if you trip up the stairs in a huff and sprain an ankle is that going to be *my* fault? I don't think so, buster.'

'That's different. We're equals!' he hollered back. 'On set I had seniority, and that boy—'

'Oh, and that's another thing that's getting up my nose. You keep referring to Ethan as a boy—but he's nineteen years old. He's a man. He has the right to vote and he has the right to choose what kind of work he wants to do. He *chose* to work with you. He *wanted* to be a part of your team. You wanted your show to be a success, and you've been blaming your ambition for the accident. You forget that Ethan wanted the show to be a success too—why else was he there?—but you don't take *his* ambition into account.'

His mind whirled at her words, but he lifted his chin and set his shoulders. None of that made a scrap of difference.

'No,' she carried on, 'you won't take *any* of that into account, will you? It's much easier to carry on the way you have been.'

Something inside him snapped. 'Easier!' He started to shake with the force of his anger. 'Tell me how any of this is easy?' he yelled. 'Every day—*every single day*—I have to fight the urge to go driving in my glorious car, resist the impulse to go down to the beach and relish the feel of salt water against my skin, turn my back on the desire to race into the kitchen and try out a new recipe that's exploded into my mind!'

With each named temptation he flung his arm out as he paced up and down in front of the garden bed.

'I chain myself to my computer all day to write a book I should be qualified and competent to write. But instead I find myself battling with it as if it's an enemy that's determined to bring me down. So will you kindly tell me how any of that is *easy*?'

She moved to stand in front of him. She stood on a slightly higher piece of ground than he did so she was almost eye to eye with him.

'It's easier than facing the consequences of the accident.'

Ice crept across his scalp.

'It's easier than attempting to rebuild your life.'

He didn't have a life, and for as long as Ethan remained in hospital he didn't deserve a life.

She gave a mirthless laugh, as if she'd read that thought in his face. 'You really feel *that* responsible for Ethan?'

That wasn't worth dignifying with an answer.

'Then this—' she gestured all around '—is easier than meeting with Ethan face to face, easier than witnessing his struggles, and easier then offering him the true moral support of a friend.'

He had to swallow before he could speak, and he felt every last drop of anger draining away. 'I have it on good authority that the last thing Ethan wants is to clap eyes on me.'

'Ethan's mother is *not* a good authority—and if you think she is then you're an idiot.'

He couldn't speak past the lump that had stretched his throat into a painful ache.

'Have you even spoken to Ethan yourself?'

He hadn't. Diana had demanded that he not plague her son, that Mac leave Ethan in peace. Call him a coward, but he hadn't *wanted* to speak to Ethan—hadn't wanted to hear the boy's recriminations.

'A real man would show up and say sorry.'

It was Russ's voice that sounded in his head now. He shied away from the thought, from what it demanded of him. What good would facing Ethan do for either one of them? He would do whatever he could not to upset the younger man. But he *could* check up on him—see how he was doing. He could ring Terry, the creative director, or one of the producers of the show. He'd bet someone from the old team would know.

He could at least ring. Not Ethan, but one of the others. How hard could that be?

'I do have one final burning question.'

He blinked himself back into the here and now to find Jo halfway up the steps to the house.

'Precisely what calamity do you think will befall us—' she shot the words over her shoulder '—if you *did* go for a drive in your car, or went for a swim, or if you *did* go and cook some delicious meal?'

She didn't wait for an answer but continued straight into the house on those long, strong legs of hers.

'So that was a hypothetical question, then?' he muttered.

Good. Because he didn't have an answer for it.

Jo sensed the exact moment when Mac loomed in the dining room's doorway. She didn't turn from where she'd set down dishes of new potatoes and buttered green beans.

'You're just in time. Take a seat.'

'On one condition.'

She turned at that. 'What?'

'That we call a truce and promise not to holler at each other for the next hour.'

The tension in her shoulders melted away. 'Make it two and you have yourself a deal.'

His lips lifted. Not quite a smile, but almost. Maybe they'd achieve one by the end of the meal.

He took a seat. 'Did you have any trouble with my instructions?'

'I don't think so. Proof is in the pudding, though, so to speak.'

She went to retrieve their steaks, oddly nervous as she set his plate in front of him.

He helped himself to potatoes and beans. Jo dug straight

into her steak, slathered in béarnaise sauce. She closed her eyes. *Oh, dear Lord, the sauce was to die for.* She'd be lining up for his cookbook the moment it came out.

'You've overcooked your steak.'

She opened her eyes. 'Try yours.'

He did.

'And?' she prompted.

'It's perfect.'

'For you, maybe.' She wrinkled her nose. 'I prefer my steak properly cooked—not underdone, the way you seem to like it.'

'This is *not* underdone. It's how steak should be cooked.'

'And the sauce?'

He frowned. 'You've cooked it a little too long and it's started to separate.'

Truly? She stared at it.

'It's a pity about the tarragon vinegar, and you used too much onion to flavour the reduction, but only an experienced foodie would know.'

He frowned at her steak again, but she ignored the silent censure. 'Relax, Mac.' She reached for the beans. 'I'm actually pretty chuffed with my efforts—and that's the point, isn't it?'

He blinked.

'I mean the people who try out your recipes—they're going to adjust them to their own tastes, right? Like I did with my steak?'

'I guess.'

'But as long as they feel they've created a nice meal they're going to be happy, aren't they? Mission accomplished.'

He straightened as if she'd zapped him. 'You're right. Nobody's going to be assessing their creations with a mark out of ten.'

'Uh, no.'

She tried not to focus on the shape of his lips, or the scent of coconut that came from his still-damp hair. Hair that was a touch too long. Hair that had felt glorious when she'd run her fingers through it and—

She reached for her glass of water and drained it.

'I think I've been getting too hooked up on every detail.'

He really did need to let up a bit.

'But as long as my targeted audience is satisfied then that's the best I can hope for.'

Yup.

He suddenly grinned. Her heart skidded, and then settled to pound too hard too fast. She took back her earlier wish that he'd smile. She wished he wouldn't. Why couldn't her heart just behave normally around him?

'So, have you come any closer to discovering your new career path today?'

This had become a habit—at dinnertime he'd throw suggestions at her about a new vocation.

'Go on—thrill me,' she said. *Not literally.*

'Chef?'

She wrinkled her nose. 'I expect I'd need to like cooking for that.'

'You don't like to cook?'

'I never became interested in it until I started watching your show. Russ made all of us watch it.' She blew out a breath. 'But I'm afraid you're not going to make a convert of me. It's all far too fiddly for my liking.'

'Gardener, then?'

'It's a pleasant enough way to while away an hour or two, but a whole day of it? A whole week of it? Month after month? No, thanks.'

Bandit pattered into the dining room. 'Then maybe you'd like a stint as a dog breeder?' Mac's grin suddenly widened. 'It could be the perfect fit. I discovered today that Bandit is, in fact, Bandita.'

'What?'

'He is a she. Bandit is a girl dog.'

Her jaw dropped. 'You're joking?'

'I take it you didn't check before you agreed to adopt him…uh…her?'

She stared at the dog. 'It never occurred to me to check. I mean he's…she's…fluffy, and has lots of fur, and it's not like it's…um…obvious. I just—'

She folded her arms and glared. 'That nice old man told me Bandit was a boy.'

'I suspect "that nice old man" has taken you for a ride.'

'Why, though? What's the big deal if Bandit is a boy or a girl? It certainly makes no difference to me, and—'

She broke off at his laughter. He looked so different when he laughed.

She moistened her lips. 'What?'

'Bandit is a girl dog who I suspect is going to be a mother in the not too distant future.'

'*Noooo…*'

'Yes.'

'So that nice old man was just trying to fob Bandit off onto some poor sucker?'

'Bingo.'

And she was the sucker.

She stared at Bandit. She stared at Mac. 'We're going to have puppies?'

'Looks that way.'

Puppies? She grinned. She ate some more steak. 'Well, that'll be fun.' In the next instant she stiffened. 'What else did that rotten old man lie about? Is she microchipped? Has she had her vaccinations?' She set her knife and fork down. 'Well, that's that, then.'

Mac frowned. 'That's what?'

'It means I'll have to take her to the vet's tomorrow for a thorough check-up.'

'It wouldn't hurt,' he agreed.

She found herself grinning again. 'Puppies, huh? Do you think there's any money in dog breeding?'

'Not really.'

Oh, well. She'd think of something on the job front soon enough.

She gestured to the food. 'I don't think this effort has disgraced me.'

'Absolutely not.'

But he didn't meet her eye as he said it. Her heart started to thump. There was loads of time yet to learn all she needed to know about *macaron* towers.

She swallowed. Béarnaise sauce one day. *Macarons* the next.

'What on earth are you trying to do?'

Jo turned at Mac's voice. Bandit twisted out of her grasp and ran a few paces away, where she turned to glare at Jo. Jo let a growl loose from her throat. 'I'm trying to get Bandit into The Beast.' She gestured to her car. 'But Bandit doesn't seem too enamoured with the idea of going for a ride. Either that or it's the V-word—V. E. T.—that has her spooked.'

She pushed her hair off her face, thinking she must look a sight before telling herself that it didn't matter one iota what she looked like.

'For heaven's sake, how hard can it be? I'm bigger than her. I'm stronger than her. And if you make one derogatory comment about my intelligence in comparison to hers you'll be getting fish fingers for dinner.'

He raised his hands. 'No comments, derogatory or otherwise. I'm hoping for a cheese soufflé. I just put the recipe on the kitchen counter.'

She hoped it would taste as good as the words sounded

coming from his lips. 'Do I need to pick up any exotic ingredients?'

'Not for today—but you'll need these for later in the week.'

He handed her a shopping list. Wrapped inside it was some housekeeping money.

'Here, Bandit.' He clicked his fingers and Bandit was at his side in an instant.

Jo scowled. Typical female. She rolled her shoulders. Actually, when she thought about it, she couldn't fault Bandit's taste.

'Up.' He patted the front passenger seat and Bandit leapt up and settled there. Mac turned back to Jo. 'There you go. I'll see you when you get back.'

He started to walk away and Bandit immediately leapt down to follow him.

'Ahem…'

Mac turned at Jo's cleared throat. He shook his head. 'C'mon, Bandit, let's try that again.'

This time when Bandit was seated in the car Mac shut the door. But when he started to walk away Bandit set up a long, mournful howl.

'Don't cry, lovely girl.' Jo reached into the window to pat her. 'It's okay.'

None of which made the slightest difference. Bandit continued to howl.

Jo swung back to Mac. 'She's pregnant. I'm pretty sure that means she's not supposed to get upset.'

He lifted both arms. 'What do you want me to do about it?'

'It's more than obvious what needs to happen.'

'What's that?'

'You're going to have to come with us.'

Mac's face shuttered. 'That's out of the question.'

Jo took one look at him and had to rest her hands on her

knees for several long moments. Pulling in a breath that helped haul her upright, she opened the car door to release Bandit—who leapt down in an instant.'

'I'm sorry, beautiful girl.' She went to fondle Bandit's ears, but the dog dodged away from her and for some reason it cut her to the quick. It was all she could do not to cry.

'What are you doing?'

Disbelief was etched across every line of Mac's face. A face, it occurred to her now, that had become a little too familiar to her.

She tried to swallow the lump in her throat, but only partially succeeded. 'I'm not going to put her through that kind of distress. Not while she's in such a delicate condition.' Her voice came out high and tight, due to the lump. 'She'll hurt herself, or spontaneously abort. Or…' She shook her head, her stomach churning. 'I'm not going to be responsible for that.'

She walked past Mac and tried to hold her head up high.

'But… But…' he spluttered.

She stopped and waited, but he didn't say any more. She turned. 'Are you waiting for me to bully you? If you are you'll be waiting a long time. You're an adult. You know what's right and wrong.'

His jaw went tight and a tic started up beneath his right eye.

'I'm going to conserve my energy for when I have to contend with Bandit *and* her puppies when I eventually leave.' That was going to be awfully traumatic for poor Bandit. The thought made her stomach churn even harder.

'You can't take her when you leave.'

Jo started to stalk away, but he strode after her.

'She loves it here. Jo, I… Look, I know it's unfair, but she's adopted *me*—bonded with *me*. I didn't mean for it to happen.'

From the corner of her eye she saw the weak excuse for a smile that he shot her.

'I'll make a deal with you. You keep the puppies and Bandit stays here with me. I'll look after her—I promise.'

'Look after her?' She whirled to face him. 'You can't even take her to the vet! I can't in any conscience leave her here—even though she loves you and merely tolerates me. Even though I know she'll be way happier here than she will be with me.'

He took a step back from her, his mouth pressed so tight it turned his lips white.

'I don't know why I expected something better from you. You wouldn't even visit your brother when he was in hospital, though you had to know it was the thing he most wanted.'

He'd frozen to stone.

There was no room in his life for compassion or love or responsibility to his family…just a manufactured guilt that took over his every breathing moment.

She turned away, not knowing why her heart hurt so hard.

CHAPTER SEVEN

Jo COUNTED OUT the eggs she'd need for the soufflé and had started to read the 'Hints on soufflés' section of a cooking website she'd found when voices floated in through the open front door.

Voices? She lifted her head and frowned. Surely not? She hadn't heard *voices*—as in more than one person speaking, having a conversation—since she'd arrived. She didn't count the way either she or Mac spoke to Bandit. Or her and Mac's often fraught and adversarial conversations.

He doesn't kiss like an adversary.

He kissed like a dream.

Stop it!

She cocked her head and listened harder. There was definitely more than one voice.

The voices grew stronger as she marched through the house. She pulled up short of the front door when she found Mac talking to an unknown man by the front steps—a man carrying what looked like a doctor's bag.

Mac didn't appear the least bit self-conscious. Could the man be an old friend?

She looked at the bag again and then it hit her. A *vet*! Mac had called out a vet.

She had to fight the urge to race outside and throw her arms around him. Oh, he'd love that, wouldn't he? *Not.* She straightened her shirt and then pushed outside as if it what was happening in front of her was the most normal thing in the world.

Could Mac conquer his fear of what the world thought of him one person at a time? She crossed her fingers behind her back.

She strode across the veranda. 'I thought I heard voices.'

'Jo, this is Daniel Michener. He's the local mobile vet.'

She hadn't considered for a moment that this area would warrant a mobile vet.

'There are a lot of hobby farms—not to mention dairy farms—in the area,' Daniel explained when she said as much. 'It's a bit hard to bring a cow, horse or an alpaca into the surgery.'

Which made perfect sense when she thought about it. 'Well, I'm really glad you can give Bandit a once-over.'

'I understand you adopted her and know nothing of her history?'

Jo grimaced. 'I was told she was a purebred seven-year-old male border collie, microchipped, neutered, and fully vaccinated.'

He laughed. 'Let's take a look at her, then.'

Mac played veterinary nurse, soothing Bandit and convincing her to co-operate with Daniel. He made a rather nice veterinary nurse, with those big hands gentle on the dog's neck. She shivered at the way he'd run a hand down Bandit's back while talking to her in low, reassuring tones. The sight of the broad man with the small, fine-boned, not to mention *pregnant* dog made her heart pitter-patter.

He glanced up and caught her staring, raised an eyebrow. She shrugged and forced her gaze back to Bandit, tried to ignore the way her breath hitched in her chest.

The vet gave Bandit a clean bill of health. 'You should expect the puppies in about a month.' He clicked his bag shut. 'My best guess, looking at her teeth, is that she's three years old—and this is not her first litter, so she'll probably be a good mother.'

Not her first?

She moved in a little closer and Mac's scent—all warm cotton, coconut and dog—hit her. It was all she could do not to swoon. She had to step back again.

'Can you tell how many puppies she's going to have?'

He shook his head. 'With a border collie, though, you can expect somewhere between four and eight.'

Eight!

The vet handed her his bill. Mac stood beside her as they waved him goodbye.

'Can Bandit stay here with me?' Mac said without preamble. 'I promise I'll look after her.'

'Yes.'

He plucked the bill from her fingers. 'She's my dog now, so I'll take care of her bills.' He strode back towards the house. 'But those puppies, Jo…' he called over his shoulder. 'They're all yours.'

Puppies? She smiled. *Eight* puppies? She groaned. What on earth would she do with eight puppies?

Maybe Russ would like one after he'd recovered from his surgery. Weren't pets supposed to be good for people— a form of therapy?

She bit back a sigh. What Russ really needed was a visit from his brother.

Mac ostensibly studied the cheese soufflé that Jo had set on the table, but all the time his mind whirled. Tomorrow Jo would have been here for a week. *What did she mean to tell Russ?*

He glanced at her. She wiped her hands down the sides of her jeans. 'Does it pass muster?'

He pulled his attention back to the soufflé. 'On first glance, yes. It's a nice colour.'

She folded her arms, narrowing her eyes.

'Okay, okay.' He raised his hands. 'I'd want it higher and fluffier if you were one of my apprentices—but you're not. This is the very first time you've made a soufflé, right?'

'Right.'

'Then in that case it definitely passes muster.'

She sat and motioned for him to serve it.

He drew the warm scent of the soufflé into his lungs. 'It smells good.'

She leaned in closer to smell it too, her lips pursed in luscious plumpness. A beat started up inside him, making his hand clench around the serving spoon.

'So this whole food-assessing thing…it's a bit like wine-tasting? You check the colour of the thing, smell it and finally taste it?'

'Though in this instance one hopes it doesn't get spat back out.'

She sort of smiled. There hadn't been too many smiles from her in the last day and a half.

What was she going to tell Russ?

'I'm trying to get away from the demanding level of perfection that's necessary in a top-notch restaurant. The people who buy my book aren't cooking for royalty.' Not like he had. They'd be cooking for their eighty-five-year-old grandmothers. 'I'm correct in thinking, aren't I, that they just want to have some fun?'

'Fun.' She nodded, but he could tell she held back a sigh.

He shook his head. How was he going to teach her the intricacies of a *macaron* when she didn't even like cooking?

He pushed the thought from his mind and sampled a forkful of soufflé.

'Well?'

He'd give it to her straight. Somehow she sensed it whenever he fudged. And she didn't seem to mind the criticism. *Because she wants to get better.* Yes, but he wasn't sure her reasons for wanting to get better were going to help her conquer the laborious process of making a *macaron* tower. He shook that thought away. If she left tomorrow there'd be no need to figure that out.

The thought of her leaving filled him with sudden darkness. He moistened his lips. He didn't want her leaving because he wanted her to tell Russ that there was nothing to worry about. That was all.

He dragged his mind back to the soufflé. 'An accomplished soufflé should be lighter. You probably needed to whip the egg whites a bit longer. But it's very good for a first effort.'

'You mean it's passable?'

He needed to work on that whole giving-it-to-her-straight thing.

She sampled it too, and shrugged. 'I don't understand the difference between beating, whipping, creaming, mixing and all that nonsense.'

It wasn't nonsense.

'What's all that about anyway?'

He stared at her. 'Would it help if I put a glossary defining those terms in the book?'

'Yes!' She pushed her hair off her face. 'I mean *I'd* welcome one.'

Done.

'And could you also add a definite length of time for how long egg whites should be whipped?'

'That depends on the size of the eggs, the temperature of the room in which you're whipping them, the humidity in the air and any number of other factors.'

She stared at him. He wished he could ignore the intriguing shape of her mouth. He wished he could forget their softness and the spark they'd fired to life inside him.

'Mac?'

He jumped. 'What?'

'I just asked if you could include a photo, then, of what properly beaten egg whites should look like?'

He wrote that down on the pad he'd started to keep at his elbow when they had dinner. With the addition of Jo's suggestions, the cookbook finally felt as if it were taking shape. He just had to remember he wasn't writing a text-book for apprentices.

In the kitchen, the oven timer dinged. He frowned. 'What else are you cooking?'

She didn't answer. She was already halfway to the kitchen.

She returned with a pizza. One of those frozen jobs she'd shoved in the freezer after her first shopping trip. *What on earth...?*

She took one look at his face and laughed. 'I'm a carni-vore, Mac. I'm sure cheese soufflé with a vegetable medley is all well and good, in its place, but give me a meat lovers' pizza every time.'

She seized a slice and proceeded to eat it with gusto. His stomach tightened, his groin expanded, and it was all he could do not to groan out loud.

She tilted her chin at the pizza. 'Help yourself.'

'I haven't eaten that pap since I was a teenager. It's full of chemicals and MSG and—'

'You don't know what you're missing.' She suddenly grinned, and it made him realise how remote and subdued she'd been. 'Have a slice and I'll put you out of your misery.'

His chin came up. 'What misery?'

'What I'm going to tell Russ tomorrow.'

He didn't try pretending that it didn't matter. It mat-tered a lot.

Without another word he took a slice of pizza and bit into it. 'Yuck, Jo!' He grimaced and she laughed. 'This is truly appalling.'

If she liked pizza that much he'd make her a pizza that would send her soul soaring—

He would if he still cooked, that was.

She reached for a second slice. 'On one level I know that. Whenever I eat pizza from a restaurant I can tell how much better it is. But this…? I don't know—I still like it.'

He finished his slice and gazed at what was left.

'It's strangely satisfying. Addictive.'

She was right. He reached for a second slice and polished it off. 'What *are* you going to tell Russ?'

He watched as she delicately licked her fingers—eight of them. He adjusted his jeans. He drained his glass of water. *Don't look. Don't think. Don't kiss her again.*

She rose and opened the bottle of red wine sitting on the sideboard. He hadn't noticed it before. He didn't know if she was making him wait to punish him, or whether she was trying to gather her thoughts.

She handed him a glass of wine and sat. 'I'm going to tell Russ that you're one of the most pig-headed, stubborn men I've ever met. I'm going to tell him you argue every point, and that whenever your work is interrupted you have creative type-A tantrums that would do a toddler proud. I'm going to tell him that you sulk and scowl and swear under your breath. And I'm going to tell him you've stolen my dog.'

He stared at her and the backs of his eyes prickled and burned. 'I could kiss you.'

Everything she'd just said was designed to allay each and every one of Russ's fears. He couldn't have done better himself.

'I'm not going to tell him that.'

The air between them suddenly shimmered with a swirl of unspoken desires and emotions as the memory of the kiss they'd shared rose up between them. He knew she recalled it too, because her eyes dilated in exactly the same way as they had before he'd kissed her the last time.

And it had to be the last time. *Don't kiss her again!*

But the way her lips parted and her breathing became shallow…it could slay a man.

She dragged her gaze away and took a sip of wine, but even in the dim light he could see how colour slashed high on her cheekbones. He searched his mind for something to say.

'Do you really mind about Bandit?'

Her lips twisted. 'More than I should, I suspect. But not so much now I know there are puppies on the way.'

Her chin came up and her gaze lasered him to the spot.

'Can I ask you a question?'

He set his glass down. 'If I get to ask one of you in return.'

She twirled her glass in her fingers. Eventually she set her glass down too.

'Deal.'

He stiffened his shoulders, because he didn't expect her question would be an easy one. That was okay. Neither was his.

'Shoot.'

'Why won't you visit Russ?'

He tried to not let her words bow him. He should have known this was what she'd ask.

'It's funny…you don't seem a particularly vain man.'

He wasn't.

'But actions speak louder than words.'

What was she talking about?

'Are you really *that* afraid of showing your ugly mug to the outside world?'

At any other time he'd have laughed at the 'ugly mug'. He happened to know for a fact that she was rather partial to his particular 'ugly mug' no matter how much she tried to hide it. Except…

Was that what she really thought of him?

His shoulders slumped. 'I'm not vain, Jo.'

She gnawed at her bottom lip, but didn't say anything.

He dragged a hand down his face. 'I made a promise to Mrs Devlin that I would lie low and stay out of the limelight until Ethan was out of hospital. Tabloid journalists would hound me like a dog if they knew I was in Sydney.'

She opened her mouth, but he continued before she could voice her protests.

'They'd find out—no matter how quiet I tried to keep it.'

'Why did you make such a promise?'

'Because the media brouhaha surrounding me and the accident was seriously upsetting for Ethan.'

'And you wanted to do what you could to make things easier for him.'

'At the time I'd have done anything either he or his mother asked of me.' He still would. He leaned towards her. 'Why don't you think what I'm doing for Ethan is good enough?'

She reached out and twirled the stem of her wine glass in her fingers. 'Is that your question?'

Dammit! 'No.'

She didn't say a word. Just sat there like the rotten sphinx, sipping her wine. She picked a piece of pepperoni from the pizza and popped it into her mouth.

He watched the action, suddenly ravenously hungry. Their gazes clashed and she stilled mid-chew. For a moment she was all that filled his vision, and then she looked away.

'What's your question?'

Her voice came out high and thready. He knew why. The same frustration coursed through his veins and made his skin itch. Would a brief physical relationship really be such a bad idea?

He forced himself back in his seat, closed his eyes and drew a deliberate breath into his lungs. He opened his eyes, but the question on his tongue about the relationship between her, her grandmother and her great-aunt dissolved, to be replaced by an altogether different one.

He leaned towards her and her eyes widened at whatever she saw in his face. 'What I want to know, Jo, is why you're so convinced that you're not beautiful? Who or what made you feel that way?'

She glanced away, traced the edge of her placemat. She opened her mouth, but he cut her off.

'I want the truth.' Not the lie he could see forming on her lips. 'If you won't give me the truth then don't give me anything.'

She swallowed and met his gaze. He stared back. He knew how forbidding he must look, but he wanted her to know he was serious about this.

'We might not be able to explore the physical relationship I'm aching to explore with you, but out here in the boondocks we can at least be honest with each other.'

Eventually she nodded. 'Okay.'

She pushed her hair behind her ears and then drained what was left of her wine—which was a not inconsiderable half-glass.

'When I was in school I was always teased for being a giant. I might have been picked first for basketball games, but I was always picked last at school dances. Boys obviously didn't like to date girls who were taller than them.'

He grimaced. Kids could be cruel.

'But when I was nineteen and at university I fell madly in love with a chemistry student. I thought...I thought he had feelings for me.' Her knuckles turned white around her glass. 'It turned out, though, that I was a bet—a dare. It was some kind of Chemistry Club challenge—the guy with the ugliest date for the Christmas party won.'

Mac couldn't believe what he was hearing. 'He... You—'
He broke off, shaking all over.

'Me and some of the other girls caught wind of it and
dumped them all before the event, but...'

But it had made her doubt her beauty. And she'd been
doubting it ever since.

She refilled their glasses and handed him one, glancing up at him from beneath her fringe, her eyes bruised
and wounded.

'I don't want to talk about this, Mac. I answered your
question and the conversation is now over.'

'No!' He exploded out of his chair. 'I can't believe you've
let a bunch of immature jerks let you feel like this—made
you feel ugly and worthless. You're beautiful and you're
worth a million of them.'

'Go and see Russ, Mac, and then we can talk about this
as much as you like. But until then—zip it.'

She rose, collected their plates and strode into the
kitchen. He wanted to go after her, shake her and tell her
those boys had been wrong. He curled a hand around the
doorframe of the dining room before he could storm through
it. If he went after her he'd kiss her. And this time neither
one of them would stop.

He strode out to the front veranda, Bandit at his heels,
into the chill night. If only he could get his hands on those
cruel twerps. If only he could prove to her that she was
beautiful.

You can. Go see Russ. For her.

He sat on the top step and held his head in his hands.
That would mean something to her. But...

Go see Russ? Though he wanted to, with everything that
was inside him, he couldn't break his promise.

Jo searched for signs of pity in Mac's face the next day,
when he gave her a brand-new recipe to try out—coq au
vin—but couldn't see any.

What did disconcert her was the way his gaze rested on her lips and the answering hunger that rose through her. She didn't want to want this man. She wished she hadn't told him that nasty sordid tale last night. She wished she'd been able to resist his appeal for honesty. He made her feel far too vulnerable.

She gazed at the recipe and gave her brain a metaphorical kick. *Think of something halfway intelligent to say.*

'So, this needs to simmer for a long time?'

'That's right.'

'Simmer, boil, poach, stew—all that nonsense should probably go in your glossary of terms.'

He wrote that down on his notepad. 'A genuine simmer is just below boiling point, but where there's still the occasional bubble surfacing.'

Right. She filed the information away.

'C'mon—sit down,' he ordered, gesturing to the kitchen table. 'There's hours before you need to get the stew on to simmer.'

'There's a lot of chopping to do,' she said, referring to the recipe.

He switched on the laptop he'd brought downstairs with him. 'Jo, not even *you* need five hours to chop some chicken and vegetables.'

He had a point. If only she hadn't done the grocery shopping yesterday afternoon she could have used that as an excuse to avoid him now. She sat, but she'd have much sooner grabbed the broom and started sweeping the laundry, or headed outside for a spot of weeding.

Anything except being in the same room as him, sitting so close to him. And if he thought they were going to continue last night's conversation then he was going to be sadly disappointed.

'What do you want?'

He raised an eyebrow and she knew she wasn't being

particularly gracious—but then she didn't *feel* particularly gracious. She felt grumpy, out of sorts, frustrated...

She stuck her nose in the air. 'I'll have you know I'm very busy with important housemaidy things.'

His lips twitched. 'Do you think you can fit the making of tea into all that important housemaid business?'

With an exaggerated sigh, she rose and made tea while he fiddled around with his computer.

When she set the pot and two mugs on the table and took her seat again he said, 'We're going to take a vocational test.'

Something inside her started to shrivel. The sooner she worked out the next stage of her life the sooner she'd leave him in peace, right?

He fixed her with the clear blue of his eyes. 'You've helped me and now I want to help you.'

The shrivelling promptly stopped. He *wasn't* trying to get rid of her?

'Ready?'

She shrugged. 'I guess.'

He turned to the laptop. '"Are you more motivated by achievement or appreciation?"' he read.

She blinked. 'Um...' She liked to *see* the results of her hard work—as in the way Mac's house now currently shone after all her dusting and sweeping. 'Achievement.'

He leaned back in his chair with a frown. 'Are you sure?'

She glared back at him. 'Of course I'm sure.'

'Why do you want to make that *macaron* tower for your grandmother, then? Aren't you hoping to gain her appreciation and help her win a bet?'

What she really wanted to do was bring her grandmother and great-aunt's differences to an end. She knew they loved each other, so why couldn't they show it?

Because of her? She'd always been a bone of contention between them.

'Jo?'

She shook herself. 'Fine—whatever. Appreciation, then.'

His glare deepened. 'You have to take this seriously.'

She lifted her hands. 'I am.'

He glared at her for a few more seconds before returning to his computer. '"Do you tend to rely on your past experiences or on hunches?"'

She was tempted to fish a coin from her purse and toss it. 'Hunches…'

He checked the appropriate box just as she was about to change her answer. *Oh, well.*

'"Are you more interested in what is real or what is meaningful?"'

He stared at her. She stared back.

'Meaningful,' they said at the same time.

He asked her over sixty questions!

At the end he gave her a score. 'And that means… Hey!' he said when she took the computer from him.

She shook her head. 'Now it's your turn.' Let's see how he liked being put under the microscope. '"Do you tend to be easily distracted or able to concentrate well?"'

He glared. 'I can concentrate just fine when I want to.'

She checked the box for 'easily distracted'. As far as she could tell Mac actively *searched* for distraction.

'"In most situations do you rely more on careful planning or improvisation?"'

He dragged a hand down his face. 'Improvisation—more's the pity. Or these recipes I'm trying to drag out of my head would be a lot easier to commit to paper.'

'"Do you prefer step-by-step instructions or to figure things out for yourself?"'

He scowled. 'If only I *did* prefer step-by-step instructions!'

She was going to have to get him cooking again. Somehow.

When they'd finished she gave him a score and then read

out the associated job suggestions. '"Artist",' she said. Chef fitted into that category perfectly. '"Teacher. Entertainer."'

'Very funny.' He retrieved the computer.

She wasn't trying to be funny, but she kept her mouth shut.

'According to your score, you'd make a good girl scout. What *is* this garbage?'

'You tell me.'

'No, no—here we go. It says you'd be a good scientist.'

'Except I'm tired of being a scientist, remember?'

'You're tired of being a *geologist*,' he corrected. 'You could go back to university and major in a different science.'

'Yay,' she said, with a deplorable lack of enthusiasm. 'Also, I want to live in a city. Find me a job in one of those.'

'Why?'

'I want to go to the cinema, and the library, and to big shopping centres and all those lovely things.' All the places she'd missed when working in the Outback.

'Here we go. As you're apparently service-orientated you'd also make a good nurse.'

The sight of blood didn't worry her. But… 'I hate hospitals.'

He took on a sick pallor. 'Me too.'

And just like that she wanted to reach out and take his hand, offer silent support and comfort. He wouldn't welcome it. He'd probably kiss her in retaliation.

Ooh!

She pulled her hands into her lap. 'Well, that's certainly provided me with food for thought.'

'It was complete and utter nonsense!'

She smiled at him. 'I appreciate the effort.'

Finally—*finally*—he smiled back.

CHAPTER EIGHT

JO PULLED THE *macarons* from the oven and set the tray on a trivet. Hands on hips, she surveyed them. These weren't pretty, like the picture on the internet. They were crooked, misshapen and kind of flat. For the love of everything green and good! How hard could it be to make these fussy little confections?

She hunched over her laptop and reread the recipe, but she couldn't find where she'd gone wrong.

She'd made a halfway decent cheese soufflé. As far as she could tell her coq au vin had been good, even if Mac hadn't eaten very much of it. And, okay, so her béarnaise sauce hadn't held together the way it was apparently supposed to, but it had tasted just fine to her.

Her hands clenched. For a week now she'd been religiously following Mac's instructions and cooking recipes with names she couldn't even pronounce. She'd figured she was ready to try her hand at *macarons*.

She cast a glance at the tray and her lip curled. Apparently not.

Baring her teeth, she made a pot of tea and then pulled another egg carton towards her. She would master this if it was the last thing she ever did.

She separated eggs. She'd need to buy more. Luckily a nearby hobby farm sold farm-fresh eggs. The way she was going through the rotten things she'd be on a first-name basis with the owners of said hobby farm by the end of the week.

Mac strode into the kitchen, staring down at a sheet of paper in his hands. Tonight's recipe, she supposed. Yay, more cooking. She forgot all about cooking, though, when she noticed how amply he filled out his beaten-up jeans. The material stretched across strong thighs and she could almost see the muscles rippling beneath the denim.

He glanced up and froze when he saw what she was doing.

Her chin shot up. Well, bad luck, buddy! She'd been making his recipes for seven days now. *Seven days of cooking*.

He turned to leave. 'Don't even think about it.' Her voice came out on a snarl. He turned back and raised an eyebrow. 'Sit!' She pointed to a chair. She could see he was about to refuse. 'I will tie you to it if I have to.'

He blinked. His eyes turned dark and lazy. Deliberately his gaze lowered to her lips, all but caressing them. 'I'm almost tempted to put that to the test.'

She had to swallow. Wrestling with him would be so very intriguing.

And foolhardy.

She backed up one step and then another. She seized the tray of *macarons*. 'Look at these.'

He did, and then grimaced.

She dropped the tray to the table and swung away to pour him a mug of tea. She pushed it across the table towards him. 'Would you like a *macaron* to go with that?' she asked drily

His lips twitched, but he didn't sit. 'No, thanks.'

'Of course you don't. No rational person would touch one of those with a twenty-foot pole. Have you seen anything less appetising in your life?'

He took a hasty slug of his tea.

She glared. Why did this cooking gig have to be so

hard? 'If you say one more thing against my béarnaise sauce I'll...'

'Tie me up?'

Images pounded at her. 'Pelt you with my *macarons*.'

He laughed. It seemed like an age since he'd laughed. 'A fate worse than death.'

She tilted her chin at the tray. 'Those suckers would probably knock you out. Please, Mac, I need your help. Can you please, please, *please* tell me what I did wrong?'

He sat and pulled the tray towards him and something inside her chest started to flutter and thrash. *Two birds. One stone.* If she could get him to do something that was halfway related to cooking it would teach her a technique she obviously needed and maybe—just maybe—it would help him overcome his resistance to preparing food again. Maybe he would find his way back to his passion and find some comfort in losing himself in it for a while.

'I suspect you didn't beat the egg whites for long enough.'

There seemed to be a theme emerging there.

'Or perhaps you didn't use enough confectioners' sugar. Or you cooked them at too high a temperature.'

There were too many variables. With a growl she finished separating the eggs—a full dozen—and shoved the bowl and a whisk at him. 'Show me how it's done,' she demanded. 'There must be something wrong with my technique.'

His face closed up and his body drew in on itself, tight and unbending. 'You know I—'

'I'm ready to beg. And it's not real cooking, Mac. It's just whisking.'

And then it hit her—how she could keep him in the kitchen with her. She moistened her lips. 'I haven't really told you why it's so important that I master this stupid *macaron* tower, have I?'

'You mentioned the bet between your grandmother and great-aunt.'

She snorted. 'Ah, the bet. It wasn't our finest hour I'm afraid. My grandmother had been flicking through a magazine and came across a picture of one and made some throwaway comment. I said it was pretty. Great-Aunt Edith then said there was no way on God's green earth—her words—that I could make one for my grandmother's next birthday. Grandma, thinking she was standing up for me, said I could do it standing on my head.'

He winced.

'Naturally, of course, I said it'd be a piece of cake.' *What an idiot.*

'And then the pearls were put up as a stake…?'

'It's like something from a bad comedy.' And she was caught squarely in the middle.

'Why did you let yourself get drawn in?'

'Habit. But lately I've been thinking it's a bad habit all round—this adversarial bent we've developed.'

'It must've been there before you came along.'

'I guess so, but I want to do something to change it. I want to mend it.'

He leaned in towards her and her heart did some more of that fluttering and thrashing.

'You know the whole "Russ having a heart attack and me suddenly re-evaluating my life" stuff. I know they love each other. So…'

'How are you going to change it?'

'I don't know yet.'

'Isn't making a *macaron* tower just falling in with their continued rivalry?'

She shrugged. 'My plan so far is that I make the best damn *macaron* tower that's ever been seen and then I take the pearls and claim them for my own.'

He started to laugh. 'I suspect that'd be something to

see.' He sobered. 'But, Jo, isn't the necklace just the object of something that goes deeper between them?'

She slumped into a chair. 'I guess.'

'Tell me about them.'

So she did. She told him about Great-Aunt Edith first. 'I mean I know she loves me. And she's the one I most physically resemble. So it's odd—I can't understand why she's been on my case since, like, for*ever*. I shouldn't wear this and I shouldn't say that, and I shouldn't act like this and I shouldn't draw attention to myself like that, and I shouldn't wear my hair like this. On and on and on.'

It wore her out just thinking about it.

'It made me rebel in every dreadful way when I was a teenager. I wore tight pants and even tighter tops—things that didn't suit me. I'm afraid she was right on that subject.'

'And your grandmother?'

'My grandmother is the opposite. She's pretty, petite, and oh-so ladylike. She's stuck up for me forever, declaring I should wear, say and do whatever I damn well please—always telling me that I look gorgeous and pretty regardless of my get-up.' She glanced at Mac. 'And I'm afraid that's not always been the best advice to be given.'

It was her grandmother's vision that she'd never really been able to live up to.

He leaned back. 'They love each other, you say?'

'Oh, yes.' There wasn't a single doubt about that. 'But after one particularly vehement argument twelve months ago Great-Aunt Edith moved out.' Which was crazy. Her grandmother and aunt belonged together.

'Is it possible your great-aunt feels like you do—overshadowed by the petite women who surround her and made to feel she's never measured up?'

As far as Jo could tell, her great-aunt was indestructible.

Or was that just the attitude she assumed?

She sat up straighter.

'That attitude—it's wrong. You're a beautiful woman, Jo, which means your great-aunt must've been a great beauty too. But if she didn't believe herself beautiful, can you imagine how she must've felt, growing up with a sister who fitted into society's "classically beautiful" mould?'

Jo's throat tightened.

'If they love each other, as you say…'

'They do.' She might not be certain of much, but she was certain of that.

'Could it be that your grandmother is showing her love and acceptance for your great-aunt through you? If your great-aunt has felt overshadowed all these years then your grandmother treating you—the child who looks so like her much-loved sister—with adoration and such disregard for what the world thinks… Well, that's powerful stuff.'

Wow.

Things started to fall into place.

Holy Cow! 'I don't know what to say.'

His eyes narrowed. 'You're not going to cry, are you?'

She tipped up her chin. 'Most certainly not.'

And that was when she noticed that he was whisking her egg whites. A fist tightened about her heart even as she noticed that his technique was way better than hers. *Keep it casual.*

'Wouldn't it be easier to use an electric beater?'

He glared and she raised her hands. 'Sorry—is that some weird food purist thing?'

Humour lit his eyes although it didn't touch his lips. 'It *would* be easier.'

'But?'

'But this kitchen doesn't happen to be stocked with that kind of equipment.'

Oh, that sealed it. She was going out and buying an electric mixer first thing tomorrow.

'Here—you try.'

She took the bowl and tried to mimic his whisking action.

He didn't grimace, but she suspected he wanted to. 'It just takes a bit of practice,' he assured her.

She wished she felt reassured.

'Oh, for heaven's sake, Jo!' he exploded a moment later. 'That whisk isn't a hammer. You're trying to whisk air into those egg whites.'

She held the bowl out to him. He didn't shrink back, but she could see what was going through his mind.

She snapped, 'This isn't *real* cooking. It's just some stupid egg whites and a rotten whisk.'

He ground his teeth together, snatching the bowl from her. 'You have an attitude problem when it comes to the kitchen.'

Wasn't that the truth?

'Look—*this* is how you're meant to be doing it.'

He demonstrated what he meant. He looked so at home with a whisk—kind of commanding and…right. She could watch him do this all day.

'Why did you grow up with your grandmother and great-aunt?'

She'd answer all the questions he wanted if he'd just keep whisking.

'There was a twenty-year age difference between my father and my mother. When I was five, my mother left. I think she was tired of hanging out with older people. When she left, Grandma and Great-Aunt Edith moved in.'

'Do you still see your mother?'

'Occasionally.' She peered into the bowl. 'She lives in the UK now. Aren't they done?'

'No. Test it.'

He kept hold of the bowl but handed her the whisk. She swirled it through the mixture.

'See?' he said. 'It's not thick enough yet.'

Right… She glanced at the tray on the table. Well, that

was one question answered. She bounced up and measured out confectioners' sugar and set it on the table within Mac's easy reach.

'And your father?'

She wrinkled her nose. 'We're not close. He moved out to a bachelor pad when I was six. He's a geologist. I became a geologist because I thought it might give us something to talk about.'

'But?'

'But I don't like being a geologist—and if he has a problem with that then he can just suck it up.'

Mac stopped whisking to stare at her.

'Relationships are two-way streets. If he wants a proper relationship with me then he needs to put in an effort too.'

'You sound kind of well-adjusted on that?'

She simply shrugged.

'Here—test the mixture now.'

She did.

'Feel how much stiffer it is? That's what you're aiming for.'

Oh, okay. So that explained the cheese soufflé too…

Mac looked ready to leave again. She handed the whisk back to him.

'My father is what he is. Grandma and Great-Aunt Edith have raised me, loved me and stood by me even when we've all been at loggerheads with each other. They're my family and they're important to me. I don't want to think what my childhood would've been like if it wasn't for them.'

'And that's why you want to bring their silly feuding over the pearls to an end? And you think a *macaron* tower will help?'

'It can't hurt.'

'Well, there's a start.' He pushed the bowl over to her. 'Perfectly whisked egg whites.'

He stood.

He couldn't leave yet! She took the sugar she'd measured out earlier and went to tip the lot into the egg whites.

Mac's hand on her wrist stopped her. 'What are you doing?'

He sounded utterly scandalised.

She forced her eyes wide. 'I'm adding the sugar.'

'You're supposed to add it *slowly.*'

He proceeded to show her exactly how to add it, and how to beat it into the mixture. She might have feigned a bit more stupidity than necessary, but it was worth it to see him work. Surreptitiously she measured out the other ingredients and had them ready whenever he needed them.

She moistened her lips. *Keep telling him stories. Don't give him time to think about what he's doing.*

'Grandma and Great-Aunt Edith are the reason I want to move back to the city. They're eighty-five and eighty-three, respectively. I want to spend more time with them.'

He glanced up. 'So the cinemas, libraries, cafés—they're just…?'

'Attractive fringe benefits.'

He continued to stare at her. It took an effort not to fidget.

'They're getting on. They're independent, and in good health at the moment, but it won't last forever. When the time comes I want to care for them. They spent so much of their lives looking after me and…well, we're family and it matters.'

Russ's heart attack had taught her what the important things in life were and it wasn't a lesson she meant to forget.

Those blue eyes flashed and she swore she almost felt heat searing her skin.

'Are you trying to make me feel guilty about Russ?'

She blinked. 'Of course not.'

He pushed the bowl towards her and stood. 'I think you'll find your mix is ready.'

'Don't go, Mac. I'm not trying to make you feel bad about Russ. I tried that the other day and I'm not one to go back over old ground. I just wanted to make sure you knew how he felt—that while he won't say anything he's hurt that you haven't been to see him. Now that you do know the rest of it is up to you.'

'There is no "rest of it", Jo. There's nothing that can be done.'

'You could at least tell him why. You could at least acknowledge that you're letting him down and apologise. I understand you feel responsible for Ethan, but he's not the only person who needs you.'

This wasn't the way to make him stay.

She stuck out a hip. His gaze fixed on it for a heartbeat before returning to her face. She tried to control her breathing.

'Look, I'm doing my best with your rotten recipes, aren't I?'

'They're not supposed to be rotten.'

'Then why do I keep dreaming of fish-finger burgers?'

He adjusted his stance. 'Your point being…?'

'I'm trying to help you out, so the least you can do is sit there and watch as I try to shape this unholy mess into pretty little *macarons*. Give me tips where appropriate and whatnot.'

He folded his arms, lowered his gaze to her hip again. When he raised it his eyes had started to gleam. 'I'll do it for a boon.'

A…*what*?

'A kiss.'

Something inside her softened. He smirked. She hardened it. Did he think she'd run away from the challenge? She hitched up her chin. She wasn't in any mood to be browbeaten.

'Done.'

A kiss on the cheek. She bit her inner cheek to stop from smiling. Simple.

'A kiss on the lips,' he said, as if he'd read her mind.

She could feel her eyes narrow. 'I thought you said kissing was a bad idea?'

'I was wrong. I want to kiss you. A lot. And for a long time. In fact I want to do more than kiss you, Jo.'

Everything inside her thrilled to his words. She should be running for the hills, but she needed steady legs for running and hers were far from steady. The temptation to follow the beat of this particular drum flooded through her. It addled her mind, but it didn't completely scramble it.

'Fine, then. A kiss on the lips. But no hands.' She didn't need even the tiniest bits of their bodies touching. 'And not until the *macarons* are in the oven.'

'Deal.'

He sat. Her heart chugged. This was craziness—absolute craziness. Why on earth did he want a kiss from a great lug like her?

'You're a beautiful woman.'

She didn't believe that for a moment, but she couldn't deny the heat that flared between them. It didn't make sense, but it existed all the same.

She picked up a spoon.

'Your hands are shaking.'

She gritted her teeth and handed the spoon to him. 'Cooking makes me nervous. Show me how you dollop this mess out to make pretty little domes.'

'You don't *dollop* it. You pipe it.'

He flung open a kitchen drawer, seized a freezer bag and snipped off the end. She watched as he masterfully filled the makeshift piping bag and then proceeded to pipe a perfect row on her newly prepared cookie sheet.

'We'll take it in turns. You do the next row.'

His hands were steady. Hers weren't. That had to be the

reason his rows looked so much neater than hers. And even while she lectured herself to pay attention and follow his instructions precisely all she could think about was what beautiful hands he had and what an idiot she'd been to make that no-hands rule for their kiss. It would be divine to have those fingers tracing across her naked flesh.

'They're ready to go in the oven now.'

Her pulse fluttered up into her throat, jamming her breath and making her knees tremble. *Don't show weakness.* She did what she could to force steel to her backbone. With an insouciance she was far from feeling she picked up the tray and moved towards the oven.

'Wait.'

She wanted to scream.

Mac clicked his tongue. 'I'd better check the oven temperature.'

It reminded her of what she'd just achieved in here. Mac had all but made those *macarons* himself.

He opened the oven door and put his hand inside. Apparently satisfied, he took the tray from her and placed it inside. When he turned back he wore the most satisfied smile she'd ever seen a male of the species wear.

'Now you have to kiss me.'

She might doubt her attractiveness to the opposite sex, but there was no denying the relish in Mac's grin. That relish gleamed from his eyes, practically spilling from his every pore. Her throat started to tighten. She couldn't trust it. Mac was a consummate actor.

She slammed her hands to her hips. 'You think it's fair to blackmail a kiss from me?'

'God, but you're beautiful when you flare up like that.'

The shrivelling started. 'And now I *know* you're not being serious. I've never been beautiful and—'

'I've never understood the urge some men have to bend

a woman over their knee and give them six of the best... until now.'

Her eyes started from her head. Her throat thickened and she had to swallow a couple of times. 'You wouldn't dare!'

He leaned in close, his eyes blazing back into hers. 'You'd better think very carefully about what you say from here on. Believe me, Jo, you don't want to test me on this.' His lips hooked up with self-satisfaction. 'After all, you don't know what boon I might demand next time.'

She couldn't look away. 'What makes you so sure there'll be a next time? If those *macarons* turn out perfectly I won't need your help again.'

'You still need to master the filling—not to mention the assembling of the tower.'

Heck.

'And if I hear you make one more disparaging remark about your appearance I promise you, Jo, you *will* be sorry.'

She believed him. He looked utterly and completely forbidding.

Mac wasn't sure if anything had ever satisfied him as much as the gobsmacked expression plastered across Jo's face.

He leaned in closer to her again. 'You are divine, desirable, and all I can think about is kissing you. And more. *So* much more.'

'Stop.' Her voice came out as a hoarse whisper.

'You know how to make me stop, my beautiful, *beautiful* Jo.'

Her eyes widened. He could see the struggle she had not to open her mouth and contradict him. His heart twisted at the uncertainty that flashed in her eyes, at the vulnerability she tried to hide. She was one of the most beautiful women he'd ever met and it hurt something inside him that she doubted her loveliness like this.

'You have a face that poets have only ever dreamed of,'

he continued. 'And, speaking of dreams… I dream constantly of unbuttoning your shirt and freeing your pretty breasts from your bra, feasting my gaze on them until I can't resist, until I lose control and have to touch them, taste them, caress them. I want to give you the same physical pleasure I get from just looking at you. Oh, and, Jo…I dream of you losing control and—'

Her lips slammed to his and Mac was determined to kiss her until she finally believed she was beautiful.

Except her lips touched his and every thought, his very ability to think, dissolved as if rational thought had never existed. All that was left was sensation. Kissing Jo was like standing on a storm-tossed headland, with the wind whipping past and thunder clapping overhead and lightning creating jagged patterns across the sky. It was crazy and elemental and not to be withstood.

He didn't try to withstand it. He'd never felt more alive in all his life.

He curved his hands around her face to deepen the kiss.

'No hands,' she murmured against his lips, before her tongue tangled with his and her hands went to the back of his neck to pull him closer.

Where he was hard she was soft. Where he was famished she spread a banquet at his feet. Where he thirsted, she bathed him in water until he felt quenched. He never wanted to stop. Kissing Jo didn't just make him feel alive. It made him feel free.

He groaned when she eventually reefed herself out of his arms. She stood there staring at him, her chest rising and falling and her fingers pressed to swollen lips. He reached out a hand to her, but she backed up and shook her head.

'Did I hurt you?' he managed to croak out.

She pulled her hand away. 'Of course not. I… It's just—' She tried to glare, but it didn't quite come off. 'I thought you promised me gentlemanly behaviour?'

So had he. 'I lost my head.' He glared too. 'This whole thing we decided…that kissing is a bad idea…that's a load of hogwash. Kissing you is the best idea I've ever had. I *like* kissing you, Jo. I like it a lot. I think there should be more of it.'

'No.'

'Why not?'

The glare she sent him should have withered him. 'Too complicated, remember?' she snapped.

She swung away to grab a couple of sodas from the fridge. She set the one he guessed was meant for him on the far side of the table from her. She opened hers and took a long swig. He couldn't drag his gaze from the long line of her throat. The longer he watched the thirstier he became.

'Mac, please stop looking at me like that!'

'I can't help it.'

And he didn't want to help it. Right or wrong, he wanted to get naked with Jo as soon as humanly possible.

'I want you and I love looking at you.'

She scrubbed a hand down her face. 'You're deliberately trying to make this as difficult as possible.'

'My body is on fire. If you want to call a halt to things, then fine. That's your prerogative. But I want your body burning as badly as mine.'

And he could tell from the tight way she held herself that it was. There was a remarkably simple solution to that. She just had to say the word. He continued to gaze at her with naked hunger, hoping she'd lose control and kiss him again.

If he asked, would she stay? Here at the beach house? With him? He'd just made *macarons* and the world hadn't caved in. Maybe—

'Fine,' she snapped. 'I'll simply remove myself from your presence.'

'You can't. You have *macarons* in the oven.'

'Then *you* go somewhere else. Take Bandit for a walk or do some work.'

He shook his head, his eyes never leaving hers. 'My house. I can go where I want.'

Her chin shot up and those smoky eyes blazed at him. His mouth watered.

'You're determined to remain here with me in the kitchen?'

In answer he merely reached out and took possession of his can of soda.

She slammed herself into a chair. 'Fine, then I'll raise something that's been playing in my mind about Ethan.'

Was she trying to tick him off? Fine. She might find it harder than she thought. 'And what might that be?'

'Just for a moment reverse your and Ethan's situations. Pretend he's the boss and you're the apprentice.'

He dragged a hand down his face. If only that were the truth. If only—

'Imagine you're the apprentice who screwed up—as apprentices do. Wouldn't you want to see your boss? For starters, wouldn't you want to know he was okay? And, secondly, wouldn't you want to know he thought you important enough to visit?'

Bile burned his stomach. Jo turned him on like no other woman ever had, but she was going to give him an ulcer too.

'Or would I just be glad to never have to clap eyes again on the man who ruined my life?'

She folded her arms. 'Would you believe your life was ruined? And if you did would you hold anyone else responsible?'

He had no idea, but according to Diana Devlin he had indeed ruined her son's life.

'Mac.' Jo rested her forearms on the table, her eyes dark and troubled. 'It occurred to me the other day that Ethan might, in fact, be plagued with the same guilt that torments you.'

Every muscle he had froze.

'*He's* the one who accidentally let a platter of seafood slide into that vat of oil. *He's* the direct cause for the start of the fire. You know it was an accident, and I know it was an accident, but does Ethan? Or does he hold *himself* responsible for the whole sorry mess?'

The thought horrified him. 'He can't!'

'Says who?' She stabbed a finger at him. 'How would *you* feel if the positions were reversed?'

His mouth went dry. How *would* he feel if he'd been the one who'd dropped the iced seafood into the hot oil? *Guilty as sin.* His fingers tightened around his can of soda, crushing it. Bubbles fizzed up and over his hand to drip to the floor.

He barely knew Ethan. They'd probably spoken a grand total of twenty words to each other. Like most of the new apprentices he'd been in awe of Mac.

Mac cursed himself anew for not taking more time to put Ethan at ease for his first couple of appearances on the show.

Jo came to stand in front of him. She smelled of sugar and *macaron* and soda. 'You want me to believe I'm beautiful.'

'Because you're gorgeous,' he croaked out.

'And in the same way I want you to realise you're not responsible for the accident.'

His heart thudded. His temples pounded. And an ache started up behind his eyes. 'Ethan's not responsible either.'

'No, he's not. It was just an awful accident. I just hope he's not lying in that godforsaken hospital bed of his beating himself up about it.'

So did he.

'Mac, you just helped me make *macarons*.' She shook her head. 'If we're being honest, *you* made them. And the world didn't come tumbling down around your ears, did it?'

It took all his strength to swallow rather than howl. 'What are you trying to say?'

'I'm saying ring him.'

But Mrs Devlin said…

This mattered too much for him to get it wrong. He *had* to find out if Ethan blamed himself. If he did then Mac had to do everything he could to make the younger man see sense. To put his mind to rest.

'Mac?'

'I don't want to do anything to make matters worse.'

She handed him a tea towel to wipe his hands. Taking his can from him, she set it on the table before wiping the spill at his feet. When the oven timer buzzed it made them both jump.

He stood frozen as she pulled the tray from the oven and set it on the table.

'Your rows are perfect.' She pointed. 'Look.'

He stared at them and something inside him swelled at their perfection, at the knowledge that he'd made them.

'Mine are less so.'

'Practice. All you need, Jo, is practice.' Practice at making perfect rounds. Practice at believing she was beautiful.

I want you to realise you're not responsible for the accident.

Could she be right? He was too afraid to believe it—too afraid that Ethan would take one look at him and turn away in disgust. But what if he didn't?

His heart pounded so hard it hurt.

Jo gestured to the *macarons* and then around the kitchen. 'You love all this.'

It was pointless denying it. She'd put that whisk in his hand and for a moment he'd felt as if he could fly. He'd tried to ignore it by focussing on her story about her family, but no matter how much he'd lied to himself it hadn't worked. In much the same way it appeared that trying to turn his back on his passion hadn't worked. He could blame his talent and his ambition all he liked, but it didn't stop him from loving cooking as much as he ever had.

'I expect Ethan must love all this too.'

Something inside him stilled.

She blew out a breath and fell into a chair. 'I understand you wanting to help him. You've both suffered a dreadful accident that's changed your lives. But…'

Mac sat too, his mind a whirlwind. 'This is a hell of a way to stop me from kissing you again.'

She bit her lip. 'I shouldn't have started this. It's none of my business.'

He didn't know if he was angry with her, or grateful, or something else entirely. 'Don't stop now.'

She stared at him, her eyes dark. 'We've got in each other's faces so much this last fortnight, with me demanding you take better care of yourself and you taking issue with my body image, and me wanting to change your view of the accident and you trying to help me find a new direction career-wise. And then there's Bandit, which has added a whole new dimension. I didn't know any of this was going to happen, Mac, and it's been intense. I've never experienced this kind of intensity with anyone in such a short time before.'

He dragged a hand down his face.

She straightened, her voice suddenly tart. 'And you needn't interpret that as me being in love with you, or something stupid like that, because that's not what I'm talking about. This is… It's not friendship, but there are elements of that. It's not lust, though that's part of it.'

She shook her head. 'Maybe it's the proximity and the isolation and the fact we've both recently been through something big that's created a kind of melting pot here.' Her chin lifted. 'Do you know what I'm talking about or am I just—?'

'No.'

She glanced down at her hands.

'I mean yes,' he growled, wanting to wipe that look from her face. 'I was saying no to your alternative. I'm saying yes, I understand what you're trying to say. I can't explain it but there's a connection.'

And he didn't want there to be one. Even though he liked her.

She grasped at the air, as if searching for the right words. Her gaze returned to his—troubled, puzzled, dazed. 'When I think about some of the things I've said to you I'm appalled at myself. I don't feel like this—the here and now we're in—is the real world.'

He eased back in his seat. His heart thudded in his ears. 'There's something else you want to say that you wouldn't normally say in *the real world*, as you put it—isn't there?'

She slumped back before straightening again. 'What the heck? In for a penny… Helping Ethan realise there's a future—that he has a future to look forward to—wouldn't that be a fine way to help him?'

Yes. Yes, it would.

'You both share a passion for cooking, right? Well, maybe Ethan would like to help you work on the cookbook.'

'He's still in hospital. He's still recovering.'

She ignored that. 'Maybe down the track the two of you could start up your own cooking show on TV—do it the way it should've been done in the first place.'

His heart tried to pound out of his chest. He leapt from his chair. 'We'd be considered freaks.'

'Is that how you see Ethan?'

Of course it wasn't. But the general public wouldn't be so kind.

'Is that how you see yourself?'

A fist tightened about his ribcage

'You tell me I'm beautiful and expect me to believe you, but you refuse to see yourself fairly.'

He was scarred. End of story.

But he didn't repel her. He met her gaze and swallowed. Maybe other people would see past his and Ethan's scars too.

'Call him, Mac. See how he's doing. Give him something to live for.'

She folded her arms when he didn't say anything. He *couldn't* say anything. A lump the size of a frozen pizza throbbed in his throat.

'Promise me you'll at least think about it?'

He gave a curt nod, feeling bruised all over.

'And tomorrow I think we should try something different. Tomorrow *you'll* come down here and cook one of your complicated recipes, barking your instructions as you go, and I'll jot them down.'

Did he dare?

'Mac, it's time to decide what's more important—your self-imposed punishment or getting this cookbook written.'

With that she left.

Mac fell back into his seat. He let out a long, slow breath from cramped lungs. Man, that really had been one hell of a way to stop him kissing her.

CHAPTER NINE

THE NEXT DAY Jo swept, vacuumed and beat rugs. She did three loads of laundry, washed dishes and wiped down shelves. She cleaned windows—inside and out. This close to the coast, the easterly sea breezes laced the windows with salt. They needed cleaning. *A lot.*

She tried to fill her mind with salt, dust and cleaning, but over and over it returned to Mac and yesterday's kiss, to the words Mac had spoken, to the hunger in his eyes. And every single time her heart fluttered up into her throat, her thighs softened and her eyes burned. Did he really think her beautiful?

She collapsed on the top step of the veranda and stared at the glorious scene in front of her, hugging a bottle of window cleaner and a cleaning cloth to her chest. She could look at it any way she wanted, but Mac wasn't feigning his desire for her. She might not be able to explain the attraction between them, but that didn't make it any less real. He found her attractive. *Beautiful.*

He wanted her.

You are divine, desirable and all I can think about is kissing you.

When he'd said that he'd made her believe it. Hearing his voice in her head now made her believe it. When she saw herself reflected in his eyes she liked what she saw. He had no reason to lie. So why couldn't she keep on believing it?

Her heart did a strange little skip.

Bandit came to sit beside her and even tolerated it when Jo fondled her ears. 'Has he shut you out too, girl?'

Jo hadn't clapped eyes on Mac once so far today and… she glanced at her watch…it was nearly three o'clock. He'd been down for coffee while she'd been pegging clothes on the line—and he'd taken the entire pot back upstairs with him. He'd obviously made himself sandwiches and taken them back up to his room too, while she'd vacuumed the front rooms. She knew he was up there. She'd heard his heavy footfalls as he'd paced back and forth, back and forth.

She scowled. It was time for him to come out of this self-imposed exile and live again.

'If he doesn't come down to cook one of those absurd recipes of his, Bandit, then he's getting fish fingers for dinner.'

'Now, *that* would be a fate worse than death.'

Bandit raced across to the door.

Jo took her time turning around.

It still didn't ready her for the shocking bolt of heat that stabbed through her. She found herself repeating over and over: *One-night stands are bad. One-night stands are bad.*

She didn't mean to be judgmental. One-night stands were all well and good between consenting adults. But instinct warned her that a fling with Mac would be a *very* bad idea. He made her feel too much. Which was a real shame, because she'd be prepared to pay a lot for the physical release he could give her, but in this instance she suspected the price would be too high.

'How are you on this fine day, Jo?'

Was it a fine day? She went to rise, but he motioned for her to remain where she was before taking a seat beside her.

'I was hoping you were about to put me to work,' she said. 'That would make it a fine day.' His eyes suddenly gleamed and she choked. She wanted to add, *In the kitchen—writing down your recipes…* but decided it would be wiser to remain silent.

'Soon,' he said, growing sober. 'I think the suggestion you made yesterday has a lot of merit. So I'll cook and you can make notes.'

Yes! And tomorrow she'd hassle him to show her how to assemble the *macaron* tower. 'Smart move. It'll save you from the fish fingers.'

'First I want to clear the air about yesterday's kiss.'

Was that even possible?

'Or at least try to explain myself.'

The shrivelling started—the dying inside. She stared directly out in front of her. Here it came—the let-her-down-gently speech. For a short time she'd believed… She shook her head and swallowed.

'I don't want you to think I want a fling with you, Jo.'

Ditto. But she remained silent. She didn't have the heart to take part in the conversation. If she had the energy she'd cut him off and ask if they couldn't just get on with the cooking.

'I like you, Jo. I like you a lot. And, yes, I want to make love with you. But you deserve more than that.'

Yeah, right. Blah, blah, blah.

'*I* want more than that.'

She frowned. That wasn't part of the usual routine. Where was he going with this?

He bumped her shoulder gently with his. 'I want more than that with *you*, Jo.'

She blinked. She blinked at the beach, at a flock of seagulls, at the field of native grass.

'Are you ever going to look at me?'

She turned to meet his gaze—his deadly earnest and vulnerable gaze. She had to swallow before she could speak. 'You're saying… Are you saying you want to pursue a relationship with me?'

'Yes.'

Something inside her started to sing.

'But…' he added.

The singing stopped. A weight dropped down on her. She swung back to face the front.

'For heaven's sake, Jo, I'm not trying to blow you off. I'm trying to tell you how I mean to go forward from here. I…I understand that I might not figure in your plans for the future, and that just because a relationship with you is what I want, it doesn't mean you're going to fall in line with me.'

She had to look at him. She couldn't help it.

He was glaring down at his clenched fists, the pulse at the side of his jaw was throbbing, and his mouth was pressed into a thin line. This man… Her heart gave a giant kick. This man was tied up in knots. Over *her*!

She swallowed. 'You know I want you, Mac.'

Blue eyes lasered into hers.

'And I suspect you know that I like you too?'

He gave a cautious nod.

'So keep talking—because, believe me, I'm all ears.'

He straightened, and then he smiled, and it pierced through to the centre of her.

He reached out and took her hand, wrapped it between both his own. 'There are some things I need to clear up before I'm free to follow my heart.'

'Ethan?'

'I need to make sure he's okay. I need to help him in any way I can.'

He wouldn't be the man he was if he didn't want that. She wouldn't like him half so much otherwise. *Like?* Oh, yes, she liked him a lot. A whole lot. And in this particular moment that thought didn't scare her.

'I have to go see him.'

Wow. She straightened.

'I mean to leave tomorrow. I'm not sure how long I'll be gone.' His hand tightened about hers. 'I'm not sure…'

'You're not sure…?' she pressed when he hesitated.

'If you're prepared to wait.' He stared at their interlaced hands. 'I don't know if you're prepared to wait until I return from seeing him. I'm not sure you're prepared to wait and see what my life and career may or may not develop into.' He lifted his gaze to hers, his eyes dark. 'Before the accident I could've offered you the world. But now, Jo, I don't have anything solid to offer you.'

She didn't need anything solid. 'I'll wait until you return from seeing Ethan.' A grin broke through her. 'I mean *someone* needs to keep an eye on Bandit. After that we can take it step by step.'

Once Mac and Ethan had settled on a plan of action, then she and Mac could look to the future. *Their* future.

He lifted her hand and pressed a kiss into her palm, his lips firm and warm. 'Thank you.'

Something inside her soared free then. She had a feeling the only thing that kept her anchored to the ground was Mac's touch.

They should go inside and start cooking. Knowing Mac, he'd have chosen something that would take ages to prepare, but she didn't have the heart—or the strength—to break the spell that wove around them. She imagined that in years to come she'd remember sitting here with him like this, holding hands in the mild winter sunlight, with the sound of the surf in her ears and the promise of their future in front of them.

'What are you hoping will happen with Ethan?' she finally asked.

'That he'll work on a couple of projects with me when he's ready to.'

'That sounds nice.'

'I'll move back to the city so we can do that. And so I can see you.'

'That sounds even nicer.' She tightened her hand in his. 'So far it sounds as if we're on the same page.'

He pressed another kiss into her palm. She wished he'd

kiss her properly, but she knew why he didn't. If they kissed they'd lose control.

'I bless the day you came here, Jo. You've made me see possibilities I hadn't considered.'

She leaned against him, relishing his warmth and strength. 'You were grieving. You were mourning the life you'd had that was suddenly snatched away, and you were mourning for Ethan and *his* life too. Grief is a process, and you're finding a way through it.'

'Thanks to you.'

His eyes held so much promise it was all she could do not to throw herself into his arms and seek an answer to the desire coursing through her. She'd wait. Because it was what Mac wanted and perhaps what he needed. But when he finally felt free there'd be nothing to hold either of them back. Her skin tightened at the thought.

'You…uh…?' She swallowed and tried to think of something—anything—other than getting naked with Mac. 'You mean to drive your car?'

'I guess.'

'It's a pretty visible car, Mac. The Sydney paparazzi know it, don't they?'

He grimaced. 'I'll hire something.'

And someone somewhere would leak that too. Mac deserved to embark on his mission free from the worries of the press.

'You can borrow The Beast if you want. Nobody'll look twice at you in that.'

'You'd trust me with your car?'

'As you'll be leaving your gorgeous sports car here, in my care, trusting you with The Beast only seems fair.' She was going to trust him with her heart. In comparison, her car was nothing.

He laughed. 'Deal.'

And then he leant forward and touched his lips to hers.

He tasted of coffee and determination, and his kiss tasted like every promise she'd been too afraid to wish for.

It ended far too soon, but she knew why. The spark between them was already too hot, too twitchy. They had to negotiate it carefully or—

Stop thinking about getting naked with Mac!

'You're beautiful, Jo.'

She didn't contradict him. She didn't want to. 'You make me feel beautiful.'

His smile was her reward. 'You don't know the half of how beautiful I'm going to make you feel.'

She groaned. A sound of need and frustration she had no hope of holding back.

He nodded. 'I'm hoping I won't be gone too long.'

So was she.

He rose, pulling her to her feet. 'Come on—it's time to cook.'

'What are we cooking?'

'*Macarons.* I have a good recipe for them—better than the one you were using yesterday—and you need to keep practising.'

She all but floated into the kitchen with him.

Mac left at the crack of dawn the next day.

Leaving Jo behind when all he wanted to do was make love to her, prove to her over and over again how beautiful she was, was one of the hardest things he'd ever done.

He gritted his teeth, resisting the increasingly urgent craving. He had nothing to offer her. Nothing solid. No kind of future. But a future might be possible, mightn't it? A future could be wrestled from the wreckage the accident had wrought.

He held to the thought tightly, because he ached for that future. With Jo.

He tapped his fingers against the steering wheel and wondered what she'd be doing. She'd planned to make more *macarons*. The thought made him smile, because she didn't even like them. She'd taken a bite from one yesterday and with an 'Ugh!' had tossed it in the bin. She'd planned to take yesterday's batch to the farm where she bought the eggs.

'Maybe someone will find a use for them.'

That was what she'd said. He laughed. The very thought of her warmed him to the soles of his feet in a way he could never have imagined a month ago. Beautiful, breath-of-fresh-air Jo, who'd breezed into his life and turned it upside down like some kind of super-heroine from a comic book.

Imagining Jo in a skimpy superhero outfit kept him pleasantly engaged for half an hour. Especially when he imagined peeling it from her gorgeous body.

He spent another hour wondering what kind of dessert would make her mouth truly water. If she didn't like *macarons* then anything too meringuey was off the list. He selected dessert after dessert, only to dismiss them. Eventually he grinned. Maybe pineapple upside-down cake? *Yes.* Something warm and rich and full of flavour. That would suit her perfectly.

As soon as he returned to the beach house he'd make her one. He'd watch every nuance of her expression as she ate it. He could spend a lifetime making food to indulge all her senses. She'd appreciate his efforts too. He had no doubt about that. And he'd relish her relish.

Before he knew it the five-hour drive to Sydney was almost complete. He could hardly wait to return to Jo, but first things first.

He drove over the Sydney Harbour Bridge, but he didn't head for his swanky inner-city apartment. He turned the car in the opposite direction—towards Ethan's private clinic.

Jo pulled her phone from her pocket to glance at it for the umpteenth time, but there were no new messages, no new texts.

In the last two days she'd sent Mac five texts. She grimaced at Bandit, who lay under the kitchen table with her nose between her front paws, evidently missing Mac too.

'Do you think five texts is too many, Bandit? Too needy?'

Jo collapsed into a chair. She flipped out one finger. 'Are you there yet?' She held out a second finger. 'Thinking of you.' She stared at a third finger. 'Sunny and fine here.' She grimaced at the fourth. 'Missing you. Ugh! Now, *that*, Bandit, was too much.'

She dropped her hand to her lap. Her last message had been a simple goodnight before she'd gone to sleep last night.

She straightened. She wouldn't be needy. Mac had a plan he needed to bring off, and in the meantime he'd asked her to wait. She'd wait—because his eyes had promised that once he'd done what he needed to do he'd devote all the time she wanted—needed—to her…to them.

She hugged herself. She still found it hard to believe that Mac wanted her.

And she wanted him.

Oh, what was the point in denying it? Somewhere along the line she'd fallen in love with him. She couldn't pinpoint the exact moment. Their first kiss? Their second? When they'd argued about fish fingers? When he'd helped her polish off that pizza? The scorn in his eyes for her cruel excuse of an ex-boyfriend?

Thanks to Mac, she saw that for what it was now—the attempt of a sad bunch of losers with no self-esteem to build themselves up at the expense of others.

Pitiful.

It was pitiful that she'd let it affect her for so long too, but it had fed into all the insecurities created by her grandmother and her great-aunt. She let out a long breath. It had been easier to believe that she was unattractive than to risk being vulnerable again. Well, no more. She set her shoulders. She'd never fall into that pattern again. Living with that kind of fear emotionally crippled a person, and life was too short.

'Way too short, Bandit.'

She stood and swiped a bottle of water from the fridge, then headed for the front veranda. She turned in the doorway. 'C'mon, Bandit—the fresh air will do you good.'

Bandit huffed out from beneath the table, head hanging low as she scuffed after Jo. When they reached the veranda Jo bent down to caress Bandit's face.

'Aw, honey, he'll be home soon.'

She sat and glanced out at the view. In the meantime she meant to savour her newfound sense of self. She was done with feeling like a freak. She was done with feeling as if she was too tall, too large, too broad—too anything! By whose standards was she any of those things? Even the tiny, gorgeous women who adorned the covers of magazines were airbrushed to within an inch of their lives— their eyes widened, their necks lengthened, their waists trimmed and their thighs shrunk.

What was *that* about? If the so-called beautiful people weren't beautiful enough, then what hope did real people like her have? None. Because the standard was no longer human—it was in the mind of some designer and that was where the real freakishness lay. She was done with trying to live up to such impossible standards.

From now on she meant to wear whatever she wanted to wear—dresses, heels, chunky jewellery—regardless of whether it drew attention or not. She was healthy, she was strong, and she was a good person. She was kind to animals and to moody men. She was independent and able to make her own way in the world.

Mac desired her, wanted her, but she could see now

that too was secondary. It didn't matter what anyone else thought. It only mattered what she thought of herself.

She threw her arms out wide and lifted her face to the sun. 'I am beautiful!' She yelled the words at the top of her lungs and then with a laugh cracked open her water. 'If anyone hears me, Bandit, they'll think I'm a certified nutcase.'

Bandit, who'd collapsed by the door, flicked an ear in Jo's direction, but nothing more.

Jo pointed a finger at her. 'Now, you have to stop being a pathetic female, Bandit. Seriously—neediness is a bad look.'

Nothing. No response at all.

'It's never wise to pin all your hopes on a man.' She wrinkled her nose and grimaced. Well, on that count both she and Bandit had failed. Spectacularly. 'Except we can trust Mac, Bandit.' She swallowed and nodded. 'He's a man among men.'

Bandit's head lifted. Jo stared at the dog and pushed her shoulders back with a proud little shuffle. Well, well… Perhaps Bandit listened to her after all. Maybe she wasn't as indifferent to Jo as she pretended to be.

'I mean Mac won't let either one of us down, and—'

She broke off when Bandit leapt to her feet with a joyful bark and scampered down the steps at full speed. What on earth…?

'Bandit, you have a tummy full of puppies!' she hollered. 'You need to be careful!'

And then she heard it too. A car coming up the drive.

Her heart started to thud. Mac was home? She bounced upright, spilling water. She wanted to race towards the sound in the same way Bandit had.

Pride, she lectured herself, leaning against a veranda post as if she hadn't a care in the world. She did her best not to bounce. She had no hope whatsoever of keeping the smile from her face, though. *Mac was home!* She couldn't wait to hear a about the plans he and Ethan had made. She wanted Mac to be filled with hopes and dreams and plans for the future. She meant to figure large there.

Mac manoeuvred the car along the rutted driveway. He didn't stop to let Bandit into the cab—which, given Bandit's over-the-top exuberance, was probably wise. Jo remained leaning against her post even when he pulled the car to a halt at the front of the house.

She wanted him to see her standing there, tall and proud in the sunlight, elevated by the veranda, and she wanted to make him hungrier than he'd ever been in his life.

When he pushed out of the car, though, that thought fled. She raced down the steps towards him, appalled at his pallor and at the darkness that seemed to drag his eyes deep into their sockets. She took his arm. She'd have hugged him, but he shook her off.

'Not now, Jo.'

She tried not to take it personally. 'You look ill. Do you need a doctor?'

He shook his head.

'Then how about you put your feet up and I'll get you a sandwich and a beer?'

'I'm going to take a shower.'

He hadn't even taken the time to pet Bandit, but he did let the dog follow at his heels.

Lucky Bandit.

Mac and the dog disappeared inside the house. Jo lowered herself back to the step. Things had evidently not gone well in Sydney.

She closed her eyes. *Patience.* She'd let him shower and rest without pestering him, and later she'd put some good food in his belly. By then he might be ready to talk. Between them they'd find a solution to this setback.

She pushed to her feet. Spaghetti and meatballs. Comfort food. That was what they needed.

* * *

Mac closed his eyes as the stinging spray from the shower rained down on him, but he couldn't get the image of Ethan out of his mind. That image was burned there to torment him for all eternity.

Six months on and the nineteen-year-old still had to wear a bodysuit, was still in pain. Mac closed his eyes and braced his arms against the tiles.

Six months might have passed, but Ethan had taken one look at Mac and growled, 'Go away,' before turning his back.

Six years—sixty years—wouldn't be enough to erase the harm Mac had done.

And then Diana Devlin had walked in and it had all gone to hell in a handbasket from there.

He scrubbed shampoo through his hair, digging his fingers into his scalp, wishing he could trade places with Ethan, if only for a day, to give him some respite.

Ethan's doctor had taken time to talk to Mac. Mac had well and truly wanted out of there by that time—going to visit Ethan had been a grave mistake—but the doctor had at least been able to assure him that the upset wouldn't impede Ethan's recovery.

That was something, at least.

In fact the doctor had said Ethan's recovery was going better than any of them had hoped. He'd even implied that Ethan could have gone home weeks ago.

Ethan hadn't wanted to. The doctor hadn't said as much, but Mac had read between the lines. They were keeping him in for 'psychological assessment'—those had been the actual words. Not unusual in these circumstances, as it happened.

Mac twisted the taps off and seized a towel, scrubbing it over his face and hair. They thought Ethan was in danger of committing suicide. No wonder Diana hated him.

The accident hadn't just damaged Ethan physically. It had damaged him mentally. That was Mac's fault.

An ache stretched his throat. He'd never be free from that. *Never.*

He threw down the towel and dressed in the nearest things to hand—worn jeans and a faded sweater. The days of bespoke suits and designer clothes were behind him. He stood at the window and stared out. Eventually he roused himself and spun back to face the room.

He hung up his towel, put his dirty laundry in the washing basket, unpacked.

You can't put off going downstairs forever.

Weight slammed to his shoulders then, threatening to crush him. Earlier, when he'd pulled the car to a halt at the front of the house and had seen Jo standing in the sunshine, proud and magnificent, his chest had cracked open and split down the middle like a hewn log.

He paced from one side of the room to the other, hands clenched and muscles corded. For as long as he owed such a debt to Ethan he didn't have the right to pursue his own happiness. He pushed both hands back through his hair, fighting for breath. What he had to focus on was making enough money to ensure Ethan was looked after.

The dreams he'd started to dream—they were dust. It was what he deserved.

But Jo? She deserved better.

He pressed his palms to hot eyes and eased himself down to the edge of the bed.

Mac forced himself downstairs for dinner. Food was the last thing on his mind, but he didn't doubt for one moment that if he didn't appear Jo would storm upstairs to demand an explanation.

The concern in her eyes when he strode into the kitchen

cut him to the quick. 'I'm fine,' he bit out before she could ask.

He took the jug of iced water and two glasses she had sitting on the kitchen bench through to the dining room. She followed a few moments later with a fragrant platter of spaghetti and meatballs.

She dished them out generous servings, but she didn't start to eat. She gulped down water, the glass wobbling precariously in her hold.

'I take it your trip didn't go precisely as you'd hoped?'

It hurt him to look at her, but he forced himself to do it all the same. He deserved to throb and burn. 'He's a mess, Jo.'

'He's been through a lot.'

'Seeing me didn't help. Seeing me just made things worse.'

'How…?' Her voice was nothing more than a whisper.

He had to pull in a breath before he could continue. 'He hates the sight of me.'

She didn't say anything. She sliced into a meatball, slathered it in sauce and ate it. Her lips closed about the morsel and need rose up in him so hard that wind rushed in his ears, deafening him. Seizing his knife and fork he attacked a meatball, reducing it to a pile of mush. He started in on a second one and then on the spaghetti.

'I can put that in the blender for you if it's how you'd prefer to eat it.'

He set his cutlery down, afraid he wouldn't be able to push food past the lump in his throat. His stomach churned too hard for food anyway.

Jo continued to eat, as if unaware of his mental turmoil. He wasn't stupid enough to believe that, though. She was eating to stave off heartbreak. A fist reached out and squeezed his chest, all but cutting off his air supply.

'So,' she said eventually, with a toss of her head, not meeting his gaze. 'What's the plan from here?'

His very heartbeat seemed to slow. It was all he could do not to drop his head to the table.

From a long way away he heard himself say, 'I revert back to Plan A.'

Her gaze flew to his and he watched with a sickening thud as realisation dawned in those sage eyes. Her eyebrows drew in and she gripped a fistful of her shirt right above her heart.

He swallowed and forced himself to continue. 'I focus on making enough money to take care of every single one of Ethan's needs for as long as he needs me to.'

'I…' With a physical effort she swallowed, but she didn't loosen the grip on her shirt. 'Where does that leave us?'

Bile burned like acid in his throat, coating his tongue. 'There can't be an "us", Jo. At least not for the foreseeable future.'

She stared at him for long, pain-filled seconds, as if she hadn't heard him properly, and then she flinched as if he'd struck her. The colour leached from her face; the creases about her eyes deepened. Heaviness settled over him. His chin edged down towards his chest. His heart was thudding dully there. How could he have done this to her? Why hadn't he taken more care?

I'm sorry! The words screamed through him, but he couldn't force them out.

She swung back, eyes blazing. 'You fall at the first hurdle and give up? Come running home with your tail between your legs?'

He wanted to open his arms and make his body a target, to tell her to hurl whatever insults she could at him. Anything to make her feel better. Only he knew it wouldn't help. Not one jot.

'Has life always been easy for you? Have you never had to fight for anything?'

She laughed, but it wasn't the kind of laugh he ever wanted to hear again.

'Russ used to brag about you—about how you were this *wunderkind* who went from triumph to triumph.' She shot to her feet. 'But the fact of the matter is all that coming so easily for you has made you a…a *loser*!'

Her words cut at him like whips. He wanted to beg her to forgive him.

'When something really matters, Mac, you keep trying until you succeed—despite the setbacks. If Ethan really mattered to you, you'd try harder.'

What she was really saying, though, was that if *she* mattered to him he'd fight harder for her. It was what she deserved.

As for Ethan… He shook his head. He couldn't force his presence on the young man again. He'd done enough damage as it was.

'But you're not going to do that, are you?'

How could he make her understand the extent of Ethan's misery? What was the point anyway? She'd simply tell him to do something to ease that misery. That was beyond Mac's powers. What he *could* do was make money to hire people who'd bring about a positive difference in Ethan's life.

'You're just going to give in.'

There wasn't an ounce of inflection in her voice and that was worse than her anger. Ten times worse.

She dotted her mouth with her napkin, tossed it down beside her plate, and left.

It felt as if his heart had stopped beating.

CHAPTER TEN

Mac barely slept, but he forced himself out of bed as the first rays of sun filtered over the horizon. He made himself dress and go straight into the master bedroom. He opened the curtains to let in the light. Shutting himself up in the dark, not caring about what he ate and not getting any exercise had been stupid things to do.

He had to stay healthy.

With that thought he cracked open the glass sliding door. Air filtered in—cold but fresh.

Only then did he turn to his computer and switch it on. A hard brick settled in his stomach, but he ignored it to examine the lists of recipes he'd selected for the cookbook. At least a dozen of them were either not started or unfinished.

That meant a dozen recipes he'd have to make while barking instructions for Jo to jot down. He pulled in a breath. That was twelve days' work, if he made a recipe a day and wrote it up in the evening. Less if he did two recipes a day. On top of that there was the glossary of terms and techniques to write up, and serving suggestions to add to each recipe.

He created a table and a timeline. He printed off a shopping list for Jo. He would get to work on the first recipe this afternoon. After that he'd talk Jo through the icing she'd need to make for her *macaron* tower. She could tackle that under his supervision tomorrow morning.

He rose, collecting the shopping list from the printer on his way to the door.

'C'mon, Bandit.'

A morning and afternoon walk down to the beach each day, perhaps along it for a bit, would keep both man and dog healthy. He set the shopping list on the kitchen table before letting himself out of the house. Quietly. It was still early.

The sun rose in spectacular munificence over the Pacific Ocean, creating a path of orange and gold. At the edges of the path the water darkened to mercury and lavender. The air stood still, and with the tide on the turn the waves broke on pristine sand in a hushed rhythmic lilt.

Mac halted on a sand dune to stare at it all. It should fill his soul with glory. It should fill him with the majesty of nature. It should…

He'd give it all up for a single night in Jo's arms.

He dragged a hand down his face and tried to banish the thought. A single night wouldn't be enough for her. It wouldn't be enough for him either, but it would at least be something he could hold onto in the bleak, monotonous months to come.

He rested his hands on his knees and pulled in a breath. Except he couldn't do that to her. He laughed, although the sound held little mirth. More to the point, she wouldn't let him do it to her.

Good.

The weight across his shoulders bowed him until he knelt in the sand with Bandit's warm body pressed against him.

I can do this. I can do this. I can do this.

He lifted his head. He *had* to do this.

Forcing his shoulders back, he lumbered to his feet and stumbled along the beach for ten minutes before turning and making his way back to the house.

The scent of frying bacon hit him the moment he opened the front door. He hesitated before heading for the kitchen.

Leaning a shoulder against the doorframe, he drank her in—the unconscious grace of her movements, the dark glossiness of her hair and the strength that radiated from her.

'That smells good,' he managed.

She didn't turn from the stove. 'Bacon always smells good.'

He could tell nothing of her mood or state of mind from either her posture or her tone of voice.

He rubbed his nape. 'I didn't think you were much of a breakfast person.' Mind you, she'd barely eaten any dinner last night.

'I'm not usually, but I make an exception when I'm setting off on a car journey.'

She moved to butter the toast that had popped up in the toaster and that was when Mac saw the suitcases sitting by the doorway leading out to the laundry and the back door.

A chill crept across the flesh of his arms and his face, down his back. 'You're leaving?'

'I am.'

His heart pounded. 'Today?'

'That's right.'

She finally turned. The dark circles under her eyes made him wince. She nodded at his shopping list.

'So I'm afraid you'll have to get your own groceries.'

A knife pierced through the very centre of him. She couldn't leave! Just because they couldn't be together in the way they wanted it didn't mean she had to go.

She set the toast on the table and then two plates laden with bacon, eggs and beans. She'd made enough for him too. Maybe she'd had the same thought—that he hadn't eaten much at dinner last night either. It warmed some of the chill out of him, but not for long.

When she indicated he should do so, he sat. He stared

at his plate. He forced himself to eat, but all the while his mind whirled. Jo couldn't leave. He needed her here. She—

She needs to eat. Wait until after she's eaten.

Two rashers of bacon, a piece of toast and a fried egg later, he pushed his plate away. 'Thank you.'

'You're welcome.'

He waited until she'd finished before speaking again. 'Why are you leaving?'

She took their plates to the sink. She wore a pair of jeans that fitted her like a glove. Had she worn them deliberately to torment him? He gulped down his orange juice but it did nothing to quench the thirst rising through him.

She pushed a mug of coffee towards him, cradling another mug in her hands and leaning against the kitchen bench.

She took a sip before finally meeting his eyes. 'I'm leaving, Mac, because I refuse to watch you sacrifice yourself on the altar of guilt and misplaced responsibility.'

He swallowed back his panic. 'I prefer to call it duty.'

'You can call it what you like. Doesn't change the fact it's messed up.'

His head rocked back.

'And I'm not going to support you in that delusion.'

Jo might not understand what drove him, but it didn't mean she had to *leave*! 'You haven't learned how to make the *macaron* tower yet.'

She shrugged. 'I did that stupid vocational test of yours again last night.'

He closed his eyes and pinched the bridge of his nose, concentrated on breathing.

'I considered each of the questions as honestly as I could and you know what? It came back with the perfect job. So thanks for the tip.'

How would he cope out here without her?

He forced his eyes open. 'What job?' he croaked, a fist tightening about his chest.

'Paramedic.'

Saving lives? Dealing with emergencies?

She'd saved Russ's life, and probably Bandit's. She'd forced Mac to turn his life around. Her practicality, her strength, her ability to respond quickly, it made her... *Perfect*. The single word rang a death knell through hopes he hadn't realised he still harboured. Impossible hopes.

Jo deserved to get on with her life.

Without him.

He just hadn't known that letting her go would tear the heart from his chest.

'The NSW Ambulance Service is recruiting soon, so I figured it's time I got on with things.'

Mac found himself on his feet, moving towards her. He cupped her face. Her skin was warm and soft and alive against his hands.

'Stay,' he croaked. 'Please. Just another week.'

In another week he'd find the strength to let her go, but please God don't ask him to relinquish her today. *Please*.

Her eyes melted to emerald for a moment before she blinked them back to a smoky sage. 'If I stay we'll become lovers,' she whispered.

'Sounds perfect to me.'

He ached to kiss her, but she planted a hand on his chest and forced him back a step.

'To you it probably does, but I'm not going to settle for second best. I will never come first with you, Mac. Ethan always will.' She swallowed, her face pale. 'I deserve to come first with the man I choose to share my life with.'

Her words forced him back another step. His heart burned. Ethan had to come first. He had to look after the other man until he was back on his feet, and there was no telling how long that would take.

If he made a lot of money—millions of dollars—he could set up a trust fund to take care of Ethan, and then he'd be free to follow his heart.

If.

He stared down at his hands. Jo had no intention of waiting around to find out if he could manage that. He couldn't say he blamed her.

She cleaned the kitchen. He'd have told her not to bother except that would only mean she'd leave sooner. He took her bags out to The Beast and stowed them in the back. He rested his head against the doorframe before striding back into the kitchen.

'What about Bandit?'

She lifted a hand to her temple and rubbed it, making him wonder if she had a roaring headache too. 'I thought you wanted to keep her?'

He shook himself. 'I mean what about the puppies?'

She seized a tea towel, shook it out and hung it on its rack. 'When they're ready to be weaned I'll come and collect them. If there are any issues let me know. I've left my mobile number, my email address and my grandmother's contact details beside the phone in the in the hall.'

She didn't meet his eyes. Not once.

His heart started to thump—hard. 'Is that where you'll be staying?'

She slung her handbag across her shoulder. 'It's my childhood home.'

He suddenly found it difficult to swallow. He stared at that handbag. She was really leaving?

'Goodbye, Mac.'

He had to swallow the bellow that rose up inside him. They couldn't end like this! There'd been so much promise and—

She reached out as if to touch him, but her hand dropped short. 'I really do wish you well. I hope…'

What did she hope?

'I hope that you succeed.'

She spun on her heel then, and shot through the laundry and out of the back door. He lumbered after her, his limbs heavy and clumsy, as if they didn't belong to him. She was so calm, so cool and untouchable. As if she didn't care. She was tearing him to pieces.

A black knot of acid burned through the centre of him. 'Is this really so easy for you?' The words left him on a bellow. 'Don't you feel the slightest sting or throb? Don't you—?'

'Easy?' She swung towards him, her face contorting. 'Easy to walk away from dreams you let me believe were possible? Dreams that—?'

Her eyes filled and her pain rose up all around him.

'Easy?' She lifted her hands as if to beat out her pain on his chest.

He wanted to wrap her in his arms and make her pain go away, soothe the desperation in her eyes and the despair that twisted her lips.

'Jo…' He swore.

'Easy?' She thumped her chest. 'When you've broken something inside me that I'm afraid I'll never be able to fix?'

His mouth dried. His stomach knotted. He wanted to hide from the accusation in her eyes, from the anguish there—anguish *he'd* caused.

'I'm sorry, Jo. I—'

She twisted her hands in the collar of his shirt and slammed her lips to his. The world tilted. She explored every last millimetre of his lips with a hunger that had the wind rushing in his ears, firing his every nerve-ending to life. She deepened the kiss as if her very life depended on it, and everything he had reached towards her.

But she pushed him away.

'I tried to play nice, Mac, and keep it civilised, but you made it impossible! I hope that kiss torments you every night for as long as you hole up out here.'

She needn't fear. It would burn him through all eternity. As would the tears in her eyes and the pain that turned her lips white.

'That's it, Mac. That's us done.'

She slammed into her car, started up the motor and roared away.

He stared after her, her words ringing in his ears. *That's us done.*

Behind him Bandit set up a whine that became a howl.

Mac spun around. 'You're too late, you dumb dog. You should've told her you loved her while you had the chance.'

Mac picked up a rock and hurled it with all his might at a fencepost. He kicked a tuft of grass, jarring his ankle when he connected a little too well with it. He yelled out his pain and frustration at the top of his lungs. But it didn't help.

The end. *Finito.* This was as far as he and Jo would ever go. He stood there, arms at his sides, breathing hard. Jo was gone. The earth might as well spin off its axis for all the sense that made.

He waited for the sky to darken and a curtain to descend about him. It didn't. The sun kept shining, the breeze continued to rustle a path through the native grass, and on the beach waves kept rushing up onto the sand.

His heart shrivelled to the size of a pea.

Jo was gone.

It was his fault.

And there was nothing he could do about it.

CHAPTER ELEVEN

Mac finished the cookbook in a fortnight rather than the projected month.

A morning walk, an afternoon walk and making sure he ate three square meals a day still left him with a lot of time on his hands. So he worked.

He didn't sleep much.

He sent the manuscript off to his editor and then cleaned the house from top to bottom. Having neglected it completely since Jo had left, that took him two full days.

On the third morning after finishing the cookbook, with nothing planned for the day, he stared at the omelette he'd made for breakfast and found he couldn't manage so much as a bite. With a snarl, he grabbed his coffee and stormed out to the veranda.

Twiddling his thumbs like this was driving him crazy. When would he hear back from his editor?

He collapsed to the step and ordered himself to admire the view.

'See? Beautiful!'

His scowl only deepened. The view did nothing to ease the burn in his soul or the darkness threatening to tug him under. He'd kept himself busy for a reason. He'd missed Jo every second of every day and every night, but keeping busy had helped him to deal with it, to cope with it, to push the pain to the boundaries of his mind.

He had to find something to do. He leapt up, intending

to stride down to the beach for the second time in an hour.
Bandit stood too. He stared at her and pursed his lips. If he
went down there she'd want to come, and with her about
to drop her puppies any day she should probably be taking it easy.

He glanced around wildly for something else to do and
his gaze landed on a rosebush. He nodded once. The garden needed wrestling into shape. He could wrestle while
Bandit dozed in the sun.

He gathered some battered implements—a hoe, a trowel
and secateurs—from the garage. He barely glanced at his
car, even though he still made sure to turn the engine over
twice a week. It reminded him too much of Jo.

Digging up weeds and pruning rosebushes reminded him
of Jo too. Everything reminded him of Jo. He wondered how
she was getting along with her *macaron* tower.

One thing about being so hung up on Jo—it meant he
had less time to brood about Ethan.

Jo's voice sounded in his head. *You're just going to give
up...? Fight harder...*

What else could he do? He'd make sure Ethan wanted
for nothing.

Except a life.

He started reciting multiplication tables.

When lunchtime rolled around he ate cold omelette and
a banana. He sat outside in the sun because the kitchen reminded him too much of Jo. So did the dining room.

'I miss her *more*,' he shot at Bandit, who moped nearby.
She didn't flick so much as a whisker.

Has life always been that easy for you?

Yep. Right up until the accident. 'But don't worry, Jo—
it's hell now.'

Which was unfair. Jo had only ever wanted his happiness.

Fight harder.

'How?' He shouted out the word at the top of his lungs, making Bandit start.

He apologised with a pat to her head. What did Jo mean? How could he fight any harder? He was fighting as hard as he could!

He paced the length of the garden bed. He was fighting as hard as he could to make money.

That wasn't what Jo had meant, though, was it?

He bent at the waist to rest his hands on his knees. He didn't know how to fight for Ethan when the other man hated the very sight of him. How could he rouse the younger man from his apathy and depression if—?

Mac froze. The trowel fell from his fingers. Ethan hated the sight of him in the same way Mac had loathed the idea of a housekeeper. Blackmail had been the only method that had worked on him. Blackmail and playing on his guilt about Russ.

He'd loathed the very idea of Jo, but her presence here had forced him to reassess how he was living, to question the bad habits he'd formed. He certainly hadn't welcomed her with open arms, but she hadn't gone running for the hills.

As he'd done with Ethan.

No, she'd forced his inward gaze outwards. She'd reminded him that he needed food and exercise for his body, along with sunlight and fresh air. She'd forced him to recognise that he wasn't betraying the task he'd set himself if he took the time to enjoy those things. She'd made him see that he needed those things if he was to accomplish that task.

She'd stormed in here and turned his world upside down. He hadn't enjoyed it. He'd resisted it. But it had been good for him.

It had brought him back to life.

Who did Ethan have to give him that kind of tough love?

His mother? Very slowly Mac shook his head. Diana was too caught up in her fear for her son and her anger at the world.

From the corner of his eye he saw Bandit polish off the rest of his abandoned omelette. He didn't bother scolding her. She'd put up with his growly grumpiness and no Jo for the last fortnight too. If omelette helped, then all power to her.

Mac drummed his fingers against his thighs for a moment, before pushing his shoulders back and reaching into his pocket for his mobile phone. He punched in the number for Ethan's doctor.

Jo carefully sealed the lid on the airtight container holding the most perfect dozen *macarons* she'd ever seen. She set them gently on a shelf at the very back of the pantry with the other six dozen *macarons* she'd spent the last few days baking. She had twice as many as she needed, but she wasn't taking any chances. Each and every one of them was perfect.

All the less than perfect ones had been placed in her grandmother's biscuit tin, and even her grandmother's enthusiasm for them had started to wane. After her grandmother's birthday dinner tonight Jo would be glad if she never set eyes on another *macaron* for as long as she lived.

Puffing out a breath, she moved back to the table and pulled a plastic cone towards her. She had another eight of these cones in the cupboard. This one she was going to ice. Easy-peasy. Which was precisely what it wanted to be after the number of cones she'd already practised on.

She pushed her hair back from her face. What on earth possessed people to spend hours—or in this case days— slaving over a dish that would be demolished in a matter of minutes? Where was the satisfaction in that?

If Mac ever rang her she'd ask him.

Her throat ached, her temples throbbed and her chest cramped—as always happened whenever she thought about Mac. And as she thought about him a lot you'd think she'd be used to it by now.

She gripped her hands together. It had been eight weeks since she'd left his coastal hideaway, but she still hadn't grown used to the gaping sense of loss that yawned through her. Some days it was all she could do to get from minute to minute. Some days it was all she could do not to lie in some dark corner and shut the rest of the world out.

But what good would that do anyone?

Please! Some histrionic part of herself that tore at her hair and sobbed uncontrollably pleaded with her. *Please, can't we just…?*

Jo swallowed hard and shook her head, blinking furiously. *No, they couldn't.*

She wished she'd been able to hold onto her anger for longer. That anger had helped initially, but it had slipped away almost as soon as she'd arrived home. Instead, the hope that Mac would come to his senses had grown—the hope that he'd call her and tell her he loved her and was prepared to create a life that included her.

Which made her a certifiable idiot.

'But a beautiful idiot,' she whispered, reminding herself that her time with Mac hadn't been entirely wasted.

Of course it hadn't been wasted. By the time she'd left he'd been healthier, stronger, and sexier than sin. Whether he knew it or not, she'd been good for him.

Oh, he knew it all right. It just wasn't enough.

She collected icing sugar—the good, pure stuff—butter, milk and food colouring. The fact of the matter was she *had* heard from Mac. Twice. A curt email on the evening she'd left, asking if she'd reached her destination safely. She'd answered with an equally short Yes, thank you. And a week later he'd sent her a recipe for a *macaron* tower.

She'd thanked him again. Very briefly. And that had been the sorry extent of their communication. She expected to hear from him soon, though. Bandit must have had her puppies by now, and those puppies must be getting old enough to be weaned.

Why hadn't he let her know when Bandit had had them and how many there were? Why…?

Because he'd been too caught up in whatever his latest scheme was for making money for Ethan, that was why.

She seized the plastic cone and snapped it in half. She dug her fingernails into it and gouged and shredded until some of the frustration eased out of her. Then she calmly retrieved another one and set it on the table. She pulled in a breath.

Okay, now she was ready to start.

The doorbell rang, but Jo ignored it. It would simply be more flowers for her grandmother. Her grandmother could answer it.

Jo set about measuring icing sugar.

Grandma popped her head into the kitchen a moment later. 'Jo, dear, would you mind coming out for a moment? We have a visitor.'

'Is it Great-Aunt Edith?' Had she dropped in early for some reason?

'No, dear, and I don't believe it's an emissary sent by her to sabotage the making of your *macaron* tower either.'

Your macaron *tower.* But Jo remained silent. Her great-aunt mightn't like losing, but she'd never stoop to foul play. Her grandmother, however, had taken to imagining dastardly plots at every turn.

Wiping her hands down the front of her shirt, Jo walked out into the lounge room—and her hands froze at rib level when she saw who stood there.

Mac!

She stared, mouth agape. It took all her strength to snap

it closed again, and the blood pounded in her ears and she had to plant her feet to counter the sudden giddiness that swirled through her.

She glanced at her grandmother, who smiled serenely.

She glanced at Mac, who smiled serenely.

Serene? Her heart tried to pound a path out of her chest. She wanted to scream. Whether in joy or despair, though, she wasn't sure.

'Hello, Jo.'

She swallowed and released the lip she'd been biting. 'What are you doing here, Mac?'

'Didn't I say, dear?' Grandma patted her arm. 'I've hired Mac to cater my dinner.'

She'd *what*? 'But…how?'

'I rang to tell you about the puppies, but you weren't in.'

Grandma hadn't mentioned that!

'We got talking. Your grandmother asked me if I'd be interested in catering her birthday dinner. And…' He shrugged.

It took every last muscle she had not to dissolve in the warmth of his eyes. The heat between them was as blistering as ever. She gripped her hands together. It would be a bad idea. Becoming lovers with this man would make her miserable.

You're already miserable.

She tossed her head and hardened her heart. 'And…?' she persisted.

'And I found I couldn't refuse.'

She would *not* be his consolation prize.

She opened her mouth, a set-down on her lips, but Mac had turned away to rifle in a basket.

He turned back with a handful of squirming fluffy puppy, wearing a pink and green bow around its neck. 'Happy birthday, Lucinda.'

'Oh, my word. Edith will have a fit!' Her grandmother

clapped her hands in delight. 'Thank you, Malcolm, what a lovely gift.'

Jo tried to prevent her eyes from starting from her head.

'And this one here is for you, Jo. I've called her Beauty.'

He placed the puppy in her arms and she had to close her eyes as his familiar scent hit her and the warmth of his voice threatened to cast a spell about her.

She took a step away from him. Liking each other had never been their problem. It was only logical that he'd still like her as much as he ever had—want her as much as he ever had. What wasn't logical was her instant response to him, given all that had happened—or not happened—between them.

It had been two months. She shouldn't love him as much now as she had then. She wanted to weep, only it filled her with so much joy to see him.

You'll pay for it tomorrow.

Her eyes stung. She moved further away from him, from all the temptation and remembered pain, to perch on an armchair with her sweet, sleepy puppy.

'Believe it or not…'

She couldn't help but glance up.

'Bandit has been pining for you.'

Only Bandit? She shook her head. 'I don't believe you.'

On the other side of the room her grandmother cooed over her puppy. Beauty snuggled down on Jo's lap, taking the base of Jo's thumb into her mouth as if determined to keep a hold of her. Jo covered her body with her free hand to let her know she was loved.

'The moment you left she set up a whine that turned into a howl.'

Truly? She gestured for him to take a seat on the sofa opposite, but he didn't move from where he stood. He all but devoured her with his hot, hungry gaze. She rolled her shoulders and swallowed.

'She hasn't forgiven me yet for letting you leave.'

Jo would. Forgive him, that was. If he said he was sorry and asked her to return with him she would. In an instant

No! That would be a bad thing, remember? She had a life. She'd have a new job soon. She had a puppy.

But she didn't have Mac.

You can't have everything.

She lifted her chin. 'Good for her.' She was *not* going to sacrifice her life to a man intent on sacrificing his own life to guilt and regret.

'How's Ethan?' It was a nasty little dart, but they both needed to remember why they couldn't be together.

'He's doing okay. I left him and Diana out at the beach house.'

He'd what?

Her jaw dropped. The puppy let out a yelp and with a start Jo relaxed her grip and bent to soothe it. She stroked it back to sleep, its fat little tummy and its utter trust weakening something inside her.

'How…?' she whispered when she finally dared to look at him. 'How did that come about?'

He glanced at his watch. 'Well, shoot—look at the time? Lucinda, you'd better point me in the direction of the kitchen if I'm to serve you at seven on the dot.'

He went out to his car, returning with two laden baskets filled with the most intriguing-looking ingredients.

He grinned at Jo. 'I understand you're my kitchen hand?'

She tried to smile back, but couldn't. 'Yay,' she said weakly instead.

'Buck up, Jo. All I want you to do is assemble a *macaron* tower.'

That was the problem. Mac didn't want her for anything more substantial. Her fingers curled against her palms. Why had her grandmother hired him? And, more to the point, why had Mac agreed to it?

They settled the puppies in their baskets in the laundry. Mac unpacked his groceries. Jo washed her hands and set about icing two plastic cones.

Mac glanced at them. 'Why two?'

He'd come up so close behind her his breath raised all the fine hairs at her nape. She wanted him to kiss her. She ached with it. But he hadn't given her so much as a kiss on the cheek, and that spoke volumes.

In her heart she knew it was for the best.

'I don't think I've mentioned yet what a sight for sore eyes you are.'

She was wearing an old pair of tracksuit pants and an oversized T-shirt that had once been blue but was now grey. She was a sight, all right, but not the kind he meant.

She spun around. 'What are you doing here, Mac?'

His gaze lowered to her mouth. Beneath tanned flesh the pulse at the base of his jaw pounded. Hunger roared through her. They swayed towards each other, but at the last moment he snapped away.

'If I kiss you now I'll be lost, and I did promise your grandmother I'd make this meal.' He ground that last from between clenched teeth. He glared at her. 'And you promised her that darn *macaron* tower.' He suddenly seized her shoulders in a strong grip. 'But after this party we're talking.'

'Right.' She swallowed. 'Good.'

Except... He wasn't going to go over old ground, was he? He wouldn't ask her to return to the beach house as his housekeeper, would he?

He had to know that wasn't enough.

His fingers tightened, although she sensed how he tempered his strength.

'What's the plan for this evening? Is there anything you'd like me to do?'

Love me.

She swallowed that back, shrugged. 'Just follow my lead, I guess. I think I have it under control.'

Fingers crossed.

They stared at each other for a long fraught moment. She swung away, her heart surging in her chest. One thing was clear—she and Mac still generated heat. Not that it made a bit of difference. Other than to make working with him in the confines of a suburban kitchen all the more fraught, uncomfortable…and exciting.

Focus on making the tower.

She'd been concentrating on this event for weeks now. She couldn't afford to let Mac derail her.

She made the *macaron* tower—carefully inserting tooth-picks into the iced cones and then painstakingly attaching the coloured *macarons*. When that was done she decorated it all with swirls of pink, green and lemon ribbon.

She stood back to admire it and almost stepped on Mac. She glanced back at him. 'What do you think?'

Ugh! Think you could sound any needier?

She tossed her head. 'It's pretty fabulous, isn't it?'

'It's beautiful.'

But he was looking at her when he said it, not at the tower. The air between them shimmered. He took a hasty step away and Jo had to bite back the moan that rose through her.

Mac cleared his throat. 'What flavours did you decide to go with?'

She kept her gaze on the tower. 'Lime with passionfruit cream, and strawberry with a vanilla buttercream.'

'Nice.'

She picked up the tower and very *very* carefully walked it into the pantry.

Then she made a second tower, identical to the first. It was just as perfect. She set it in the pantry beside the first one.

Mac raised an eyebrow. She merely shrugged.

'Jo, dear.' Her grandmother came bustling in. 'Guests will start arriving in forty minutes and you've yet to shower and dress.'

'And take the puppies out for a pee and a romp in the back yard,' Jo added. 'Go ahead and finish getting ready, Grandma. I won't be late. I promise.'

CHAPTER TWELVE

Jo ROMPED WITH the puppies for fifteen minutes, but all the while she was aware that Mac was in her childhood home and…and…

And what?

She settled the puppies back in their baskets and went to shower. She'd splurged on a new dress for the occasion. And heels. She'd almost be the same height as Mac in them.

Almost, but not quite.

Her grandmother was shooting last-minute instructions at Mac when Jo returned to the lounge room. During her absence Great-Aunt Edith had arrived. They all broke off to stare.

Jo turned on the spot. '*Now* I'm a sight for sore eyes,' she shot at Mac.

Her dress was a simple shift in a startling geometric pattern of orange, purple and black. It stopped a couple of inches short of her knees. She'd never worn anything so short before, and certainly not with heels. She had legs that… Well, they practically went on forever—even if she did say so herself.

Mac's eyes blazed obligingly. Fire licked along her belly in instant response.

'Nice,' he croaked.

'Good Lord, Jo! What *are* you wearing?' Her great-aunt tut-tutted. 'It's far too short for a girl of your height.'

'The shop assistant assured me it was perfect for a girl of my height,' Jo countered.

'You look very pretty, Jo, dear,' her grandma said.

Great-Aunt Edith glared. 'But is it *seemly*?'

Jo glanced back at Mac, who could barely drag his gaze from her legs, and a female purr of satisfaction rose through her. 'Oh, I expect it's quite the opposite, Aunt Edith, but I believe that's the point.'

Before her aunt could remonstrate further the doorbell rang and Jo went to answer it, putting a sway into her step for Mac's benefit.

Eat your heart out.

When she returned he'd retreated to the kitchen and she could breathe easier again. He needn't think he could come around here and get her all het-up without expecting some kind of payback.

Five additional guests had been invited to dinner, all of them longstanding friends of her grandmother's and great-aunt's—people Jo had known all her life.

Each of them stared at her as if they didn't recognise her when she answered the door. They'd stare a whole lot more before she was through this evening.

She went to serve drinks, but Mac was there before her.

'Who *is* that young man?' her great-aunt demanded of her grandmother.

'Aunt Edith, this is Malcolm MacCallum—the famous chef,' Jo said. 'I was his housekeeper for a short time not that long ago.'

'Humph. I remember. I can't believe you'd waste your education on such a lowly position as housemaid.'

'What does it matter?' her grandmother piped up. 'As long as she was happy.'

Happy? Jo shoulders started to droop.

'And I can't believe you're turning your back on the possibility of promotion, not to mention stability, by switching vocations so late in life.'

Late in life? Jo choked.

Mac's lips twitched, and her great-aunt's eyes narrowed. 'Precisely how well do you know this Malcolm?'

She made her smile bright. 'Very well.'

Great-Aunt Edith drew herself up to her full formidable height. 'I'd like to know—'

'I'm afraid it's none of your business.'

'Jo!' her grandmother remonstrated.

'Or yours either, Grandma.'

The sisters stared at each other, evidently nonplussed.

'How long before we eat?' Jo shot out of the corner of her mouth.

Mac cleared his throat. 'If everyone would like to move into the dining room, I'll serve the entrée.'

Jo silently blessed him, and moved towards the kitchen to help, but with a gentle shove he pushed her towards the dining room.

'I have it covered.'

Right. Was he ever going to tell her what Ethan was doing at his beach house? And did it have any bearing on them—him and her?

There is no you and him.

Her grandmother sat at the head of the table and her great-aunt at the foot. Her grandmother's allies sat on the right side of the table—which was where Jo found herself— and her great-aunt's ranged down the left.

Like a battlefield.

As if this were a war.

And then it started.

'Do you think it's *wise* to wear such high heels when you're such a large girl, Jo?'

'Eadie, don't be such an old-fashioned prig. Our Jo is the height of fashion.'

Everyone else around the table weighed in with an opinion.

'I think that dress and those heels are perfect,' Mac said, serving mussels in garlic sauce.'

Both sisters glared at him, united for a moment in their mutual suspicion. Jo hid a smile.

In the next instant, however, the entire table had lost themselves in the delight of the food, forgetting all about Mac. Across the table he caught her eye. He mouthed 'perfect' before disappearing back into the kitchen. Her pulse skittered. Her heart throbbed.

When everyone had finished the entrée her great-aunt said, 'Jo, I really think you need to reconsider this career change you've been talking about.'

'Oh, Eadie, stop fussing. If this is what Jo wants—and if it'll make her happy—then so be it.'

'Heavens, Lucinda—a *paramedic*? Any Tom, Dick or Harriet can train as one of those. Our Jo is better than that.'

'Your Jo is quite simply the best,' Mac said, having whisked their entrée plates away and now serving lamb so succulent it melted in the mouth.

'She'll become a drudge,' her great-aunt said.

Grandma shook her head. 'Her choice.'

'I'd quite happily become *her* drudge,' Mac said.

Jo nearly swallowed her tongue.

'Who *is* he?' her great-aunt demanded.

'He's Mac.' She had no other explanation.

'He's her admirer,' Grandma said.

'If Jo had what it took to catch a man she'd have done so years ago,' scoffed Great-Aunt Edith.

'Ha!' snapped Grandma. 'Jo has her head screwed on right. Life is far easier when one doesn't have to pander to a man. Not that *you'd* know about that, Eadie.'

Ouch! Jo winced on her aunt's behalf.

'If Jo married me I'd be a very lucky man.'

Jo's fingers tightened about her cutlery and her stomach churned. What game was Mac playing?

'If you married him you could eat like this every night,' one of her grandmother's cronies said.

They ate then, mostly in silence, all relishing the amazing food.

Eventually Great-Aunt Edith pushed her plate away. 'Ladies, don't forget to leave room for dessert.' She shot Jo a smirk. 'I take it there *will* be dessert?'

'But of course.'

'Ah, but will it be the *promised* dessert?' She folded her arms and glared down the table. 'What *I* want to know is if she's managed to pull off what she promised she could. Lucy? Did she or did she not make you a *macaron* tower?'

Her grandmother smiled benignly. 'Where are the stakes?'

Jo rolled her eyes when the contested pearls were placed with ridiculous ceremony in the middle of the table.

Mac cleared the plates. 'I'll pour the dessert wine,' he said, moving to the sideboard. 'Jo, you can bring in the dessert.'

'The dishes?' she asked him.

'All cleared.'

'The puppies?'

'Safely tucked away in the laundry.'

Good. Right. She drew in a breath, rose, and moved to the kitchen.

As carefully as she'd ever done anything in her life, Jo picked up the first tower that she'd made and backed out of the pantry. She paused outside the doorway to the dining room for a moment, to pull in a breath, and balancing carefully on her new heels entered the room.

Gasps rose up all around her.

She set the concoction in front of her grandmother and

with a quiver of relief stepped back again. Mission accomplished.

'Happy birthday, Grandma. I love you.' She kissed her grandmother's cheek.

They sang 'Happy Birthday', but throughout the song she couldn't help but notice, even though Great-Aunt Edith's voice was the loudest, how her aunt's gaze kept returning to the tower in awe. And she recognised something else there too—hunger and yearning.

When the song finished Jo left the room and returned with the second tower. She set it down in front of her great-aunt. 'I made this one for you Aunt Edith, because I love you too.'

'But…' Grandma spluttered. 'It's not Eadie's birthday.'

'Maybe not, but you both deserve pretty, beautiful things. To me, you're both the most beautiful women I know, and you've helped to make me the woman I am today.'

They stared at her, but neither spoke.

'My real gift to you today, Grandma, is to bring this ridiculous feud of yours and Aunt Edith's to an end.' She reached across the table and took the pearls. 'These now belong to me. I have no cousins. It's what Great-Grandmother would've wanted. Besides…' She clasped them around her throat. 'They go perfectly with my outfit.'

The sisters' jaws dropped.

'Those towers consist of your individual favourite *macaron* flavours. The combination is perfect—much better than if they were just one or the other. Just as the two of *you* are perfect together.'

Both women's eyes had grown suspiciously damp.

'I love you. I know you both love me. I also know you love each other—even if you find the words too hard to say. Great-Aunt Edith, it's time for you to come home. This is where you belong and this is where you're wanted.'

Grandma blew her nose loudly. 'She's right, Eadie.'

Great-Aunt Edith cleared her throat—twice. 'Lucy, I can't tell you how glad I am to hear it.'

'Excellent.' Mac broke into the moment. 'Now that *that's* settled, I'm stealing Jo away.' He raised a hand before anyone could argue with him. 'She's not fond of *macarons*, so I've made her a dessert of her own.'

He took her arm.

'Jo?' her grandmother and her great-aunt said in unison.

'It's okay,' Jo said. 'I'll shout if I need rescuing.'

With that, she allowed him to pull her into the kitchen.

He turned with a grin that turned her heart over and over.

'That was masterfully done,' he said.

'Yes.' It had left her feeling powerful. 'What dessert did you make me?'

He handed her a plate. 'Pineapple upside-down cake.'

She took a mouthful and closed her eyes in bliss. When she opened them Mac was staring at her with a naked hunger he didn't try to hide. It only made her feel more powerful and assured…and bold.

She tipped up her chin. 'When are you going to tell me you love me?'

He met her gaze uncertainly. 'I thought I'd been saying it all evening.'

He had.

Her great-aunt and her grandmother came bustling into the kitchen.

'My dear, I do believe it's terribly poor form to just leave the table like that.'

'Yes—listen to your grandmother. We raised you better than that.'

'I agree. But I'm afraid there are puppies to attend to. Unless you'd rather deal with the puppies yourselves?'

'Maybe Malcolm could…?'

'Not in a caterer's job description, I'm afraid,' Mac said, edging Jo towards the back door.

'Puppies?' asked Great-Aunt Edith.

'Come along, dear, and I'll tell you about them. Malcolm brought one for me and...' she glanced at Jo '...one for you, Eadie dear.'

Grandma had just given away her puppy!

'There are more puppies back at the beach house,' Mac whispered in her ear.

Jo let out a breath. Okay.

Before Grandma and Great-Aunt Edith could form another argument, Jo took Mac's hand and led him outside.

'You left the puppies behind,' Mac said.

'But I do still have hold of my dessert.'

She released him to eat another spoonful. She took a step away from him so she could breathe and think.

She lifted her plate. 'This is divine.'

'You're divine.'

Mac stared at the woman he loved and wondered if he'd done enough to win her.

If he hadn't he'd just do more. He'd do more and more and still more if he had to—to convince her that they belonged together, to prove to her that he could make her happy.

She led him down to an old swing set and sat on the swing. He leaned against the frame and feasted his eyes on her. He burned to kiss her, but while it killed him he had no intention of hauling her into his arms until he was one hundred per cent certain it was what she wanted.

She had questions. Rightly. It was only fair that he answered them.

'You somehow managed to manipulate my grandmother into asking you to come here today?'

'Guilty as charged.'

'Because you were worried I might fail with the *macarons*?'

He had no intention of lying to her. 'I came here today to help you in whatever capacity you needed me to.'

She'd outdone herself with those *macaron* towers, though.

She pursed her lips, staring at him. 'So you worked out early on that I was trying to get Grandma and Great-Aunt Edith arguing on the same side? Against me?'

'It was a good plan. But it seemed only fair that someone should argue on your side too.'

If she'd let him, he'd always argue her case.

'Why is Ethan at your beach house?'

She sat in the moonlight, eating pineapple upside-down cake in that sexy little purple and orange number, and for a moment he couldn't speak. The urge to kiss her grew, but he tamped it down. After all this time away from her just being able to look at her thrilled him.

The night was mild for this time of year, but not exactly warm. He slipped his jacket off and settled it around her shoulders.

The flash of vulnerability in her eyes when he moved in close stabbed at him.

He eased back, his heart thumping and his mouth dry. 'Everything you said to me before you left was a hundred per cent on the money.'

He closed his eyes. What if he hadn't done enough? What if his best wasn't good enough? What if she simply wished him well and turned away? How would he cope?

'I don't want to play games, Mac.'

His eyes flew open.

She rose. 'If you don't want to talk then I'd like to go back inside.'

He was being pathetic. Spineless. Waiting for a sign from her first.

A real man wouldn't hesitate.

Earn her!

'Please don't go, Jo. I was just gathering my thoughts. It's been a crazy couple of months and I'm trying to work out where to start.'

She searched his face. Slowly she sat again. 'Tell me what happened after I left.'

He leant back against the swing set's A-frame. 'I threw myself into finishing the cookbook. I finished it in record time.'

'Congratulations.'

'And then, with nothing to keep me occupied, I had a lot of time to think.'

'Ah.'

'And some of the things you said tormented me—like trying harder where Ethan was concerned. So I started wondering what more I could do to help him.'

'And...?'

She stared up at him and her lips glistened as if she'd just moistened them. Hunger roared through him.

'It took me longer to work out than it should've.'

'And what did you work out?'

'That he needed to be shaken up the same way you shook me up.'

Her lovely mouth dropped open.

'I talked to his doctor first. I had no intention of barging in like a bull in a china shop like I did the last time. The doctor and I came up with a plan to bring him to the beach house, and then we got Diana Devlin on-side.'

'I bet that wasn't easy.'

He and Diana might never be the best of friends, but they'd come to an understanding.

'Once the doctor told her he thought it'd be for the best she was behind the plan a hundred per cent.'

Jo leaned towards him. 'How did you convince Ethan to go with you?'

'I used emotional blackmail. Just like you had on me. By the way, Russ sends his love. I'm staying with him tonight.'

'You've *seen* Russ?'

'I've seen quite a bit of Russ.'

'He's not mentioned it to me.'

Because Mac had asked him not to. He hadn't wanted to get her hopes up. He hadn't known how long things with Ethan would take.

She sagged, one hand pressed to her chest. 'I'm so glad.'

'I am too,' he said quietly. 'There are some mistakes I'm never going to make again. But back to Ethan. I told him his mother needed a holiday, but that she refused to go without him. I told him she'd fall ill if she wasn't careful.'

Her mouth hooked up. 'Nice work.'

His chest puffed out.

'And he's improving?'

'It's taken a while, but, yes. The sea air and the fact he can see how good the break has been for his mother have both worked wonders. It's the puppies, though, that have really been working magic.'

She leant back, her eyes wide. 'Wow, that's really something.'

It was. 'Every now and again he starts to talk about the future. We even had an argument last week about what recipes I should put in my next cookbook.'

Her urgings to keep trying, not to give up, to try harder, had made a man of him. Regardless of what happened from here, he was glad—and grateful—to have known her.

'He doesn't blame me for the accident, Jo. He's learning not to blame himself either.'

She set her now empty plate on the ground and rose to stand in front of him. 'That's wonderful news.'

His heart started to race. Hard.

'He still has a way to go. There'll be more skin grafts

down the track. But eventually he'll be able to return to work. When he's ready I mean to help him any way I can.'

She moved another inch closer. Mac swallowed, his hands clenching at his sides.

'I don't know—' His voice cracked. 'I don't know if you can live with that. You might see it as me putting him first.'

She shook her head. 'I see it as you being a good friend—a true friend. I certainly don't see it as a sacrifice or self-immolation or a sign of guilt.'

He stared at her. 'That's good, right?'

'That's very good.'

He couldn't drag his gaze from the smoky depths of her eyes. Was she saying what he thought she was saying?

He seized her face in his hands, unable to resist the need to touch her. 'What are you saying, Jo?'

No, wait!

'No, wait,' he said. 'Let me tell you what *I'm* saying. I'm saying I love you, my beautiful girl.' He brushed her hair back from her face. 'I'm saying I want a life with you. I'm saying that fighting for you—by fighting to work out the right thing to do where Ethan was concerned—has made a man of me. I'm saying that if you give me a chance I will prove to you every single day that you are my first, foremost and most cherished priority.'

His hands moved back to cup her face.

'You are my number one, Jo. Please say you'll let me prove it.'

She pressed a hand to his lips. Her face came in close to his, her eyes shining and her lips trembling. 'I love you, Mac,' she whispered.

He wanted to punch the air. He wanted to whirl her around in his arms. He wanted to kiss her.

'No man has ever made me believe in myself the way you have. No man has made me feel so desired or so beautiful or so right.' She swallowed. 'Yes, please. I really want the chance to build a life with you.'

He stared down into her face as every dream he'd been too afraid to dream lay before him in a smorgasbord of promise.

Jo's eyes started to dance. She leaned in so close her words played across his lips. 'This is the part where you kiss me.'

He didn't wait another second, but swooped down to seize her lips in a kiss that spoke of all he couldn't put into words. He kissed her with his every pent-up hope and fear, with the joy and frustration that had shaken through him these last months since he'd met her. And she kissed him back with such ardent eagerness and generosity it eased the burn in his soul.

He lifted his head with a groan, gathering her in close. 'I love you, Jo. I nearly went crazy when I thought I'd lost you.'

Her arms tightened about him. 'You haven't lost me. I'm in your arms, where I belong, and I'm not planning on going anywhere.'

'You mean that?'

'With all my heart.'

And then she frowned. 'Well, I mean, I *do* start my paramedic training next week, so I'll have to leave your arms literally, but you know what I mean.'

He dropped a kiss to the tip of her nose. Her very cute nose. 'But you'll keep returning here? To me?'

Her fingers stroked his nape. 'There's nowhere I'd rather be,' she whispered.

'I can commute between the coast and Sydney,' he said.

'And I can commute between Sydney and the coast,' she said. 'But, Mac, we need to make sure that wherever we go we always have room for friends and for puppies.'

A grin started up inside him until it bubbled from him

in a laugh. 'I'm glad you feel that way, because Bandit had ten of the little beggars.'

Her mouth dropped open, so he kissed her again. When he lifted his head—much, *much* later—she smiled dreamily up at him.

'Did I mention that I happen to love the way you kiss?'

'No.'

So she proceeded to tell him. Which meant, of course, that he had to kiss her again.

When he lifted his head this time he found himself growling, 'Promise me forever.'

She reached up to press her hand to his cheek. 'I promise you, Mac—' she stared deep into his eyes '—that for as long as you make me pineapple upside-down cake, I'm yours. Forever.'

Her voice washed over him like warm honey and he started to laugh...and it filled his soul.

* * * * *